JAVELIN
The third John Kerr thriller

JAVELIN

ROGER PEARCE

Publications

urbanepublications.com

First published in Great Britain in 2017 by Urbane Publications Ltd
Suite 3, Brown Europe House, 33/34 Gleaming Wood Drive, Chatham, Kent ME5 8RZ
Copyright © Roger Pearce, 2017

A CIP catalogue record for this book is available from the British Library.

ISBN 978-1-911583-74-5
MOBI 978-1-911583-75-2

Design and Typeset by Julie Martin
Cover by

Printed and bound by CPI Group (UK) Ltd, Croydon, CR0 4YY

urbanepublications.com

For Olwen

With the exception of capitalism, there is nothing so revolting as revolution.

George Bernard Shaw

Prologue

Enjoying the bright autumn sunshine from the riverbank, Detective Chief Inspector John Kerr watches a pair of swans emerge from the shadows of Hammersmith Bridge and glide to the shore. The tide is low and their coats shine white against the mud as they patrol the shore for bread from the Anchor pub before taking to the water again.

Kerr is in a lightweight navy suit, the jacket folded on the chair beside him, and a white cotton shirt, open at the neck. He has purchased a bottle of Barolo with two glasses from the bar and sits at a rickety wooden table on the terrace, a strip of raised deck hugging the chest high flood wall. The pub is of rough whitewashed stone, with '1728' carved into the blackened oak lintel and a horseshoe on the studded door. Upstream to his right, three brightly painted houseboats lie alongside each other in the mud, woodsmoke curling from one of the chimneys. Kerr's companion is late so he is already on his second glass, doing his own thing, just as she would expect.

John Kerr is a career Special Branch officer who spends his life fighting terrorism and extremism. It is the end of a week in which he has debriefed three agents, soothed Europol over Brexit, batted off a complaint from MI5 and blown the covert policing budget. This morning his boss, Commander Bill Ritchie, has nominated him for a promotion board to detective superintendent. Neither of them is hopeful.

Thirty paces to his left, at a right angle to the river walk beyond the sculling club, is a dirt track fronting a block of flats. He sees Robyn skid to a halt in a maroon Volkswagen Polo, narrowly missing the metal posts bordering the path. The swans have just come ashore again and the racket sends them thrashing into the air. Robyn is the mother of Kerr's daughter, Gabrielle, and she looks cool in tight jeans, ankle boots with three inch heels and her glossy, dark hair tied back. She has not seen Kerr for over six months. 'How's it going?' Her rental car key clatters onto the table as she kisses him on the cheek three times, Italian style, then surprises him by sliding her tongue between his lips.

Robyn fills her own glass, replenishes Kerr's and sits, legs crossed, facing him into the sun. Designer shades flip down from her forehead and her free leg swings while she talks. Robyn is playful but keeps her canvas work bag strapped across her body; it tugs at the buttons of her blouse and spoils her cream linen jacket. Kerr shifts his jacket to make room on the chair but Robyn prefers to cradle the bag in her lap.

Kerr watches a black motor scooter pull up on the far side of the Polo, annoying the swans again. The riders look young, in jeans and black T-shirts, a girl with long blonde hair and a stubbled boy on the pillion, and Kerr notices her pink canvas shoes. She carefully lays a black rucksack on the ground before joining the boy on a bench with a view of the river and terrace. Neither flinches when one of the swans flaps onto the flood wall and hisses at them, spreading its wings. This gets Kerr's attention: surely every kid knows a swan can easily snap your arm?

Robyn is chasing the Barolo. She is Glaswegian but has lived in Rome for over two decades and works for Spirito e l'Anima, an EU charity reporting on human rights abuses. She is in transit from Belfast, where she has been researching sectarianism against Catholics, and will return home tomorrow, Saturday. Kerr has taken the tube from the Yard and throws Robyn's key another glance. Why the rental car? She is deeply tanned and in good spirits. Kerr wonders if she is seeing someone.

The faster Robyn speaks and drinks, the stronger her Scottish accent. The barman wedges the door open in the warm air and gives her a wave as she tells Kerr about Belfast's separate schools and bus stops, the peace walls, tribalism and the powerful undercurrent of violence, things that Kerr has known about for a long time.

The couple on the bench are still drawing Kerr's attention. It is their inactivity that attracts him. Homebound traffic trails from the south side of the bridge and the river path is busy with dog walkers, cyclists, boaties and workers drifting to the pub on an early getaway. A couple on Coronas are fooling around taking selfies and everyone seems energised by the autumn sunshine except these outsiders, who neither speak to each other nor use their iPhones. Then the boy's eyes lock with Kerr's for a second before he forces them back to the sweep of the river.

Robyn pours them both more wine and wants to know what Kerr thinks, so he places his hand over the car key and tells her she won't be driving anywhere tonight. 'Why are you always checking up on everyone?' she says with a laugh. Then she jiggles a chunky crystal bangle up her forearm, eases the bag aside and leans in to remove a speck from Kerr's scarred cheek. 'So what happens now?' she says, which surprises him again, for Robyn had suggested the time and place. Her fingers rest there, stroking him, and her face says she isn't planning to go anywhere.

Abruptly, she walks into the pub. Through the open door Kerr sees the barman slide her another bottle of Barolo and unhook a set of keys from the wall behind him. With a discreet 'follow me' nod Robyn heads down the path. Disarmed, Kerr slips her car key into his pocket, grabs his jacket and catches her by some giant steps built into the flood wall. Robyn clambers up to a rickety wooden pier and leads the way to the middle of the three houseboats. A topiary bush in the shape of a heron keeps watch where the tiller should be but Robyn steps easily aboard, gripping a butcher's bike for support.

She unlocks the door and waves him inside. Layers of varnish darken every surface and a whiff of oil and bilges hangs in the air. While Kerr gets his bearings, Robyn takes two plastic wine glasses from the galley. In the forward cabin he checks out a comfortable looking double bed, but Robyn stays in the saloon pouring the wine. 'Make yourself at home,' she says, like someone who already has. He sees that she has finally released her bag, as if she feels safe here, and left it beside the stove.

Kerr wants to know how she has use of the boat but Robyn is in full flow again about her Belfast project. By the time she makes her move water is lapping against the hull on the rising tide. 'Shall we?' she says, lifting her blouse over her head and shaking her hair free. This cracks them up, for they are the words Robyn had used the very first time, on the floor of Kerr's Ford Transit in a field outside Skegness. It had been noisy outside as well as in, with rain hitting the roof like shrapnel and a German rock band blasting them from six coaches away.

They leave a trail of clothing on their way to bed and she joshes him as he stubs his toe. When they have found their rhythm she rolls on top, pacing him, arching her back, then taking his hands from her breasts and interlocking their fingers. Through a gap in the curtains Kerr can see Hammersmith Bridge, suspended in the dusk like a giant Meccano set, but she pulls him back to her. 'Just me,' she says, urgently. 'Only me.' Her body quickening, she grips his hair, holding his head still. She wants their eyes to connect, too, but there is something unfathomable behind hers that transcends the sex and disconcerts him.

The boat lifts from the mud as they climax and floats with a bump against its mooring, which makes them collapse with laughter. A second later, with Robyn tight against his chest, a shadow dances across the bed from the window. Footsteps patter above them, then Kerr hears a scrabbling from the stern as Robyn stretches over him and screams something in Italian. Throwing his head back he sees a flash of long blonde hair, then scooter girl's pink shoes as she snatches Robyn's bag. Kerr scrambles from the bed, shouts at Robyn to stay put, grabs his clothes and gives chase.

Naked on deck, Kerr searches for the thief. The strength is ebbing from his erection but there is enough light and life to raise a cheer from the nearest drinkers. The girl is sprinting along the path, heading for the motor scooter. Kerr pulls on his trousers, slips into his shoes and leaps from the flood wall.

As he runs past the pub, he sees pillion boy turn to look at him, then yell into the girl's ear as the engine fires and they shoot away. Pulling up his zipper Kerr feels the lump of Robyn's car key in his pocket. He weaves, half-naked, between a clump of evening walkers and cyclists, charging for the Polo.

Robyn's key fob is defective, costing him valuable seconds, and the Polo is boxed in. Wrestling with the door lock he hears the echo of the scooter's buzz as the thieves escape. With no space to turn around, Kerr spins up the towpath in reverse, then throws a handbrake turn in a shower of grit and dust.

As he shoves the stick into first he clocks the scooter at the junction with Hammersmith Bridge Road. The boy is shouting into the blonde curtain of hair again, urging her on. Recklessly accelerating into the traffic they brake hard to avoid colliding with a tipper truck, then try to overtake a 209 bus as they funnel between the suspension towers onto the bridge.

Kerr forces his way into the main drag. Pressing the horn, on headlights and hazards, he skims past a line of traffic and forces a white van off the road. The driver flashes him, lighting the target in Kerr's sights. On the bridge's apex fifteen car lengths away traffic has come to a halt with the scooter trapped behind the bus, giving Kerr a clear run.

Accelerating on a collision course, Kerr snaps on his seatbelt. Then he realises the thieves are not kids at all. The boy has dismounted and faces Kerr in the firing position of the professional gunman, legs apart, arms outstretched, gripping a pistol in both hands. Beyond him the girl revs the scooter and he can see Robyn's bag strapped across her chest.

As Kerr swerves, he hears the *crack* of the first shot. The bullet makes a clean hole in the windscreen, smashing the mirror, grazing Kerr's left temple and thudding into the rear seat. The damage is serious, but Kerr is not thinking about Hertz as he rams his foot to the floor. The second shot is rushed. It pings off the engine block, enters the driver's compartment and exits within an inch of Kerr's left calf. The girl steers the scooter to safety past the bus, leaving her partner alone on the bridge.

Kerr brakes hard but the Polo is still doing twenty when it collides with the bus, the seat belt scorching his skin as he is thrown forward, his head finishing off the windscreen. He releases his belt and rolls from the car, crawling along the tarmac to the back of the Polo. The gunman is less than five paces away, between the bus and the two massive suspension chains. No sign of the girl. Passengers are crying with fear as they stream to the south bank and safety.

The gunman is in the firing position again as Kerr gives a roar and charges him. Another pair of shots, then Kerr is on him, wrenching at the weapon with both hands. It is a Glock, probably the same model used by his team. Kerr rips it towards the sky, then down with a sharp twist, tearing the gunman's trigger finger from its socket.

Kerr's attacker howls with pain. He is well built, but Kerr's adrenaline makes him the stronger. As the Glock clatters to the road Kerr has his right hand against the gunman's throat, banging his head against the chain. Traffic is still rumbling northwards and the bridge sways beneath Kerr's feet. He drags the gunman by the hair onto the footway and throws him against the handrail, forcing him backwards until his face is framed by the river.

Then, from nowhere, the girl's arm is tight around Kerr's neck, the barrel of the Glock cold and hard against his temple. Her strength surprises him as he pitches himself against her, crushing her against the chain. A bone cracks but she still has the gun and ducks onto the road. She knows the firing position, too, and looks calm as her accomplice joins her. Kerr grabs the rail, preparing to take his chances in the river.

The silence is broken by a loud hissing sound coming from a black rectangular box on the tarmac beneath the Polo, followed by a stream of grey smoke. Kerr reacts instinctively. 'Bomb!' he yells, the terror in his assailants' eyes telling him they already know. As he moves to deal with the threat Robyn sprints from his right, firing pepper spray at the terrorists. They cover their eyes and escape along the side of the bridge as Kerr springs to the bomb, shouting at Robyn to get down.

The device is the size of a shoe box but heavy as a brick, and Kerr slides it onto the palm of his hand like a valuable piece of china. It must have fallen from the car in the crash and the magnet sticks to Kerr's watch. He uses up precious seconds clambering back to the footway, then catapults it over the rail like a discus thrower. The bomb explodes a second later, its fragments peppering the top of the bridge.

The terrorists have reached the scooter, four cars beyond the bus. Kerr wants to arrest them but Robyn grips him tight. The buttons on her blouse are all wrong and there is no sign of her bra. Gently taking the pepper spray, he shoots her a quizzical look.

Behind them, blood streaming from his face, the bus driver hurries along the stalled traffic, yelling at everyone to get off the bridge. At the north approach a police car is stranded, its blue light reflecting on the water. Ignoring his bloodied face and chest, Kerr lies on the tarmac to check the Polo for a second device. Clear. He takes Robyn's hand as they walk slowly down the pathway to meet a pair of overweight cops lumbering towards them. 'Sorry about this,' he says, suddenly hit by a cold stab of fear.

Robyn looks at him hard. 'What makes you think this was about you?'

Chapter One

Monday, 10 October, 11.13, Finsbury Park

The safe house lay within shouting distance of Finsbury Park mosque and the spot where, in the shadow of 9/11, radical cleric Abu Hamza had preached hate in the street while traffic found an alternative route. It was hidden in the basement of a three-storey Victorian semi and had its own private access, a slanting brown door built into the flight of steps to the main entrance. The space was cramped for the two young men who lived there, and they had to take it in turns to occupy the bed, the unlucky one making do with a futon. A black recycling bin and overgrown shrubs in pots filled the narrow front yard, leaving the basement in perpetual gloom. The sun occasionally found its way through the bars of the rotting sash window, but on this rainy morning the terrorists had tacked a bed sheet to the frame as they worked beneath a single low energy bulb.

The men were brothers, eighteen and twenty-one, and their arrival in London on the last Saturday in September had drawn them closer. This morning's attacks would be the first in the campaign and they listened carefully to the travel updates on LBC. Both were nervous, for their speciality was dealing drugs in Belfast, not planting bombs in London. The Englishman who gave out the orders had been reassuring, right from the moment he recruited them at his grimy tyre and exhaust workshop near Willesden, saying their inexperience did not count because they were just the delivery boys. 'Like Ocado, or knocking out a kilo of charlie. Place the commodity and walk away,' he had told them the night before, lifting two lethal improvised devices from his wheelie bag onto the rocky pine table, followed by a pair of loaded Glock pistols. 'We've done the difficult bit for you.'

The bombs were contained in plastic school lunch boxes, one lime green, the other polka dot blue, with nails packed into the moulded fruit compartments. A timer power unit switch protruded through a slot cut into the side of each box, primed to detonate the explosives thirty minutes after activation.

The older brother was called Fin, though this was not his real name. Beside each bomb he had laid two double sheets from Friday's edition of the *Metro*, taped together lengthwise. Wearing latex gloves, Fin carefully folded the newspaper around the polka dot bomb, leaving the switch accessible, and slipped it into a clear plastic bag with the *Metro* logo clearly visible. Then he stood back, waiting for his younger brother to do the same. 'Go on,' he said, 'it's not going to bite you.'

For the journey into central London they slid each bomb into a supermarket Bag for Life, then zipped into their lightweight hooded waterproofs. The younger brother's work name was Kenny. These days he was always in such pain from an injury to his right leg that Fin would often give him an extra turn on the bed. Seeing the boy's face crumple now as he adjusted the support strapping around his knee, Fin laid a line of cocaine on the table with a twenty pound note.

The boy snorted, sniffed and downed a glass of water. He took his pistol and concealed it against the small of his back, just like Fin: the gun did not trouble him, for they had both carried firearms since their mid-teens. Gingerly, he picked up his Bag for Life and stood tall. 'Let's do it.'

They raised their hoods against the rain as they climbed the four cracked steps to the street, sending a rat scurrying beneath the dwarf wall. Finsbury Park tube was a ten minute walk to the left, but their orders were to take a longer route in the other direction, passing St Peter's church at the opposite end of the street from the mosque before swinging right to follow a quiet cinder path bordering the main line. Kenny always walked with a limp these days, stone cold sober or high as a kite, so Fin took the direct route, towards the mosque, past the surrounding flats which had been home to jihadis fighting a quite different enemy.

Monday, 10 October, 11.34, Caledonian Road

Detective Sergeant Alan Fargo boarded the 73 bus and ushered his elderly mother and sister into the last priority seat as they crawled away from Kings Cross. The bus stop was close to the former police flat they shared off Caledonian Road, a stone's throw from Regent's Canal. Pauline, who had Downs, was thirty-four today, so Elsie was taking her to Brighton for a short break before winter set in. Because it was a special day, Elsie wore the brooch Fargo's dad had given her on their Ruby anniversary, a dolphin of cubic zirconia. Victoria station was only five stops away but Elsie had spent her entire life in Falmouth until being widowed and resolutely refused to travel underground, even if it quadrupled the journey time. She pretended this was to protect Pauline, though whenever Fargo sneaked his sister into the Yard to enjoy the view from the eighteenth floor she seemed to love the crowds on the tube ride home. It was standing room only for Fargo, and Elsie's umbrella, unfurled after the walk to the bus stop, flopped damply against his leg as he beamed down at them and took another call from the office. Like John Kerr, his boss, Alan Fargo was a career Special Branch officer who ran the heavily restricted Terrorism Research Unit, known simply as Room 1830. Monday morning was always busy with admin and operational catch-ups from the weekend, and his phone vibrated again as they drew into Victoria bus terminus, forty minutes after leaving Kings Cross. It was a bad day to be late but he was still smiling as he offloaded their wheelie cases, sprung the handles and checked the online tickets. He would see them to the mainline platform in good time for the 12.51 and collect his altered trousers on the way back to the office. Since falling in love, joining a gym and ditching fast food, he had lost over forty pounds; none of his clothes fitted, and Alan Fargo had never been happier.

Pauline insisted on pulling her own case, so Fargo reminded

her to use the pedestrian crossing at the front of the terminus lanes while he assisted Elsie. Instead, he saw her take the shortest route and collide with a bedraggled young man coming from the station. The jerk must have missed her with his face concealed beneath his hood, but made no attempt to apologise. Fargo had always been fiercely protective when anything happened to his younger sister, but his anger evaporated in a second. 'Poor boy,' he heard Pauline say as she watched him limp towards their bus.

•••

Monday, 10 October, 12.23, Strutton Ground

'Honestly, it was a lovely afternoon and we had fun.' Half a mile away John Kerr was enjoying family time, too. In their first catch-up for nearly a month he sat with Gabi, his daughter, at the window table of Cantina Carla, on the corner of Victoria Street and Strutton Ground market, opposite New Scotland Yard. Gabi was a violinist with the Royal Philharmonic Orchestra, just back from a European tour, and had dropped by for brunch on her way to a rehearsal at the Barbican. Kerr had waited outside, spotting her across the street in her skinny jeans, denim jacket and ankle boots like Robyn's. He had grabbed her battered violin case, hugged her tight and ducked every question about the attack in Hammersmith.

Gabi leaned in close. 'Dad, why do you always have to be so evasive?'

'Let's see what the real detectives come up with,' said Kerr, instinctively checking his BlackBerry.

'Why aren't you on Apple, Dad? So how did you two leave things?'

'What did Mum say?'

'To ask you.'

'Well, it was great.' Kerr sipped his coffee and smiled. 'We're going to do it again very soon.'

'So Mum was friendly, yes? I mean, you're always saying she's mad at you.' Gabi glanced at Kerr's *colazione* with extra mushrooms and tomatoes. 'Are you really going to eat all that?'

'We got on really well. You know, *conversed*,' said Kerr, leaning in. 'Like you tell us to.'

'About me, I suppose?'

Kerr speared a mushroom. 'Don't think you came up.'

Gabi's foot knocked against the violin case. 'What then?'

'Human rights. You know what Mum's like.'

'And you both got pissed, I suppose?' Kerr had persuaded Gabi to go for eggs Florentine, but she pushed the toasted muffin to the side of the plate. 'As per usual?'

'We talked, shared a bottle of wine.'

'On the boat. Yes, she told me. And?'

Kerr looked awkward. Through the window he spotted Gemma Riley, his head of comms, leaving the takeaway sandwich bar in Strutton Ground. Chic in charcoal grey trousers, flat patent shoes and a white cotton blouse, she sprung a giant 'London 2012' umbrella, paused to buy fruit from the market stall and hurried back to the Yard.

'Dad, I'm talking about when Mum's bag got nicked.'

Kerr glanced across the road again. 'Like I said…'

'So you are going to meet up again, soon?'

'Probably.' Kerr was eyeing the muffin. 'Yes, definitely.'

'How can you be this laid back,' said Gabi, shaking her head, 'when Mum's so totally freaked out?'

'She doesn't need to be.'

'No? After what you and…whoever did to her car? She says Hertz have probably banned her for life.'

'Gabi, this was someone trying to get *me*.'

'Try telling Mum that.'

'I already did.'

'So call her again today. After this. Say I told you to.' Gabi stared at Kerr's damaged face and sighed. 'Jesus, why do you two always make me feel like *I'm* the parent?'

Kerr smiled. Gabi shared a flat near the Royal Albert Hall with two other musicians but often stayed over at Kerr's apartment in Islington or visited Robyn in Rome. These days she was always trying to bring them together. The coffee machine gurgled and hissed behind the counter and he saw Carla looking at him. She gave a thumbs up. 'Everything good?'

'Brilliant.' They had been out a couple of times after work and Carla sometimes brought him crêpes on the house. Kerr laid his cutlery neatly on the plate. 'Gabi, don't worry about us. Everything's hunky-dory. How was Russia?'

'No, Dad.' Kerr heard Gabi's shoe knock against the case again as she leaned across the table, her voice little more than a whisper. 'Tell me who bloody well tried to kill you.'

Chapter Two

Monday, 10 October, 12.27, Victoria Bus Terminus

On the tube the bombers had travelled the seven stations to Victoria in separate carriages, standing with the bags between their legs, Fin keeping an eye on his brother through the glass door. There was an escalator to the surface but the final stage to the mainline concourse was up two flights of regular steps, which slowed Kenny down. Fin walked ahead to their vantage point outside The Globe Tavern, in the far left corner of the terminal. He was already slouching against its black tiled wall like a regular drinker by the time his brother emerged between the taxi rank and The Pasty Shop, still sheltered from the steady rain by the station's wrought iron and glass canopy. He watched Kenny make a beeline across the bus lanes, shifting the Bag for Life from one hand to the other as he bumped into a plump woman pulling a wheelie case.

Fin had chosen a spot outside the range of the CCTV cameras. Safe in the lee of the pub, he tried to relax while he got his bearings. Stretching away from him were the four bus lanes, glistening in the rain and separated by glass shelters restricting visibility from the station concourse. At the opposite end of the terminus he located the German investment bank Rafal Eisner Capital, six storeys of minimalist steel and smoked glass. Its Reception was half the area of a tennis court and even from this distance he could easily make out the 'RECap' logo, an illuminated oval of gold and eggshell blue suspended above the receptionist's head.

All around him was constant traffic, with buses arriving every couple of minutes, most passengers hurrying to the tube and mainline stations. Fin waited for another bus to hiss past, then hopped into the road to get line of sight on the locations for the bombs. Confirm.

He surveyed the ground for risks, signs of officialdom. Midway between Fin and the bank a couple of drivers were stretching their legs before the next departure. To his half-right, beside an open top sightseeing bus, a travel guide wearing a bowler hat stooped to assist a clutch of Japanese tourists. Beyond him, sheltered by the station canopy, stood a pair of shortish, hi-vis transport police, their trousers weighed down by the paraphernalia of the everyday cop. They loitered, chatted and chewed gum for a couple of minutes before disappearing into the station. No threat.

Fin turned to his brother and studied him for a moment. In the darkness of the hood Kenny's wide eyes were vivid blue, lit by the cocaine, but his face was jagged with fear. 'You ready?' Fin gripped his arm. 'Know what to do?'

'Is it gonna work? You trust him?'

'Trust *me*,' said Fin. He reached into his bag and activated the power switch, then waited for Kenny to do the same. 'Time is a bit of the fucking essence here, kid,' he whispered as his brother hesitated, then repeatedly pumped his arm, as if inflating his courage. The moment Kenny bent down to flick the switch Fin checked his watch: 12.33. Fin made a final scan of the station entrance as another bus swept into the terminus, then gave his brother a gentle shove. 'Go.' He watched Kenny step across to the third bus lane, removing the bomb from its bag as he closed on the first trash receptacle. It was a transparent polythene sack attached to an oval rim, a safe alternative to the metal bins once used by IRA terrorists to conceal their bombs. Fin could see that it was empty apart from a couple of crisp packets, empty cigarette packs and discarded copies of the *Metro*. A parked bus shielded the site from the station, its engine noise and exhaust fumes keeping passengers at bay. Fin heard his brother cough as he walked slowly past and placed his bomb on top of the rubbish, twisting it to expose the newspaper's logo.

Fin watched him leave the terminus, walking alongside a secondary entrance to the tube. As passengers emerged from the Underground into the rain umbrellas popped up all around, bright as fireworks, and Kenny was soon lost to view. Fin paused, scanning for new threats. The same two cops had reappeared, still talking, and he watched a traffic warden wave a lost Mercedes driver from the Buses Only sign at the far end of the terminus. A young woman hurried towards him, hair as red as the buses, with leggings and shoes to match. She shouted something into her mobile, spat a wad of chewing gum on top of Kenny's bomb and passed Fin without a glance. The cops were interrupting each other now, airing some grievance, their minds a long way from here.

Fin and Kenny would move unnoticed. No-one would see anything until much later, after the Yard had scrabbled around for every second of CCTV.

In the distance, Fin watched a dark cloud disappear behind the Victoria Apollo Theatre as the rain intensified and people quickened their pace, heads lowered. When the cops retreated beneath the canopy he decided to take his chance. Face and head buried deep inside the hood he timed his move to coincide with a departing double decker, which covered him to the second garbage bag only a couple of bus lengths from the bank. It was full, so Fin acted the street scavenger as he bent down to rearrange the rubbish and leave his bomb at the bottom.

Passing the bank with the Victoria Palace Theatre dead ahead, he turned left and hugged the inside of the pavement until he came full circle to the rear of the pub. He could see Kenny in the distance, heading south down Buckingham Palace Road. Across the street was Lower Grosvenor Gardens, a triangle of green protected by iron railings, with gravel paths, wooden benches, neat hedges and a statue of Marshal Foch on horseback, caught within three busy roads. Without waiting for the lights to change Fin dodged the traffic, took the nearest entrance and hurried through the gardens, as if taking a short cut.

Fin's diversion was the signal that the bombs had been delivered, and he spotted the Englishman in a blue Trapper hat and long black coat observing him from the doorway of Threads wine bar across the street, mobile at the ready. Resisting the urge to turn and watch him dial, Fin swung away after his kid brother, hurrying to find a pub with TV to watch the breaking news.

Chapter Three

Midway through the early shift Gemma Riley was feeling peckish and had just taken a bite of her salmon baguette when the call came through. It was on 2715, the non-emergency number used for security trace requests or enquiries from other police units. Gemma was head of the SO15 communications room, known simply as Reserve, a square office on the sixteenth floor covering three windows and separated from the corridor by a see-through partition from floor to ceiling.

From her workstation by the window overlooking St James's Park, Gemma looked round at her assistant for the day, an obese health and safety loser from property services with trousers an inch too short who had introduced himself as 'Slim'. With her regular number two on maternity leave, Gemma was having to mentor a stream of security vetted fill-ins with zero intelligence expertise. Slim had arrived fifteen minutes late, announced his gastric band operation 'any day now' and spent the morning on the other extension, 2716, while Gemma discreetly vaporised the air with eau de cologne to mask the smell of cigarettes. He was on it now, slurping milky coffee from a chipped Keep Calm and Carry On mug he had brought with him, so Gemma picked up.

'Special Branch?' A man's tense voice, calling from the street. Traffic in the background, people talking nearby.

'Who is this?'

'Bomb in Victoria station. Thirty minutes.' Gemma dropped the baguette into her drawer and reached forward, grabbing a pen. The accent was fake, a mixture of English and Irish. 'What kind of bomb?' Behind her, Slim was talking loudly about the imminent sale of New Scotland Yard, so she spun round and prodded his beefy shoulder. 'Where?'

She heard the swish of car through puddle, then a woman's fading laughter. 'I told you. Thirty minutes. The code is Topaz.'

'No. I mean where in the station? I need the exact place. Please don't hang up.'

Click.

A Special Branch civilian officer long before the birth of SO15, Gemma was a genius hoax detector. Threats to set ablaze, blow up or annihilate on behalf of Jesus or Satan were routine, especially after an actual terrorist attack, though the usual number was 999 or the Anti-Terrorist Hotline. Even Crimestoppers, for the seriously deluded. But the coldness of this man's call sent a tremor down her spine. That, and the word 'Topaz'.

In a heartbeat she jabbed a single number, the link to the Yard's central communications complex, immediately reaching one of the operators. 'Good afternoon this is Gemma in SO15 comms. We just had a Livebait on one of our dedicated lines. Location is Victoria station, no other details.' Gemma glanced at the clock. 'Thirty minute warning at twelve thirty-nine.' As Gemma spoke she was working the keyboard. 'The word is Topaz. Just a sec.' She paused, waiting for the code to flash up on her screen. 'And it's a negative with us. I'll do some more work on it and get back to you.'

'What's a Livebait?' asked Slim as Gemma cut the call. It sounded like he was eating.

'Code.'

'What for?'

'A coded bomb threat.'

Slim had his finger poised, ready for another call. 'That's just confusing.'

Gemma swung to face him. 'Not now.'

'Topaz' was still bugging her, an infant tugging at its mother's sleeve. She pushed away from the telephone desk to the Special Branch Registry terminal a couple of windows away, judging the distance and rotation to perfection. Logging on as she shifted into position, she found what she was looking for in thirty seconds.

'Slim, or whatever your name is, don't move from there.' She rolled back to her desk and turned to face him. Mousy hair twirled from his crown like soft ice cream. 'It's going to be very busy in here, so get your arse in gear. Anything you don't know, ask.'

Born in Romford, Gemma had spent her adult life gravitating west, stretching her vowels on the way. Slim had two podgy fingers deep inside a crisp packet and looked truculent as he extracted a final mouthful, spilling crumbs onto the mottled grey carpet. Gemma reminded herself to speak with John Kerr when this was over.

She opened her drawer, pushed the baguette aside and took out a laminated sheet of A4. The protocol for rapid dissemination of a terrorist attack was DEN, or 'digital emergency notification', a kind of virtual reality telephone tree using email or text. Gemma preferred the personal touch: to make absolutely sure the message got through she maintained her 'personal code red schedule', ringing key people to tell them the state of play. On Kerr's advice she had also inverted the priority list, notifying field officers before management.

'Jack, where are you, please?' Her first call was by radio to Jack Langton, Kerr's head of surveillance, who travelled everywhere by Suzuki.

'Lambeth, coming into the Yard.' Gemma could hear the whoosh of busy traffic as she repeated the message, then an immediate growl of acceleration as she told him the code word. Langton was taking the call seriously, too.

'Okay, I've got four out and about, three mobile and Melanie on foot. Tell John I'll starburst from Victoria until we get sorted.'

In a Starburst operation, surveillance officers fanned out from the focal point of a terrorist incident to deal with suspicious activity near the scene, or respond to eyewitness sightings in the fallout. 'Also, Gemma, Topaz was one of our jobs, ninety-six, seven, something like that.'

'I know. I just searched it.'

'Alan will give you the detail.'

'He's going to be late in this morning. Oh my God', said Gemma, remembering. 'Jack, he's coming from Victoria.'

Langton bounced straight back, his deep Geordie voice reassuring. 'I'll look for him.'

Alan Fargo's extension in Room 1830 was the third on Gemma's list but she was already dialling his private mobile, the number she knew by heart. It was engaged.

•••

Monday, 10 October, 12.43, Victoria Train Station

The dispatcher at the Yard assigned the highest grade to Gemma's alert. Within sixty seconds firefighters and paramedics covering Victoria station had activated the joint contingency plan; less than four minutes from the initial call the evacuation of Victoria mainline station was being ordered over the public address system as railway staff streamed through the concourse to cover the exits. Deep underground, tube drivers announced that trains would not be stopping at Victoria, and passengers already surfacing were channelled into Victoria Street. The orders by loudhailer and tannoy were jumbled yet unmistakable, for Londoners always travelled beneath the shadow of terrorism.

The earlier flood of commuters had subsided to a steady stream, and they exited the station by several routes. Some were guided from the east perimeter into Wilton Street, or from the opposite side to Buckingham Palace Road. A few took the escalator to the upper level and hurried through the shopping mall towards the coach station.

The majority, the unlucky ones, settled for the familiarity of the front entrances, trailing through the bus terminus into the killing ground. Waiting patiently at the gate to Platform 12, between the Gatwick Express and Upper Crust, Elsie and Pauline Fargo were slow to move. Confused, rooted to the spot, the old lady clung to Pauline's arm as over-amplified voices collided around her. In front of them the concourse stretched almost as long as a football pitch, but their Brighton train was already in the platform, only a few paces away. Pauline watched her mum stare longingly at the red tail-lights, as if they might still make it to the seaside.

Eventually it was Pauline who took charge. Her brother would know what to do, but when she speed-dialled Fargo she got the busy signal. She took stock, telling herself to breathe slowly. People were barrelling through the main exit between Boots and the ticket office, and she imagined her mother being trampled beneath the human tsunami. To the right, in a much broader passage leading past the tube entrance between Vodafone and a bureau de change, things seemed less chaotic, with passengers eddying patiently around the entrance before funnelling to safety. She tried Fargo again as she led the way there, supporting Elsie as she stumbled on a stretch of uneven floor. Then they were in the open air, the rain cool against Pauline's cheeks as she looked around for her brother, still believing he would come to the rescue.

•••

Monday, 10 October, 12.46, Strutton Ground

'I'm going to be in Rome all next week, Dad,' said Gabi. 'It's just Mum and me.'

Through the window of the café Kerr saw Alan Fargo cut diagonally across Victoria Street, taking advantage of the red light. He was carrying a dry cleaning bag, mobile clamped to his ear. There were sirens in the background, central London's regular mood music. 'That'll be great.' Kerr took a bite of his dessert. Carla had brought pancakes with melted chocolate and a croissant for Gabi. 'What's the forecast for Rome?'

'Bugger the weather, Dad. I want you to join us.'

'Robyn already mentioned it,' said Kerr, still peering across the street. Fargo finished his conversation but seemed to have another call waiting. Kerr could see the agitation in his face as he propped himself against the Yard's perimeter wall. After a few seconds he cut the second call, then immediately dialled again and hurried back along Victoria Street.

'And?'

'Think I'm tucked up next week.'

Gabi was also tracking Fargo now. 'What's the matter with Alan?'

'Probably forgotten something,' said Kerr.

'Fly out for the day, then. Lunch. So we can be a proper family for a few hours. Is that too much to ask?'

'Sure,' said Kerr. There was a faint *thump*, the noise a tipper lorry makes hoisting a loaded skip on board, then a crisper sound like a pub discarding its empties. It sent a flock of pigeons flapping into the air from the green across the street. 'I mean no, course it's not. I'll see what I can do.'

Gabi reached for his hand. 'Promise?'

Fargo had stopped. He was staring in the direction of Victoria, his face ashen. 'Did you hear that?' said Kerr.

'It's a crane or something. There's loads of construction going on. Try and make it Thursday. It's her birthday.'

'I know.'

'Don't lie.' Gabi nodded towards Fargo. 'Alan will cover for you. Or Jack, or Melanie. They always do.'

By now they both had a fix on Fargo, who was shouting into his mobile. Kerr gave Gabi's hand a squeeze. 'Hang on a tick.' Pedestrians were turning to peer down Victoria Street and a market trader had stepped into the rain to stare, absently wiping his hands on a tea towel.

Then a motorcyclist was speeding towards them up Broadway, leaving the Yard to his left. Bike and biker were in nondescript black but Kerr immediately recognised Jack Langton. Kerr watched him swerve before the junction to mount the opposite pavement, scattering pedestrians at the bus-stop as he raced for Alan Fargo. Then Fargo was astride the pillion, head unprotected, the dry cleaning stuffed into his coat and his arms tight around

Langton's waist as they bumped off the kerb and shot out of view, the Suzuki's roar smothering every voice in the café.

Kerr had switched his BlackBerry to silent when Gabi arrived. He reached into his jacket on the back of the chair, checked the screen and saw two envelopes and a missed call as he eased round the table. 'Sorry, love, gotta go.' He threw Carla a wave as he slipped a wedge of cash into Gabi's hand. 'Settle up for me, will you?' He bent to kiss her. 'Say hi to Mum.'

Chapter Four

Monday, 10 October, 12.54, Victoria Bus Terminus

Fin's bomb detonated nine minutes early, just as the evacuation was reaching its height in a procession three or four deep. The sounds of the actual detonation did not reach Kerr. There was a crack and a blinding flash of light, followed by a roar and rattle like machine-gun fire as the nails raked everything in their path. Men and women dressed for the office were cut down as cruelly as soldiers before a firing squad, visitors clutching maps and cameras flattened like stalks of wheat in a storm.

The shock wave, hot as a furnace, reverberated off the station wall. It stopped the ancient clock above the arch but gained another pulse of energy for itself, tricking people, ripping the limbs from innocents beyond the terminus who thought they had escaped, who would have been saved had they ignored the call.

Fargo's mother and sister almost made it. Six metres from the bomb a lump of dried mortar jammed a wheel on Elsie's case, tipping it over, so they paused outside Rafal Eisner Capital Bank while Pauline rang her brother's number again.

The explosion swept through the bank's elegant frontage unimpeded, collecting them in its path as Pauline left her final voicemail. It also picked up a young shaven-headed veteran in an Afghan Heroes sweatshirt who had stopped to help Elsie, and a girl pushing her baby in a zipped-up buggy. The force blew them into the bank's Reception and then, unforgiving, covered them in vicious green shards of glass.

Fin's bomb created a neat circle of devastation, with vertical surfaces peppered by shrapnel and the sides of the nearest bus bulging grotesquely away from the blast. It shattered windows all around, raining glass onto the soaking ground where it glittered like hoar frost. The bomb killed the four men and three women directly in its path and tore away the limbs of a dozen others.

Beyond them, survivors circled in slow motion, zombielike, clothes ripped away, blackened faces and bodies lacerated by nails and flying debris, their ears ringing in the silence.

Langton covered the eight hundred metres to Victoria station in fifteen seconds, overtaking two ambulances as he skidded into the terminus. The still air of the bomb's aftermath had grown thick with converging sirens and a BMW 3 Series area car had been abandoned haphazardly by the terminus exit, doors wide open, blue lights still flashing. Nearby a crew stood beside their marked Vauxhall Astra, trapped by the walking wounded screaming for help.

Langton and Fargo rode straight past them into the carnage, tyres crunching across the blanket of glass and debris. They came to a halt less than five paces from Kenny's bomb, engine idling as they took in the scene. Then Fargo was shouting into his ear, almost throwing the bike off balance as he dismounted. 'Over there!' he yelled. 'That's where they brought them out.' They both stared at a twenty metre stretch across the terminus exit, the escape route that had become a death trap. The crew from the area car, a man and a woman, were already sifting through sagging flesh for signs of life, their hands crimson. A halo of blue lights encircled the terminus as emergency crews awaited clearance to enter the scene, so Langton guessed these two young cops were disobeying orders. He saw the male officer waving at Fargo. 'You have to get back, mate,' he shouted, but Fargo was bending over the victims and did not even look up.

Visibility restricted by his helmet, Langton found a man in a pinstriped suit clutching his part severed leg, so Langton made a tourniquet of his scarf around his thigh and yelled for a paramedic. The eyes of the dead stared back at him, glassy, surprised or reproachful in the instant before shutdown. 'Alan, we're too late,' he said, taking Fargo's arm as the white-faced cop threatened to arrest them.

Retreating to the motorcycle, Fargo pulled away from Langton and ran to the gaping hole that had been the front wall of the investment bank. The floor was completely covered in debris, but Fargo spotted his mother immediately. 'Over there,' he said quietly, as Langton appeared at his side. Elsie Fargo lay on her back, the sparkly brooch still attached to her collar. She looked peaceful, eyes closed, swimming with her dolphin in an ocean of broken glass.

A baby's whimper led them to Pauline, lying dead beside an upturned stroller three metres away, half buried, her bloodied right arm limp across the cover. She must have spent her last moments crawling through glass to rescue the infant, for her hands and arms were badly lacerated. Langton crunched across the floor, calling for the baby's mother, but the only sound came from the tiny, invisible trace of life deep inside the buggy.

'Bomb! We've got a secondary!' More shouting, this time through a loudhailer. 'Everybody away. Clear the area *now*!' Langton looked around as Fargo carefully extracted the child, the pink fleece clashing with her screaming red face.

In the open to the right he could see a black Range Rover with tinted windows, one of the SO15 bomb disposal vehicles. In the terminus, an unprotected bomb technician was trotting from a garbage sack at the far end, calmly waving the rescuers away.

Langton took the tiny bundle and waited for Fargo to remove the brooch from his mother's body. 'There's another one,' he said gently. 'We have to get out.'

The rescue teams were rushing from the scene as they emerged into the rain, where an inspector clutching a roll of tape tried to send them into Victoria Street. 'That's my bike over there,' said Langton, pointing.

The inspector wore rimless glasses, the lenses smeared by dust mixed with raindrops. 'Leave it.'

'We're in the job.' Langton handed him the baby and nodded at the wrecked bank. 'She's the only survivor in there.'

Jack Langton was a head taller, intimidating in his helmet and leathers, but the cop looked like he wanted to dump the baby and punch him. 'That's a crime scene. What the fuck were you doing there?'

He sounded officious, but it was obviously the stress talking. 'Saying goodbye,' said Langton, curling one arm around Fargo and pushing the cop aside with the other.

When Langton started the Suzuki, Kenny's bomb was nine seconds from detonation; had Fargo stumbled or delayed another instant, they would have been eviscerated. It exploded as they accelerated out of the bus lane, the shock wave scorching Fargo's bare neck as it chased them down the street.

Chapter Five

Mobile on the go, resisting the rubbernecker's urge to follow the sirens, Kerr had raced back to the Yard in less than three minutes. He removed his jacket to shake off the rain as he returned the security officer's nod of recognition and paused to locate his warrant card. Kerr and Shavi had known each other for years, but a terrorist incident always brought everyone out in a rash of extra ID checking, as if the Yard was facing imminent attack. The bomb scanner inside had obviously been reconfigured, too, with the dimly lit corridor now a cavern of red lights, beeps and body searches as external visitors waited for clearance.

Tension was also crackling through the Back Hall, the main reception area, with all the phones on the go and front desk staff taking extra time to issue passes. It was not a good day to visit the Yard. Kerr recognised a knot of secondees to a Met celebrity inquiry, young homicide detectives diverted by allegations of geriatric rape. In identical trench coats and Italian shoes they checked texts and made calls, competing for updates on the tragedy half a mile up the road.

Kerr swiped himself into the lobby. It was grab-a-sandwich time and a crowded lift was just leaving. 'Hold it,' he called to a sea of deadpan suits clutching paper bags. The front man pretended to search for the button but Kerr already had his foot in the gap. Squeezing into the crush, he faced the doors for the silent ride to the eighteenth floor, his breath misting on the brushed steel.

In search of accurate information Kerr headed straight for the Fishbowl, his BlackBerry vibrating and chirping. The floor was quartered into open plan offices around the lift shaft and Kerr's working space occupied the far corner of the unit that watched returning 'foreign fighters', radicalised British men and women suspected of planning jihad on the streets of London.

The Fishbowl was a glass partitioned former store room only slightly larger than a prison cell. It was crammed with Kerr's desk, laptop and landline, two additional chairs, kettle from home and emergency bottle of rum from Jamaica. A narrow safe protected his Glock 19 automatic pistol and ammunition. Nothing about the room was regulation, and Facilities had decided that even the floor area exceeded his entitlement. The Square Foot fascists had been on his case all summer, until silenced by Alan Fargo with evidence of offenders in their own department.

Kerr had caught the texts and missed messages on the run back to the Yard, returning Gemma's call from the exact spot Fargo had occupied moments earlier. By the time he folded himself behind the desk, cleared his BlackBerry and opened his email he had a clear picture of the events leading up to the bombings. Had Kerr been in danger of underestimating the catastrophe, the figure who suddenly darkened his door removed all doubt. Dark hair dishevelled, crash helmet cradled in his right arm, Jack Langton had removed his neck warmer and held it against the side of his throat, from where a streak of blood curled around the knuckle on his wrist.

'Christ, Jack.' Kerr reached across the desk to the nearest chair and swept away a pile of time sheets and expense claims awaiting his signature. 'Sit down.' The kettle was half concealed on the floor and he flipped the switch with his foot. Nearest him on top of the safe was a giant RPO merchandise cup Gabi had bought him, but he discreetly slid it back and spooned Langton's coffee into a regular Interpol mug.

Still in his biker's leathers, Langton revolved the helmet on Kerr's desk to reveal a deep indentation that had almost penetrated the metal. 'Two hundred quid down the tubes,' he said, holding his hand against the wound as he checked the cloth.

'Put it on the sheet,' said Kerr, with a nod at the papers on the floor. 'I'll sign.'

'Sure.' Langton opened the neck warmer, revealing the black

fabric ripped and shiny with blood. 'Shrapnel. Nails, I think, but it's not bad. Anything on my back?' He stood up again and Kerr saw that the left shoulder and calf were ripped.

'Afraid so.'

'Bike got hit, too. Just after the flaming respray.'

'We'll get it redone,' said Kerr. Langton rode a Suzuki GSX R1000 and Kerr had only ever known it to be caked in dirt. Kerr wanted to ask about Fargo and a thousand other things but knew he had to let Langton work through his shock. He took his time with the coffee. 'Where's Alan?'

'I dropped him at Tommy's A and E. He got hit in the face and neck.'

'Bastards.'

'We were lucky.'

Kerr took a breath. 'What about Pauline?' Kerr had got to know Fargo's sister from her visits to the Yard and had often taken them home in his Alfa Romeo, sometimes dropping into his apartment on the way.

Langton shook his head and looked down. Kerr let him alone for a moment, but the click of the boiling kettle seemed to revive him. 'We found her. Elsie, too.'

Kerr topped Langton's coffee with a slug of rum from his bottom drawer. 'Alan?'

'He just picked up Pauline's final voicemail. You can hear the bomb go off.'

'So who's…?'

'Gemma's up there with him. But he's coming back in,' said Langton shortly. 'Soon as they stitch him up.'

'Of course,' said Kerr, nodding slowly. 'And how about you, Jack? Want to talk about this now, or take a break and get cleaned up?'

'What do you think?'

'Okay.' Kerr sat back. 'Remember Operation Topaz?'

'Of course. 1997.'

'Six.'

'Our last operation in London against the Real IRA. Bombs at electricity sub-stations around the M25. Timed to knock out the capital's power supply in one strike. And they almost succeeded.'

'Correct. So is this morning a coincidence, or do you think they've come back?'

Langton sipped his coffee and winced. 'Do you?'

'MI5 raised the mainland threat level in May,' said Kerr. 'But you're the man on the ground.'

'Put it this way,' said Langton, feeling round for the tear in his jacket. 'I can't remember the last time we had an Irish surveillance target.'

Kerr pointed at his screen. 'May 2001, according to 1830. But they've been dead quiet ever since.'

'So far as we know.'

Kerr was looking over Langton's shoulder into the main office. 'Let's ask the expert,' he said, as Langton swung round.

A heavyset man in a dark suit, the jacket flapping open, trousers baggy and creased, was heading at speed for the Fishbowl. The head of Kerr's source unit, the man everyone knew simply as 'Dodge', was stabbing the air with the forefinger of his right hand as he spoke hands-free on the phone, his angled head burying the mobile in the flesh of his neck. Dodge had been a highly successful agent handler in the Royal Ulster Constabulary Special Branch who had relocated to London with his wife and daughter after two attempts on his life. These days, he did the same work for John Kerr.

Dodge was speaking on high volume, his untamed growl audible through the Fishbowl's open door from ten paces. He rested his head against the doorframe while finishing the call, legs crossed at the ankles, jangling the change in his pocket.

Kerr exchanged a glance with Langton. Dodge was obviously speaking to a friend in the Police Service of Northern Ireland, or PSNI, the replacement to the RUC.

'That was Billy Docker,' said Dodge, replacing the phone in his breast pocket. 'Nothing going down in west Belfast. You all right, Jack?' he asked, inserting a podgy finger through one of the shrapnel holes in Langton's jacket as he squeezed behind him for the other spare chair.

'He's quick off the mark.'

'And Phil called me from South Armagh the minute the news broke,' said Dodge, offloading a pile of surveillance logs onto the floor. 'The Irish border is also a nil return.'

'Any others?'

'Yes. Ouch, that's bad.' Dodge had grabbed the helmet from the table and was studying the dent. He leaned over to check for damage to the back of Langton's head. 'I've already had three conversations and another two missed calls.'

'So they still love you over there.'

'They can read the signs. The code, the station, and all coming after Hammersmith Bridge. They know the shit London's going to be throwing at them. And Gemma played me back the bomb threat. How long ago did you hire me, John?'

'Too long.'

'Well that call is the most rubbish attempt at Irish I've heard since getting off the plane,' he said, nudging Langton. 'Even worse than your man here.'

Kerr pointed to the coffee but Dodge shook his head. 'So is anyone laying this at the IRA?'

'It's stronger than that, John. This is definitely *not* the IRA. That's what PSNI is saying. Anyone who matters, at least. Phil sounded pissed off I'd even asked.' Dead on cue Dodge's phone rang. He sat back in the chair, crossed his legs and listened intently for thirty seconds. His black shoes were scuffed and dull, the leather of the right heel worn from driving. 'I'll get back to you,' was all he said as he rang off. 'That's a no from north Belfast. Nothing's floating around there to suggest a return to violence.

You know how it is these days, guys. Belfast is a café society, poncy bars, pedestrian malls and not a body searcher in sight.'

'With Derry a cultural icon,' said Langton.

'If you believe that shit,' murmured Dodge as Kerr's phone rang.

'We'll be right round,' said Kerr, putting the receiver down and swinging sideways to open his safe. 'That was Gemma. They're back.'

'Where? 1830?' said Dodge, incredulous.

'And telling me to bring the BG,' said Kerr, bending down to spin open the safe and remove a slim, heat bound document marked Secret.

The *Blue Global* was the UK's monthly intelligence assessment drafted by the Joint Intelligence Committee. Circulation was restricted to the highly vetted Whitehall intelligence circle and the copy routinely forwarded to 1830 had been lying in the Fishbowl since Friday afternoon.

'So no-one in PSNI is putting their hands up, right?' said Kerr as the three of them walked round the corridor. 'Is that what you're saying, Dodge?'

Dodge had fallen a step behind, reading a text on the move. 'No indications of any dissident activity, period,' he said, 'including on the mainland.'

'But what if PSNI has taken its eye off the ball?'

Dodge held up his mobile. 'These are good people, John.'

'Or the intelligence function has been so degraded there's less coverage than anyone's making out,' said Langton, shrugging at Dodge. 'I'm not blaming Phil, or Billy. Or any of them…'

'Is it possible the dissidents got clever again without anyone noticing?' said Kerr, swiping them into Room 1830. He took a step back to let the others go first, thinking fast. 'Is there a big fat hole in Ireland where the intelligence used to live?'

Chapter Six

The Terrorism Research Unit, Room 1830, was a square double aspect office on the south side of the Yard with the two farthest walls extending six windows from the corner. The office overlooked the old Battersea Power Station and Vauxhall, though someone had dropped the venetian blinds a long time ago: thick with dust, discoloured by age, their dented slats shut out all natural light apart from a lopsided triangle in the far window. A haphazard cluster of old-fashioned fluorescent strips flickered, hummed and buzzed with tinnitus-like persistence. They covered everything in a dirty white shroud, penetrated only by the glow of a dozen computer screens pulsing with secret intelligence.

Fargo shared the room with six officers. There were four regulars to assist him with intelligence assessment, terrorist finance investigations and cell site analysis, and a pair of newcomer detectives, specialists in cybercrime who looked like they had come straight from college. They were crammed into a corner next to Fargo's reading room, a glass partitioned space even smaller than the Fishbowl, but as Kerr looked around they seemed perfectly at home.

Jacket hanging unevenly from the back of his chair, shirt sleeves rolled up, Alan Fargo was sitting at his desk diagonally to the left of the door. He drank from a can of Red Bull as he worked his computer, his black framed glasses reflecting the light from the screen. The left side of his neck was dressed with white cotton and a plaster and there were two red weals on his cheek.

As the door thudded shut behind him, Kerr watched Fargo sit back and look at each of them in turn. His pale blue shirt, open at the neck, was stained with blood and debris. 'Before you ask, yes, I'm okay. And no, things won't get better away from the office.' His voice was slow and measured, the accent stronger than usual, as if he was speaking from Falmouth. Kerr waited as he wrestled with his bottom drawer, pulled out a clean shirt and held it up to them, as if a change of clothes would make everything all right. 'I'll get a shower later. Okay?'

Kerr dropped the *Blue Global* onto his desk.

'Cheers,' said Fargo, as if this was a Monday like any other and Kerr had just made his morning. But Kerr was not fooled. Fargo's face was empty, all expression and emotion drained away, and when he turned from the screen there were shadows behind his eyes. It was a look Kerr recognised, the blank grief of parents after the discovery of their murdered child, the killer still roaming free.

The tone missing from Fargo's voice was incomprehension. 'I'll get myself sorted as soon as we find who did this,' he said, nodding his head back and wincing as the dressing pulled.

By 'we' he was referring to 'Mercury', the GCHQ server named after the Roman god of messages, eloquence, trade and trickery. Installed by Cheltenham's engineers six months earlier, it stood directly behind Fargo's desk, a featureless dark red rectangle the height and width of a human. Protected within a Perspex shell like a piece of modern artwork, almost fluorescent in the dull room, Mercury was the UK's ultra-modern hi-tech channel for circulating top secret and encrypted intelligence between Fargo's office and MI5, the Security Service. It had replaced 'Excalibur,' a caged monster of grey steel twice the size but with half the processing power, whose imprint was still visible on the tiled floor.

Dodge circled behind Kerr to lay a hand gently on Fargo's shoulder, and the gesture seemed to energise him. Fargo drained his Red Bull, crushed the can before tossing it into the bin, pushed his chair back and grabbed the *Blue Global*. 'Let's talk in here,' he said, minimising his screen and easing past Langton into the reading room.

'It's like this, guys,' he said while they were still squeezing round the table. 'I appreciate your concern. Really. But it's better if I stay here. The only way I can help Mum and Pauline now is to find out who did this. For the other victims, too. This is what I'm here for, and right now it's the only way I can function.'

'Nice try, but you're staying at mine tonight,' said Kerr.

'Already sorted, actually,' said Fargo, and colour flooded his face for a moment as Kerr nodded in understanding. He touched his cheek and gave a rueful smile. 'She's been raiding Reserve's first aid box since we got back. I'm well looked after.'

'Does Bill Ritchie know you're here?'

'He's got COBRA. Already left. They called it within an hour of the bombs. Home Sec's chairing.'

'COBRA' was Whitehall-speak for 'Cabinet Office Briefing Room A' at 70, Whitehall, the nation's modest equivalent to America's Situation Room in the White House. Usually chaired by a minister, it was the first stop for managing a national crisis such as a terrorist attack, attended by experts from the Yard, MI5, MI6 and GCHQ. COBRA sprinkled ministers with machismo, checked their dodgy decisions and spread a safety net against political fallout. It ranked high on the options menu of successive prime ministers, who invoked it for anything from flooding to volcanic ash.

'That's a bit swift,' said Langton, with a short laugh. 'So everyone's panicking that the IRA are back...'

'Which they're not,' said Dodge.

'...and they never told us first,' said Langton. 'Alan and I saw everything back there. No suicide bomber remains. Devices placed in rubbish bins. A coded warning intended to mislead. This isn't ISIS. MI5 can't pitch up at COBRA and make out this was a couple of jihadi thugs with rucksacks and a chip about Syria.'

Kerr looked at Fargo. 'What's Mercury telling you?'

'Nothing, and that's the point.' Fargo grabbed the *Blue Global* and flipped through it. 'Have you read this yet?'

Kerr shook his head. 'Tomorrow.'

'Don't bother. It starts off with Syria, Yemen, Afghanistan and Iraq. Al-Qaeda in west Africa. Then section five, the usual on terrorist fundraising, followed by radicalisation of sex-starved boys in Bradford wanting to bomb the crap out of us.'

'Which these definitely weren't.'

'Quite. Then it goes all *Computer Weekly*, Chinese spies hacking into big business servers.' He slid the document across the table. 'Irish extremism is like the epilogue. All about flags, marches and the Disappeared. Remnants of the paramilitary groups no more serious than violent criminals, too busy drug dealing and kicking the shit out of each other to pay us a visit.'

Kerr frowned. 'So why did they raise the threat level?'

'The usual.' Fargo shrugged. 'Covering all the bases before the EU Referendum.'

'So if this is what it looks like, everyone's unsighted.'

'Caught with their pants down,' said Langton.

Dodge's mobile was vibrating again as Kerr studied him across the table. 'And no-one picked up *anything*?'

A gold lighter rotated in Dodge's left hand as he checked the screen. 'I should take this.' He looked like he needed a cigarette, too.

Kerr was shaking his head. 'Not possible,' he said, quietly.

Chapter Seven

Monday, 10 October, 16.38 local, Cool Rivers Country Club,
Ngong, Kenya

Mark Bannerman absently circled his last slice of ostrich meat around the plate, leaving a faint red smear on the white china. 'So will you bring him to me, Rico? Spruced up? Fed and watered?'

The African held out his palms and laughed. 'How can I refuse?' His hands were small and neat, with well-manicured nails, and a rose gold signet ring clinked against his plate.

'That's settled then,' said Bannerman, spearing the ostrich.

They fell silent as the wine waiter, impeccable in black trousers and white jacket, crossed the lawn to refill their glasses. Bannerman's tiny gesture for another bottle was unnecessary, for by now the discreet staff of the Cool Rivers Country Club knew the men's exact requirements.

The sun drifted from behind a cotton wool cloud and bleached the table cloth a starker white. Old-fashioned sun visors angled from Bannerman's spectacles like an extra pair of eyelashes. He flipped them down, leaned in and clinked glasses. The deal maker looked Rico straight in the eye, but kept his own hidden behind the lenses. 'Always good to do business with you, my friend.'

As usual, they were drinking Whispering Jack chardonnay from South Africa's Western Cape. Rico had introduced his elegant British counterpart to the wine within a week of Bannerman's posting as second secretary to the British High Commission in Nairobi, less than an hour's drive to the east. Over the years the wine had become their private joke, the perfect tipple for a couple of spooks, a parody of their profession.

A pastel murmur of laughter, flirtation and propositioning hovered in the warmth over the dozen or so tables set apart around the lawn. But conversation between the two men over by the acacia tree never rose above a dark shade of grey, as unobtrusive as the honey bees foraging in flowerbeds bordering the lake.

Bannerman was wearing his usual cream linen suit with green socks, pale blue tie and worn suede shoes. A battered straw Panama lay on the grass beside them, covering one of his mobile phones. His counterpart was a middle-ranking operative in Kenya's secret intelligence agency, known as the National Intelligence Service, NIS, and had special responsibility for 'Icecap,' its top secret special interrogation section. African internal politics were notoriously difficult to read, but Bannerman had access to the NIS small print that told him Rico was on the rise. For their official meetings at NIS headquarters Rico power-dressed in a navy chalk stripe three piece suit and crisp white shirt with the collar swept back and a plain tie. But their private, off the record encounters were always social affairs. This afternoon Rico, too, looked relaxed in linen trousers, open-necked patterned shirt and expensive brown slip-ons.

'So how many in the lock-up?' enquired Rico. 'Apart from your good self?'

Bannerman raised his forefinger. 'A trusted friend from London.'

'Reliable?'

'Deniable.' Bannerman looked west beyond the lake and across the vast plain to the Ngong hills. Wispy cloud crossed the sky like streaks of lint, parting around the highest reaches to throw shadowy contours around the slopes. 'My dear Rico,' he murmured, seeing the follow-up question forming on his guest's lips. 'Cheque's in the post.'

Rico laughed. 'I think my director expects something specific?'

'Diplomatic bag on the ten twenty-five. We'll courier it to him before bed-time. Happy now?'

Mark Bannerman was an Arabist in his late fifties, enjoying the twilight of a distinguished career in MI6, the British Secret Intelligence Service. The Nairobi station provided him with a beautiful colonial style house in Langata, less than five miles from the restaurant, where he enjoyed beautiful views of the Ngong hills from his verandah and, in bed, regular sex with his housekeeper. Bannerman knew the NIS approved of him because he had secret access to their internal memoranda. Soon after his arrival the NIS director had written about him as 'a post-colonial grandee from Britain's privileged upper tier', a description that had sent a ripple of laughter through SIS headquarters at Vauxhall Cross.

The twice divorced son of an Anglican bishop from the Church's neocon wing, Bannerman had at least two decades on his guest. Privileged and elitist, the only child from Tewkesbury had begun life a world apart from the fifth son of a smallholder in Migori, near Lake Victoria. In their youth, each had graduated with a First in PPE from Cambridge, and now their professional lives had converged in the mission to hunt down Islamist terrorists.

The Africans liked Mark Bannerman because he was not American. The CIA station chief still lectured them on George Bush's war of terror at their fortress embassy in United Nations Avenue, but Mark Bannerman drove them to the countryside to buy them lunch. 'If Daniel can be available after tea on Thursday,' said Bannerman, lazily watching the waiter approach with their wine, 'that would be extremely decent.'

'Daniel' was the NIS pseudonym for Mukhtar Abu Fazul, a twenty-three year old Al-Shabaab militia man suspected of complicity in planning the attack on Nairobi's Westgate shopping mall in September 2013. Lifted forty-eight hours earlier from his hiding place in Kariobangi, a dirt poor suburb in the north-east of the city, Fazul now languished, unrepresented and untraceable, deep inside the stained concrete walls of an army interrogation centre off the Kiambu Road to the north.

They paused again for the waiter. In exchange for secret British government funds for an upgraded NIS IT system, Bannerman and another SIS officer from London were to be allowed unfettered access to the shackled Mr Fazul for as long as it took.

'I promise we'll behave,' said Bannerman. 'Just a friendly chat.'

'And the "loose ends" you mentioned. We tie them together, yes?'

'What are friends for?' Beneath his hat Bannerman's mobile was buzzing. 'So shall I tell them we have a deal?' Bannerman leant down to pick up the phone, then waited for Rico's nod. 'Good man. *Mi scusi*.'

Bannerman drifted off in the direction of the lake, examining his mobile as if seeing it for the first time, another part of the act. 'Giles, we're on,' he said, softly.

'Have you seen the news?' The voice in London was of golden syrup.

'Of course not. I'm still at lunch,' said Bannerman, checking his watch: almost five o'clock. 'I've pencilled in Thursday, so tell Ronnie to pack a bag and get his arse over here.'

'You haven't heard about Victoria?'

'Too bloody busy doing your dirty work,' said Bannerman as an image of Vickie Elder, the Service's deputy head of station in Damascus, floated into his mind. He checked he was out of earshot from the cluster of tables. 'What is it this time? Drinking or over the side?'

'The railway station. Bombed.'

A pause. In its website, the Cool Rivers Country Club made much of its 'signature pink flamingos' and Bannerman watched a couple of them now, wading through the shallows at the far side of the lake. 'And what's that got to do with Kenya?' Bannerman cursed inwardly, for he knew what was coming.

'The sisters think it's IRA.'

'On what basis?'

'Unconfirmed. They're still totting up the corpses.'

'Well you can fucking count me out.' Giles Lovett was the senior man, though pay grades cut little ice with a man enjoying his final posting and Bannerman had a more credible field record. 'Tell them from me.'

The voice in London had acquired an edge. 'Security Service made a special request through the Home Sec.'

'This is Five panicking again. And perhaps someone should have bloody asked me first.'

'You're at lunch.'

'For Christ's sake leave it a couple of days, Giles.' In his agitation Bannerman had crossed onto the soft turf near the water's edge. He took a step back as water oozed over the suede of his right shoe. 'Things will settle down.'

'Mark, you're either not listening or being obtuse. I'm talking a full house. Home Sec, Foreign Sec. And C personally. It's agreed. You're coming back.'

'Buggeration.' High in the sky beyond the flamingos an eagle had spotted prey. He flipped the shades up to watch it circling and hovering.

Mark Bannerman had served with distinction in Iran, Israel and Lebanon. His finest work, however, unreported and unsung, had been in Northern Ireland as the principal British intermediary with the IRA and secret negotiator for peace. In the mid-nineties, while the Real IRA planned and executed its terrorist campaign on the mainland, Bannerman had been secretly shuttling between London, Dublin and Belfast in the effort to find the endgame to a generation of slaughter, building a skeleton deal around arms decommissioning and a ceasefire in return for early release of terrorists and political self-determination.

As the months turned into years, the brutal murders continued and the political chasm grew wider, but Mark Bannerman neither lost faith nor uttered a word of condemnation. Night after night he chivvied, cajoled, charmed and compromised his terrorist interlocutors. He got drunk with them, bargained, made concessions and threats, then faithfully repeated their message to London.

By the end, Bannerman had done whatever was necessary to bring them to the table. The spy as conciliator had forged peace through pragmatism. It would be a step too far to say the Real IRA trusted Mark Bannerman; but gradually the spook with the silver spoon became the only representative of Her Majesty's Government with whom they would do business. He had become the acceptable face of the enemy.

'We want you in the air tonight,' said Giles. 'Briefing here tomorrow then straight across the water. Congratulations. You'll need your running shoes.'

The handful of politicians who knew Bannerman said he had walked a tightrope. Vauxhall Cross viewed things differently. Within SIS he soon became known as the Marathon Runner because, for them, it was the sheer scale of his achievement, rather than its sensitivity, that would secure their legacy.

'Does anyone actually know for sure this is dissident?'

'The cops and Five are completely unsighted. Everyone in full denial mode.'

'So make them do the leg work first. Let's get some certainty here.'

'That's what we want from you, Mark. The *actualité*.'

'Very funny. And the answer's no. I do the job on Daniel first. With Ronnie.'

'Mark…'

'Come on Giles, I've worked my nuts off to get this far with Rico.'

'Well done again. Now go home and pack.'

'Just give me two more days. Then I'll dance a fucking jig if you want.'

'Tell your man that Ronnie will bring someone else out from London.'

Bannerman gave an involuntary glance back towards Rico, who was also on his mobile. 'NIS won't accept that.'

'So cancel the money. You're checked in on BA64. Twenty-three fifty from Jomo Kenyatta. You'll feel better after a glass of champagne but make sure you get a good sleep. Penny will pick you up our end.'

'Penny? This is not the way…'

'Mark, please don't make this sound like an order.' Click.

In the distance, Bannerman watched the eagle suddenly swoop to earth and fly off with its wriggling prey. 'And why don't you fuck yourself, Giles,' he murmured to himself as he turned to deal with Rico.

Chapter Eight

Monday, 10 October, 14.04, SO15 Reserve,
New Scotland Yard

Kerr had taken a call on his BlackBerry from Gemma Riley but needed to speak with her face to face. He waited in 1830 while Dodge took two more calls from contacts in Belfast and made one of his own to Armagh, then hurried down the fire escape stairs to Reserve. Dodge claimed to have Northern Ireland covered, but Gemma was his primary source in London. Speed was vital. He had to tap into her memory before it drained away in the whirlpool of mistaken sightings, red herrings and false trails that destabilised every terrorist investigation.

Through the glass partition he saw Gemma multitasking at her desk, phone tucked beneath her chin as she worked the keyboard and scanned a list on her notepad. Evidently, she had also found time to shout for back-up: squeezed between the computer terminal and the shredder were two young officers Kerr recognised from the public order unit on the seventeenth floor, one making calls while the other searched the Registry database.

Kerr's target was exactly as Gemma had described him, sitting nearest the window, the back of his shirt untucked and dark grey with sweat. He was dialling a battered iPhone with a badly damaged screen, cracks radiating from a hole the size of a ball bearing.

'Slim?' Gemma's stand-in assistant immediately turned the phone face down on the desk and revolved slowly in his chair. His legs were splayed wide, stretching the trousers tight over his thighs and crotch, and a heavy shoe with a tarnished metal buckle caught Kerr's shin. Slim was slow to take Kerr's hand and, when he did, his grip was soft and clammy.

'Who wants to know?' he demanded, a fragment of potato crisp trembling on his lower lip.

'I'm John Kerr.' Something sticky had transferred itself to Kerr's palm. 'You should leave now.'

'I'm on till four,' said Slim abruptly. Beside the phone Kerr spotted a betting slip receipt for the 1.50pm race at Haydock Park. The horse was 'Shooting Star', and the bet £5 to win.

'You left your post uncovered,' said Kerr as the phone began reverberating on the desk. 'We don't do that here.' The incongruous James Bond theme filled the room as Slim picked up, and Kerr made out the name 'Perry' through the shattered screen.

Slim held the phone up, waiting for Kerr to back away. 'I need to take this.'

Kerr grabbed Slim's wrist, cancelled the call and tossed the phone back on the desk, sending a sliver of glass onto the floor. 'Property services are getting you back a day early,' he said, sweeping an empty crisp packet and fast food container from the desk into the trash.

Slim looked truculent, but the voice sounded weak. 'That's not the deal,' he mumbled, taking a fix on Gemma for some back-up.

Kerr pulled Slim's jacket from the back of the chair. 'We just came under attack and you sneaked out to place a bet,' he said calmly. The jacket was dog-tooth check with shiny elbows, and it released a wave of sweat and stale cigarettes. 'So you're out.'

Slim heaved himself to his feet and looked around the room. 'No wonder you Special Branch types are in the shit.' This time he spoke up, his voice surprisingly high pitched for such a heavy man.

As Kerr jerked his thumb to the corridor Slim grabbed the phone, snatched his jacket, struggled into the sleeves and forced his personal coffee mug into one of the pockets. He shot another glare at Gemma, who was in mid-conversation but managed a simultaneous shrug and wave without missing a beat.

Kerr watched Slim until he entered the lift, then rolled his chair over to Gemma and waited for her to finish her call. Behind her, sunlight suddenly flooded St James's Park as the rain clouds drifted north. She swung round to close the blinds but Kerr checked her, shifting sideways to avoid the glare. 'Sorry, but he buggered off for a good twenty minutes,' she said, 'just when it was getting manic.'

Kerr pulled one of her tissues and wiped his palm. 'I'll work something out. Have you got the recording?'

'I had a listen with Dodge, then sent it to tech for enhancement.'

'What do you make of it?'

'We've got a male speaking from a busy street in the rain. Rubbish attempt at an Irish accent, according to Dodge.' She checked her notes. '"Englishman on a bender in Dublin putting on a Belfast accent." Something like that.'

'He told me.'

'Nothing sounds authentic,' said Gemma, sliding Kerr the torn pages from her pad. 'This is what I managed to get down at the time. Crowded street, constant traffic noise with people talking around him. He's not disguising anything. Why stand in full view getting soaked when he could be home and dry?'

'Because he's watching?'

Gemma nodded. 'There were heavy vehicles swishing past. Buses or lorries.'

'Let's see what the CCTV throws up. Anything else?'

Gemma frowned in concentration. 'That's it. Unless tech come up with anything better.'

Kerr drew a little closer and lowered his voice. A couple of metres behind him Gemma's emergency helpers were discussing a name thrown up from Registry. 'What about Alan?'

'Doc said he's okay physically,' said Gemma. She showed him a roll of lint and bottle of antiseptic at the corner of her desk. 'I tidied him up again when we got back. And he's, you know, fully functioning. Right?'

'Seems to be.' Kerr rubbed his shin where Slim's shoe had connected. 'Do I send him home?'

'Don't waste your breath. Alan still thinks PTSD is a nasty

rash.' Gemma gave a short laugh and grabbed Kerr's hand. 'John, do you have any idea how stubborn he is?'

'Obviously not.' Kerr exhaled and peered across the park. 'And from today no-one knows him better then you.' He smiled at her and they both stayed silent for a moment, thinking of Pauline, ignoring the voices in the background.

The love affair between Gemma and Alan Fargo had surprised Kerr and delighted the whole team since its birth over a year earlier. Theirs truly was the attraction of opposites. Gemma had always been a free spirit in the capital's fast lane, a living, breathing directory of clubs, bars, restaurants, exes and phone numbers. But her newest lover had never married or even enjoyed a long-term relationship, so far as Kerr knew. Until now, with few interests outside his vital work at the Yard, Alan Fargo had always been Kerr's fixture, unwavering, locked into the same grey channel between home and the office.

Fargo had only opened up to Kerr once, in the Booking Office Bar at St Pancras Station on a return trip from Paris. 'She's like a firework display, John,' he had volunteered over his second Kentucky Spritzer. 'You know, New Year's Eve on the Thames, when it goes on and on. Expensive, crazy. It's bonkers. Sounds and colours you never dreamt of and you can't guess what's coming next.'

By this time, in early January, Fargo had already lost thirty pounds and was beginning to reflect Gemma's brightness. With overwashed white shirts ditched for fresh pastels there was a different aura around him, a lightness, as if sunshine had reached him through 1830's dusty, lopsided blinds. Gemma Riley, a decade younger but with light years' more experience, had turned his friend's life around, and Kerr knew she would rescue him from his grief.

'He's staying at mine for the next few nights,' she said. 'We'll pick up some clothes and stuff later. And I'll be holding his hand when he identifies the bodies.'

'Very good. What about a spell of compassionate? He must still have some loose ends in Cornwall?'

'Alan's already told you where he needs to be, hasn't he?'

One of the detectives tapped Kerr on the shoulder and held out the phone. 'Kerr.' He listened briefly, then handed it back. 'Gotta go. Commander's waiting upstairs.' On the way out he paused by Slim's vacated desk to glance at the betting slip. 'Loser,' he said, screwing it up and tossing it into the bin as he hurried away.

'John, wait!' Kerr was halfway to the fire escape stairs when Gemma called out to him. Behind her in the office two phones were ringing but she ignored them and scampered down the corridor. 'Horses.'

'What?'

'In the background. I heard them over the traffic. You know, the clippety clop. There were two, I think. Perhaps we should be looking further afield? You know, flagging up riding schools in the suburbs, that sort of thing?'

'Let's wait for the cell site analysis. But feed it in downstairs, will you?' He smiled. 'And run it past Alan?'

•••

The outer office on the eighteenth floor was empty, with Donna's work space clear except for a red coffee mug, fresh lilies in a vase and a photograph of her two smiling nieces in their school uniforms. Half-hidden beside her chair was a tan leather shoulder bag. Bill Ritchie's PA and gatekeeper had just returned from a fortnight in Jamaica, catching up with her family, and Kerr guessed she must have popped out to the sandwich bar. Resisting the urge to sneak a check of her computer, he knocked and entered the main office before Ritchie could give his customary yell of welcome.

The commander of the SO15 intelligence unit occupied a spacious carpeted corner office diagonally opposite Room 1830 with panoramic views of St James's Park and London's northern reaches as far as Kite Hill, the highest point on Hampstead Heath. The room was a rectangle extending six windows by four, allowing plenty of space to accommodate the dark wood conference table with its eight chairs and, alongside the inner wall, a grey safe towering over a round occasional table with two threadbare easy chairs. The man himself stood half concealed behind the open safe door, popping tablets from two blister packs. He beckoned Kerr inside as he drained a glass of water.

The two men went back a long time, since Kerr's lengthy undercover operation, when Ritchie had acted as mentor, protector and cover officer. For five years he had been the voice of reason and sole authority figure in the double life of Kerr the extremist, and these days, whenever Kerr played the maverick, Ritchie would complain that little had changed. In private their relationship still transcended rank, except when Kerr stepped seriously out of line. Kerr slid a chair from the conference table and sat down without being asked. 'How did it go?'

'With the Home Sec in the chair?' Ritchie tossed the sachets into the safe. 'How do you think?'

'I imagine she's pretty delighted about Irish dissidents bombing London.'

'Steamed in brandishing a big stick with "IRA" written all over it but no-one came up with any hard evidence.' Ritchie expertly pushed the safe door shut with his shoe and headed for his desk in the corner farthest from the door. 'So she's bashing the good guys instead.'

'That desperate?'

Ritchie nodded as he sank into his chair. 'Obsessed.'

The flakiness of Avril Knight around the Irish peace process was the worst kept secret around Parliament and her promotion to Home Secretary had been an unwelcome surprise on both sides of the Irish Sea. With the EU money tap soon to be turned off, everyone knew her murmurings about 'recalibrating the balance of power at Stormont' meant forcing concessions from the republicans at any price. She reserved her strongest anger for what she called an amnesty to IRA paramilitaries 'OTR', shorthand for terrorists still on the run. 'These thugs murdered your colleagues,' she had told her driver and protection officer one night through a mist of gin and tonic, 'and we indulge them like teenage truants.'

Ritchie reached for his trademark yellow legal pad and looked at his notes. 'Derek Finch kicked off with casualty numbers and the recovery operation but she cut him short. Knight is only interested in demonising republicans. Bombers in London using an IRA operation name? In her eyes, conclusive evidence, the best news she's had in a long time.'

Through the window Kerr watched an Airbus 380 making its final approach into Heathrow, the sun glinting off its fuselage. 'Eleven people died this morning. So far. Doesn't she care about that?'

'To Avril Knight, body counts are a debating point. She *needs* the dissidents to be responsible for this.'

'But they're not. Is she really going to use Victoria to bring pressure on Stormont?'

Ritchie spread his hands. 'Would you expect anything else? Our atrocity down the road is Knight's best opportunity yet, so she's pissed off that we're not delivering for her.'

'Unbelievable.'

'Knight smells blood and all we're offering is lavender. Give me a minute,' said Ritchie, writing notes on the pad in his bold hand. The commander's work station was a creaking oak desk almost two metres square, with a surface of green inlaid leather. It had been occupied by Lord Trenchard, the Commissioner, during the early 1930s, and then by successive heads of Special Branch until consigned to the Yard's furniture store by hot-desking modernisers. On promotion, Ritchie's first act had been to walk the floors shaking hands with every officer; theirs was to raid the store overnight and return Trenchard's desk to where it belonged.

Ritchie finished his notes and joined Kerr at the conference table. 'What's Dodge telling you?'

'It's not dissident. Nothing from across the water.'

Ritchie nodded. 'Politically it's the same story, which gets her even more worked up. Press releases spewing out of Stormont like confetti, all parties committed to power-sharing, etcetera. Every politician jumping in with "peace in our time" patter, and Knight doesn't like it. Remember Lisa from Northern Ireland Office? Treated her like something under her shoe.'

'Who pitched up from MOD?'

'Bloke I hadn't met before. His first COBRA and he made the mistake of talking about jihadis, like this is down to kids taking revenge for Syria. Knight practically bared her teeth at him, like she was going to rip his nuts off. She's only got one question, John. It's crudely rhetorical. And we're all giving her the wrong answers.'

'Did she ask you?'

Ritchie shook his head. 'But I told her anyway. We go where the intelligence leads us, and what we have so far is inconclusive. The code word is only one piece of the jigsaw.'

'I bet she loved that,' said Kerr with a short laugh, imagining the scene in the crowded briefing room.

The commander gave a 'who cares?' shrug that made Kerr smile. Bill Ritchie had covered Irish republican terrorism since the eighties, and Kerr enjoyed seeing him in his element. His promotion to the top job over a year ago had been sudden, dramatic and unexpected. There was a different look about him these days, a leaner, fitter version of the rumpled head of ops who had steered the Branch with his sleeves rolled up and, for the past two years, lived with the quiet conviction that he would die from prostate cancer. The elixir of success had lightened his mood, tightened his body, groomed his hair and packaged everything in a single-breasted navy suit. With his cancer at bay, Bill Ritchie took his meds, attended his check-ups and revelled in the heavy workload that came with his second chance.

'Who came from MI5?'

'Toby Devereux, looking like he'd just thrown up. Same conclusion as Dodge, but took twice as long to spin it. Plus the usual overview guff about "terrorist remnants," thugs diverting to bog standard criminal activity.' Ritchie scanned his notes. 'Initial readout from MI5 analysts in Belfast shows no traces of individuals or groups travelling to the mainland. No suspicious movements by targets under investigation.'

'So a zero report.'

'Knight looked like she wanted to rip Toby's heart out, but I backed him all the way. Then he let drop that MI5 have a direct line into the enemy camp, as if they'll have everything sorted by teatime.'

'What kind of line?' said Kerr, sitting forward. 'Telephone intercept? Microphone?'

'He said "secret and reliable," so I guess it's human, an asset with access to the dissident leadership. Presumably to tell them no-one from Belfast had a day out in London.'

'So he's using his source to prove a negative?'

Ritchie shrugged again. 'Who knows? He went all cryptic and asked to speak with Knight in private, away from the riff-raff. You know Devereux. He'll be backing it both ways.'

'Bill, he's a bit late for that,' said Kerr. 'Wait till Knight finds out he's been talking about lowering the threat level.'

Ritchie looked across sharply. 'When?'

'Three, four days ago. Part of a post-Brexit review, apparently.'

'Good timing, just as the bombers were inserting the detonators,' said Ritchie. 'And no-one's fronted him?'

'I'm checking with 1830…,' he said, then paused as Donna entered the office, still in her outdoor jacket, followed by Alan Fargo. He had changed his shirt but looked even more battered than before.

Ritchie stood up and shook his hand, gripping his upper arm politician style. 'Alan, I'm truly sorry for your loss. Have a seat.'

'Thanks, sir. I'm fine,' said Fargo, glancing between them. 'Just thought you should know this situation could still be live. They've got two more possibles just inside the station forecourt. Shopping bag and rucksack.'

'Abandoned in the rush?' said Ritchie, staying on his feet.

'They're hoping so. Also a plastic bag on a bus in Victoria Street,' he said, nodding through the window. 'Heading for the station. Top deck, rear offside seat.'

'Thanks.' Ritchie slipped his jacket off and slung it on the back of the chair. He was just as Kerr remembered him from the old days, except now he picked an invisible speck from the collar, smoothed his powder blue tie and looked five years younger. 'Is Jack Langton okay?'

'He's as good as me,' said Fargo.

'Dodge on form?' said Ritchie. 'We're going to need every asset in his little black book.'

'Everyone raring to go,' said Kerr.

'So let's get to work.'

Chapter Nine

Because of heavy early morning traffic flying into Heathrow, Mark Bannerman's Boeing 777 circled in a holding pattern for nearly fifty minutes before being cleared to land. Emerging from the bank of heavy cloud he stared gloomily out of the window as the first officer invited them to admire the view of Tower Bridge and Parliament to the right, lit up by a stray shaft of sunlight. 'Fuck,' he murmured, getting a fix on Vauxhall Cross as they descended alongside the Thames into Terminal Five.

It had been a tough night. Bannerman had left his house later than planned, keeping the embassy driver waiting for over an hour while he worked the Internet, and arrived at Jomo Kenyatta airport too late for a livener in the business lounge. Anticipating his return within forty-eight hours, even sooner if he could make everyone see sense, he had brought only his Ted Baker soft leather holdall, a present from the son he rarely saw. Another embassy official had been at the gate, someone from the consular section Bannerman vaguely recognised but ignored. The staffer had disappeared to the back of the plane as Bannerman swung left for champagne cocktails, a steady intake of gin and tonic and a sleep wrecked by the screaming infant of a couple still in their safari rigs. By the time they landed it was well past seven-thirty, eighty minutes late on a day when every hour counted.

The one bright spot was seeing Penny Redman again. She was only five foot four but he spotted her the moment he walked through the automatic doors, waiting outside Krispy Kreme beyond a phalanx of suited chauffeurs holding whiteboards and minicab drivers with names on strips of cardboard.

She walked ahead out of the concourse, heading for the upper parking garage. For twenty years Bannerman had teased Penny that she owned more trouser suits than Hillary Clinton: this one was navy blue with white piping over zip-up boots and matching shoulder bag. She covered the ground with short, rapid steps, as if trying to lose him, and Bannerman felt a pang for their shared past.

He found her feeding the parking pay station as he exited the opposite lift but stayed back as she zigzagged across the garage to a silver VW Golf GTI, half-hidden between a white courier van and a black taxi. The interior light stayed off as she opened the driver's door and, as he squeezed in beside her, she leaned across to kiss him on the cheek. 'Welcome back,' she said, taking a folder from her bag and sliding it onto his lap. 'Homework.'

He watched her wriggle out of her jacket and reach to lay it on the rear seat over his holdall. 'When are you going to invent a reason to bloody visit me?'

'Mark, behave,' she said, drawing his eyes from her blouse. She checked her watch, started the engine and reversed expertly from the space. 'We've got less than five hours.'

'Plenty of time.'

'Wait till you've read that.'

Bannerman and Penny had bumped into each other in Tehran, crossed paths in Jerusalem and shared beds in Marriott hotel rooms across Europe, until someone tipped off Bannerman's wife. Penny was fluent in French and Farsi, but their main contact had been in Dublin from 1994, when she had regularly shuttled from London to help him lure terrorists to the peace table.

'You're the boss.'

'Afraid not,' she said as she wheeled out of the car park and lowered the window to insert the ticket at the barrier. 'And Giles Lovett wants a word as soon as.'

Bannerman shivered at the inrush of cool air, pushed his seat back and shuffled low. 'Stuff Giles.'

She popped a piece of gum into her mouth and tapped the pack against his arm. 'Work.'

He took a strip of gum and began to read. The folder was cloth covered in deep purple with a ridged diagonal black cross from corner to corner, the regular format for MI6 documents in transit. Inside were twenty-three numbered pages of pale blue A4, each marked 'Secret and Personal for MB – Prebrief.' The document was a review of the Northern Ireland situation divided into political and security sections headed 'Talk in the Chamber' and 'War on the Ground.'

His long legs crossed at the ankles, head down in concentration, Bannerman stayed silent until Penny reached the M4, cleared a speed camera and accelerated hard into the outside lane. 'You're not dragging me into the Office, surely?'

'I'm taking you home.'

'Thanks.'

'You need a shower first.'

The first section unpicked the relationships between politicians at Stormont, the row over the so-called 'letters of comfort' to fugitive paramilitaries, and political threats to the peace process. The comment looked original, SIS internal, without the sense of cut and paste that devalued most Whitehall assessments.

It had begun to drizzle and the wiper juddered on Bannerman's side of the windscreen. 'Who put this together?' he said, suddenly. They had reached the tailback from Chiswick Flyover as Penny made the outside lane. 'Penny, is this all you?'

'Try not to sound so bloody surprised.'

'I'm not.' He wasn't. Bannerman believed that, in another age, Penny would have made Chief. She had been recruited when MI6 barely existed at Century House, a dingy, rundown office block near Southwark, and a woman director would have been even more incongruous than the petrol station in the forecourt.

Nowadays, post Iraq with its huddle of compliant, compromised spooks on the Number Ten sofa, Penny would make the perfect C, faithful to the secret mission and scathing of the dodgy politics. But in the early eighties, for all her talent, the odds had been too heavily stacked against her. There was nothing to break through, she once told him, because the glass ceiling had yet to be discovered.

Bannerman scanned the open source material until he came to the security report. This covered MI5's assessment of the power struggles among a 'ragbag of dissident remnants' from the Real and Continuity IRA factions, terrorist involvement in criminality, and recent attacks against police and prison officers, including images of bombs recovered intact. Penny had included sensitive SIS human intelligence offering a crushingly pessimistic exposé of murder plots, power struggles and conspiracies that rarely broke the surface.

The section closed with a brief account of the Victoria bombings, complete with photographs. 'But this only happened yesterday,' said Bannerman.

Penny shot him a look. 'Lucky we didn't *both* spend last night on the razzle.'

'It's brilliant,' said Bannerman, rubbing his eyes. The final page was a full-length image of a bulky, powerful man in his late twenties. He wore muddy jeans with a red and blue checked shirt, a woollen hat reaching down to his stubbled cheeks and safety boots, the steel toe caps glinting in the sun. Bannerman peered at the squinting face. 'Is this him?'

'Later,' she said as they fed onto Kew Bridge.

Penny Redman lived in a one bedroom flat on the first floor of a double-fronted Edwardian house opposite the primary school in East Sheen, with Richmond Park only a five minute jog to the south. Lime trees bordered the street and Penny's downstairs neighbour had planted a row of pink and white azaleas by the front fence. On a good day, the mainline train from Mortlake ferried her to Vauxhall Cross in less than twenty minutes, so Penny had extended the lease and stayed put for over twenty years.

At the top of the staircase her front door opened onto a small lobby with stained oak doors leading to the living room, modest kitchen and ensuite bedroom. Bannerman made himself comfortable while Penny locked her document away in the small combination safe beneath her bed and disappeared into the kitchen.

The living room was rectangular with dark red walls and a wide bay window that overlooked the school playground and faced the sun in the afternoons. Penny had brought two rugs home with her from Iran, a Kilim flat weave that almost covered the polished wood floor and a finer, Persian knot carpet attached to the wall opposite the original tiled fireplace. Her furniture was mostly oak and walnut, with the drop leaf dining table and chairs, sideboard, bureau and bookcases all acquired from Richmond's antique shops. By the window two brown leather armchairs flanked an ancient Chesterfield.

Bannerman knew his way around, for he had camped out here on his recall to London, bringing himself back to life with Penny while burying his marriage. Old copies of *The Economist*, *New Statesman* and *Private Eye* crammed every surface with photographs of godchildren and nephews, and logs strewn each side of the fireplace completed the intimate, cluttered feel that Bannerman loved.

The rumpus of children arriving for school filtered up through the trees as he dumped his bag on the floor by the sofa and stretched. From the kitchen, the tang of frying bacon purged the staleness of the flight. 'I'll take a bath if that's okay?' he called out, watching the street became clogged with four-by-fours.

'Help yourself.'

Penny had recently installed a new power shower, wash basin and toilet, but the centrepiece was the free-standing Cambridge bath she had acquired in her first year. It filled quickly, while Bannerman brushed his teeth and undressed. His mobile rang and he padded back into the living room, crouching down to conceal his nakedness from the window as he reached inside his jacket. Expecting it to be Rico from Nairobi, he pressed Ignore as soon as he saw the Office number.

By the time Penny entered with a tray of tea and two rounds of bacon sandwiches in thick white bread, Bannerman was half-submerged, soaping his hair. Water had spilled onto the tiled floor, so she took care as she balanced the tray on a wooden footstool and pulled up the slatted wooden chair she normally sat on to dry herself. She handed him a fluffy white hand towel from the radiator.

'Thanks.' Bannerman dabbed his face, dropped the towel onto the wet tiles and reached for his mug of tea, no milk. He took a sip, grabbing the nearest sandwich with his other hand. This was the meal she had made him when he turned up on her doorstep three years before and he studied her as he ate, wanting to be certain she remembered, too.

Penny took the other round, settled onto the chair and straightened her trousers, preparing for business. She had pulled off her boots and more water slopped onto her bare feet as Bannerman sat up. 'The man you asked about is Tommy Molloy,' she said, pulling at a stringy piece of fat. 'He's the one they'll take you to.'

'Any connection?'

'Sean Molloy's nephew.'

'Well he looks bloody wild. Don't say they've dragged me all this way to deal with a nutter?'

'He doesn't want to meet you, either. We made the approach to Sean yesterday afternoon.'

Bannerman squeezed the bread flat and took another bite. 'How?'

'Through Dublin. Same channel as before. Same alert status. He picked up in less than ten minutes.'

'Sean always was responsive. But things were different then.'

'And we're still paying his pension.'

Bannerman glanced at her naked feet. She had bunions, neat hemispheres polished from rubbing inside her boots, and her toenails were painted bright red. 'Coming in?' he said, spreading his legs.

Penny drank her tea. 'Mark, you need to concentrate. Anyway, Tommy *will* show.'

'Says who?'

'Sean will have him killed if he doesn't. He'll listen to what you have to say.'

Bannerman was chewing rapidly, washing the bacon down with tea. Bubbles of soap wobbled on his right eyebrow. 'Which is?'

'We need to know if dissident republicans did this.'

Bannerman laughed. 'I've just been reading that they didn't. Your words, Penny. Everyone in the Emerald Isle denies it, right? Or did I miss something?'

'They want you to make sure.'

'Who? Five?'

'In case something got missed along the way.'

'You mean they've taken their eye off the ball and want me to find it for them.'

'To discover if the IRA have been kicking it around in London,' said Penny.

Bannerman sighed. With both palms he streaked his hair back, forming a Dracula V on his forehead. 'Who fired the distress signal to C?'

The present incumbent was James Harrower, a user-friendly ex-diplomat. He had let it be known around the Office that he wished to be addressed by his first name, but this was a step too far for spooks of Bannerman's vintage, raised on Cold War paranoia and MI6 deniability.

'It went straight to Number Ten,' said Penny.

'Let me guess. From Toby Devereux?' A nod. 'And what answer is he hoping for?'

'He's briefed COBRA they have no definitive intelligence against the IRA.'

'And how pissed off did that leave our hawk at the Home Office?'

'Very. But Toby can't be seen to be trashing his own assessment, obviously.'

Bannerman frowned. 'What does he *actually* believe?'

'That Victoria station has their fingerprints all over it. Metaphorically speaking. A "rebuttable presumption" at Thames House, apparently.'

'It's arse covering, Toby Devereux in a tizz because the bombers sneaked over from Belfast while he was fretting about social networks in Rotherham.'

'Whatever. No-one can afford to wait until the dust settles,' said Penny. 'The political implications are massive. If you confirm their fears tomorrow…if the unionists get into a strop and Sinn Fein walks away…'

'And how heavily am I supposed to lean on Tommy Molloy?'

'You're not.' Penny leaned across and took his arm. 'Listen. You have to tread carefully. None of your jokey post-imperialism icebreakers.'

'What's his track record?'

'Prime suspect in three murders over the past decade. Plus shootings and punishment beatings. Conspiracy to supply explosives and drugs.'

'So why isn't he banged up?'

'Insufficient evidence, I suppose…not sure. The whole thing doesn't smell right.'

'Perhaps he's working for the Garda Siochana and no-one told us.'

Penny shrugged. 'There's probably tons we don't know. He's not active now but the current bunch of thugs in Belfast are terrified of him. Anyone who crosses Tommy Molloy disappears. He's unpredictable, irrational. But if the IRA have come back to attack London he will say so.'

'Unless someone tops him first,' said Bannerman, finishing his sandwich.

Penny leaned forward in the chair, deadly serious. 'Don't be flippant about this. Tomorrow won't be like dealing with Sean. I was against you going anywhere near the bloody place.'

'Okay, Penny. What's my back-up from Dublin?'

'No cover. You're on your own, like before.'

Another phone was ringing in the living room. This time it was Penny's landline and she was back in less than twenty seconds. 'Giles,' she mouthed as she handed him the phone.

'Yup.' Bannerman activated the speaker so that Penny could hear.

'Welcome back,' said Giles, then continued when Bannerman failed to answer. 'You didn't pick up earlier.'

'Too busy reading Penny's excellent paper.'

'We want to fill you in here, too, before you leave. How soon can you be at the Office?'

'No can do. Sorry. Just leaving for London City.'

'You can drop by with Penny on the way.'

'Giles, I have to be in Belfast in three hours.'

'Why?'

'Catching up with someone.'

'Who?' There was a pause and Bannerman could hear voices in the background. 'You know the stakes here, Mark.'

'Corpses at Victoria, outrage at Stormont,' he said shortly. 'Blowback at Westminster. I can imagine.'

'We want you to go in hard.'

'Hard.' He watched Penny vigorously shaking her head. 'I thought you wanted a negotiation?'

'This is the deal. If they're not responsible for this, then fine. Everything hunky-dory and we all go home. But if this gangster Molloy dissembles…'

'Dissembles?'

'…and we find out they did it anyway, then Her Majesty's Government will retaliate.'

'Oh, I shan't be mentioning HMG, Giles.'

'Let's be aggressive and not take any shit. Have you got that, Mark?' Bannerman stayed silent again, reminding himself why he disliked Giles so much. 'That's what we want you to say. No shilly-shallying. We fight fire with fire. That's the message. From James.'

'Ah, I see.' The extrovert James Harrower had been profiled in a couple of Sunday broadsheets as tough, no-nonsense and pragmatic. The new broom actually seemed to relish his televised select committee appearances, jacket off, cuffs out, Blair-like and blokeish. 'And what am I offering in return? That we don't send the SAS to execute them? Like the good old days?'

'No need to be facetious.'

'Nice speaking, Giles, but have to run or I'll miss the flight.' Bannerman reached down and pulled out the bath plug. 'I'll drop by on the way back to Nairobi. Love to all.' Click.

Penny handed him a bath towel. 'Now you can see why I'm so against this.'

Bannerman was slowly shaking his head. 'Giles brings to mind a bully three years above me at boarding school,' he said, handing her the phone. 'Always on the lookout for a spliff and a blow job.' Ignoring the towel, he raised himself up and turned to her as the water gurgled around his calves.

She touched the smooth skin inside his thighs. 'I don't have any cannabis.'

'No, it's alright, love,' he said quietly, looking down, enjoying the pulse of hot blood.

Penny stayed in her chair, watching him, snatching a glance at her watch. 'Shall we go to bed?'

Chapter Ten

Philip Deering's modest offices on the third floor of a mansion block in Chapel Row, Mayfair, close to the US embassy, were inconvenient in many ways. The claustrophobic lift still had its original metal concertina gates and occasionally jolted to a halt between floors. The three rooms were poky, poorly insulated, damp and spartan for the specialists and PA who worked there, the annual rent astronomical. Yet Deering dismissed any notion of leasing modern offices further west, towards Kensington or Holland Park, because location in the capital's wealthiest centre had cachet. A Mayfair address was the gold standard in his delicate line of work, and high value clients squeezing with their anxieties into the conference room always left comforted by its old world charm. For that alone, Deering was happy to climb the stairs and quietly elevate his fees.

He liked to lunch in Harry's Bar, dine at The Wolseley and drink in the Punch Bowl or Running Footman, but top of the list was the working breakfast at Claridges in Brook Street, a ten minute stroll away. He was heading there now through the drizzle, in deep conversation with 'Sunny' Jim Walker, the morose chief financial officer and money laundering wizard he had rescued from the rubble of the global banking crash.

Philip Deering was sixty-six and a retired major general, though from his appearance few would guess his age or position. So determined was he to reinvent himself that even his Sandhurst contemporaries, still peering at life through the regimental prism, in civvy outfits as blatant as mess-dress, would barely have recognised him.

'Do you think he'll turn up?' said the accountant as they reached the junction with Grosvenor Street. 'Must be frenetic over there right now. Horrendous.'

'A tenner says yes.' Traffic was heavy and the pedestrian light showing red, but Deering spotted a gap and crossed anyway. Walker was too hesitant and Deering waited for him at the opposite kerb, outside the Post Office.

'But will he buy it?'

Deering nodded. 'He's greedy.'

The major general had been assiduous in masking his Service life, a bubble of power, status and entitlement. There was no spit and polish on Deering's shoes or chalk stripe in his suit, and the grey, crinkly hair was in need of a trim. In the space of a single summer the plummy-voiced, unchallenged supremo had left town for good, ousted by the deal-maker in tasselled loafers and high street raincoat. 'Shabby-chic' his wife jokily called him, dressed to match the furniture in their Fulham home. Amelia, the present Mrs Deering, was third in line to Deborah, the colonel's daughter he had married as a young subaltern, and Kaltrina, a sexy Albanian interpreter who had caught his eye while serving in Kosovo in the summer of '99. Amelia was the widow of Deering's closest friend in 1 Para and had a couple of car-crash liaisons behind her, too. They had been going strong for eleven years and Deering knew this marriage would last because his fallen comrade bound them together, loyalty ensuring faithfulness.

Breakfast was served in the hotel's beautiful art deco Foyer and Reading Room, and Deering's usual table was awaiting him, in a corner beside a giant blue flower arrangement just inside the soaring entrance arches. His position gave an uninterrupted view of the beautiful Chihuly chandelier, ornate lobby fireplace, and any guest drifting within eavesdropping distance. At first glance the choice of place appeared unnecessarily open: all the tables were set apart, and those alongside the far wall offered complete discretion. But only Deering's spot allowed a rapid getaway without drama, should the business deal take a dangerous turn.

Philip Deering was the founder and CEO of Wymark Corporate Solutions, a boutique company offering services in business intelligence, corporate risk and protective security. There was no website or other marketing because Deering accepted commissions by word of mouth only. Consumers included a Russian oligarch reeking of KGB, the risk and compliance heads of three investment banks, a football coach, a couple of hedgies, a phone-hacked celebrity and a high-ranking fugitive from Egypt's Arab Spring. His most recent signing was a trust fund manager intent on suing her husband to death.

Wymark's core associates deployed an army of freelancers to carry out its work: due diligence for the patron or disinformation against the rival; personal protection or invasive surveillance. The fee structure covered every permutation. To the privileged few who took their chance in the creaking Chapel Row lift Deering used 'boutique' because it sounded non-Army and implied a uniquely personal service to satisfy 'niche requirements.' And he uttered 'niche' as a whisper that boundaries could be pushed, favours pulled and laws stretched to satisfy Wymark's élite hierarchy of clients.

Walker ordered tea, almond croissants and brioche while waiting for their guest, checking every few moments for the anticipated 'no show' text while his boss surveyed the foyer. Suddenly Deering spotted a flurry of movement by the fireplace. With a laugh like a small explosion he slid the chair back and got to his feet in one movement. 'You lose, mon ami' he murmured to Walker as he dabbed his mouth and let the napkin drop. By the time their guest reached the arch Deering's hand was already outstretched, his face glowing with bonhomie. 'You made it,' he said, 'Marvellous.'

Derek Finch, deputy assistant commissioner and head of counter-terrorism, dubbed the 'Bull' within the Yard because of his untrammelled aggression, took the remaining chair facing into the restaurant, unbuttoned his jacket and let the waiter pour his tea.

'Sunny and I watched you on the seven o'clock bulletin,' said Deering when they were alone. 'Never thought you'd make it.'

Finch gave a modest shrug. 'Just another day.' He smiled,

placed his mobile on the table and did a take of the room, a minor celebrity checking his fan base. 'This is important.'

'And after yesterday's trauma our need is all the greater.'

Finch ordered eggs Benedict and Deering his usual omelette made with Scottish haddock, Sunny contenting himself with muesli and yoghurt. This was not the first time they had broken bread together. Deering's overture in late spring had been supper in the top room of The Other Place, a private club in a narrow alley off the Strand, behind the Adelphi Theatre, where Finch had swallowed the bait even before the arrival of the hors d'oeuvres.

'So what do you think?' said Deering.

Finch was piling soft butter on a chunk of brioche. 'I don't think this affects our time scale.'

'Sorry, Derek. I mean the investigation. If it's not too…'

'You saw the news,' said Finch, eating the bread in one mouthful.

'But this is the return of the IRA to our shores, right? Known code words, the same MO? Is that your working assumption?'

'Everyone's in denial,' continued Finch, chewing rapidly. He glanced at his watch, a chunky, expensive Breitling. 'COBRA can't even face the thought.'

'So you're the breaker of bad news.'

'Oh, I'm not jumping to conclusions.'

'Quite.'

'And no way is this for politicians to decide.'

'Absolutely. Good to hear.'

Finch straightened his cuffs and drained his tea. In a few months he would be flying in Philip Deering's slipstream, yet the two men had reached this point from opposite trajectories. The badges of prestige shunned by Deering still meant everything to Derek Finch, who deployed his double breasted pinstripe suit with monogrammed silk ties and retro braces to shout power and success.

The youngest offspring of a bus driver and care assistant,

Finch had scrambled his way into the Yard's inner circle by self-promotion, trashing of rivals and a borderline pass in Criminology at Cambridge. Shaky around political correctness, unsound on diversity but a fixture in the Masonic Lodge, Finch had slipped through on a raft of bullshit and tokenism that fooled no-one, including the cronies steering him. Yet for all his success he lacked Philip Deering's inner confidence, seeing every provocation as a red rag. The runt of the litter had shredded flesh to become leader of the pack, but everyone still despised him as the Bull.

Deering stayed silent, hands lying still on the crisp white table cloth while Finch briefed him on the investigation. He spoke openly, as if Deering and his associate had a need to know, only pausing briefly while the waiter brought their orders. On the coded bomb warning he was word perfect. Vigorously polishing his fork with the napkin, he held nothing back about the forensic recovery at the scene, difficulties in identifying the most mutilated victims and the placing of the bombs in polythene rubbish sacks. He led them through the scene, speculating that the second device had been intended to murder his bomb disposal officers, then walked them around the detail of his exchanges with MI5 and GCHQ.

Deering worked hard to disguise his contempt for the man. The sole purpose in cultivating Finch had been to extract such disclosures, yet the scale of his indiscretion always took him by surprise. Scotland Yard's head of counter-terrorism was exploiting insider knowledge to pitch for the plum job Deering had already offered him. He was behaving like a prostitute inflating the price, and Deering had rarely listened to anything so flagrant and undignified. 'Thank you for being open,' he said when he had heard enough. 'And for trusting us. I think we can offer you something in return.'

Finch's face clouded in midbite. 'Haven't we already agreed that?'

Deering nodded, reminding himself that if Finch ever made the conversion to Wymark's security consultant, he would require a tight leash. 'I'm talking about the here and now,' he said, forcing a smile. 'Sunny and I believe we can add value to your inquiry, or at least narrow the search.'

'Sorry. Not with you.'

'The perpetrators. I would have called you, but here we are anyway. Serendipity.' Deering tried his omelette and glanced at Walker. 'I've had a call from an associate across the water. A friend, actually, from the old days. Intelligence Corps.'

'Which section?'

'14 Det.'

'Long gone.' Finch had begun liberally spooning hollandaise sauce onto his eggs.

'But with operatives still very connected.'

'Where is he now?'

'Doesn't matter. This friend has access to people on the ground, Derek. Far deeper than the police or MI5 and a hundred percent more reliable.'

'And what's he telling you?'

'Yesterday's attack was planned and carried out by republican dissidents controlled from west Belfast. That's the shorthand. You can throw out any other theory.'

'Names?'

'Let's be patient. These thugs never disarmed. No-one with a scintilla of insight ever doubted their capability to bomb London.'

'Including us,' said Finch, unconvincingly. Fork still in hand he scratched the bridge of his nose, revealing a Help for Heroes wristband in the tri-service colours. 'So when do I get to interview him?'

'You don't. He's Wymark's asset. Code name Sidewinder, and that's all I can give you.'

Finch lay his cutlery down and gave a small laugh. 'Look, you know I have to assess the source, give him a score.'

'And how many do I get out of ten?' said Deering, enjoying the other man's awkwardness. 'Accept my word. Please. The call is less than two hours old, a heads-up from our impeccable source. You'll meet others like him when you come aboard.'

'Philip, if you're telling me you have material info…'

Deering leant in. 'My informant is a veteran soldier who never closed the door because he loves his country,' he said crisply. 'Let's just leave it at that. The government thought they had Ireland sorted, didn't they? Surrender to every republican demand. Betray the unionists. Power-sharing around Sinn Fein's agenda. Line drawn, game over.'

'Police never stopped monitoring them…'

'…and the IRA never stopped making threats but everyone ignored them because the truth was inconvenient. Some of us always knew they would come back one day.' Breakfast over, Deering lay his cutlery neatly across his plate. 'Yesterday they did just that. Fact. The IRA got real again and innocent Londoners are paying the price.'

'Will he find out more?'

'I imagine so.'

'Well, I'm grateful. Obviously.'

'That's not all.' Deering threw a glance at Walker, who handed him a white A3 envelope. 'We'd like you to have this on account,' he smiled, sliding it across the table. The package was bulky, only just fitting beneath the rim of Finch's plate. 'And Sunny also transferred another ten into your bank this morning. An advance on salary for when you join us. But mostly a sign of good faith. Of friendship.'

The envelope lay untouched while the recipient looked from one to the other. This counted as a potential flight moment for Deering but he stayed deep in his chair, legs stretched out, fingers interlinked. The heart of Wymark's operation was the integrity testing of public officials with secrets for sale, and bribery was the oxygen. A lifestyle check on Derek Finch had revealed a poseur chasing a lifestyle higher than his income and with credit card debts through the roof. His recent leap up the property ladder from neo-Georgian semi to mock-Tudor mansion had coincided with the failure of his wife's office cleaning business. He was already three months in mortgage arrears, and Spanish attorneys were threatening to foreclose on his holiday villa.

A profile of such ruinous, eye-watering recklessness should have arrested the attention of Finch's vetting officers; instead, it was Philip Deering who studied Finch's hand, knowing he would reach out to save his acre in Bromley and slice of heaven in Andalusia.

Finch's mobile was vibrating but he ignored it as he buried the envelope in his breast pocket. It took a couple of fumbled attempts because the bundle inside was so thick.

'Naturally,' said Deering, 'I shall channel you the product from Sidewinder as it comes in. My act of public duty,' he chuckled, 'before your escape to the private sector.'

Finch stared from one to the other. He looked physically diminished, as if he knew they knew. 'And how do you want me to help in the meantime?'

It was the surrender Deering had been expecting, the deflation from braggart to mere instrument. 'My proposal is that you reciprocate with a daily update on your investigation. The sort of thing we heard just now.'

'How?'

'I suggest we speak each evening by secure phone? To compare notes, in confidence. A sort of rolling of the pitch for the day you join us.'

As soon as Finch had left them alone Deering ordered two Kir Royales. 'Christ, Sunny, we have to kiss a lot of frogs in this business.'

'None as ugly as that one,' grumbled Walker, reaching into his pocket to settle their bet.

Chapter Eleven

Wednesday, 12 October, 12.17, Europa Hotel, Belfast

In Mark Bannerman's memory the Europa in Great Victoria Street, Belfast, endured as the most bombed hotel in Europe. To English TV viewers who had never visited Northern Ireland the blasted structure and its boarded-up windows came to symbolise the Troubles; and for a wave of reporters, government officials and reckless tourists, dangerous nights risked within its battered walls had been a rite of passage, a war story pepped-up by the breakout of peace. For two decades, check-in at the Europa had been a trip to the front line.

The hotel sat adjacent to the Grand Opera House, which had also suffered blast damage from Europa's bombs, and a grenade's throw from the railway station. Viewed from the street, its central core had a wing with four pillars extending obliquely on each side, like arms outstretched in welcome. Bannerman had stayed here twice, about six weeks before the final, devastating attack in 1993. The pockmarked ruin that had once shamed Belfast now enjoyed multiple stars on TripAdvisor, with plate glass everywhere and a plaque in Reception telling the world Bill Clinton had slept upstairs. While Bannerman was spying around the globe the Europa had grown unrecognisably chic, the icon of a city transformed.

He relaxed with a coffee in the fifth floor junior suite the Office had reserved for him, waiting for the call. Despite the travelling, he felt refreshed. The previous day's recreation in Penny's bed had cost him the scheduled 15.40 flight from London City with Flybe and it had been well after ten when he checked into the hotel, time enough for a nightcap in the Piano Bar before a dreamless sleep.

The suite had a small, separate lounge, but Bannerman sat on one of the upright chairs between the bed and the window, the holdall at his feet. He was entitled to one of the deluxe rooms to the rear of the hotel, with a view of the Black Mountains, but the operational plan required clear line of sight to the hotel forecourt and the street. It had rained for a while mid-morning but the sun was gaining the upper hand, drying the slick pavement and warming Bannerman's knees through the glass. Traffic was light, with buses and trucks passing easily in the wide thoroughfare, and a convoy of cyclists from the right veered wide to avoid a puddle radiating from a blocked drain. Squeezed between two pubs across the street were a hair salon stacked on a bookmakers; beneath him, the shiny black roof of a stretch Merc, still speckled by rain, glided through metal bollards into the space once cratered by a massive van bomb. A taxi rank occupied the opposite kerb to his left, and workers on early lunch were risking the rain to converge on Sandwich Express. Earpieces in place, hands in pockets or working iPhones, they overflowed the shop in a neat queue trailing back along the pavement.

Bannerman had stayed in bed until eight, flicking between Sky News and BBC Breakfast but thinking mostly of Africa, then showered and dressed in a fresh shirt with the tan cords and blue linen jacket he had worn the day before. Penny had advised him to keep his profile low by ordering room service, but he had gone for breakfast in the Causerie restaurant to the right of the lobby, checking for watchers while enjoying his first Ulster fry in a decade.

A pay-as-you-go Nokia rested in his right palm, slipped him by Penny at the airport drop-off as they kissed goodbye. Noticing flecks of mud still clinging to his suede shoes from the lunch with Rico, he resisted the urge to call Nairobi on his SIS encrypted mobile to check the Office had hooked up with him.

Suddenly the Nokia was purring in his hand, Unknown Number. 'David' was all he said, as directed. He listened for a moment, then peered through the window to his left. Loitering in the middle of the sandwich line was a young woman in combat trousers and denim jacket, wearing a baseball cap with a knot of hair above the back strap. He had clocked her with the rest on his initial scan, two or three minutes earlier. Mobile to her ear, she looked directly up at him, then cut the call and walked slowly away. Bannerman kicked the holdall beneath the bed, grabbed his jacket, slipped the room key into his shirt pocket and made for the lobby.

He spotted the girl again as he emerged through the hotel's revolving door. She was waiting for him across the street, just beyond Subway and a modest travel agency, Belfast by Bus. Ignoring the pedestrian crossing he kept to his side, strolling in front of the opera house. Jacket hooked over his shoulder, he acted like a visitor with all the time in the world as he paused by the 'What's On' hoarding to study the posters and steal a look around. Penny had warned him the pick-up would be like this, a female working alone, no surprises or hostiles sniffing at his heels, but Bannerman always listened to the survival instinct that had extricated him from more threats than he could remember.

He maintained this leisurely pace even when she took a right turn by the clock tower above the Assembly Rooms and disappeared from view. By the time he reached the corner she was fifty paces away, lingering outside a menswear shop before vanishing again behind the building. He crossed the street and followed in the lee of the stone wall, pausing by an electrical supply shop just inside the junction.

The meeting place turned out to be no more than a potholed lane just wide enough for one vehicle, with shuttered, defaced buildings on the left side facing a high metal fence and padlocked gates. A barrier prevented access from the far end, sixty paces away, and beyond that towered the patchy green dome of Belfast City Hall in Donegall Square. The lane was deserted apart from a beaten-up black taxi halfway along, its diesel engine spluttering against the walls. The suspension sagged on the driver's side and he could make out a stocky figure behind the wheel, visor down.

The clapped-out engine gave a cough as Bannerman stepped away from the safety of the wall, and he felt the first pulse of anxiety.

The nearside passenger door swung open and he clambered inside without hesitating. The girl was sitting in the far corner, diagonally to the driver. She looked more like a student than a courier, but the cream canvas bag cradled in her lap might have held coursework or a gun. Bannerman offered his broadest smile, pulled the door shut and sat beside her. 'Nice to meet you,' he said, neatly folding his jacket in his lap.

Face impassive, the girl held out her palm. 'Mobile.' As soon as he handed her the Nokia she expertly flipped the back panel and removed the battery.

'No calls home, then.'

The hand appeared again, the voice sharp. 'And the other one.'

Bannerman searched inside the jacket for his work mobile, an ancient Samsung Galaxy, battered and scratched on the outside, its innards reconfigured by SIS coders. Pressure on the Calendar app transformed the phone into a recording device as he surrendered it; and the moment the girl flipped out the battery she activated a back-up power cell secreted above the camera lens. Bannerman had routinely used this trick for meetings in Tehran and, sometimes, against Rico's director: on this mission, the button was second nature. Sitting back in the seat, he watched her dump the batteries in the door pocket and hide both phones in her bag.

The taxi was damp and dirty, with a sliding glass partition separating them from the front, and there was a whiff of stale vomit. The pale-skinned driver did not turn his head or make the slightest movement. Bulging shoulders strained the seams of his white T-shirt, and the bull neck was as wide as his head. He looked dangerous, but drove off the instant the girl caught his piggy eyes in the mirror.

Bannerman tried another couple of perfunctory remarks, then gave up and stared out at the city, reduced to a bleak monochrome through the tinted glass. They were heading west for the river, the engine echoing off the canyon of buildings, and ran into a heavy shower on the centre of Albert Bridge. Only one wiper worked and it stuttered across the windscreen as they descended into the Short Strand, reminding him of the drive with Penny a little over twenty-four hours earlier.

They filtered off the bridge, keeping the river to their left, then followed the high walled perimeter of the bus depot into the heart of republican territory. Bannerman soon lost his bearings, confused by rows of new housing punctuating the Victorian terraces that had once lined every narrow street. The enclave was as small, claustrophobic and impoverished as he remembered it, its warring factions kept at bay by tall steel fences euphemised as 'peace lines.'

The faces of republican martyrs commemorated in Gaelic looked out from giant murals on the ends of many terraces and, from street corners, watchful eyes of the living tracked their vehicle through every turn. Suddenly they swung into a cul-de-sac of new starter homes, sweeping round the turning circle in one go and stopping by the end house.

Bannerman studied a low, curving wall inset with ceramic images of paramilitaries. 'Is this it?'

A balaclava had appeared in the girl's hand. Bannerman gave her a long sideways look. 'You said no dramas.'

'Put it on.'

Two young men had appeared at the junction twenty paces away, observing. Bannerman shrugged and stretched the coarse black cotton in his hands, looking in vain for eyeholes. It smelt of sweat and stale breath as he pulled it over his head. Wondering who had preceded him, he felt another beat of alarm.

The taxi moved off again as he sat forward to struggle into his jacket, then steadied himself with both hands as they regained the street. Disorientated, nauseous from the stench, he tried to breathe through his mouth, but the suction pulled at the material and made him gag. The girl slapped his hand away when he tried to reach a couple of fingers beneath the hood. 'Do that again and we'll tie you.'

After a couple more sharp turns he felt a bump, as if they were mounting the kerb, then the taxi rolled to a halt with the engine switched off. It rocked when the driver's door slammed shut and Bannerman felt a stream of cool air as someone grabbed his wrist, pulling him outside. Rain drummed on the hood, compensating for his suffocation and loss of sight. He heard a gate squeak open, then something brushed against his trousers, as if he was being pulled through brambles, and he was inside again. No voices. Kitchen odours of burnt toast, blocked sink and stale dishcloths filtered through the hood, and he kept bumping into things as he was led deeper into the house.

Then he was pushed down into a soft chair. The hood was whipped away, snagging his nose, and he caught the driver disappearing through the door as he looked around to get his bearings, taking deep breaths to recover his senses. Bannerman found himself in the musty, rundown front room of a Victorian house. Purple velvet curtains had been pulled shut, with everything thrown into shadow by a single frosted bulb in the ceiling. The reek from the hood still lingered and he blew hard into a large blue handkerchief, trying to clear his passages.

He was sitting in a dark brown armchair to the right of the window, facing a bulky silver TV. A bottle of Evian had been left in the cup holder built into the armrest, but the seal had been broken and the rim tasted of someone else's mouth. On the floral carpet between him and the door were two dining chairs, evidently placed there for his interviewers. Apart from a crucifix on the opposite wall and an image of the Virgin, the room was impersonal, giving no hint of who lived here, with streaks of dust on the table beside him suggesting a recent clear-out of family photographs.

He heard the front door open and slam shut, then voices. Tommy Molloy entered the room followed by taxi girl, and he clocked the canvas bag now strapped across her shoulder. Through the gap in the door, lined up neatly at the foot of the stairs, he glimpsed a woman's mauve Crocs and two pairs of children's trainers. Bannerman started to stand but Molloy stopped him dead: there were to be no handshakes, no preliminaries at all.

Molloy sat down and stretched his legs, crossing his beefy arms. From Penny's photograph Bannerman immediately recognised the working boots, steel toe caps glinting beneath the light bulb, the brightest objects in the room. The woman sat to Bannerman's left, nearest the door, and he saw the bag drop to her feet. No-one said a word. Molloy was wearing the same work clothes and looked clammy, as if he had been labouring in the rain and come straight from the site. Away from the sun his eyes were wider, but the look just as belligerent. Bannerman let silence cloud the room, waiting for the targets to break first. There was a sudden *crack* and the rickety chair almost collapsed as Molloy lurched forward, his boots smearing the carpet with mud. The voice was harsher than granite, the face so close that Bannerman could taste tobacco on his breath. 'Why are you here?'

Bannerman leaned back in the armchair, cross-legged, and swept back his hair. His interrogators looked down on him, but he had done this before and felt in control. 'Surely London covered that?'

'I want *you* to tell me.'

'First things first, Tommy,' said Bannerman, blowing his nose again and tucking the handkerchief in his sleeve. 'This business with the hood. There was no need for the condemned man routine. Your uncle never did that.'

Though Bannerman had fired his rebuke as a provocation, the gangster's overreaction took him by surprise. Molloy shot forward again, jabbing a warty finger in Bannerman's face. 'But he's not here, is he? Fuck it, you're dealing with me now.'

Bannerman did not flinch as it occurred to him that, for all the bluster, Molloy's position as IRA thug-in-chief might be less secure than MI5 realised. 'Alright. We need to know urgently if the IRA put the bombs down in Victoria station,' he said levelly. 'I believe you have the answer.'

'Why would you think that?'

Bannerman held out his palms. 'Which part?'

'Don't be clever.'

'Okay,' said Bannerman mildly as another wave of hostility washed over him. 'The code words used in the warning have been used in dissident IRA operations. The bombers placed a secondary device, probably to trap the bomb disposal guys. A favourite tactic around here, right? And number three, the target was a bank, same as a lot of IRA attacks since the credit crunch. Is that enough?'

Molloy sat back again, regarding Bannerman's tanned face. 'And why did they send me a ponce like you?'

'What's your answer?'

'You've heard the reports, same as me. Every fucker's denying it here and across the water.'

'Tommy, I'm being friendly. The politics of this are incredibly sensitive.'

'For London, yeah. I bet they are. For the British fucking government.'

'And?'

'The Real IRA has never put its weapons beyond use.' Molloy tapped Bannerman's knee. 'You can tell them this. The day we resume hostilities against England no-one will have any doubt.'

Bannerman glanced at the girl, as if Molloy was already a lost cause, but she stared back, unblinking. 'I'm simply asking, did that happen on Monday and I missed something?'

'And if we did?'

Bannerman steepled his fingers, a tutor marking down his dullest student. 'There would be serious repercussions, naturally.'

Molloy gave a loose, phlegmy laugh, then coughed loudly. 'Your English soldiers coming back for another fight, you mean. Is that what they sent you to tell me?' He looked at the woman, shaking his head in disbelief. 'You really want another bloody nose like last time? What a joke.'

'It's more than that, Tommy. It's Brexit. How many millions does the European Union dump into Northern Ireland? No idea? It's about one forty, give or take. But Europe's bleeding hearts will soon be scuttling back to Brussels, taking their moolah with them. So it comes down to this. If you've been up to your old tricks, power-sharing will collapse. That's a stone bonker, believe me. And if the protestants walk from Stormont, Westminster is not going to pick up the tab.'

'And that's supposed to scare me?'

The spook observed Molloy for a moment, searching in vain for similarities with his uncle. In his long career Bannerman had encountered many psychopaths around the world, and this slab-faced bully boy who had shot, bludgeoned and terrorised his way to the top of the dung heap was no different from the rest. Released from the stifling anxiety beneath the hood, Bannerman felt a sudden rush of temper. 'No. Of course. Men like you don't do "scared," do they?' He uncrossed his legs and lurched forward so violently that one of the springs gave way. The words came in a flood, a storm drain channelling a declaration of war. 'You have a lot of soldiers on the run, Tommy. OTRs. Twenty? Thirty? If it turns out these attacks are down to you, we will take active steps against them. That's a sacred promise. In secret, anywhere in the world, until the end of time. No more amnesties, no more secret deals with bombers and murderers. Understood? No more get-out-of-jail-free cards. Let the bastards rot.' Suddenly the woman's chair crashed back as she turned and left the room without a word. Bannerman clocked her bag on the floor and lasered back on Molloy.

'You'll never be able to...'

'Shut up. I haven't finished. And guess what? The drugs trade in Belfast suddenly becomes the number one police priority. Overnight.' Penny's voice was inside his head, but the drip, drip of her words of caution had evaporated with his fear. 'Heavy jail penalties for traffickers, keeping our brightest youngsters safe from criminals like you. How does that sound? And if you're still into the red diesel scams, forget it.'

Molloy's head swayed from side to side, the eyes locked on Bannerman's.

'That's the message, Tommy. It's what my masters are telling me to say.'

'Their English lickspittle.' He glanced at the handkerchief flopping from Bannerman's sleeve. 'They send a man like you to intimidate me?'

'Dress it up how you like. I've been around a long time. A success story. Ask your uncle Sean.' Outside he heard a car draw up, then the squeak of the front gate. 'And if I'm right, how long till they knock you off? What's your sell-by, Tommy? A week? Thirty-six hours? How soon do you get *your* bullet in the head?' Bannerman sat back in the chair again. 'Fuck you, man. I'll soon be reading about you and thinking back to our friendly chat.'

He eyed Molloy's boots, waiting for the onslaught, but instead the door was flung open and taxi girl reappeared, followed by a second woman in tight jeans and a green, coarse-knit patterned sweater with an uneven oval neck. She was older, mid-thirties, but he could tell by their complexion and build that they were sisters. 'Leave us,' she said to Molloy, though he was already surrendering his chair. It was a command, spoken with more muscle than anything Molloy had inflicted, and Bannerman realised for the second time how wrong London had been.

She sat down and faced him, hands folded in her lap.

'I'm David.'

'Don't bother.' She shook her head. 'But I know why you're here. What has Tommy been telling you?'

'It's what he hasn't said that troubles me.'

'Well you're barking up the wrong tree.'

'An attack in London is more effective than twenty bombs over here, right? Isn't that what you used to say in the good old days? A strike at the heart of Empire, and all that?'

'We're not responsible for your bombs,' she said, shortly.

'That doesn't quite cover it. Sounds like politician speak. Who are you?'

'You come here from London making threats but offer nothing in return.'

'Not so.'

'Another English betrayal.'

Bannerman showed her the face he kept in reserve for moments of unexpected stress. He hadn't the faintest idea what she was talking about, which left bluff, a lie or concession. 'So what do I tell them?'

Abruptly the woman stood up, followed by her sister. 'Dublin promised us a lot more than your threats and menaces.' She turned by the door and regarded him with disdain. 'You don't understand what I'm saying, do you? The bastards sent you here without telling you.'

Bannerman could hear movement in the narrow hallway. 'What do I tell them?'

'A fancy carrier pigeon is no use to me.'

Chapter Twelve

When Dodge was not out on the ground looking after his agents he worked in a narrow rectangular room just along the corridor from John Kerr. It extended eight paces from the door to a double window overlooking St James's Park, though Dodge rarely hung around long enough to enjoy the view. Kerr and Bill Ritchie valued every shred of human intelligence (HUMINT) as potential gold dust, so Dodge had installed three tall gunmetal security cabinets along the side wall, and also acquired (by means unknown) a steel office door with a digital lock as elaborate as Alan Fargo's in Room 1830. The place was really a fortified store, protecting the files of every Special Branch agent over half a century, from the revolutionary left to al-Qaeda, and was so cramped that Dodge had to shuffle crabwise to reach his desk by the window. When unlocked, the cabinet doors swung open within an inch of the opposite wall, concealing any occupant from the corridor.

The two women and two men in his source unit team were based in the same open plan office that housed the Fishbowl. Hot-desking in a space at the opposite end from Kerr, squatters among the teams monitoring Syrian returnees, jihadi websites and London mosques, they still found themselves in his line of sight. Dodge regarded the cultivation of agents as an art, needing the finesse of a rose grower working miracles with blighted soil. He had survived in Ireland through meticulous attention to tradecraft, but imposed only two rules on his troops: they had to work any agent recruitment in pairs, woman with man, and store every disc, video, audio or scribbled note in one of his precious safes.

Today, apart from his diversions to the Fishbowl and 1830, Dodge had spent the entire morning on the phone, listening to the Irish friends and security experts he had worked alongside for so many years. With the landline red hot and the mobile on permanent charge, the intel about London's worst terrorist attack since 7/7 was consistent: the outrage was *not* the work of the IRA. That was the message he had been hammering into John Kerr since ten o'clock.

The final call came through as he was returning along the corridor with a paper cup of coffee from the main office. The accent was English and the words stopped him in his tracks. It was the voice of a man, sure of himself.

'I want to speak to Dodge.'

'Who is this?' No-one outside the Yard knew his nick-name.

'I have information about the bombs in Victoria.'

Phone clamped to his ear, Dodge reached his office and jabbed the lock. 'Okay,' he said, turning to ease open the heavy door with his backside. 'How did you get this number?'

'From Frankie.' The voice was soft, with a stress on the last word. Dodge was shuffling past the third and final safe as the name hit him. He froze, as if someone had reached inside his rib cage and seized his heart. The coffee slipped from his hand and spattered his suit, but Dodge scarcely noticed as he crashed the final step to his desk.

'How do you mean?' He collapsed into the revolving chair, almost tipping onto the floor. 'What are you saying?' Bunched over the desk he rammed the mobile against his right ear, clenching the other hand against his forehead.

'We need to meet.'

One of the women on Dodge's team appeared in the doorway, craning round to see him. 'Spare a minute?'

Dodge covered the mouthpiece. 'Not now.' He could feel himself beginning to hyperventilate. 'Close the door.'

The officer lingered for a moment, concerned, curious. She looked about to step into the room and say something, so Dodge waved her away and waited for the door to swing shut.

'Where?'

'Covent Garden. There's a café by the museum called Concetta's. I'll meet you there in twenty minutes.'

'Too tight.'

'I'll wait for you.'

'Who am I looking for?'

'I'll find you.'

Dodge sat for a moment staring across the park, waiting for the hammering in his chest to subside. Then he snatched his mobile and headed out, skidding on the spilt coffee. He left alone and told no-one where he was going, breaking his own cardinal rule. The first lift was full, the second slow to arrive, and the revolving door on the ground floor seemed even more sluggish than usual. Emerging into Back Hall he clocked Alan Fargo with his late lunch in a brown paper bag and a new can of Red Bull. Fargo had evidently spotted Dodge, too, and was waiting beside the Book of Remembrance, fiddling with the dressing on his neck.

'Can't stop,' growled Dodge, hurrying past as Fargo started to say something. Sensing Fargo's eyes on him, Dodge paused to glance over his shoulder as he reached the exit. From here the two lesions on Fargo's cheek seemed to coalesce into a single red weal, bright as a traffic light. It made Dodge turn away, shamed by his friend's look of bewilderment.

He took the tube for the two stops from St James's Park to Embankment, lighting up the moment he hit fresh air. The shaded side of Villiers Street was still slick from the morning's showers and he almost slipped again on the flagstones. He tapped out another cigarette as soon as he turned off the Strand into Maiden Lane, checking his watch outside the Maple Leaf pub, on the perimeter of Covent Garden: just after half two. He had time. He shouldered his way to the bar through a bunch of Canadians watching ice hockey with bottles of Moosehead lager and ordered a shot of Jamesons, then another. When he turned to leave the visitors took their eyes off the screen to make way for him, instinctively wary of the sweating, agitated Brit. Back on the street he circled the elegant neoclassical buildings of the old market, struggling to calm himself as he squeezed through a crescent of spectators in front of St Paul's church, all eyes fixed on a dreadlocked juggler balancing on a ladder.

He spotted Concetta's the moment he turned the corner, between Accessorize and the Lower Courtyard, a stone's throw from the London Transport Museum at the opposite end of the square. It looked tiny, like an old-fashioned village shop, with a dwarf brick wall beneath latticed windows to the left of a blackened oak door. Dodge needed another whiskey, but it was the smell of fresh coffee that hit him as he went inside, dipping his head and almost tripping down a small step. The right wall was lined with green banquettes, tables and pastoral scenes of Tuscany, opposite a high wooden bar serving tea, coffee, pastries and brightly coloured cup-cakes. About a dozen middle-aged customers occupied the tables in pairs or small groups, casually dressed and buzzing with conversation. Purse in hand, a woman in a pink waterproof turned from the bar to check something with her husband, who held up two fingers in a T.

At the far end he saw a red-brick arch leading to a separate space, a sunken, dimly lit area filled by a communal oak table with an eclectic assortment of chairs in front of two soft leather sofas. Alongside the left wall, just past the toilets, was a laptop-friendly wooden ledge with high bar stools. Dodge's cold caller was looking straight at him, alone on the farthest stool in the corner, and Dodge almost stumbled again as he negotiated the steps inside the arch.

He was in his late thirties, wearing jeans, sneakers and a light blue shirt, cuffs neatly folded over, with a sleeveless yellow pullover. The man who had galvanized the bombers and called in their attack to Gemma looked completely different, clean-shaven with dark, gelled hair combed back, the nails scrubbed and hands moisturised, all traces of the workshop eradicated. He stayed seated when Dodge reached him. 'That wasn't hard, was it?' he said, taking a sip of espresso. The voice was different, too: softer, educated, northern English. A blue Tommy Hilfiger man bag dangled from his stool.

There was only one other person in this area, an old timer with tobacco fingers and straggly, tea-stained beard clutching a giant mug and squinting at the *Independent*. Dodge would have preferred to stand but the caller had already pulled up the adjacent stool and waited for him to heave his bulk onto the seat. It took Dodge three attempts and he caught the other man's smirk as his shoes scrabbled for a hold on the footrest. The cold call, and now this: for the second time in thirty minutes Dodge had surrendered control, and it sickened him.

'What do you want?' said Dodge, still shifting to get comfortable. He had finished up with his back to the café, the position of greatest vulnerability.

'To work for you. Like one?' He raised his cup, then leaned in, sniffed and studied Dodge's eyes. 'Or another proper drink?'

Dodge looked away to the bare wall, hiding himself. 'I don't even know who you are.'

'I'm offering you information about the thing at Victoria,' he said quietly, with a glance at the old man.

'It doesn't work like that.'

'So why did you come?'

Dodge leaned in close. 'You know why I'm fucking here.'

Frankie. The name hung between them, floating like a feather. The other man laid his hands on the ledge, quite still. There were no rings, bracelets or wrist watch, and a down of golden hairs covered his forearms.

'I don't even know who you are,' said Dodge, eventually.

'Bobby Roscoe. No-one ever calls me Robert. You won't find me in any of your magic boxes. And I already ditched the phone.'

They faced each other again. There was a sudden roar from the street, then just the interior hum again, as if someone had slammed the noise box shut: evidently Dreadlocks had done something spectacular with his ladder. 'So how do I reach you?' said Dodge.

'Like now, I'll find you. We'll go for a whiskey next time.' He held out his palms. 'Want to know what I've got?'

Dodge nodded.

'Basically, you're on the wrong track,' said Bobby quietly. 'This is about bashing the banks, not uniting Ireland.'

'And?' Dodge regarded him carefully, trying to read the other man's petrol grey eyes but coming up with a blank. 'Who put them down?'

'If I knew that I'd be naming my price, wouldn't I? Next stop, Rio. I'll get more.'

Dodge shook his head. 'I haven't got the space for this shit.' He shifted on his stool, longing to get away, rooted to the spot.

'Do your guys have anything better?' The smirk again. 'Didn't think so.'

'And what if you're just another fucking time waster?'

'Arrest me.' Bobby gave a harsh laugh. 'But that's never going to be on the cards, is it? Both of us know that.' He checked his watch, drained his coffee and slipped from the stool. 'Time to go. You want proof this is the real deal, Mr Dodge? Check the news day after tomorrow. Then you'll see how genuine I am.'

'Not yet.' Dodge swung round and grabbed Bobby's arm, sensing the old man eyes on them. 'How did you get my mobile? I have to know.' He meant it as a demand but the words came out plaintively, dripping away with his self-respect.

'Frankie, you mean?' Roscoe slipped the bag over his shoulder. 'Ah, that's for another day.'

The rebuff was Dodge's ultimate humiliation. It was not supposed to be like this, the handler manipulated by the untried asset, the rule book flipped like a pancake, and he felt a surge of panic. 'Why are you doing this to me?'

'Friday,' said Roscoe, gently resting a hand on Dodge's shoulder. 'I'm telling you, I'm the best you'll ever get.'

Chapter Thirteen

Wednesday, 12 October, 15.03, Short Strand, Belfast

When the two sisters abandoned him, Mark Bannerman was alone in the cramped front room for no more than three minutes. Leaning forward in the armchair, senses on high alert, he heard the front door open and close three times, then voices drifting from the hallway into the kitchen, two or three men and a woman. The kettle was boiling and someone cursed as a piece of crockery smashed on the floor. The voices were muted yet angry, with the woman's the most insistent, but he could not catch the words over the kettle. As it clicked off, Bannerman concluded they must be discussing him, and not in a good way.

Then the door was flung open and the younger sister, taxi girl, reappeared with her bag safely over her shoulder. She shifted the two dining chairs aside and moved in close.

'Any chance of a cuppa?' he asked, smelling coffee on her breath. Deadpan eyes like stones, she produced the hood from the bag, sending him another throb of alarm. Bannerman stared up at her, his face creased in disappointment. 'Surely not?'

She jabbed the cloth in his face until he took it from her. 'You have to wear it.'

When he was blind again he felt the girl's fingers close tightly around his wrist as she led him back through the house. The kitchen had acquired more odours since his stumbling entrance, tobacco, stale alcohol and live sweat, and he bumped against a hard body as he neared the door. He braced for a shove or strike from the people he could sense in his way, but the only sound was his own amplified breathing and the rattle of crockery as he glanced off a drawer.

He remembered to shorten his steps over the lumpy threshold until cool air draped around his throat, relieving the fetid heat beneath the hood. Brambles tugged at his trousers again as the taxi choked to life, and he heard the front gate scrape over concrete, as if one of the newcomers had pushed it too far. Then the girl was dipping him inside the taxi, the button on her denim sleeve trapped between her palm and his pate, and he almost toppled over as they accelerated away.

The return journey was much shorter, no longer than four or five minutes by Bannerman's estimation to the moment the engine cut out. He had no idea what to expect: a bullet, a blow or some kind of message. He waited for the girl to free him of the hood, then did it himself, blinking through the tinted glass to get his bearings. He found they had stopped in another cul-de-sac, similar to the first, and guessed the taxi had hugged friendly territory all the way. 'So what happens now?'

'Not up to me.'

Bannerman swept a hand through his hair. 'Do we get to repeat the pleasure?'

The girl was searching in the door for the batteries and shrugged as she dumped them on the seat. 'Like I said.' Then the phones tipped from her bag.

'I wasn't trying to be difficult back there, you know,' said Bannerman. He could tell she was waiting for him to fumble with the batteries, so scooped the phone wreckage into his jacket. 'Can we stay in touch, at least?'

She pointed past his right ear. 'Up there to the Strand, turn left for the bridge.'

He looked at her, then the driver's massive back. On cue, the engine spluttered to life. 'Is that it?'

'There may be something else tonight. I don't know. But not in the Europa.' She handed him a business card. 'Check into this hotel on your way. There's a reservation for you in the name of David Alton.'

Bannerman glanced at the card and slipped it into his jacket. 'Fair enough.'

'If we speak again, it's with you alone. No-one else. And we know you like playing the big shot, don't you? No denying it. If you breathe a word to London everything's off.' She leaned across to shove the door open and waited until he was standing in the roadside, then slid across and grabbed the handle. 'And get them to buy you a decent phone,' she said just before the taxi drove off in a smog of diesel, reminding him to press the Calendar app again.

•••

Wednesday, 12 October, 15.37, Europa Hotel, Belfast

It was just over a mile to the Europa, but Bannerman decided to walk, sucking in fresh air from the river as he crossed Albert Bridge without a backward glance. The sun had turned the Lagan blue since the drive three hours earlier and he paused for a few moments at the centre to collect his thoughts, reflecting how much the city had changed. In front of him the Black Mountains, once the backdrop to a desolate waterside, now overlooked expensive riverside apartments with glass and steel balconies. He dived into the Central Railway Station, also refurbished since his last visit, and perched on a metal bench to fire up the Samsung. There was a text from Penny – 'pse call' – and another from Rico in Nairobi: 'told ur man daniel stays til u bak.'

Bannerman allowed himself a smile. Rico's bosses, perhaps even the man himself, had evidently told Ronnie and whoever he had brought from London that any interrogation of their NIS prisoner would be denied until Bannerman's return. This was two fingers to Vauxhall Cross, a breakout of Kenyan autonomy that would have gone down extremely badly with Giles Lovett.

He found the Donegall, the hotel on taxi girl's card, in less than ten minutes. It was part of a red-brick Victorian terrace in May Street, east of Donegall Square, a stroll past St George's Market. Incongruously sited between an optician's and a breast clinic, the hotel had been remodelled in the minimalist style: the mirrored Reception was dark brown, not much larger than a domestic living room, with double glass doors leading to a modest breakfast space at the rear. The exhausted looking receptionist, severe behind a stainless steel desk in an overwashed white blouse, offered a tight smile but only fleeting eye contact, and checked him into Room 406 on the top floor without asking for a credit card.

Back at the Europa he was too late for lunch in the lobby bar, so ordered a large Bombay Sapphire gin and tonic with a dish of olives in his room. He kicked off his shoes, slumped onto the sofa and speed-dialled Penny on her encrypted mobile. 'All fine,' he said, as soon as she picked up. 'And they disclaim it. Are you in the office?'

'What's the language?'

'Our Tommy says if his foot soldiers do anything our side of the water we'll know about it. Paraphrasing, obviously. Haven't listened to the playback yet.'

'What's he like?'

'Not as charming as we thought. But they didn't give him time to show his softer side.'

'Who?'

'A woman barged in, trampled all over Tommy and completely blindsided me.'

'*Who?*'

'Someone definitely not in the bios you made me read.' Bannerman popped a couple of olives and took a slug of gin. 'I'll write it up later but we're looking for two sisters. They're absolutely running the show over here, Pen. Got to be a record somewhere.'

'I'll go back to the skirts.' This was an old MI5 nickname veterans like Penny and Bannerman still resorted to at times of displeasure.

'Anyway, she said the IRA were not responsible for Victoria.'

'Did you press her?'

'Nothing doing.' He could hear the glug of water being poured and wondered where Penny's desk was these days. 'So I think they're both a no, but not as unequivocal as I'd have liked. Sorry.'

'It's alright. I wanted you to tread carefully. How did they treat you?'

'I've known worse.'

'The truth, Mark.'

The lie came more easily. 'Kid gloves all round. Tell you about it later.'

'So how soon do we hook up with them again?'

'Penny, you're kidding me,' said Bannerman, idly twirling his Donegall key card. 'These people don't want a relationship of any kind. It's not like before.'

'But they denied Victoria. They wouldn't do that without a *quid pro quo.*'

'What do you mean?' Bannerman was thinking back to his interrogation in the house.

'A trade-off for not spilling innocent blood. Come on, you know them better than anyone.'

Bannerman grunted, deep in thought, suspicious.

'You can get the seventeen-forty if you hurry.' Penny's voice faded for a second and he imagined her swinging round to check the time. 'I'll pick you up.'

'It's okay. I'll get some dinner here and catch the first flight tomorrow.' He took another drink. 'Penny, what kind of trade-off?'

'A concession, of course, like they always do. Something political and completely over the top.'

'Is there any kind of secret deal being worked between HMG and Dublin? Promises for the future?'

There was a pause in London, which might have been cover for a lie or space to think. 'No,' she said, cautiously. 'Means nothing.'

'Because the woman implied there was. She claimed Dublin promised them a lot more than my "threats and menaces".'

'Charming.'

'Exact words, and I didn't have a clue, obviously. Embarrassing. I mean, is MI5 holding out on us?'

'I'm sorry, Mark.'

'It's unprofessional. I got dragged back from Nairobi at their request, right? They're the people who wanted this. Is there some agent thing they haven't told us about? What the fuck's going on?'

'I'll get Giles to speak with Toby. Ping me the recording and we'll go through it tomorrow.'

Bannerman rang off, finished the olives and pressed playback, listening intently. The quality was poor, with some of the words inaudible, but the gist was plain enough. He particularly wanted to hear what the sisters had said when they left the room, but there was nothing except a low hubbub, as if taxi girl had been alone or left the bag somewhere in the house.

Bannerman needed a long, hot shower to purge himself of the day's filth, but decided to wait until he reached the Donegall. Instead, he drained his glass and wandered through the suite, collecting his belongings. Picking apart every phrase, Bannerman realised his meeting with Tommy Molloy and the two women could never be spun as a success. Threat had toppled civilised dialogue, reducing him to a crude ultimatum.

These days the spook was thinking about his legacy, and Marathon Runner had a much finer ring than *English lickspittle*. In Nairobi, Goldman Sachs and ExxonMobil were beginning to show interest: the oil giant had let it be known they respected Bannerman and would actively pursue him when the time came. He stood for what they admired as the 'entrepreneurial wing' of SIS, the type to get the job done, a world apart from the consular and army re-treads crowding the vol-au-vent-prosecco circuit.

When he was ready, he unlocked his phone. Should it ever escape from Vauxhall Cross, fancy carrier pigeon was unlikely to fly very high in the macho worlds of oil and finance. He pressed the Calculator app to delete the recording, grabbed his holdall and headed for the lift, hungry to redeem himself before the day was done.

Chapter Fourteen

Taxi girl's name was Siobhan Cody. She was thirty-two years old but looked and acted in her late twenties, except when she was on a mission for the army. Colleen, her sister, was six years older, with clean hands but a much meaner face, nature's payback for keeping the likes of Tommy Molloy in check. The sisters were known for their assistance to impoverished Catholics, not dissent against the British élite, and their photographs featured in the local press rather than MI5 headquarters. So deep was their cover that they were eulogised, not spied upon.

The taxi driver was Declan 'Tanker' Quigley, a mountainous lorry driver and red diesel smuggler with a mashed face, tent peg teeth and photofit eyes who also worked within the community. Under the direction of Siobhan and Colleen, Tanker enforced discipline through an escalating regime of beatings, kneecappings, disfigurement, torture, stabbings and shootings. Tanker had more blood on his hands than the surgeons who repaired his victims, according to Tommy Molloy.

Tanker was also responsible for the acquisition or disposal of transport, often at very short notice. Within the past two hours he had taken possession of a five year old Honda Interceptor VFR800 motorcycle stolen in Liverpool by a car ringer from County Antrim. He was riding it now across the Albert Bridge, heading for the Donegall with Siobhan Cody on the pillion. They wore the same clothes as before, though Tanker had zipped a black bomber jacket over his T-shirt.

About fifteen metres short of the hotel he swung through a pair of lopsided metal gates into the potholed yard of Taxi Dermot, a dilapidated Portakabin with peeling green paint and the door wedged open. They parked behind a long axle Mercedes Sprinter van positioned to conceal the motorcycle from the road, placed their helmets beside the front wheel and walked away with a side-glance at the owner, whose eyes stayed fixed on the bookings screen.

Cody received the call on the stroke of five, as they were approaching the rear of the hotel from Little May Street. 'System black' was the message, confirmation that the hotel's CCTV was down. Thirty seconds later they entered an unlocked rear door into the breakfast room and swung right for the goods lift, pulling on clear rubber gloves as the ill-treated doors clanked shut. Cody had ditched the baseball cap and used a paddle brush on her hair.

The fourth floor corridor was deserted and Tanker stood out of sight as Cody knocked on Room 406. She made it sound tentative, pressing her ear against the wood until she heard sounds of movement inside, then taking a step back. Sensing Bannerman's eye at the peephole she waggled her fingers in a flirty wave, the girl across the bar. She expected a voice telling her to go away, or a door tightly chained, but the old man surprised her with his openness. Wet hair slicked back, feet bare, he wore the hotel's towelling bathrobe and a broad smile, as if she were bringing room service or sex. 'Almost caught me in the shower.' He looked pink, sounded tipsy and acted like he was already taking her surrender. 'Knew we hadn't seen the last of each other.' Pepper and salt chest hair curled beneath the shawl collar and a shred of green was trapped in his teeth.

'Did you tell anyone?' she demanded, holding back.

'Just you and me,' he said, making a show of inviting Cody inside. He was still smiling as she flitted past him and Tanker's boot connected with the closing door, scoring a double hit against his face and toes, catapulting him backwards. He would have collapsed but for Cody, who used the momentum to drag him further into the room.

Tanker loomed over Bannerman before he could react, grabbing the robe with both hands and throwing him onto the bed like a parcel as he howled in pain. His nose looked broken, streaming blood onto the white duvet, and his toes had evidently been trapped hard beneath the door: they dangled from the side of the bed, stripped of skin, with one of the large nails hanging by a thread. Head and lungs lifted as he drew breath to yell at them, so Cody grabbed a handful of hair and jabbed him hard with her fist. She heard his front teeth shatter, then blood from his burst upper lip flooded his jaw as he fell back, defeated.

Neither of his attackers needed to look around, for they had worked here before. The king bed was to the left of the door, beyond a frosted glass hanging space holding Bannerman's jacket and trousers. A curved steel and glass bureau with sunken lighting was built into the opposite wall and the window alcove neatly housed a dark leather easy chair with round occasional table. The carpet pattern meandered in swirls of blue and brown, and muted abstract prints hung from the eggshell walls. A small TV angled from the corner high above the bureau, an afterthought. Cody clocked Bannerman's unpacked holdall and his Samsung phone on the bureau beside a tumbler, a pair of empty miniatures and an open can of tonic.

In a single practised move they spun him round to the left side of the bed, with Tanker kneeling on the mattress beside him. Bannerman was clutching his nose and trying to say something but Tanker had already produced a roll of black masking tape from his jacket. He tossed it to Cody and held Bannerman's head still while she tore a strip and sealed his bloody mouth. She leaned over until their faces were almost touching, relishing the fear and despair in his eyes, the realisation that he had been deceived. 'Sending you back was a mistake, right? It's the vanity that's going to kill you.' She liked watching him try to speak, a blister of tape rising and falling. 'You really think you can come here making London's threats for them?' Bannerman began to struggle, trying to sit up, so Tanker slapped his face and raised a warning finger.

Cody bent over again. 'I'm going to ask you, like we did back at the house, and this is the only thing that will save your life. Do your masters in London and Dublin agree? Will they make good on their vow?'

She waited for him to shake his head, then glanced at Tanker. The headboard and bedside tables were made of brushed steel with matching lamps, complementing the style of the bureau. Coming round the foot of the bed, Tanker rolled Bannerman onto his left side, shifted the lamp and stretched his right forearm onto the table. The weapon was weighing down his jacket pocket. It was an old-fashioned police truncheon, still attached to its flaking leather strap but with lead in the business end. While Cody gripped Bannerman's wrist he brought the club down hard on his knuckles, immediately following with a smash onto his fingers, a process Tanker called the 'double tap.' Bannerman's shriek penetrated the gag, expanding the blister into a bubble, then sucking the tape back inside his mouth.

Tanker tossed the club onto the bed, took hold of Bannerman's hand and crushed the shattered bones together. The bathrobe had come apart in the struggle leaving Bannerman exposed, limbs shuddering and quaking, his torso convulsed in agony. Tanker maintained his grip until Cody motioned for him to pause. 'Well?' she said, when Bannerman was flat on his back again. Bannerman had begun frantically shaking his head, so she held his forehead still, peeled back the tape and looked into his eyes, coolly regarding his terror. Face smeared bright red, Bannerman's nostrils flared in the desperate effort to suck air through the stream of blood and the words came in a fractured gasp. 'Don't know…swear…haven't got a clue what…what talking about.' She re-sealed the tape, rolled him on his side again and held his left hand against the table as Tanker repeated the attack, then calmly replaced the club in his jacket. Cody stood watching him in silence for almost a minute. 'This is what we mean by enforcing the deal,' she said finally, as his body began to subside.

Tanker checked his watch and spoke for the first time. 'Cameras back on in ten.' He produced a flick knife with a black metal handle and steel band, his other weapon of choice, spinning it expertly in his palm. 'Do you want me to, or are we going to fuck about here all night?'

Cody's answer was to grab Bannerman's left arm and start to pull him, but Tanker brushed her aside, wrapped his arms around Bannerman's thighs and whipped him from the bed. His head made contact with the bureau before he hit the floor, and he lay prone, his strength ebbing away, the robe soaking up blood from his hands and face like a giant blotter.

The bathroom, to the right of the bureau, continued the theme of waves and ripples. It was essentially a wet room with a wash basin, toilet and shower, separated from the living area by a wavy panel of frosted glass. Tanker dragged Bannerman there by his feet and pulled the bathrobe clear. The knife reappeared as he stood over Bannerman with one foot on his chest, then the blade sprang clear, its *snap* echoing off the tiles. Bannerman was starting to move again in a final clutch at life, so Tanker bent down, placed the knife carefully on the floor, stretched Bannerman's arms above his head and waited for Cody to stand on his shattered hands. More sounds of torment gurgled in his throat, but fainter now. His legs began to thresh again, as if Cody's cruelty had diverted his strength to the opposite extremity, so Tanker used the club to smash his right shin, the bone's crack reverberating like gunshot.

The blade was a stiletto, with a tightly serrated edge. Holding it high in his right hand, Tanker straddled Bannerman's waist, gripping him tight between his thighs. He cut quickly, a single downward slash on the right side of Bannerman's chest, extending from the collar bone to the waist. As Bannerman's whole body contracted in trauma Tanker attacked the other side, two slashes diverging from a point near the collar bone, then a third, horizontal line slicing through his left nipple to form a crude letter A. He was careful not to cut too deeply, for he wanted Bannerman alive.

The body was growing still and the eyes fading, so Tanker slapped him again and Cody leant round to the washbasin, splashing water from her cupped hands over his face. It slopped onto his chest, then stained the tiles in a dribble of diluted blood. Tanker made his central cut from the belly button, slashing upwards to the throat, then curving right in a swirl that matched the motif of the carpet. He completed the tail of the letter R in a deeper flourish that set off a final, useless revolt. Bannerman's limbs went rigid and he trembled as if in an electric shock, the convulsion so violent that Cody lost her balance and Tanker felt his own massive frame lift for a second. Then everything changed again as the body fell quiet and his head lolled to one side, eyes wide open. Tanker smiled as he hauled himself to his feet and dropped the knife into the basin, happy that his victim had stayed with them right to the end.

The shower head was adjustable, fixed to a vertical steel rail secured to the wall by four evenly spaced brackets. Tanker took the waist tie from Bannerman's robe and looped one end around his neck, rapidly tying it in a bowline knot. He dragged Bannerman beneath the shower, reached under his armpits and pulled him up while Cody hooked the other end of the tie around the highest bracket and passed it to Tanker. Raising Bannerman's corpse with his left arm, Tanker took up the slack on the tie until Bannerman was hanging with his shattered toes just touching the floor. 'Is it going to hold?' said Cody, as Tanker tied the other end and tested the bracket.

Tanker ripped away the gag to release a gloop of blood and saliva that stretched like chewing gum before pooling around the drain.

'For this skinny bastard? No problem.'

Cody disappeared for a moment to search Bannerman's belongings. Through the frosted partition she could see the silhouette of his hanging body, a spectre, gently swaying as Tanker made his final aesthetic adjustments. There was no wallet or paperwork in the jacket, just cash and credit cards, and nothing but clothes in the holdall; only the phone was worth taking. She took from her bag a rectangle of cardboard the size of a cereal packet, folded down the middle, with a loop of string attached.

In the bathroom, Bannerman's naked body was hanging with his head dropped to the right, and his face looked distended, as if it might explode at any second. Tanker had wiped excess blood from his chest to accentuate the IRA tattoo, and stood aside to rinse the blade and admire his handiwork. Cody unfolded the card, hooked the string over Bannerman's neck, then loosened it until it hung around his thighs, leaving the artwork and his penis exposed. Printed neatly in red on the cardboard were three words: 'find another scapegoat.' She pointed her mobile, then reached forward to make final changes, tweaking Bannerman's head until his bulging eyes stared directly at the camera.

'Aren't you forgetting something for your man?' said Tanker as the camera flashed.

'Shit,' said Cody, searching in her bag. She took out a tangerine, wedged it between Bannerman's teeth and took three more shots, like an estate agent searching for the best angle.

They washed the blood from their shoes, stuffed the gloves into a plastic bag and escaped by the stairs. Six minutes after murdering Britain's Marathon Runner they were on the motorcycle again, sprinting across Queen's Bridge to the Short Strand and safety.

Chapter Fifteen

Wednesday, 12 October, 19.27, The Fishbowl, New Scotland Yard

'So is it deliver or collect?'

Mobile wedged under his chin, Kerr checked the time on his desktop. 'I'll pick it up on the way.'

'You'll be late home, you mean,' said Nancy to the ping of another incoming email, Kerr's third from Alan Fargo in less than an hour. He could hear the children racing down the hall. 'Upstairs! Now!'

Kerr peered at the screen and smiled; he liked to hear Nancy talk about him coming home. 'Only a bit. I have to drop by 1830 on the way out.'

'Sure about that?'

'Alan's got info about Hammersmith I need to check.'

'I'll get them ready for bed.'

'Can't wait to see you.' Nancy was teaching Kerr to cook, but tonight they had promised each other curry and sex.

'They want you to read more *Horrid Henry*. Is Alan going to get through this?'

'Yes. Non-stop work,' said Kerr, reading Fargo's message again. 'Stuff like this.'

'Send him my love. And don't forget the movie.'

'Got it,' he said, and paused from transferring papers into the safe to grab a paperback from his desk.

Nancy was the ex-wife of Karl Sergeyev, now the Foreign Secretary's close protection officer, and Kerr had been in a relationship with her for over a year, enjoying secret sleepovers at her three-bedroom Victorian semi in Hornsey Vale. Nancy had worked in the Special Branch Registry since leaving school, sacrificing her career a decade earlier for the charming Russian she had always known would cheat on her.

Separated, her life turned upside down, Nancy had finally found work as a GP's receptionist to help pay the mortgage. As well as raising their two young children, she had joined a weekly art class and held onto her dwindling circle of girlfriends at the Yard.

'And Alan will let Robyn know, right? If it's anything important?' Kerr could hear the children again, making mischief around her. 'Not you.'

'It's okay, sexy,' he said as he spun the dial, looking forward to being with her. 'Home with you soon.'

•••

Kerr entered 1830 to find Alan Fargo sitting with Detective Sergeant Melanie Fleming, deputy to Jack Langton and leader of the Reds, the most experienced team of watchers. On the floor beside her was a charcoal Michael Kors tote bag holding a pair of black patent court shoes with a tacky parka and grey sneakers. Hair held back in a brown scrunchy, make-up removed, Melanie was barefoot in jeggings with an expensive silk blouse and pearls, having evidently altered her appearance on the surveillance plot.

'Snapdragon?' said Kerr. She looked a cross between Primark and Harvey Nicks, and he did a double take.

Melanie nodded. 'He took the train from Rotherham so I stayed on him. Jack biked it down and we picked up again at Kings Cross.' She pulled on one of the sneakers. 'The meet was a café in Grays Inn Road. Contact a white female.'

'Any trace?'

Melanie shrugged. 'Jack thinks the whole thing may have been social.'

'Good work, anyway.'

Melanie and Fargo were studying four A4 size photographs on a desk to the left of the door. This was the workstation Melanie had occupied with such impatience on a spell of recuperative duty, before being sent on the undercover mission that had almost killed her. She took a DVD from the bag, *The Americans*, and slid it onto the desk. 'You wanted this for tonight?'

'Cheers.' Kerr nodded. 'Right, what have we got?'

Fargo's hair was damp, and he had evidently showered, shaved and changed his shirt since their first session that morning. Despite nearly two days and nights on the case, broken only by TLC from Gemma and catnaps in her bed, he looked refreshed. Kerr peered at the dressing on the side of his neck. 'Aren't you supposed to keep that dry?'

'It's fine,' said Fargo, releasing a whiff of Lynx as he reached out to rearrange the photographs. Three showed the innards of a single improvised explosive device, IED, taken from different angles. A fourth showed a single rectangular metal plate, blackened and distorted, with a jagged edge where one of the corners had been ripped away.

'Bomb Data Centre forwarded these while I was in the shower. This is the lab's reconstruction of Hammersmith, with a mass of text on the email to explain everything. Most of it vaporised in the explosion or ended up in the river, but a piece of steel fell back onto the tarmac.' Fargo pointed to the fourth photograph. 'They think it's the base of the bomb, here, length twenty-six centimetres.'

'Which is?'

Fargo reached for one of Melanie's court shoes. 'Roughly that.' Fargo indicated various symmetrical marks on the base plate. 'The lab used the holes and indentations to map the likely positions of the timer, circuit board and detonator, then rebuilt the bomb. You can see patches of solder here and here.'

'But only a best guess,' said Kerr, unconvinced.

Fargo crossed to his own desktop and scrolled down the screen. 'They also found a piece of wire burnt onto one of the bridge suspension chains, still with its insulation and a speck of solder at the end. Plus fragments of battery wedged in a lorry tyre, blue shreds of plastic, probably the timer, and a sliver of circuit board.

Oh, and a piece of magnet with traces from the underside of the Polo.'

'Explosive?'

'Yes. PETN on the base plate.'

Kerr peered at the closest photograph. 'So who made it?'

Fargo locked his screen and rejoined them. 'Not the IRA. Every bomber in the world leaves a profile, right? A signature way of doing things? These materials don't fit any IRA device going back to the early seventies.'

'Anyone else?'

'They checked every terrorist group. Real IRA, al-Qaeda, al-Shabaab, ISIS and hundreds of others. No forensic or engineering match to any known device in the world. Hammersmith looks unique.'

Kerr frowned. 'But how can they be so sure, just from that lot?'

'It was fitted with a trembler.'

'What?'

'A booby trap.'

'Okay. So what's new?'

Fargo selected one of the reconstruction images and picked out a steel ball the size of a marble. 'This piece tore through the roof of the 209 bus, split the driver's face open and embedded itself in the front chassis.' Fargo traced this finger across the photograph. 'It was soldered to the end of a beam spring, just here, designed to trigger the bomb at the slightest movement, the instant it made contact with the steel plate. Except in this case the trembler activated the timer, not the detonator.'

'Saved your life,' said Melanie.

'And this design,' said Fargo, collecting the photographs together, 'really *is* unprecedented. They used a very sophisticated piece of engineering against you…'

'…or Robyn.'

'…or Robyn. But the only common feature between that and any other known device is the explosive.'

'What about Victoria?' said Kerr, intrigued.

Fargo shook his head and Kerr saw the grief etched into his face. 'It looks like we're, you know, hunting two different sets of operators here. We've proved a negative, really.'

'Okay. Tell them thanks, Alan, yeah? And get some rest.' Kerr gave Fargo's arm a squeeze. 'Promise?'

Waving the DVD at Melanie in thanks, Kerr remembered the paperback he had brought her from the Fishbowl, Mohsin Hamid's *The Reluctant Fundamentalist*. Recently he had begun encouraging his team to share books and films to ease the tedium of long nights on stand-by. 'Enjoy,' he said, dropping it into Melanie's bag and heading for home.

He was at the door by the time Melanie spoke. 'Actually, have you got a minute?' Kerr turned, eyebrows in a question mark. The cybercrime desk was empty because the officers had left for an overnight at GCHQ, but three of Fargo's crew were still working at the far end of the office. Melanie gestured to the reading room. 'In here?' Fargo was already logging on to Mercury. 'You, too, Al.'

Fargo rarely allowed sensitive documents to leave his control. Officers who needed to brief themselves on 1830 product had to use the reading room, a corner space so cramped that Fargo, last in, had to close the door before he could pull his chair from the table and sit down.

Kerr sneaked a glance at his watch and looked between them. 'So?'

Melanie cleared her throat. 'Have you seen much of Dodge lately?'

'Yes. He's put on weight, never stops talking and thinks I don't know he smokes in the office.'

'What I'm saying is, have you noticed anything different?'

'None of us are feeling particularly good after what's happened,' said Kerr, with a glance at Fargo. 'We need sources and right now Dodge is the main man. I'd expect him to be preoccupied.'

'I mean before that. The past few weeks. He's strange. There's something wrong. Tell him, Al.'

Fargo immediately looked awkward. 'I bumped into Dodge in Back Hall yesterday, wanted a quick word about Mercury. It's just that he came across as…distracted, you know? Looked like he wanted to say something, then completely blanked me. But I put it down to…well, I suppose he may be embarrassed about my situation. It's probably nothing.'

'No, Al, it is something, and we're not helping him by keeping quiet. Helen Farr told me she caught him on the phone this afternoon and he looked like a ghost.'

Kerr felt a spark of irritation. 'So you've been asking around, yeah?'

'Actually, no,' said Melanie. 'He was really off with Helen, and Dodge is never like that. Waved her away, then dashed out without telling anyone or leaving a contact number, which is obviously a complete no-no on the source unit. And what about his drinking?' she continued before Kerr could interrupt. 'When did any of us see Dodge hammered? The total pro, hollow legs, last man standing, brain on red alert while everyone else falls over. Couple of weeks ago I turned up late for a leaving do in The Albert and found him outside in the street completely slaughtered. Had to light his cigarette for him. Wouldn't let me take him home and God knows how he ever made it.'

Kerr looked her in the eye. 'Finished?'

'Fact is, he's breaking enough rules to sack himself,' said Melanie. 'We all love Dodge to bits but he's losing his grip. And you know what the Job's like with drink these days. I'm right, aren't I, Al? There's something bad going on here.'

'Or he's a middle aged man who's mislaid his mojo,' said Kerr. 'Domestic trouble, perhaps. It happens. And we shouldn't be having this conversation.' For a moment he silently regarded Melanie, still rebuilding her own marriage since her undercover mission. 'How is Rob, by the way?'

'We're good. Thanks.'

'So I'll watch out for him,' said Kerr, pushing his chair against the airvent, then easing sideways as his mobile rang. It was Ritchie's office. 'Donna?'

'Are you still here?'

'What about you?' he said, instinctively checking his watch again. 'It's almost eight.'

'Boss wants to see you. It's urgent, John.'

'Okay.' Fargo was already standing to make way for him. 'Can I go now?' he said, as Melanie stayed in her chair.

'Talk about Dodge getting home that night, where does he live?'

'Ruislip.'

'Wrong. That's the one we know about. Three bed semi near the church and that lovely green, right?'

Kerr shrugged at Fargo, still squeezed against the door. 'We helped him move in.'

'And twenty-six West Drive is still his registered address. But he moved three weeks ago to Harrow.'

'Melanie, you're out of order.'

'Two bedroom apartment, first floor refurb in an old private school. Gated, secure, and v posh. I checked and it was going for seven two five and a half.'

'And your point is?'

'Ruislip was rented, John. So where did Dodge get that kind of money?'

'And what makes it right for you to spy on one of my deputies?'

'I'm telling you he's got a problem,' said Melanie. 'Someone has to.'

•••

Slipping the disc into his jacket, Kerr called Nancy on his way round the corridor. 'I've got it.'

In the background, he could hear one of the children calling his name. 'And the bad news?'

Kerr's BlackBerry vibrated, and the name on the screen grabbed his attention. 'Commander wants a quick word.'

'I'll get them to deliver.'

Nancy cut the call, making it easy for him to pick up from Washington DC. 'Rich?'

'How you doing, my friend?' The voice was upbeat, for Rich Malone, former regional security officer at the US embassy in Grosvenor Square and Kerr's most trusted contact across the pond, always sounded like the bearer of good news.

'What's up?' said Kerr.

'I heard about Alan and, hey, we're truly sorry. Tough break.' Malone even made condolence sound like his Boston Shamrocks had just scored. 'How soon can you get over?' he continued, before Kerr could reply.

'What have you got?'

'Can you talk?'

'Of course.'

'I can imagine it's all hell breaking loose over there, right? Listen, I have intel for your ears only.'

Kerr paused by the toilets. Rich Malone was an accomplished intelligence officer in the US Department of State. With action in Pakistan, Vietnam and Yemen, the former cop had the brain and scars necessary to assemble counter-terrorism's jigsaw. He also kept the bullshit filter switched on, which guaranteed Kerr's full attention.

'So we need to go secure?'

'John, we need to go personal, as in you getting your ass over to Washington.'

At the end of the corridor Kerr could see Donna through the open door in Ritchie's private office. She looked busy, probably editing one of Ritchie's emails, and he wondered again what had kept her back so late. 'What's wrong with flashmail all of a sudden?'

'Listen, I'm not doing a favour for the Brits on account of I don't know where this leads, and no way am I going *mano a mano* with the frigging BSS.' This was the British Security Service, American-speak for MI5. 'What I have is for you alone. I'm asking you, pal.'

'So I'll work something for early next week,' he said as he reached Donna's desk.

'How about tomorrow? Quick in and out? John, this is important.'

Kerr noticed Donna was wearing a new silk scarf and freshened make-up. She picked up the phone to let Ritchie know he had arrived but Kerr covered her hand. 'Give me a second,' he said, putting Malone on hold.

'You're wearing that face again,' said Donna, deadpan, before he could ask.

'Can you get me on the first Washington flight tomorrow? Strictly between us?'

'Keep it from the boss, you mean?' Donna gently freed his hand. 'For that, I need the phone.'

Kerr picked up the BlackBerry. 'Rich? See you for lunch.'

Malone sounded relieved. 'Send me the flight and I'll have you picked up.'

Donna was already dialling and waved him past her. 'Be ready, John,' she said. 'It's not very nice.'

Ritchie was on the phone as he entered and closed the door, but immediately beckoned Kerr over to the chair beside his desk, cutting the call short. The office was in gloom except for a pool of light from Ritchie's desk lamp in the far corner, suggesting his boss had not moved from his chair for a couple of hours, so Kerr switched on the main ceiling lights. Ritchie, in shirt sleeves, had a single document in front of him beside his yellow notepad, one of Donna's secret green folders. He picked it up as he swung round to Kerr, using Trenchard's bottom drawer as a footrest.

'Remember Toby Devereux bragging about a direct line into the dissidents?'

Kerr nodded.

'Not any more.' Ritchie handed Kerr the folder. 'Anyone we know?'

The eyes bulged and the whole face was distorted by the tangerine wedged in the mouth between its teeth, but Kerr recognised the victim in a heartbeat. 'Mark Bannerman. I went out to Nairobi after the shopping mall attack, remember? On the terrorist finance angle? That was Mark. Where did this come from?'

'PSNI. It happened a couple of hours ago. Toby Devereux didn't notify them in advance that he was going over. Nor did Vauxhall Cross.'

Kerr stared at the bloated death mask. 'This is a good bloke, Bill. An operator. Cleared the way in Tehran, well before the regime change with the Yanks stealing the credit.'

'He should have stuck to Farsi.'

'You know about him too, from the nineties.'

Ritchie took the photograph back and held it beneath the lamp, the shadows beneath his eyes deepening in the light. 'All that beneath the wire stuff in Belfast?' he said as the memory returned. 'This is him? We never met but they gave him a nickname, "Roadrunner," something like that?'

Kerr nodded. 'And Toby sent him back for a replay.'

'When they should have known things are a lot different now,' said Ritchie, jabbing the sign around Bannerman's thighs. 'Crazy.'

'How did they find him so quickly?'

'They didn't,' said Ritchie, holding up the photograph. 'The killers sent this direct to his chief.'

Chapter Sixteen

Wednesday, 12 October, 20.43, St Jude's Presbytery, Haringey

To prepare for the confrontation, Vanessa Gavron positioned her almost new white convertible Saab 9-3 in a one-way street about twenty paces from the junction with Green Lanes, a busy thoroughfare in the borough of Haringey. Ducketts Road, a five minute walk from Turnpike Lane Underground station, was marked with residents' bays, all full at this time of the evening, so Gavron had parked illegally with her front offside wheel perched on a speed bump. This was necessary in order to snatch the best photographs of her target, and the journalist renowned as the 'Doorstepper' had never let officialdom throw her off course.

The darkened street narrowed at the junction with Green Lanes in a block paved crossing with black iron posts each side, and traffic along the main road was busy, with many of the shops still open. On the far side were the lit windows of Café Venezia beside Sunderban Curry House, and she screwed her face at the errant apostrophe in Sunbed's and Tints. Beyond the corner to her right was St Jude's Roman Catholic Church, a red-brick monstrosity glowering over Ladbrokes and Altemaar Gold.

The church presbytery, in which Gavron had a specific interest, lay directly opposite, a dilapidated Victorian pile with pitched slate roof, peeling window frames and bricks as dark as St Jude's. The windows and scrubby front garden were overshadowed by a yew tree, gnarled and sombre, that leant towards the porch like a giant signpost. The house lay in pitch blackness except for a glimmer of light through the stained glass fanlight over the front door.

Ducketts Road itself, straight as a die, was lined with terraces of modest Victorian houses in varying states of disrepair. On the way down, Gavron's passenger had remarked that her Saab was at least five years newer than any of the other vehicles they had passed: he noticed such things because he liked cars more than people, and one of his short-lived jobs in a working life that never passed Go had been a courier driver for FedEx.

Donal Quinn was in his early twenties and had spent the past nine years in New Jersey until Gavron had tracked him down a week earlier, persuaded him to return to London with her and paid for his Virgin Atlantic ticket out of her own pocket. Fingernails chewed to the quick, his face scarred from teenage acne, Donal wore a grey New York Yankees sweatshirt with a navy baseball cap the wrong way round.

They were separated by almost a generation, but had been sitting with their hands joined since Donal's first sighting in over a decade of Father Michael. The priest had turned into the street just before eight, later than Gavron expected from her previous observations, hurrying home from Confession at St Jude's. Gavron had heard the boy's sharp intake of breath over the camera shutter as his tormentor emerged from the dusk, black cloak fastened with a metal clasp and flapping over his cassock, wispy hair lifted by the breeze.

'Donal, it'll be okay.' For the next forty minutes the journalist old enough to be his grandmother had spoken with the quiet urgency of a lover, calming the victim's fear, steeling the survivor's courage. Gavron had been unlocking childhood memories from blighted grown-ups while Savile and other rapists were still hiding in plain sight, long before the police had been jerked into action. Through the years of scepticism and cover-up she had listened to men and women unable to hold down a relationship at home, difficult to manage at work, their sex lives stone cold or suicidally risky, and believed them.

Over three days of isolation with Donal in her Bankside apartment, Vanessa Gavron had mined the seam of fear his brain had shut down long ago. As the words at last began to flow, she had found herself amused by his Irish American patois, incensed by the scale of his abuse and fired up to expose the guilty.

Afterwards, with both of them wrung out, Gavron had convinced him things were different now, that the new world would believe his nightmare beneath the Gothic roof of the Olive Tree children's home outside Belfast.

'You see what I see?' Donal had rasped as the priest disappeared beneath the yew tree. 'Satan dressed as the fucking Man of God.'

They were probably someone else's words, but Vanessa Gavron would write them up, along with all the others. The garb of this particular devil, she now knew, included the musty striped pyjamas he had worn when young Donal brought his morning cup of tea. There had never been grooming or befriending, just a hand working hard under the blanket, the other pulling the boy's head onto him, tainting him for life with his stale, whiskey breath.

'You ready?' The driver's door clunked open. 'Let's hear what he's got to say for himself.'

'No…I'm sorry.' Gavron had the interior light switched off but the boy had turned his face from her. 'Can't do it.'

Gavron silently regarded him. 'Donal, that's absolutely fine, dear.'

'Next time,' he murmured, his eyes flickering another apology.

She reached for his hand again. 'Look after the car for me.'

The black front door was oak, with a heavy iron knocker, two frosted glass panels covered by cheap pleated curtains and an old ceramic doorbell marked Press. It made no discernible sound but, as she gave the knocker a double tap, the stained glass above the door brightened and rapid footsteps approached down the hall. Two heavy bolts clunked back, then someone was pulling at the door. It was jammed, probably swollen from the recent rain, but juddered open with a hard push from one of Gavron's gold buckled pumps.

A spindly woman in her sixties stood silhouetted in the light, drying her hands on a faded floral apron tied around a black cotton shift. 'Yes?' The housekeeper wore scuffed black lace-up shoes over thick stockings, her greying hair stretched back in a bun. She looked unfriendly, so Gavron did not waste a smile.

'I'd like to see Father Michael.'

'He's having his supper.'

Gavron was already looking past the woman's shoulder into the long hallway. The walls were covered in a sickly green wash with a smattering of ecclesiastical prints in cheap frames, and the only lighting came from a helix bulb curling from a dusty conical shade. To the left was the narrow staircase with a threadbare carpet runner, opposite the darkened front room, but Gavron guessed the priest was to be found through the brown door to the morning room at the far end, beneath the landing. 'He will want to see me,' she said, staring her down.

The house-cum-gatekeeper fiddled with the apron strings behind her back while she took in Gavron's grey pin-stripe trouser suit with revere collar and imitation pearls, as if calculating the visitor's status. 'Who shall I say is calling?'

'It's personal,' said Gavron, one foot on the threshold.

Perhaps the old woman smelt trouble, for the apron stayed where it was, but the face turned hostile. 'It's late.'

'Personal for Father Michael, I mean. To do with a confession.'

'Well it's not possible.' Eyes hard as flint, she peered beyond Gavron into the street, still sniffing out danger.

'Anything's possible.'

The woman's skinny right arm was already reaching for the door. 'I told you. The Father is not available.' She sucked in her cheeks, tightening the skin of her forehead, her whole face suddenly vacuum wrapped. 'You'll have to come back in the morning.'

'What are you,' murmured Gavron with a smile, 'his frigging guardian angel?'

The housekeeper looked down at Gavron's loitering foot. 'Another inch and you'll be trespassing.'

The door hit the wall with a crash and bounced back against Gavron's outstretched palm, though her eyes never left the housekeeper's. 'Any more shit from you and I'll wring your scrawny chicken's neck.'

'What's going on down there?' A yellowish light fanned from the end of the hallway as Gavron held the front door wide. Still in his clerical shirt and collar, Father Michael approached down the hall, dabbing his mouth with a white linen napkin. 'What is it, Mary?'

'I'm Vanessa Gavron, Father, and I'm…'

'I know who you are.' The priest took his place beside the housekeeper, blocking the entrance with one arm across the frame, his underarm dark with sweat. He wore brown furry slippers with a yellow smiley on the uppers but looked red-faced and angry. 'I've seen your photograph. Read your poisonous smears against the Church.'

Gavron stepped forward into a mist of his whiskey breath, as if the housekeeper had never been there. 'I'd like to come in, Father.'

'It's alright, Mary.' He patted the housekeeper on the shoulder, sending her back to safety, making room to square up to Gavron. 'There's nothing to say. Lies and tittle-tattle. You know it, too,' he said, wiping his mouth again and looking into the street, eyes glassy from drink. 'Otherwise you'd be standing here with the police.'

In all the faded colour school photos Gavron had researched over the years Father Michael looked jovial and avuncular, a man incapable of impropriety. But in real life, stooped with age as he guarded his territory, she was struck by the arrogance that had enabled him to abuse for so long. 'We need to talk tonight, Father,' she said, evenly.

'No, we do not,' he said, hissing the words as the door began to close again. 'So fuck off and leave me alone.'

Gavron calmly wiped her cheek. 'You think you can keep this buried?' She had her foot ready again, but the priest's eyes had shifted beyond the pool of light, suddenly wide in recognition.

'Donny. Is it you?'

Gavron swung round in time to see the boy emerge from the shadows around the tree. She braced herself for another battle over the front door but the only movement was a flash of white as the napkin dropped to the floor. The three stood perfectly still, the silence broken by the cooing of pigeons on the roof as Gavron took the boy's hand and held him a pace from the doorway.

Then something stirred in the priest. 'What are you doing here?' He turned the question into a demand, intimidating, the housemaster still commanding his pupil. 'With this woman?'

Suddenly Donal's hand ripped away from Gavron and he was standing in the threshold. He froze, struggling for the words, then took a deep breath, lifted his head and spat directly into the old man's face. 'Don't ever call me that again. My name is Donal. Donal Quinn.'

The priest stood rooted to the spot, Donal's spittle trail glistening on his cheek. 'Wait in the car,' said Gavron, gently tugging at the boy's arm, feeling his whole body tremble. She watched him walk away without a backward glance and fold himself into the Saab. 'I brought Donal back with me from America,' she said quietly as Father Michael slowly pulled a clean handkerchief from his sleeve, like a magician, and wiped his face. 'Today the past has caught up with you. He's not afraid, Father. You can see the hatred in his eyes.'

'No. It's nothing. All the boys had pet names.'

'I know.'

'I've been appointed to Rome, for pity's sake. You'll fucking destroy me.' This time the words came in a wheeze as the energy seemed to drain from him. His face rearranged itself in the gloom, as if weighing confession and denial. 'Have you been to the police?'

Gavron shook her head. 'It's the boy and me. That's how he wants things. For now.'

'Blackmail, then?' Father Michael studied the spittle in his handkerchief. 'What is it you want?'

'Your story,' said Gavron. She handed over a card. 'To know what happened.'

She sensed the housekeeper's shadow hovering in the background and wondered how much she knew. 'It's alright, Mary,' called the priest, without turning. 'Nearly done.'

'No, Father,' said Gavron, quietly. She reached to brush a stray breadcrumb from his other cheek, making him flinch. 'You should go back inside and finish your supper. Drink some more whiskey. But be sure to give me a call.'

Chapter Seventeen

Wednesday, 12 October, 20.53, home of Melanie and Rob
Fleming

Melanie Fleming and most other SO15 officers had been on duty almost without a break since bombings in Victoria two days earlier. There were no obvious suspects but Room 1830 maintained what Fargo called The Mushroom, an ever expanding schedule of extremists capable of manufacturing and delivering similar lethal devices.

Outside Victoria station, the work continued non-stop. A minute after the all-clear from the bomb disposal officer, with smoke still hanging in the air and corpses scattered on the ground, Derek Finch's scientists had donned their white overalls and begun work to recover forensic traces from the scene. In the meantime, frenetic activity filled the evidential vacuum, a racing cycle of witness searches, MI5 liaison, agent deployments, data mining, Facebook traces, telephone checks and media briefings. Until the longed-for intelligence breakthrough John Kerr had to make judgments about operational priorities, but it fell to Jack Langton, as his surveillance leader on the ground, to make them happen. For the operatives working to prevent another atrocity the list seemed endless, the mission impossible.

Her warnings about Dodge apparently unheeded, Melanie had hurried out of 1830 a few minutes after John Kerr. Over the previous two nights she had snatched less than nine hours' sleep and was tired from the day's lone surveillance from Rotherham. She had chatted with Alan Fargo a little longer while changing her clothes, then called Rob, her husband, to let him know she was on the way home.

The Flemings lived in an Edwardian halls-adjoining semi in Elms Avenue, Muswell Hill, twenty minutes' walk from East Finchley tube and close to the local schools for their two sons, aged six and four. The four bedroom house had come on the market in a probate sale six years earlier, and they had stretched their incomes to breaking point to seal the deal.

For half a century the previous owners had kept it more or less frozen in time, and the house had avoided the horrors of ripped out fireplaces, artex ceilings, plastic and minimalism. Melanie and Rob had loved bringing their new home back to life, restoring the sash windows, ceiling roses and cornices, installing a modern kitchen and making space for an ensuite.

At five the next morning Melanie had to be on a surveillance plot in Kilburn, so she drove home in one of the Red team vehicles, an ageing Vauxhall Corsa. On the way she stopped at their local stores for the family shop: fruit and vegetables from Stayfresh in Fortis Green and the rest from Sainsbury's, just off the Broadway. By the time she pulled up outside the house behind their white Ford Fiesta it was almost nine o'clock, with the curtains drawn and a welcoming light in the porch.

Melanie's fortunes had changed drastically since the undercover mission the previous year, when her double life had been ruled by tradecraft. In those days she would conceal her battered Renault in a lock-up nearly a mile away, beyond Cherry Tree Wood, and sneak home on foot through the park. The brutality curtailing that operation had almost destroyed her. She still kept a sharp lookout on every journey home, though time was healing: these days it was more to admire the ornate woodwork around the porch than to spot a vengeful knife or gunman. She was beginning to relish her own, everyday life again. Weighed down by shopping, nudging open the garden gate with her hip, Melanie Fleming was content.

Rob opened the door before she could find her key, kissing her as he grabbed the plastic bags. He peered inside. 'Bananas?' He was still dressed for the office in dark grey suit trousers with a tieless lemon shirt, the cuffs folded back.

'Bugger.' Melanie could taste the Stella Artois from his lips.

'Sorry, love,' she said, holding on to the banister as she kicked off her sneakers.

Rob was already halfway to the kitchen, padding along in his socks, and the limp in his right leg seemed more pronounced. 'It's okay,' he called over his shoulder. 'They're asleep.'

Melanie wrinkled her nose. 'Is that what I think it is?'

'You're in for the night, yeah?'

It was Rob's turn to cook, and chilli con carne was one of his three options. Melanie followed him into the kitchen and kissed his neck, catching sight of the Homebase carrier bag with tins of magnolia paint for the hall and landing, now firmly on hold. 'Early start tomorrow.'

Rob did not react, for he was also a police officer, an expert in rural surveillance missions that meant digging in and enduring all weathers with minimal protection. Erratic days and nights were routine, especially after a terrorist attack.

Not so long ago their professional lives had collided in the most horrifying way, leaving them both with life-threatening injuries and their marriage buried in recrimination. Melanie had recovered from her chest wound, though Rob's shattered knee had cut short his secondment to the National Crime Agency, the drenching fields replaced by an overheated classroom as he taught Met rookies the fundamentals of surveillance. He hated every minute of a routine that delivered him home by five-thirty, burying his indignation while he read to the children, took another drink and waited for his wife to return.

The dining room was at the back of the house with French windows onto the well-stocked garden, but had evolved into a kids-only zone. The bright Turkish rug over the floorboards was scattered with toys, and a couple of LeapPad learning tablets with red earphones occupied the cherry wood table. The family generally ate in the kitchen, where Melanie had opted for a traditional pine table rather than a slate kitchen island.

While Rob worked at the hob, she made a pretence of throwing away her shopping list, checking out three empty cans of Stella in the recycling bin beneath the sink. She took cutlery from the drawer and pulled back her chair facing the garden window as Rob dished up. 'I'll just pop and kiss the boys good night.'

Rob swung round with the two steaming plates of chilli. 'Have this first. They're fine. Mum gave them their teas and dropped them back around six.'

'That's good. She okay?' Since her bitter divorce Brenda Fleming had downsized to an ugly sixties flat on the Great North Road, close to the tube, and covered the daily childcare interval between school and Rob's return from Hendon. The devotee of stay-at-home motherhood was now a dedicated granny and five star thorn in Melanie's side.

'Asking when you're going to surface again.'

'I bet.'

'The kids keep telling her they miss you, apparently.'

'Great.' Melanie played with a chunk of congealed mince, put her fork down and went over to the counter to pour a glass of red. 'Thanks a lot, Brenda.'

'You know what Mum's like,' said Rob, popping another lager as he flicked the TV to Sky News. 'She thinks you're trying to have it all.'

'Yeah, right,' said Melanie, sitting down again and raising her glass. This was classic Rob, channelling his resentment through Brenda to stoke Melanie's guilt. 'Did the doc confirm Tuesday?'

Rob nodded. 'Day case. I won't be able to drive myself, obviously.'

Melanie had taken a forkful of chilli and was fanning her mouth. 'I already said I'll pick you up.'

'It'll be early. Half four-ish.'

'No probs.' She leant over and gave his good knee a squeeze. 'You'll be back on the plot in no time. Living in a ditch. Peeing into a bottle.'

As part of their physical recovery Melanie had purchased family membership at the local LA Fitness. Rob went for an early session most evenings and all four of them enjoyed Sunday mornings or afternoons in the pool, depending on Melanie's work schedule. Seven weeks earlier, with his knee almost back to full strength, Rob had torn a meniscus on the treadmill, pushing back any hopes of a return to operational duty. His mood, dark and accusing, had returned with the physical setback, like a wasp finding an open window. 'You're kidding,' he snapped, eyes flashing. 'I can hardly manage the flaming classroom.'

'I'm sorry, Rob.'

'How many more times? It wasn't your fault.'

'I don't mean that. I'm talking about the gym. You overstressed it.'

Rebuilding their relationship had been a peace process in constant session, the truce always on the verge of collapse. Melanie, ambitious and talented, had agreed to stay clear of undercover work, and Rob had resigned from his pistol club in Hornsey, vowing never to touch another gun as long as he lived. It was proving a stretch for them both, a tougher deal than the house.

Rob took a deep breath, retreating from hostile ground. 'I'm not saying…here he is again.' Rob turned up the TV volume as Derek Finch filled the screen and Melanie's mobile rang. 'Who the hell's that?'

Melanie shrugged at the unknown number.

'Leave it.'

'Hello,' said Melanie, waggling her fingers at the remote in Rob's hand. The female voice was urgent, the words flowing in a stream of anxiety. Melanie only managed sympathetic murmurs and a final splash of reassurance. 'Course I can,' she said, eventually. 'See you in a mo.'

Rob was staring at her in disbelief as she rang off. 'You're not going out again?'

Melanie shook her head, attacking the chilli. 'Lou's coming here.'

'Who?'

'Louise. Justin's girlfriend,' said Melanie, chewing fast. 'You know. Justin Hine? Head of our tech ops?' She drank some wine to wash the food down. 'I'll take her in the front…you've met him.'

'It's gone nine o'clock.'

'She's got no-one else to turn to,' said Melanie, grabbing the remote to catch up with Finch's press conference at New Scotland Yard. Hemmed in by a battery of microphones, the head of counter-terrorism was answering one of the unseen hacks over a pair of heavy black designer spectacles, a recently acquired theatrical prop that kept slipping down his nose, flared and glistening in the TV lights:

'…as I said yesterday, this is the worst attack on the British mainland since 7/7 and we may be facing the return of a threat we hoped had disappeared from our shores. On behalf of the Metropolitan Police our hearts go out to the victims and their grieving families. This is an ongoing and complex investigation. All the signs lead me to believe that Monday's atrocity is the work of Irish republican dissidents. I have to face the possibility that the IRA has become Real again. I am keeping an open mind but that is my working assumption.' He seemed to pick up on a woman's muffled voice beyond the lights. 'Yes, of course, we are working closely with the security services. And no, I'm not prepared to say more about threat calls immediately before the bombings because the details are sensitive and may soon become *sub judice.*'

The questions came thick and fast as Finch's press officer tried to keep order. Did you have advance intelligence of a renewed Irish dissident campaign? Did anyone claim the bombings afterwards? How closely are you working with the Police Service of Northern Ireland? Could the attackers be from the Middle East? ISIS? Radicalised returnees from Syria and Iraq?

Finch had a stab at them all, scanning the briefing in his blue ring binder for clues. He evidently viewed himself as a star TV performer, though Melanie guessed that, to the world outside New

Scotland Yard, he came across as incoherent, shifty and defensive. Whatever the Bull's 'working assumption' about the Real IRA, Melanie had spotted the next turn in the rolling news: obsessed with brainwashed Brits, jihadi wannabees and raving Twitterati, police and MI5 had become distracted from other deadly threats.

It fell to the chief reporter from the *Belfast Telegraph* to voice the question on everybody's lips. 'Mr Finch,' she said, her long hair drifting into view at the bottom of the picture, 'isn't it a fact that you and MI5 have taken your eye off the ball in Northern Ireland?'

The attack exposed the Bull's twin default positions: bombast and overstatement. Glaring at her for a second, he whipped off his glasses and elevated them in his right hand, poised to emphasise every phrase. In his agitation he nudged one of the microphones twice and had to repeat himself over the echo. 'Let me make it perfectly clear to you,' he said. 'The Metropolitan Police Service is not complacent. We and our stakeholders are committed twenty-four seven, working together to keep Londoners safe. No-one has dropped their guard for a single moment.' Then the spectacles were greasing down his nose again as he abandoned his notes and peered beyond the lights, hunting the camera lens for a final, extempore speech. 'I say this. The people of London know that I will not rest until the perpetrators are caught. Everyone should be reassured that the reach of my Counter-Terrorism Command is global. So yes, all options are on the table. I shall go wherever the evidence leads me, day or night...'

'Tosser,' said Rob, turning the volume down as the doorbell rang.

Melanie was already out of her chair, draining her wine. 'Hang on here. Shan't be long.'

Louise Wilson shared a flat with Kerr's technical specialist in Parsons Green, within easy jogging distance of Putney Bridge but a good hour by tube from Muswell Hill. Melanie knew this because she and Louise bumped into each other once or twice a year, whenever Kerr managed to get his team together for a drink at the Morpeth Arms, a couple of hundred metres downstream from Vauxhall Cross.

Louise was a physiotherapist and stood on the porch with a light jacket over her scrubs and an oversized canvas shoulder bag, her long blonde hair tied back in a bun. Through the spyhole she looked pale and drawn but managed a big smile as Melanie opened the door.

'You're a long way from home,' said Melanie as they exchanged a hug.

Face to face, Louise sounded hesitant. 'I had an evening clinic at the Royal Free, so I thought…I was going to call John Kerr actually.'

Melanie led her into the living room, kicking aside the children's trainers. 'Well it's lovely to see you again.'

'…but then…I know roughly what the job can be like and Justin loves every minute.' She sat on the sofa, tucking the bag neatly by her feet. 'I don't want to be imagining problems where there aren't any.'

'Red or white?'

Melanie saw Lou's hand drift to her stomach as she shook her head. 'I'm fine, thanks… I suddenly remembered you lived just up the road and thought…Anyway, how's Rob getting on? Did he follow up with that physio I…'

'He's fine, too.' Melanie pushed the door shut and perched at the other end of the sofa. 'Lou, what's the matter?'

She took a deep breath. 'Do you know where Justin's working at the moment?'

'We're all full on with the bombings, obviously.'

'I'm talking since June. I know he's been given some special project, the usual hush bloody hush, but I hardly ever see him and when he does show up he's a complete pain in the arse.'

'That's awful,' said Melanie with a frown. 'How much has he told you?'

Louise shrugged. 'Closed book. Things were always iffy cos

of my shifts but now it's insane. I mean, why is it always him working every weekend? Okay, I know he's strapped for cash with his pilot training and we both need the overtime. Fair play, but this is different. There's something else going on. I'm just wondering… was he put on some operation to watch these bombers and it went wrong? Last time home he threw a complete strop. Can you tell me? Is he…did he lose track of the terrorists and…I dunno…now he's blaming himself or something?'

'I'm sure it's not that.'

'So what the hell's going on?'

Melanie sat silently for a moment, listening to Rob clattering about in the kitchen. 'Probably best if I have a quiet word with the boss.'

Louise nodded. 'I'm getting near the end of the road, Melanie. In two and a half years it was never like this. We've only done it once since he started this job and it was like, you know, he couldn't be bothered. Rubbish.' She looked Melanie in the eye. 'Thing is, has he got someone else?'

'Is that what you came to ask me?'

'No. Christ, that was so out of order.' She grabbed her bag. 'I'd better be going.'

'And you're pregnant, right?' said Melanie, quietly. 'How far?'

'I just told you.'

Chapter Eighteen

For his dash to the United States Kerr flew on BA217, departing at 09.55 from Heathrow's Terminal Five. Donna had booked the flight by phone with her BA finance contact on an Exceptional Deferred Payment, a protocol agreed between Special Branch and the airline after 9/11 to keep such flights secret.

EDPs were never intended for concealment from Bill Ritchie, though Kerr guessed Donna would have no qualms about the deception. This was not because she had divided loyalties or questionable integrity: in addition to her high security vetting she was a regular churchgoer, a clear-eyed Christian unfazed by the smudges and blots of intelligence work. If asked, she would say Kerr had raced off at short notice to interview an Irish walk-in at Dover ferry port who had asked for him by name. That was the phony alibi Kerr had concocted with her the night before from Nancy's kitchen, phone in the crook of his neck as he curled spaghetti into boiling water.

'Thanks a million, Donna. I really appreciate this.'

'I went the extra mile for you. Again.'

'It's just a few hours.' Kerr had heard a couple of young children quarrelling in the background, a boy and a girl. She had broken off a couple of times to calm them and, because Donna kept her private life pretty much a blank sheet, curiosity had finally overcome him. 'Sounds like you've got your hands full there.'

Donna had dodged his prying with a little laugh. 'Let's hope I'm still in a job when you get back.' It was the voice she had just used on the little ones, proving she was serious.

Before going to bed Kerr had renewed his US visa waiver on Nancy's desktop (a final reminder from Donna), printed his economy boarding pass and spoken with Rich Malone in

Washington. Leaving the Alfa in the long stay car park he had headed straight for security, travelling light with only a book in his jacket, C.J. Sansom's *Winter in Madrid*. He had reassured the inquisitive searchers about his lack of baggage while they examined his BlackBerry, then stopped by Wagamama for coffee and kedgeree. Reaching the gate six minutes after final boarding he had only realised the full scale of Donna's efforts at the door of the Boeing 777, where the flight attendant ignored his boarding pass, welcomed him by name and invited him to turn left.

Held at the gate for twenty-five minutes awaiting clearance for take-off, Kerr sipped champagne and skimmed his complimentary copy of the *Daily Telegraph*, still full of speculation about the bombings. When business was normal, he enjoyed flying. With the arming of the doors, the push-back and taxiing, came a sense of release, an abstraction from the constant pull of decision-making. But this morning his lock-down in the sky left him ill at ease as they rolled down the runway, warm air fluttering over the massive starboard wing. Uncomfortable about Donna covering for him, he also felt guilty about abandoning his team in the middle of the crisis. Since noon on Monday every moment had counted, with memories, sightings, suspicions and vigilance degrading by the hour. Kerr's duty lay in the Fishbowl, not a leather armchair at thirty-seven thousand feet. The fasten seat belt sign pinged off and a man in pink stockinged feet padded towards the washroom, tucking his shirt in his waistband.

Loosening his buckle as he conjured up Bill Ritchie's inevitable words of reproach, Kerr knew that when the time came he would stand by his decision to travel and the deceit that accompanied it. Against the Bull's preoccupation with IRA dissidents was the possibility that the solution lay not across the Irish Sea but on the other side of the Atlantic. Working with allies was his remit as a Special Branch officer, the justification for his race across the ocean. The flight attendant emerged from the galley with another tray of drinks. What was so sensitive that Rich Malone could not use normal channels? He returned her smile, took the offered glass and peered through the window. The sun danced on the wing and projected the aircraft's silhouette on the blanket of clouds beneath, his escort over the waves. Who knew what might be waiting for him in Washington? While Finch chased his prejudices in London Kerr had to place his trust in Malone, running with the important alongside the urgent.

As they turned left, high over Scotland, Kerr switched on his BlackBerry to flight safe mode and pulled his thoughts back to the Yard. On Monday morning, exactly one week after the attacks, he would sit his selection board for detective superintendent, sponsored by Bill Ritchie. To assist with his preparation Donna had forwarded him three apps with bullet points for the current crop of Met policies. 'All he needs now is a miracle,' Ritchie had evidently told Donna as she pressed Send.

Kerr scrolled through the material in bewilderment. Deliverables, core competencies, diversity strategies, paradigm shifts and missions critical tumbled through his brain and had him on the lookout for the cabin crew again. The final program described a smug world of dignity at work and respect for employees, a Shangri-la of integrity, equality and fairness beneath a pagoda of self-satisfaction. It was half-truth posing as Total Policing, as if the scandals of phone hacking, Plebgate, leaks, cock-ups and bullying had never happened. Kerr tossed the BlackBerry onto the vacant seat beside him, opened his novel and asked for a gin and tonic, scarcely recognising his own organisation.

They were over an hour late into Washington Dulles International, the delay in London exacerbated by strong headwinds in mid-Atlantic. Directed by the same flight attendant who had welcomed him on board, Kerr was the first to leave the aircraft, the day's stack of emails from London buzzing inside his pocket as he eased to the door. Waiting at the end of the ramp was a woman clutching a laminated ID badge who also addressed him by name as they shook hands. She was wearing a dark suit, court heels and a business smile. 'Hope you had a comfortable flight.' She gave a lift to the last word but walked off before he could answer, escorting him to Arrivals in polite silence.

The queue at Border Protection seemed to snake for miles but she diverted him to a corner station marked Flight Crews and Diplomatic. Waiting landside while the Homeland Security officer took his prints and photograph, she led him through Customs to an unmarked door opening onto the concourse behind Starbucks, ten metres clear of the waiting crowds. The slim hand stretched out again as a man appeared at Kerr's right shoulder. 'Sam will take it from here,' she said, melting away before he could thank her.

His new escort had the look of limousine chauffeurs the world over, fiftyish, deferential, suited and booted, with a paunch over thin legs, Bluetooth in his ear and hair greying from decades spent in city traffic. Nonplussed by Kerr's lack of luggage, Sam led him to a black Cadillac XTS sedan parked in a Strictly No Waiting zone beyond the airport's sweeping roof and opened the rear door for him. Interstate 66 was clear and the driver fast, a giant rhinestone wedding ring pulsing to some silent melody as they flashed across the Capital Beltway interchange.

They covered the twenty-five miles to Washington's outskirts in less than half an hour, a few minutes longer than it took Kerr to scroll through his mail. Though well into the evening at home, emails were still filtering through. He checked the senders first, alert for tipoffs from Donna or recriminations from the commander, then separated operational team updates from the clutter of meeting requests, spam, trash and calendar reminders. There was a bunch of missed calls from his team and an alert from HR confirming Monday's selection board, set for eight-thirty in Room 407, Victoria Block. Meanwhile, the afternoon sun was shining over Washington, so he relaxed and watched the capital's iconic buildings drift into view.

Chapter Nineteen

Rich Malone called when they were three minutes away, speeding across Theodore Roosevelt Bridge and down towards Foggy Bottom. Renamed the Harry S Truman Building at the turn of the century, the State Department was a sprawling, asymmetrical monolith of reinforced concrete and limestone cladding. Despite the courtyards and classical horizontal columns, it had never shaken off the forbidding look of a monument to the Cold War. Ignoring the main forecourt, Sam parked in a loading bay outside a steel door marked Strictly No Access. He locked the car and personally escorted Kerr inside, collecting his Visitor pass from the security station. Kerr checked his watch: he had touched down exactly an hour ago.

Rich Malone's office was on the east side of the fifth floor corridor, within reach of the executive offices. 'Hey, fit and ugly as ever,' he yelled, loping round his light wood desk. Somehow he managed to deliver Kerr a playful punch in the stomach, grab his hand and yank a chair away at the same time, all without losing eye contact. In private they had been on hugging terms, European style, during Malone's final months in London, but those days had evidently gone. 'Things go smooth at the airport, yeah?'

'Rich, everyone's been brilliant,' smiled Kerr, folding his jacket onto the back of the chair.

'And Sam made it without wrapping you round a fucking bridge,' said Malone with a wink at Kerr's driver, as if the road from the airport was machine gun alley. He had just covered all this on the phone, though repetition opened up a few minutes of good-ol'-boy backchat with Sam. Malone was a sharp diplomat who had qualified for the Bar at night school, but he loved reprising his night detective role in Boston's Drug Control Unit. In London such banter had been a regular act, what Jack Langton billed as Malone's 'Irish American Brit Shtick.'

Kerr took a look around. The room and its furniture were almost a replica of Malone's office at the embassy in Grosvenor Square, minus the Union Jack, British police helmet and a couple of square metres of grey carpeted floor space. In the corner by the window the Stars and Stripes stood beside a glass table crowded with the framed invitation to a Buckingham Palace garden party, letters of thanks from the White House and shots of Malone shaking hands with smiling Administration officials. The Bureau of Diplomatic Security seal occupied the opposite wall above the logo of the International Law Enforcement Academy office in San Salvador.

'As it comes, right?' With the driver dismissed, Malone was pouring coffee at a console behind his desk as Kerr sank into a black leather sofa. 'Sam's a great guy,' chuckled Malone. 'Got shunted by a taxi outside Watergate last week and we're not letting it go.'

Malone took the opposite sofa and slid a mug bearing the blue US Senate emblem across the low table between them. Since departing for Washington seven months earlier he had gained around twenty pounds and a buzz cut that accentuated the greyish scar above his left eye. A fawn roll neck sweater with matching chinos and moccasins replaced the sharp suit and black tasselled shoes, as if he had taken time out from vacation. 'Great to see you, buddy.' He sprawled back and stretched his legs.

'What is it?' said Kerr. 'Dress down Thursday?'

Malone beamed and made a gun of his fingers. 'Couple of hours on the range first thing. Hey, I can't believe you made it,' he said, as Kerr smiled and held his arms wide. 'And you're pissed that I dragged you here, right?'

'You'll have a good reason,' smiled Kerr, trying the coffee.

'Fucking right,' said Malone. 'You want to get straight to work?'

'Unless you want to talk on the way back to the airport.'

'Excellent,' said Malone, sitting forward on the sofa. 'Like I said yesterday, this is intel for your ears only.'

'Who from?'

'The Drug Enforcement Administration.' He leaned further towards Kerr, shins pressing against the table, the sweater tight as lycra around his paunch. 'As it happens the guy is a personal contact working out of San Salvador,' he said, gesturing to the emblem on the wall.

'What's the grading?'

'Secret and reliable. You think I'd have asked you here otherwise, with all that shit raining down in England?' He paused, as if he had thrown Kerr a challenge, waiting for his nod. 'Do you remember a guy called Sean Brogan? Ex-Real IRA from the nineties? He's classified as a fugitive in the US but you say "on the run," right?'

'OTR,' agreed Kerr, ducking the first question, his eyes unwavering from Malone's. 'You want me to run a check with London?'

'Not necessary,' said Malone. 'You ever heard of the Revolutionary Armed Forces of Columbia?'

'FARC. Yes,' said Kerr, frowning at the recollection. 'The IRA trained them in bomb making, weaponry, urban warfare etcetera. Three got arrested at Bogota airport in, I dunno, two thousand?'

'And two.'

'Then escaped back to Ireland?' said Kerr.

'Eventually, correct. And we now find that Brogan carried on the good work where they left off.'

'Without getting nicked?'

'Ancient history. We're looking into it,' said Malone, making a face. 'The new intel is that Mister Brogan has reinvented himself as FARC's link man for their cocaine smuggling operations into Europe.'

'Okay. What's the route?'

'West Africa. Lagos, Nigeria. Mostly in container ships, but also swallowers on flights from Bogota. The stomach can take two kilos, would you believe? Anyway, FARC have been striking deals with Islamic State, Hamas and Boko Haram to fund terrorism. Plus, Hizbollah has been laundering drugs money through them for years. But the angle for you is Europe. A lot of the powder is smuggled across the Med from Morocco and Algeria.'

'Into?'

'Spain, Holland and Italy. Plus England, obviously. Ships to Southampton, aircraft to London, Liverpool, Birmingham. The mules at Lagos hold onto their guts a bit longer and fly into Heathrow direct. But I guess you know most of this stuff, yeah?' he said quickly. 'The supply routes, I mean, not Brogan.'

Kerr looked quizzical. 'We've just had two bombs in the centre of London. Why am I sitting here listening to this?'

'But do you know who paid for them?' said Malone calmly.

Kerr studied him for a few moments. 'You're saying West African drugs dealers are behind this?'

'No. Money launderers in Western Europe. But it's still narco-terrorism.'

Kerr blew out his cheeks. 'So why couldn't you send me this on the wire?'

Abruptly, Malone bounced off the sofa and returned to his desk. 'I'll tell you, my friend. But let's take a break.' He checked his phone and tapped his keyboard. 'Can I get you anything? Some pasta? A beer?' The armrest jerked up and down and couple of times, a Malone habit from London that showed he was worked up.

'Rich, are you telling me Sean Brogan is involved in London?'

'Later. It's a nice day and I've logged out.' Malone rounded the desk again and handed Kerr his jacket. 'How about we stretch our legs?'

They left the building by the same door and walked quickly south to Constitution Gardens, heading past the Vietnam Veterans' Memorial towards the Reflecting Pool. The air was still warm beneath a clear sky and Kerr slung his jacket over his shoulder. On the way, Malone pressed him for every detail of the investigation in London. Having witnessed one of Derek Finch's blustering performances on CNN, he was hungry for Kerr's take on the significance of the threat calls, code words, suspects and the resemblance to previous IRA attacks. But his real interest was Kerr's take on the probability of further attacks: was Victoria a one-off or the start of a campaign?

In less than fifteen minutes they found themselves at the very edge of the pool, between the Abraham Lincoln Memorial and the Washington Monument, its obelisk a brilliant white against the pale blue sky.

Kerr looked around but the nearest potential eavesdroppers were a couple of dawdling kids holding hands and drifting away from them. He stood square on to Malone, the late afternoon sun tapering their shadows across the water. 'So what is it you couldn't tell me back there?'

'I don't know if Brogan is involved in this or not. But I have other information from my DEA contact about a possible… *possible*…terrorist attack in London.'

'Another one, you mean.'

Malone shrugged. 'I have a potential target, and that's about all.'

'And this is State covering its back.'

'It's friendship protecting yours,' said Malone sharply. 'The intel belongs to DEA and they've buried it with an embargo. No third party disclosure, especially to the Brits. I only know because my pal thinks like you and me. I'm out on a limb here, John.'

Kerr held his palms wide. 'I apologise.'

'So here's what I know. Source is a Columbian male, code name Goldhawk.'

'A member of FARC?'

'Enforcer,' nodded Malone, 'with drugs and money laundering on the side. DEA recruited him recently under duress. Early hours of Tuesday Goldhawk was at a meeting in Bogota between Brogan and a John Doe. Caucasian in his late thirties. We're urgently working on the ID.'

'What nationality?'

'European.'

'Irish? Is this an IRA meeting, Rich?'

Malone sunk his hands in his pockets. 'The conversation was in Spanish but the JD was not fluent. Goldhawk was there for security only, and they kept him outside the door.'

'What type of premises?'

'A brothel in Santa Fe, off Carrera Septima. It was noisy on the landing so he only caught bits and pieces. The location was set up at the last moment so no photographic. And the context is… problematic.'

'He was wired, yeah?'

'Except the DEA's state of the art fucking equipment malfunctioned. My contact debriefed him from memory. We're left with what Goldhawk says he heard, and that's my problem. The John Doe was doing most of the talking and it was about a hit in London.'

'But this conversation is…what…twenty hours after Victoria? Perhaps he was talking about that?'

'No. The JD mentioned a target. Corona. Used the word two or three times.'

'And?'

'Goldhawk says this refers to an attack on the Royals. That's the context. You think I'm overreacting?'

Kerr shook his head.

'Untried source, no corroboration,' said Malone. 'DEA are hoping they can rescue some of the recording. But in the meantime…well, you can see why they won't disseminate this right now. It's a reputational issue and they're embarrassed. Imagine the shitstorm from your side. John, this might be nothing. For all I know this Goldhawk guy heard the word wrong, or perhaps he's playing games. But there could be a link, right?'

'You're telling me this John Doe is my prime suspect?'

'Who knows? If Monday was the opening shot the next attack could be imminent.' Malone scanned the route they had just walked, as if checking for surveillance. There was the usual scattering of tourists and joggers. An elderly couple with a little dog in a winter coat walked slowly past, the man stooped like a question mark. 'That's why I called you. If my Director ever finds out we've had this conversation…'

'She won't,' said Kerr, naturally suspicious, also taking in his surroundings. Further to the east, the late afternoon sunshine draped itself around the dome of the Capitol Building, smooth and brilliant white, the icing on Washington's cake. Uneasy, Kerr looked his friend in the eye. 'Can you introduce me to Goldhawk's handler?'

'Not possible, bud,' said Malone quickly,

'So can I have a copy of the debrief? There must be a written record?'

Malone slowly shook his head. 'Sorry. But if they rescue the recording and make the ID you'll be the first to know.' He checked his watch. 'Look, I have a scrum down with the arms control guys in thirty minutes.'

'What's the coverage of Brogan?'

'The guy is…difficult,' said Malone, suddenly hesitant. 'Lives his life off the grid.'

'That's not what I asked,' said Kerr.

'John, I've told you all I can.'

'Can I brief Bill Ritchie?'

'Are you fucking kidding?'

'So what am I supposed to do with this?'

Malone scratched the back of his head as ripples from a fallen leaf corrugated their reflections. 'I dunno. Check the family's movements, beef up the security detail. It's precautionary, John, just for a couple of days.' He looked awkward, as if he was having a change of heart. 'Fact is I never wanted to burden you with this.'

'It's okay. I appreciate it,' said Kerr, wondering why the Americans were holding out on him.

'When's your flight again?'

'Plenty of time,' said Kerr, but Malone already had his mobile ready, swinging round to check the build-up of traffic alongside the park.

'It's getting busy,' he said quietly. 'Better give Sam a call.'

Kerr never made it back to Malone's office. Fifteen minutes later the driver greeted him with a turkey pastrami sandwich in a side street off Constitution Avenue, close to the US Institute of Peace and handy for the Interstate 66. And by the time he ushered Kerr into the back seat of the Cadillac Malone was his old self again, all handshakes and smiles. 'Be good, buddy, and stay in touch, yeah?'

The return journey to Dulles took over an hour in heavy traffic but Kerr made it to check-in with time to spare before the eight-twenty departure on BA264. He had spent less than five hours on US soil. In the car a voicemail from Melanie sent him a pulse of concern: 'Hi John. I'm getting the international dial tone. Everything alright? Can you give me a call when you get back? Something's come up about Justin. Anyway…yeah, that's it. Thanks. Bye.'

They were calling the flight by the time he cleared security and found a quiet corner to make his own call. The number was filed in his contacts under Zero, a work name that featured nowhere in Dodge's agent records. He let it ring for thirty seconds, then redialled before giving up and heading to the gate.

Chapter Twenty

For their second assault the older brother, Fin, wore a dark suit with frayed cuffs, a slight tear inside the left leg and the musty whiff of a charity shop. The Englishman delivered the suit personally, unpacking it from his battered wheelie case with a faded white shirt, black woollen scarf and down-at-heel black shoes a size too small. They had to unpick the seams in the turnups to cover Fin's long legs, but he looked authentic enough to slip in and out of the City's Ring of Steel with its edgy cops, surveillance choke points and forest of security cameras.

At the bottom of the case was a brown leather man bag containing Fin's bomb, a rectangular plastic takeaway carton with 'vindaloo' scrawled on the lid and Semtex explosive packed inside. There was an identical device for Kenny in a plastic Waitrose carrier, but his delivery would require no particular dress code. 'Usual shit order for you,' said the Englishman, ignoring Kenny's nervous look of inquiry as he pointed out the black arming switches cut into the plastic.

The brothers knew their visitor simply as Bobby, and this morning he was in the same dark grey sweatshirt, stained jeans and steel capped boots he had worn in his workshop on the day he hired them. At the safe house he never stayed longer than twenty minutes and this morning handed over another packet of cocaine as soon as they had rehearsed the morning's attack to his satisfaction.

Hatred of the English had been drilled into the brothers since childhood, though they were cautious to conceal this from Bobby, on whom they depended for their survival in London. Muscular, confident and aggressive, their protector acted like he was the go-to guy for terrorism in London, though his attitude was confusing, an odd mix of friendship, jocularity and disdain, even on the first

Sunday morning when he had driven them across London to reconnoitre the targets. In Belfast Fin had come up against men whose mere presence electrocuted him with fright, drugs enforcers mostly, or gangsters close to the paramilitaries. With Bobby, for all his posturing, it was different. He acted street hard but sounded educated, too clever to be fixing exhausts and changing tyres, reminding Fin of the uppity BBC parasites feeding off the Falls Road in his youth. Like a fight dog chained to a post, the Englishman aroused curiosity, not fear. He talked as if the brothers lived or died through him alone, but Fin suspected a superior force was pressing down on Bobby, too. Perhaps the hotshot transporter of bombs was nothing more than a delivery boy, an insignificant courier just like them. Bobby was an enigma, but the question whether he was Mr Big or cannon fodder never arose because, in Fin's underworld of drugs and violence, everything came down to raw strength. If the English oddball drove his kid brother too hard, or the deal turned sour and the cocaine stopped coming, Fin would take him out with his bare hands.

For all the bluster, the brothers were relieved to see Bobby again. Holed up in their basement while the manhunt swirled above them, he was their first human contact in four days. On Monday, after planting their bombs in Victoria, they had crossed Vauxhall Bridge to watch the breaking news at the Angel, a scruffy sixties pub serving a low rent tower block behind Spring Gardens, close to where the Real IRA celebrated the millennium with a mortar attack on MI6's flashy home base. Four pints of Guinness later, with the Underground at a standstill, they separated and randomly boarded buses at Vauxhall's terminus, Fin taking the 87 for Aldwych, Kenny the 344 as far as Southwark Bridge. From there they meandered to Holloway and covered the final mile to the safe house on foot, Kenny arriving two hours after his brother, well after dark. Since then they had been lying low, isolated and on edge.

Leading them down the crumbling steps for the first time,

Bobby had described their subterranean safe house as a 'classy refurb,' a tag they immediately found to be a wild misrepresentation. On the long haul from derelict hovel to modern apartment the two dark rooms had remained at squalid, with ripped plaster littering the rough wooden floors and lifeless arteries of electrical cable poking from the walls and ceiling, cracks radiating like giant blood vessels across the plaster.

In the back room a sash window looked onto a dirty, whitewashed wall. To the left was a part constructed kitchen space crowded by builders' trestles, piles of rubble, a microwave and noisy fridge crammed with ready meals. The only furniture was a pair of black canvas camping chairs, each with a Glock pistol in its cup holder, and a folding table, on which sat the TV. The builders had yet to work on the bathroom, accessed through a sliding door opposite the kitchen, where the shower over the avocado tub dripped constantly but the toilet never flushed.

The front room, reached through a curved arch, contained the bed, futon and pine table Bobby used to demonstrate their bombs, and large sections of the wall plaster had disintegrated, exposing the brick. Neatly stored opposite the main door, wrapped in plastic and out of sight from the front window, were a brand new oven, bathroom units and bags of shiny fittings. The building spec, dog-eared and stained, lay on top, a stapled batch of A3 sheets depicting an airy, minimalist bachelor pad with designer kitchen, Beluga lights, Hansgrohe taps, wet room and pull down bed.

Fin glared at the pictures every day. They held out a promise to a stranger while he and Kenny lay trapped in a fog of permanent gloom, with only a single lamp stretching their shadows across the ceiling night and day. They were cold and stir crazy, sustained by shepherds pie and cheap whiskey, dependent on the Englishman for their white powder and LBC for a lifeline to the outside world. The chill aggravated the pain in Kenny's injured knee, though he bore every hardship in silence; but to Fin, scornful and embittered, the images of luxury were an insult. Peering through the makeshift curtain as Bobby leapt up the steps and disappeared into the street, Fin knew the Englishman was mocking them.

The headlines filtered from the back room as he shuffled into his suit and bent down to help Kenny with his leg strapping. But as the news sank in, he grinned and threw his kid brother a wink: four days on, explosions at Victoria still trumped beheadings in Syria. He helped Kenny to his feet, slid the bombs aside and cut two celebratory lines of cocaine.

When they were high and ready, Fin loitered by the front gate, adjusting the Glock in the small of his back before raising a gloved hand to give Kenny the all clear. It was a beautiful autumn morning, with a cloudless sky and a cool breeze blowing directly into their faces as they walked north towards Finsbury Park station. The shoes pinched Fin's feet and the suit waistband was tight against the pistol, but he relished the freedom, releasing his shoulder from the weight of the bomb every few steps to gulp down lungfuls of clean air. Kenny, in grey hoodie, baggy jeans and the trainers he wore in Belfast, walked more slowly than usual, his injured right leg stiff from lack of exercise. The deterioration seemed to dislodge the pistol, for he kept reaching back with his free hand. Not far from the safe house a ridge of wet leaves and rubbish had settled against a maroon Nissan Micra, and a crude handwritten sign taped to the windscreen, 'MOT New Tires Tax £899ono,' reminded Fin they might soon need transport just to get Kenny to the station.

A middle aged man in dark blue sweatshirt and jeans crossed to their side of the road just as a dog appeared from the line of parked cars, a spaniel or foxhound, scampering on a long lead. Tail wagging fast it came straight for them, woofing around Kenny's Waitrose bag like a champion Semtex sniffer. Fin's eyes never left the owner, cautiously feeling for the Glock as he weighed the threat. The man was in his thirties, stringy and shaven-headed, the type Fin had seen handling dogs in airports, with eyes that turned mean as Kenny overreacted by hugging the bomb to his chest. 'You're not gonna get far,' he said, disentangling the dog and jagging his face as he moved away. 'Chock-a-block with Old Bill.'

As soon as they were clear Fin gripped Kenny's arm. 'What the fuck's the matter with you? It's not us they're after, is it?'

'Should have gone the long way, like Bobby told us.' Kenny sounded scared as his eyes lasered dead ahead. 'Shit, what have you got us into?'

On the approach to Finsbury Park mosque a crowd of about thirty demonstrators were spilling onto the street from the square bordering Seven Sisters Road, expanding in their direction. They were yelling something Fin could not make out, but many were waving home-made placards against the new Terrorism Act. As they cleared a parked removal lorry Fin saw three heavy duty police carriers abandoned haphazardly on the opposite pavement, sealing off a small, mid-terrace Victorian house. In a flash he realised they had stumbled upon a massive police screw up. This was gun-to-the-head persecution versus human rights in an area of high sensitivity, and they were walking straight into it.

With the gap narrowing, Fin stole a backward glance towards the safe house. A white patrol car had swung across the street in front of the church, blocking any vehicles from entering. Then a black BMW 3 Series swept past them, skidding to a halt between the carriers and demonstrators, its blue light still turning, and Fin knew his brother had been right: they should have taken the quiet path alongside the railway line, as ordered. 'Too late,' he murmured, adjusting the bag on his shoulder as they drew level with the target house. 'We keep moving.'

The arrival of the BMW provoked the demonstrators, channelling their sporadic shouts into a rhythmic chant that surfed over the brothers and sent pigeons flapping from the rooftops. Then the air jolted with tension as the crew emerged with a stock of crime scene tape to block their path. The passenger was old school, hat pushed back and breathless, with shapeless trousers and a non-regulation gut below his stab proof vest. Head cocked to his radio as he called up reinforcements, he looped the tape around a fence post and began unrolling it across the street.

The train station was tantalisingly close, just beyond the mosque on the far side of Seven Sisters Road, and Fin kept walking slowly forward. 'Relax,' he whispered as they reached the BMW, sensing his brother flinch again. 'They're rounding up the usual suspects, pissing everyone off. We go right under their noses.'

The young BMW driver, hatless, red-faced and belligerent, waved Fin back as he lifted the tape for Kenny. 'Sterile area. No one enters or leaves,' he yelled against the clamour, as Fin made a face and shrugged at the illogicality of it all. Then the tape snapped as the protestors surged forward and a forest of arms pulled the brothers to safety.

Fin clapped a protective arm around his brother's shoulders. 'Couple of hours,' he said as they melted with their bombs into the crowd, 'and they'll be rolling it out all over again.'

At the station they swiped Bobby's new Oyster cards and just caught the eleven minutes past eleven for the journey to Moorgate, travelling at opposite ends of the quiet front carriage. Fin lay the bomb between his legs but, by the time they rattled into Highbury and Islington, Kenny was protecting the plastic carrier on his lap, his feet resting on the seat opposite until a fragile looking woman with a *Daily Mail* leant over to rebuke him.

From the station they headed south, cutting across a neat oval of grass in front of The Globe pub to zigzag through the maze of narrow streets on the other side of London Wall. Losing his bearings for a moment, Fin turned into a dank, rectangular yard, the ancient burial ground for a tiny church half-hidden behind a yew tree. They sat across from a lopsided angel missing a wing, an uneven row of pitted headstones and, tucked snugly against the iron railings, a mobile snack bar. Fin bought two cans of Sprite, checked his position on a tourist guide pinned to the side of the bar and squeezed beside his brother. 'Not far,' he murmured, popping the cans. 'It's the DLR, okay? Lewisham train.'

Kenny nodded as he gulped his drink, dribbling a line of Sprite down his cheek. 'Docklands. Five stops.' He wiped his chin on his sleeve as the bar owner splashed a bucket of soapy water over the uneven flagstones. 'Back by tube. Jubilee. You don't have to keep telling me.'

They separated near the bottom of Old Jewry, a few paces short of the junction with Cheapside. Watching his brother walk ahead and disappear left towards Bank station, Fin tied the scarf in a Parisian knot and slipped on a pair of tinted glasses with thick plastic frames.

Walking quickly now, he swung right into Cheapside and immediately found his landmark, the ornate black clock of St May-le-Bow, suspended at right angles to the church tower, its gold hands at a couple of minutes after midday. He crossed the street just beyond Tesco Metro, passing Lloyds Bank and Santander. His target was beyond the church, where the pavement grew busier with chain stores and building societies, all sheltered by a plate glass awning.

The boutique finance house Dolphin and Drew lay across the street, beyond a bus stop and a bicycle stand, twice the width of the adjoining parfumerie and posh chocolate shop. Fin used a slow moving double decker as cover while making his final security check, then crossed the street and doubled back, shrugging his scarf a little higher and taking a Samsung mobile from his jacket.

The bank was four storeys high and double-fronted in tinted glass, with huge pots each side of the revolving door, one containing a huge yukka, the other a vine, and more foliage spreading from oversized planters. It transformed the entrance into a minor botanical garden, pleasing to the bank's élite clients and the perfect screen for a bomber. The door was power assisted and Fin made out he was mid-call, listening intently. Deceptively deep, the entrance hall smelt like the inside of a greenhouse. He stepped aside to avoid a couple making for the exit and stood still, eyes discreetly tracking for security cameras and guards. Head lowered, he adjusted his glasses and made an imaginary point with his hand, rotating to conceal the dangling bag.

Reception was at least fifteen paces away, to the right of three security barriers monitored by a camera, and the counter left only the top of the receptionist's head visible. A lone security guard leant there, using one of her phones while an impatient group of visitors waited for their passes.

Each side of the door was a rectangle of six deep armchairs in soft leather only a shade lighter than Fin's bag, with coffee tables holding banking journals and the day's *Financial Times*. To the left, a couple of thirty-somethings were cosying up with takeaway Starbucks, the man studying a graph on his tablet while the woman used her iPhone, but the other bank of chairs was empty. With the phone still protecting his face, Fin took the chair closest to the greenery and reached for the newspaper, casually laying the bag on the floor. The pink sheets were creased and disordered and he slipped a section from his lap to cover the bag. The guard was still on the phone, obscured by the waiting clients as Fin's hand traced around the plastic carton and flicked the switch to arm his bomb. Then he slowly stood, melted into a line of workers breaking for lunch and weaved across the street, the Samsung still high against his cheek.

Cheapside had become busier in the past few minutes, with longer queues at the bus stops and sandwich bars. His escape route was Bow Lane, a narrow thoroughfare that would lead him to the tube at Mansion House. On the corner, twenty metres away from a docking station for Boris bikes, he paused. The clock above the church said seventeen minutes past twelve and the Englishman was exactly where he had said he would be, sitting astride a bike, suited with an open-necked white shirt, trousers tucked into his socks.

Bobby ignored Fin as he bumped down the kerb towards St Paul's, but the mobile was already in his hand.

Chapter Twenty-One

Gemma Riley felt shattered, but not through work. The fallout from any critical incident was nothing new to the civilians in Communications and Registry, experts who fielded the calls, identified subjects of interest and enabled people like John Kerr to do their job. No-one could say if Monday's bombs were a one-off or the first strike in a long terrorist campaign, so the women and men in Gemma's line of work learned to pace themselves for a marathon of long hours, short weekends and zero social life.

This morning, running on empty, she finally accepted it was empathy, not terrorism, that was draining her. Alan Fargo had been working non-stop since the tragedy, out of necessity and to hold his anguish at bay, and needed no persuasion to stay with her. Each night, reaching her flat well after ten, they had rustled up dinner before falling into bed and making love. Two mornings ago she had walked with him to the mortuary at Horseferry Road, minutes from the Yard, holding his hand while he waited to identify the bodies of his mother and Pauline, then trying unsuccessfully to dissuade him from returning to work. Already filled with admiration and compassion, it dawned on Gemma she was nearing a threshold she had never crossed in her entire life.

She had allowed herself to become intimate with co-workers before, the precariously married, usually, or unattached narcissists, but every fling had been poisoned by deceit and betrayal. With Alan Fargo it had been different from the start: he was shorter than the type she normally favoured, plumper, more serious-minded and less self-aware, diligent about his responsibilities at work and home. A year ago she had been thrown off course by his shy kindness and efforts to please, the thrill of previous connections eclipsed by their slow burning romance. Today, at the end of a terrible week, engulfed by grief and sorrow, the realisation she had fallen in love was exhausting.

A light was blinking on the console. '2715, good morning,' she said for the umpteenth time that day, tensing forward as the male voice at the other end of the line jabbed her memory. This time there was no preamble about Special Branch.

'Bomb at Cheapside. Dolphin. Twenty minutes.'

In a jumble of reflexes she raised her free hand to silence the talking behind her, scrawled to test her pen, marked the time and tugged at the sleeves of her new lambswool cardigan. 'Where? Say again?'

'I told you. In the City.' Same man, the hybrid English-Irish accent again, a mishmash of counterfeit vowels. The pitch was higher than the first time, more stressed and hurried.

'Is that Dolphin as in the fish?' said Gemma calmly. 'What is Dolphin? Please don't hang up. I need a proper address.'

'Twenty minutes. Topaz.'

She heard wind disturbing the mouthpiece, suggesting the caller was on the move. 'That's impossible,' said Gemma, glimpsing the second hand as she scribbled. 'What sort of bomb? How many? More than one?' Silence.

The instant the line went dead Gemma poked the button for central communications complex and called over her shoulder. 'Someone get hold of John Kerr now!' As the operator picked up she was already websearching 'cheapside dolphin'. She kept her voice to a monotone, enunciating every word with scarcely a pause. 'Hello this is Gemma in SO15 comms with another Livebait. The threat is to Cheapside, repeat Cheapside in the City, codeword Topaz, same as before so we're treating as genuine. Caller gives a twenty minute window from one minute ago, that's twelve nineteen.' She paused at the operator's sharp intake of breath. 'Yes, two-zero minutes, unless it goes off early again. Target is Dolphin. Can you read that back,' said Gemma, scrolling through the screen as the operator repeated her information. 'For info I think this must be Dolphin and Drew Investment Bank,' she continued, 'number one oh three. North side, west of the church. Hold on... yeah...has to be. I'll send you anything else I can get. Thank you bye bye.'

Gemma checked the clock again. It had taken less than a minute to make her report but the second hand seemed to have gathered speed.

•••

Friday, 14 October, 12.22, Cheapside, City of London

The City's Ring of Steel was actually made of concrete, an ugly network of chicanes on access roads designed to slow and photograph every vehicle entering the famous Square Mile. Installed in the nineties after catastrophic IRA bombs at the Baltic Exchange and Bishopsgate, its aim was to deter the wicked and dissuade the banks from deserting London for Frankfurt, Paris or Zurich. The police presence was relaxed after the IRA ceasefires but ramped up again the day after 9/11, when securocrats peered up at the City's towers and saw Armageddon.

The legacy was a functioning, regularly tested machine that slipped into gear within fifteen seconds of Gemma Riley pressing Go. The Yard's communications centre was awash with contingency plans, checklists and menus of options for everything from bombing to chemical attack, and all in alphabetical order. Crammed into blue plastic ring binders were threat levels, exercise scenarios, bikini states and army back-up protocols, with appendices of blood banks, body bag stores, emergency rooms and mortuaries.

On the ground, the location was all the frontline officers needed to hear. In the City's crowded, narrow canyons their sirens bounced off the office towers from all directions, magnifying the pulling power of Topaz. Multiple patrol cars approached St Paul's from the west and Bank station from the east as they forced a path through the congestion to isolate the threat area, splitting the pack to accelerate down the centre of the street or, if that proved impossible, scattering pedestrians as they bumped onto the pavement. Within six minutes a car had blocked off each end of Cheapside, while other crews set up pre-planned diversions.

•••

Friday, 14 October, 12.26, Dolphin and Drew Investment Bank, Cheapside, City of London

The security guard at Dolphin and Drew was a fiftyish Gulf War veteran known as Stan. His junior, a temp who had been shooting up in the underground garage when Fin delivered his bomb, was still on his break and ignored his radio when police called in the threat. Everyone higher up the chain was on voicemail, so Stan ordered an evacuation on his own initiative. 'This is not a drill,' he repeated three times over the system, his anxious voice rolling through every floor.

It was a controversial decision. Many on the bloated crisis management circuit said it was safer to shelter inside the building than flee into danger. But years ago Stan had faced a real-life crisis, a deranged accountant sacked for fraud and illicit sex who returned to shoot his boss dead. In Stan's opinion, only flight gave anyone a chance against a hidden bomb or a nutter waving an automatic pistol, and he was already imagining the carnage of Rafal Eisner Capital in his own foyer. Last year's practice drill had proved Dolphin and Drew could be emptied in ten minutes, so he looked at the clock, made his calculation and did what he thought was right.

A BMW patrol car screeched up just as Stan lifted the shiny leaf of a rubber plant and located the bag. Employees were streaming past him with their coats and phones, chatting and laughing, so he stood straight and yelled at them to get clear. There were two officers in the car but only the driver entered the bank. She was smart, in white shirt sleeve order and creased trousers, and spoke calmly into her radio as soon as she saw Stan pointing at the bag.

She glanced at his name badge and shook hands, gently pulling him clear of the bag. 'Stan, I'm Mandy,' she said, keeping a hand on his forearm. 'How do we know when everyone's out?'

'A rep on each floor tells me.'

'Have they?'

Stan shook his head as he watched her quickly circle the bag and take photographs on her iPhone. 'Gives the bomb technician a heads-up,' she said, pointing at the revolving door. 'Can you fold that back? So we can get the robot in?'

Stan nodded.

'Good. Thanks.' She tapped something into her phone, murmured into the radio again and turned back to Stan. 'Where's your assembly point?'

'Wood Street.'

'Too close. Has to be two hundred metres, minimum,' she said as her partner appeared alongside. 'Think we may have another live one, Dee. Let's send everyone down to St Paul's.' She peered through the window at the traffic still drifting slowly past and the clumps of pedestrians lingering at bus stops on each side of the street. 'And that lot. And the retail on the other side.'

There were more sirens now, punching the air from both ends of Cheapside, and two more patrol cars skidded to a halt as her partner hurried out to brief the crews. The guard felt Mandy's grip tighten against his arm but her voice was kind, as if she could sense the fear constricting his chest. 'Listen, Stan, I want you to get on the loudspeaker and tell whoever's still up there the threat is real, okay? Then you get away yourself, same as the others.'

Stan looked doubtful and nodded towards the lift lobby. 'It's my job to make sure, you know. There's always a few take the piss.'

'No time. Nothing more any of us can do till the experts get here.' She looked him in the eye. 'Your job is done. I'm telling you to keep yourself safe. Is that clear?'

•••

As before, Gemma's first call had been to Jack Langton so that he could immediately activate Starburst, the deployment of surveillance officers around Cheapside to look for unusual or suspicious activity. She was working down her notification list as a jacketless Kerr appeared on the other side of the glass partition, BlackBerry at his ear. He had a day's growth of stubble and, beckoning him in, it occurred to Gemma she had not seen him since Wednesday evening.

'What you got?' said Kerr as soon as he was through the door. His pale blue shirt crumpled, the sleeves untidily rolled up, Kerr looked weary and unkempt, as if he had been hunkering down in the Fishbowl and forgotten to take a shower.

'It's a bank. Dolphin and Drew in Cheapside.'

Kerr rolled up a chair, tossing his phone on Gemma's desk. 'How long do we have?'

'Twelve minutes max. Jack's on the plot.' The outside line began blinking at her again.

'Yeah, we just spoke.'

'They've found a bag in the Reception,' she said, her hand reaching for the phone. 'Still getting people away…Hang on…2715 good afternoon, please hold.' She put a hand over the mouthpiece to finish her sentence for Kerr, then the voice on the line was pulling at her again, wiping everything else. She pressed the speaker button so Kerr could hear. 'Come again?'

'Bomb at Canary Wharf. Fifteen minutes. The word is Emerald.'

'Where? Is that "at" or "in"? Inside a building? At the tube station? Please don't hang up. You have to give us more.'

As the line clicked Gemma dialled central comms for the second time in less than six minutes. She was searching the computer as she relayed the threat information but Kerr checked her hand. 'Tell them it's no trace,' he murmured.

Gemma look quizzical, then nodded. 'Code word Emerald is a negative with us,' she said, then rang off and turned to him.

'I'll tell you later,' said Kerr, grabbing the mobile. 'Let's warn Jack.'

Then all the lines were flashing at once and the door swung open behind them. 'Bomb gone,' said a calm female voice, before either of them could react. 'It's Cheapside.'

•••

Friday, 14 October, 12.28, Dolphin and Drew Investment Bank, Cheapside, City of London

The Semtex in Fin's bag detonated eleven minutes early, while Dolphin and Drew stragglers were still bumping into each other in their belated rush for safety.

A window of twenty minutes offered low odds to clear one of the City's busiest streets; with a gap of nine, no-one stood a chance. The first officers on scene, élite fast response drivers like Mandy, had remained with their partners in the area long after it became lethal, red mist clouding health and safety. One of them found a loudhailer; a couple of others pulled on hi-vis jackets and sprinted up and down Cheapside in a frantic race against the clock, barging into shops and offices and yelling at people to get clear.

For other professionals, their lives already peppered with contingency plans, emergency drills and actual disasters, the callout had been instantaneous. Fire crews scrambled from Shoreditch, Soho and Westminster at the press of a button, and paramedics, most already on the move, converged from every direction. With civilians, things moved more slowly, for atrocities were breaking news that happened to other people. As precious seconds dripped away, Mandy and the other cops had to break through complacency, disbelief and confusion as they ordered shoppers and suits to run for their lives.

The explosion cracked the air, lifted the whole building and scorched the killing zone in white heat as the bank's frontage disappeared, its glass shards scything everybody within forty paces.

A white Transit van left the street, collected by an invisible giant hand whose fingers crushed the sides before hurling it like a toy through a bookseller's window. Its petrol tank exploded in a ball of orange flame, just as the glass canopy above the row of shops shattered onto a string of people running for safety, killing three adults and two children. The blast caught birds in mid-flight, triggered alarms and mangled a line of parked bicycles into deadly shrapnel, rocketing a set of handlebars into the clock face above St Mary-le-Bow. Smashed windows from a hundred offices swamped Cheapside in a sea of glass: lopsided cars lay adrift with shoes, chairs, strollers and other flotsam, but its choppy surface sparkled in the midday sunshine. Disfigured corpses lay scattered like victims of an air crash, their limbs buried or blown away, stripped to their underwear as if they had fallen from the sky. Others, terribly mutilated, too traumatised to scream, moaned quietly as paper and detritus sucked from the offices above floated to the ground. A few, short of time, had tried to cheat the bomb by taking refuge in a side alley, but the shock wave found them and shredded their bodies into bloodied lumps of flesh.

The blast showed no mercy to its seventeen victims. It charged glass, brick and metal with lethal energy, then pulverised any human its missiles did not slice, pierce or burn. Stan had been adapting the revolving door when the bomb exploded and ended up on the other side of the street, his severed trunk still in the circular frame like a prisoner in some weird time capsule.

The bomb left many with 'life changing injuries,' the post-Iraq euphemism for dismemberment, brain damage and everlasting trauma. Among the dead was Mandy, decapitated as she paused to call in the robot, a roll of Police Line-Do Not Cross tape in her hand, its tail fluttering in the breeze.

Chapter Twenty-Two

Friday, 14 October, 12.47, Room 1830, New Scotland Yard

To officers in John Kerr's profession, every terrorist success was an intelligence failure. That had been lesson number one on the Special Branch course, straight after the coffee and welcome BS, and it lay at the core of Kerr's professional life. Derek Finch used it as a personal rebuke against Bill Ritchie, even when things were going well and yet another deranged plot had been thwarted. It was always the secret intelligence from Ritchie's team and MI5 that uncovered global jihad's newest recruits, urban kids unhinged in cyberspace, arrested in their bedrooms and banged up in Paddington Green. But in Finch's eyes victory was always impaired by shortfall, the source unreliable, its product too late or incomplete.

According to Gemma, the two bosses were with the Commissioner right now, updating her on Monday's attacks. As he left Reserve and made his way up to Room 1830, Kerr feared the worst. A year ago, the Bull had wanted his own placeman as commander of the SO15 intelligence unit and had never forgiven Ritchie for outmanoeuvring him. In the heat of this crisis, Kerr guessed he would exploit two breakdowns in five days to exact revenge: for a schemer as vain, self-serving and tribal as Derek Finch, even tragedy had an upside.

Despite the gruelling pace of the past twenty-four hours Kerr felt energised by the emergency at home, catching Dodge's voicemail for the third time as he raced up the fire escape stairs. His night flight from Washington had caught a strong tailwind over the Atlantic only to be held in the morning skies above Heathrow. He had not cleared immigration at Terminal Five until well after ten, too late to hurry home for a shower and change of clothes, so had driven straight to the Yard.

Entering Room 1830 he felt another rush of adrenaline. It was a full house, the whole place buzzing as Alan Fargo's team of six played catch-up to the clamour of sirens in the streets below. Two giant wall screens showed Sky and BBC News at low volume, both repeating amateur footage of the scene while the professionals organised themselves. Through the window looking east Fargo's officers had their own view, a spiral of black smoke decomposing as it drifted towards them.

Fargo was working the computer, sleeves rolled up, shirt stark white against Mercury's red glow as he explored its forest of secret databases. Evidently expecting company he had already pulled up another chair and threw Kerr a watery glance. Since his attachment to Gemma he had been experimenting with contact lenses, though his nose still carried indentations from the specs he had worn for decades.

'Rough night,' said Kerr, rubbing his chin as Fargo's eyes lingered a second longer than necessary. Kerr was mildly surprised to see a half-eaten chocolate chip cookie lying on the desk, for everyone knew Fargo followed a strict diet these days. But it was 'Salisbury Patisserie' on the white paper bag that really grabbed his attention, in ornate script above a drawing of the Cathedral.

Fargo blinked a couple of times and slid him a single sheet of paper. 'Emerald.'

'Bombs on the beaches?' said Kerr as he sat down, barely glancing at the note. 'Nineteen eighty-seven?'

'Eight-five,' nodded Fargo. 'Devices hidden in the sand all along the south coast aimed at the bucket and spaders.'

'And this was the name for our joint op with Garda Crime and Security. I remember the briefing.'

'Correct. Topaz and Emerald are both Special Branch operational codes.'

'Which boshes the coincidence theory.'

'And secret. Never released outside the eighteenth floor. So the bombers also demonstrate a security breach here. It's neat,' he said as their eyes drifted to the TV.

Kerr jabbed his index finger at the screen. 'And now we know for sure this is directed at banks, not transport. It's Rafal Eisner rather than Victoria station. Dolphin and Drew, not, I dunno, any other soft target you can think of.'

'Both of them have form in the financial crash,' said Fargo, working the computer again. 'Rafal Eisner is based in Munich with branches here and in Amsterdam. Heavily criticised by the Bundesbank for unethical practices prior to 07, through massively risky and complex financial products. There's a technical summary from the Financial Conduct Authority, if you're interested.'

Kerr shrugged.

Fargo switched to another database. 'This is a Mercury zipscan on Dolphin and Drew in the last ten minutes, but there's plenty more open source stuff to plough through, plus regulators' reports. Dolphin is headquartered in Boston, with offices here and in Paris. A low profile, high-end investment house for heavy rollers. More hedge fund than bank. Dodgy, incomprehensible loan practices, "credit default swaps on steroids," according to a pointy-head in the Fed Reserve. Everything's on the charge sheet except toxic mortgages, but Dolphin rode the fiscal stimulus and survived. It was recently censured again because of its European Realignment Programme, which is even nastier than it sounds.'

'Was this the calling in of loans?'

'At extortionate interest rates, putting a lot of diligent people out of business here and in France. Marriages destroyed along the way and quite a few suicides.'

'Dolphin was caught up in that?'

'They took cover behind the British defaulters. But just as guilty, it says here.'

'Have they been targeted before?'

'Only by regulators.'

'But the Real IRA have attacked banks in the North. Ulster Bank, three, four years ago?'

'And Santander, bombed twice. But nothing on this scale. No-one here even noticed.'

'So are you telling me this is Irish dissident, too?'

Fargo began to say something, then turned away as his computer beeped with incoming. 'We should wait for Melanie.'

'You what?'

'She's on her way,' he said, staring at the screen again. 'Heads-up. Suspicious device found at Canary Wharf. Waitrose bag with a plastic food carton inside.'

'And?'

'It's got the explosive dog excited.'

'Which bank?'

'None of them,' frowned Fargo. 'Just outside the station arch, to the left. Looks like it was kicked beneath a hedge. Dumped. Maybe whoever just panicked and got out. They're doing the usual at the station, clearing the area to send in the wheelbarrow.' This was Fargo's term for the explosives officers' robot.

'It'll be a hoax.'

Fargo peered at the clock on the computer, then double-checked his watch. 'Yeah, we know their timing's shit but it should have gone by now.'

'Not that. I mean it's Topaz for the actual bombs and Emerald for the negatives. They're letting us know, just like before.'

They sat quietly for a moment, studying the TV pictures of carnage in the City, then Fargo bent down to shift a plastic laundry bag from the floor by Kerr's feet. 'The trousers I was supposed to collect on Monday,' he said, looking away.

'You sure you're okay working on this, Al?'

'Is it personal, you mean?' Fargo blinked several times and nodded at Kerr's chair. 'Sometimes Pauline used to sit right there, remember? Helping me out?'

'It was a treat all round.'

'My sister loved every minute and it made Mum happy, too.' Fargo's eyes looked past Kerr's shoulder as the door opened. 'Here's

Mel,' he said, then dropped his voice to a whisper. 'Of course it is. But everything's fine.'

Melanie waved around the room and rolled up a chair, fixing Kerr with a long stare. 'God, you look awful.'

In jeans with a white T-shirt and dark blue sweater, Melanie was fresh-faced, despite what she must have witnessed a few minutes earlier.

'Anything?' said Kerr.

Melanie shook her head. 'Jack dropped me outside. They're doing a final sweep further east, then coming back in.'

'Apparently you're going to tell me if this is Irish dissident or not.'

'Am I?' She ran her fingers through her hair, pressed flat by the motorcycle helmet, and glanced at Fargo. 'Haven't you…?'

'We only got as far as the banks,' said Fargo. 'John, you know Mr Ritchie's been pressing for info about the bomb make-up.'

'Still waiting.'

'Everyone's being reticent. The explosives officers keep referring me to the Bomb Data Centre, like they're obviously under orders. BDC says wait for Mr Finch's official summary. But the gist is going to be that both bombs were plastic explosive, professional and positioned to cause maximum loss of life.'

'CCTV of the bombers?'

'No direct line of sight from any camera because of the buses moving between them and the station. They're studying every image, obviously, so we're still hoping for a match.' He jerked a thumb at the window. 'Especially if the same guys did the City.'

'So is Finch going to say this is dissident republican?'

Fargo took a breath. 'With the coded warning, Victoria bears the classic hallmarks of an attack by the Real IRA. That's what my contact tells me.'

'Which goes against everything Dodge has told us, plus the denials from Stormont – anyone seen Dodge, by the way? – and is obviously premature. But I can see you decided to dig a little deeper, Alan, right? Because it's personal.'

'Dodge called in sick,' said Fargo, as Kerr reached across, took a chunk out of his cookie and held up the patisserie bag. 'Still fresh. So which of you went to Porton Down without asking?'

Fargo began to speak but Melanie got in first. 'You weren't around. We were looking for you all day. I sent you a message about Justin.'

'I got it.'

'On international dialling.'

'This is down to me,' said Fargo quickly. 'I couldn't get away and Jack said he'd sort it when you surfaced.'

'And?' Kerr spread his hands, looking between them. 'Did you track down Polly Graham?'

'We had a chat in the ballistics lab,' said Melanie, 'and she sends her best. She examined the scene with the explosives officers first thing Tuesday and took away a vanload of stuff, plus photographs and video. Long story short, Porton have traced plastic explosive residues on a number of items. Semtex.'

'Anything about the bomb make-up?'

'Only to confirm two devices in separate waste bins beside the terminus. Multiple bombs makes it difficult to measure the explosive used in each, but they're obviously working on that. Forensics here are still sifting for clues about the detonator, timer, circuitry, etcetera. Thing is, even without that, Polly's preliminary readout doesn't fit with the official story.'

She took the bag, quickly passed it around and reached in herself. 'For starters, the Victoria explosive is traceable through the Czech maker's tag. It's called Semtex SA11, manufactured a couple of years ago, well within its shelf life and definitively *not* part of the cache seized in Belfast last year.'

'And Dublin before that?'

'Same again. That stuff was ancient, probably from the Libya shipment from Gaddafi in eighty-six.' She paused to bite the head off a gingerbread man. 'Starving. Bottom line, there's no suggestion any Irish dissident group had access to the Semtex used on Monday.'

'Does Derek Finch know this?'

Melanie shrugged. 'I don't imagine Polly was giving me an exclusive. God, those poor people,' she said as a flurry of voices drew them back to the TV.

Both channels had organised themselves by now, with reporters outside St Paul's Cathedral and live coverage of office workers swarming from Canary Wharf, hurried along by police with loudhailers and the chilling news from Cheapside.

'Any idea of victim numbers yet?' said Kerr.

Melanie shook her head, still fixed on the TV screens. 'Jack may have more. From what I saw before they sealed the street this is going to be even worse than Monday.' She swung round to Kerr. 'And that's something else about this whole IRA thing. Mr Finch is wrong, isn't he, about wanting to cause maximum casualties? Irish dissidents go for military targets or police. You know, look what they did to Mark Bannerman. Savage and unambiguous. But the IRA have always given a warning against civilian targets in London, enough time to get people away.'

'Except when they screwed up,' said Fargo.

'Yet nothing like this.' Kerr pushed his chair back. 'I need to try Dodge again. Is he at home?'

Fargo touched his arm and glanced at Melanie.

'Sorry, that's not it,' she said, flicking a crumb from her leg. 'Polly did find a match. The Semtex used on Monday comes from a reserve stockpile nicked in France a couple of years ago. It was government owned, totally legit, stored just outside Marseilles. Their bomb disposal were using it to destroy munitions left over from the war. I suppose the Irish could have lifted it. In theory, I mean.'

Kerr frowned. 'But there's still plenty of Semtex stashed around Belfast. We know that from Dodge.'

'Easy access,' shrugged Fargo. 'Why risk the English Channel and the Irish Sea when you can pop to the corner shop?'

'I think these attacks are pulling us in the other direction,' said Kerr. 'The Euro's waiting to freefall again and the blame game is as toxic as ever. Liaison have been telling us for ages that the collapse is still breeding extreme groups right across Europe. Look at the rhetoric. Banksters. Everyone still hates them. Brexit changes nothing.' Kerr stole a glance at Fargo. 'Can you get back to liaison, Al? Greece, to start with. Then France and Spain. Let's get our heads together.'

'Already on it. Gilbert in Paris just confirmed the Semtex theft. I've got a call in to Demitri.'

'Good. Mel, I'll give Polly a call later but I need you to tell me if Cheapside carries the same Semtex marker as Victoria.'

She nodded and offered him the last cookie. 'So are we forgiven?'

Kerr murmured something and studied Sky News for a moment. 'If European terrorists are hitting banks in London, why false flag it to the IRA?'

Fargo turned away to the screen again. 'That's a good question for Mr Finch, right?'

Chapter Twenty-Three

Bobby Roscoe's workshop lay on a stretch of urban wasteland between Willesden Junction and North Acton stations, with the railway along the eastern border of Old Oak Common Lane separating it from the main road. To the other side of the lane was the historic site of Paddington's old sidings and engine sheds, the whole sector now swallowed up by the mammoth Crossrail project. Betta Tyre and Exhaust stood between the two, set back from the thoroughfare beyond a decaying, weed strewn concrete yard large enough to turn heavy vehicles. A sloping placard in faded blue and green, with the B missing from Betta, gave the only clue that Roscoe was still trading, and these days he did not welcome new customers.

Thrown up four decades ago beside First Great Western's metal boundary fence, the workshop was a cold, windowless structure of whitewashed breeze block beneath a sloping corrugated iron roof, the main entrance set at right angles to the road. With railway property each side and the Grand Union Canal a hundred metres to the north, Roscoe's failing business was isolated and private, screened by a tangle of brambles and *leylandii* from anyone with business at the civilised end of the lane.

Secured by a roll top metal door, the workshop had a narrow inspection pit to the left and was just wide enough to accommodate three cars parked closely together or a medium sized lorry, so long as Roscoe left the door partially open. Today it concealed a white Citroen Jumper van and blue Honda SH300 motorcycle. Against the darkened back wall, behind piles of retread tyres and new exhausts, Roscoe hid the secondhand MIG transformer, wire feeder and torch he used for his unofficial job as welder.

Roscoe had been adapting the van for three days with scarcely a break, strengthening the rear suspension and fitting extra load tyres. It looked used but clean, the exterior identical to the thousands of other Jumpers on the streets of London. Behind the white panels, however, Roscoe had welded a steel platform to the chassis and bolted on a right-angled triangular frame, its sloping edge designed to house the launch pad.

He had been making finishing touches to the frame when Fin and Kenny stole into the workshop from North Acton Underground station, and the interior smelt hot as he flipped his visor and immediately lambasted the younger brother for dumping his Canary Wharf device short of Dolphin and Drew's satellite office. 'You need to man up,' he had snarled, red-faced and sweating as he cut the flame, threw off his gloves and set them to work, anger removing any doubts about their relationship.

The gloomy office in which Roscoe had hired the brothers three weeks earlier lay in the far right corner behind a grimy Perspex screen. It was just large enough for its battered captain's chair and desk strewn with oil-stained invoices. Roscoe fidgeted there now in his blue overalls, the chair squeaking as he listened to live reports of the bombing on his Roberts portable radio and watched the brothers work in the yard, still seething at Kenny's loss of courage.

They were building a shelter extending about a car's length from the entrance, for Roscoe had concluded that, however secure the man-made perimeter of rail, road and water, the workshop was still vulnerable to airborne surveillance from a helicopter, fixed wing spotter plane or drone. Three days before the Victoria attacks he had supervised their construction of the oak frame, a giant set of goal posts with the feet buried in cement and the top secured to the workshop roof by five equidistant spars.

Now he watched as Fin, still in his suit trousers, cordless screwdriver clipped to his belt, balanced on a ladder against one of the spars and reached down to Kenny for the second of four black plastic corrugated sheets, each three metres long and the width of his outstretched arm. Fin slapped the other end to the workshop roof, adjusted the fit, roughly screwed it to the frame and repositioned the ladder for the last section.

The clatter reverberated through the workshop, increasing Roscoe's agitation. He had just received his final orders for what his masters called 'operational sequencing,' and co-ordination was crucial. He checked his watch again, caught in the race between the running order and time. When he could wait no longer he took a packet of cocaine and a prepaid phone from the bottom desk drawer and walked out of the workshop, powering up the mobile. 'It's more than you deserve,' he said, tossing the drugs at Kenny.

'You never told us his one was a dud,' said Fin from the top of the ladder. 'It's not fair. You should have said.'

Roscoe looked up at him, taken aback. 'Disobey me again and you're dead.'

'From you?' said Fin with a rough laugh. 'I don't fucking think so.'

The brothers had left their Glock pistols inside the workshop, perched on the saddle of the motorcycle. Roscoe walked round the van, grabbed the nearest and aimed at Fin's head, eyes unblinking. He stood quite still for several seconds, arms locked, daring him to react, then kicked away the ladder and watched Fin scrabble for the cross bar, legs flailing. He let him dangle there, reading Fin's eyes as he chose between confrontation and defeat, calculating whether he would make a move for the other Glock.

When he was quite sure, Roscoe lowered the pistol, walked out of earshot to the railway boundary and dialled.

•••

Friday, 14 October, 14.33, Derek Finch's Private Office, New Scotland Yard

The sandwich bar in St James's station closed early on a Friday but Bill Ritchie's PA was just in time for a chicken baguette and tuna continental on brown, both with extra fillings because the proprietor fancied her. However busy their day, Ritchie always insisted that Donna steal an hour away from the office: it had become a tacit agreement, so she no longer offered to forego her break. Bombs in the City or calls from the top brass made no difference, and detectives ringing Donna to open a window in the boss's diary, or social callers, would often find Ritchie's voice at the end of the line. Unfailingly courteous, he never actually tampered with the diary: the parcel of time might be his, but the schedule belonged to Donna.

The tuna was for Donna's opposite number in the Bull's private office, three floors down from hers. Barbara Santer was in her early forties with two children at primary school and nowhere to call home. Never married to her partner of a decade, deserted six days after New Year, she had returned to the Yard when her money ran out before Easter, a common law wife devoid of rights and still reeling from the shock.

The two women spoke several times a day and met every Friday for a sandwich or salad. Barbara was darkly attractive but looked permanently exhausted, in need of a makeover and a fresh start. She had inherited an office that was cramped, soulless and untidy, with files and binders covering every surface. A giant map of the world filled one wall, with the top right corner flopping over Russia and the Southern Ocean filled with post-it notes. Barbara's desk curved around the far right corner, with a twenty-two inch computer screen, a wall calendar stuck at August and a dusty artificial orchid with a broken stem. Office and occupant looked equally cheerless, and today Donna could tell she had been deeply affected by the events of the past five days, distressed by the bombings and troubled at being so close to counter-terrorism's front man.

In the body of the room was a tiny coffee table with a pair of low easy chairs, but the two friends always found it more comfortable to eat at Barbara's desk. They went through the usual my-turn-to-pay banter while Barbara cleared the spare office chair of papers and made a show of hunting for her purse. As her friend poured the coffee Donna recognised the same maroon sweater over a tired cream shirt, the front stretched and bobbled from repeated wear. The dark grey trousers were shiny on the bottom and short on the leg, and something had snagged her tights just above the right ankle.

The Bull's management style was poles apart from Bill Ritchie's: Barbara had to field three calls as she unwrapped her sandwich, then blew out her cheeks and slumped back, exasperated. Ignoring her protest, Donna leaned across and diverted the phone to Reserve, rolling her chair closer for a sneak view of Barbara's computer. The screen was split between emails and Finch's calendar, so Donna secretly nudged the space bar to prevent it from locking.

'What does he think you live on? Air?' she murmured, nodding at the closed interconnecting door.

'He's still out, charging all over the place,' said Barbara, unfolding a paper napkin. 'I saw him on TV from the City about two hours ago, then nothing. Everyone's trying to get hold of him. I'm only his bloody diary secretary, after all.'

Barbara Santer had been drafted in from the Yard's small witness protection unit on the fourteenth floor three months earlier, upon the overnight departure of her predecessor. Her developed vetting status qualified her to work for Derek Finch, and she had endured sexual harassment almost from day one. Having disclosed next to nothing about her private life, Barbara concluded he must have had access to her vetting papers, for he seemed to know everything about her situation, especially the fact that she was newly single and staying with her mother. Finch's predatory conduct was a hot topic between the women, though Barbara always refused to take things further. 'You think anyone's going to believe me over the head of department?' she had said early in their friendship. 'Take it from me, people like him do whatever they want.'

'Not these days.'

'Donna, I got rid of one shagger for another. What's new?'

For both women the past week had been frenetic, an administrative whirlwind of meetings, briefings and calls from Home Office, MI5, Northern Ireland Office, the Cabinet Secretary and the Commissioner. With no knowledge of the government machine's impenetrable Who's Who, Barbara had been ringing her more experienced friend every day for advice and support.

Donna wiped her mouth with the paper napkin and steered the conversation to work. 'How's he been since Victoria?'

'Rubbish as ever. I blanked him again Friday afternoon when he asked me out for a drink and he's practically ignored me ever since. It's even worse now the pressure's on and he's tired.' Barbara blew out her cheeks and nudged the computer screen. 'He never gives me enough info to keep a proper calendar. If I schedule something he barges in and cancels it. Sometimes doesn't even tell me. I'm blanking callers all the time because I never know where he is, whether he's coming or going. This is the most shit manager I've ever worked for. And I'm so sorry about letting *your* boss down on…when was it?'

Donna took a bite of her baguette. 'Tuesday morning.'

'That's it,' she said, scrolling up the page. 'Day after the bombs and he just disappeared. I hadn't got a clue.'

'We know what he's like,' said Donna, peering at the window in the diary. Between nine and ten, in the space she had tried to reserve for Ritchie, was a mobile phone number. She stole another glance, pulling it into her memory. 'Honestly, it's no problem.'

'Is for me, love. Totally embarrassing.'

Donna screwed up the sandwich wrapper, licked her fingers and picked up her handbag. 'Just popping to the loo.'

In the cubicle she used her eyeliner pencil to scribble the number on a tissue, then drifted back to Barbara's office. She stayed another ten minutes before returning to the eighteenth floor.

Waiting for the lift, Donna felt relaxed about her deception. In late July, when John Kerr had quietly asked her for information against Finch, he had never been explicit about his reasons but she had never thought to refuse, or check whether he was acting on behalf of Bill Ritchie. Donna had been in the Branch long enough to read the truth, that Kerr was gathering proof of the Bull's corruption.

Donna genuinely saw no conflict between loyalty to Kerr and friendship with Barbara: in both, she was utterly sincere. In the early days, her head full of stolen names and numbers, she had occasionally felt a flicker of self-reproach; but now, as her friend confided in her more and more, she consoled herself that, one day, the Bull's exposure and disgrace would also bring justice to Barbara.

Chapter Twenty-Four

Dodge's new family home in Harrow was a high spec two-bedroom apartment on the first floor of Suffolk Hall, a refurbished Victorian preparatory school in sprawling private gardens. The living room was the old headmaster's study overlooking the public park, and the flat immediately beneath had once been the refectory. There were only twelve units, six on each floor.

Dodge had brought his wife and daughter here from their rented semi in Ruislip in the last week of September. He had been secretly negotiating the purchase since early summer, but for Nicola and Clare the move had been as sudden, unexpected and unexplained as their overnight extraction from Belfast in 2002. Nicola's interrogation on the first evening, admiring the park from the headmaster's sweeping bay window over double shots of Jameson's, forced his admission that the apartment had cost their life savings, his resettlement compensation from the Royal Ulster Constabulary and the equity from the sale of their houses in Belfast and Edinburgh, plus a sizeable short term mortgage. She had assumed their move to a property protected by CCTV, wrought iron gates and a mobile security patrol was connected to his job, though Dodge's working life had always been a secret diary she never cared to open.

Both women were happy with their upgrade to luxury. A qualified paralegal in Belfast, Nicola now worked as a conveyancer for a firm of solicitors in Pinner, and her new commute on the 183 bus was easier than the tube from Ruislip. Clare, their daughter, was a second year law undergraduate at London University and still came home on the nights she was not sleeping with her boyfriend. They carried on with life as before, sorting through the jumble of crates, cardboard boxes and displaced furniture, while Dodge drank more, reverted to a pack a day and withdrew into the gloom she recognised from his time in South Armagh, where the IRA had tried to murder him.

This morning Dodge had skipped breakfast and was still mooching around barefoot in a threadbare maroon dressing gown, sipping black coffee as he checked his iPhone and Sky News while Nicola got ready for work. He had barely slept since Wednesday's meeting in Covent Garden, constantly re-running the conversation with the man who had called himself Bobby Roscoe. *Check the news day after tomorrow.* Now that day had arrived, and the words whirred non-stop around his brain.

At the front door Nicola pinched one of his fleshy cheeks and planted a kiss on the other. Even at home his women called him Dodge. 'You look like death,' she said, kindly. 'Want me to call you in sick with man flu?'

Nicola was wearing her mock pearl necklace and earrings with a turquoise, mid-length dress he did not recognise. 'Go get your bus,' he growled, giving her backside a playful slap.

'Sun's out,' she said, checking her make-up in the hall mirror. 'Make yourself decent and sit on the balcony. Have a day off the booze.' She kissed him again and he inhaled her perfume. It was a fragrance he had not given her, another reason to remember it was Friday.

'See you about eleven?' she said, as if he might refuse.

The dressing gown parted as Dodge coughed and swung away, exposing chubby breasts in a grey thicket of chest hair. The hacking was from cigarettes, not flu, and lasted several seconds as he nodded back.

Friday was Nicola's 'night out with the girls,' a cover for her adultery with the firm's family lawyer, a man with a wife and young kids who specialised in divorce and child custody. Dodge had known about the affair for months, almost from the start, and thought the guy was taking suicidal risks with his marriage and career, like an accountant swindling his own company.

For Nicola it was different. She was seven years younger than

Dodge, still curvy and vivacious, and had sacrificed everything for him. He never gave her reason to suspect he knew, draining her guilt into his own reservoir of shame and blaming himself for their sexless marriage. 'Have fun,' he said, wiping his mouth on the back of his hand, then turning to give her a hug.

Through the kitchen window he watched Nicola press the green exit button by the gate and waited in vain for her to turn and wave. The moment she disappeared up the road he rang the office.

Nicola forbade him to smoke inside so he made more coffee and lit up on the balcony, phone in hand, before slumping in front of the living room TV. *You'll see how genuine I am.* By not reporting the contact, the source unit's chief had broken every rule in his own book; and in concealing the information, however sketchy, he had betrayed his duty of care. Dodge stared blankly at coverage of anarchy in Syria and tribal warfare at Westminster, his eyes tracking the loop of breaking news beneath, hoping against hope. Three hours and a chain of cigarettes later, still undressed, he barely made it to their ensuite toilet when Gemma's message about Cheapside flashed onto his phone, and threw up again as the news exploded on TV. Shame flooded through him as he watched Dolphin and Drew burn. *This is about bashing the banks.* The Yard could have warned the City, circulated one of their confidential notices to every financial house. To save his own skin Dodge had chosen to keep silent, and these slaughtered victims were the price of his fear and cowardice. Head in hands he sat forward on the sofa, his dressing gown speckled with vomit, transfixed by the carnage he could have prevented. This was his fault: it was as if he had placed the bombs himself.

He showered and dressed, preparing for the summons he knew would come. The instructions were as terse as the first time, though he had never heard of the venue and recited the address back twice, street and name, to be sure he had it right. Dodge's car was a battered silver Audi A4 without satnav, and he made a couple of wrong turns on the outskirts of Wembley. As he drew closer he felt sick again, forcing the car into a crowded bus lane and retching into the kerb.

Gabriel's Bar was on a side road off Acton High Street, between Chi Chi Hair Design and Chicken Express. Roscoe had told Dodge to park fifty metres away on a residents' bay, but instead he found a pay and display car park behind Lidl and walked through to Fortune Road. Directly opposite the bar, fronting a small park with swings and a slimy ornamental pond, was a disused Victorian public convenience with tiled staircase, a Gentlemen sign missing three of its letters, and concertina gates with years of litter piled on the inside. Gabriel's was a pub from the same era, with towering plate glass windows, ornate external woodwork painted black and the giant letters of its former name, The Grey Horse, just visible above the curtained windows of the upper rooms. At first sight the bar seemed as derelict as the toilet, with peeling stucco and the thickly whitewashed windows of a store that had ceased trading. The only sign of life was the name in ornate gold lettering above the entrance to the left, as discreet as a private members' club in Mayfair.

The door swung open more easily than Dodge had expected, pulling him onto the threshold. He paused a moment for his eyes to adjust to the gloom and his ears to the vividness of Radiohead, a pulse that instantly revived his final days in Belfast. The polished oak bar hugged the right wall, swinging round before the entrance in a giant inverted J. Soft light from three chandeliers showed at least thirty drinkers hanging out in couples or small groups, business types slumming it with builders, Bloody Mary versus Stella, and every head swung round to regard him, drawn by the sudden shaft of natural light. The walls of square wood panelling and ruby flock wallpaper were divided by a dado rail. High on the wall opposite the bar a muted TV showed footage of the bombings, but the hubbub beneath was pure Friday night live. Two men in identical yellow waistcoats were working flat out behind the bar, one young enough to be in college, the other in his fifties, lean and shaven-headed (Gabriel?), plus the only female on the premises, a girl with nose piercings, a scorpion tattoo on her upper arm and bright red hair, who shot him a big smile.

It took Dodge a moment to locate Bobby Roscoe, sitting alone at one of the round tables between the crowd and the toilets. He half-stood to attract Dodge with a little wave, as if they were old friends who met up like this all the time. Dodge eased his way through the bar, his grumbling excuse me's struggling to be heard above the hubbub, and every face that turned to him was friendly or challenging.

Unshaven, in dark blue working overalls with a smear of grease on his cheek, Roscoe looked completely different from the groomed man who had summoned Dodge to Covent Garden. On the table were two glasses of whiskey, both double shots, and he slid one across as Dodge sat down. 'As promised,' he said, unsmilingly.

Dodge pushed the drink aside, splashing whiskey onto the table. 'Driving.'

'Risking your job, you mean?' said Roscoe. He slid the glass back and leant in above the music, the northern accent harsher than before, more pronounced. 'Believe me, a touch of Jamies is the least of your problems.'

Dodge downed the whiskey in a single gulp, waiting for the kick as Roscoe's eyes lifted to the TV.

'Tragic,' said Roscoe quickly. The screen's flicker disturbed the dark atmosphere like neon but Dodge had to crane his neck round to see the pictures. 'Shocking. But like I told you, right?'

Dodge felt the hard 'g' driving into his brain. Manchester. 'How did you know?'

A couple of drinkers were squeezing past them, brushing Dodge's shoulder, so Roscoe waited a moment before leaning across. 'What's my *access* to these wicked bastards, you mean?' He took a drink and threw Dodge a ragged smile. 'Now that's a very big question.'

Perhaps it was the taunt that made him snap, or the anguish of the past three days terminating in his remorse and self-loathing. Before he could stop himself Dodge was on his feet, upending the table as he scrabbled for Roscoe's throat, words of pure hate sticking in his own. But Roscoe was even quicker on the draw, surprising Dodge as he caught his wrist and slowly pressed him backwards, like the victor in an arm wrestling contest. Heads were taking notice again and a pumped-up guy in white vest and combat pants paused on his way to the toilet, ready for action. Roscoe raised his hands in contrition, mouthed an 'okay' at Gabriel behind the bar, straightened the furniture and rescued the glasses.

'You need to calm down,' said Roscoe when they were settled. 'I told you when. Doesn't mean I know *who*.'

'You despicable bastard.' Dodge leaned in, breathless, weak from sickness and anxiety. 'I should have arrested you on Wednesday.'

'But now you can't, because you haven't told anyone about us. Right? Not a single soul. Too late to cover your arse now. And I'm guessing you didn't record us, either?' Roscoe waggled his iPhone and made a tutting sound. 'Unlike Yours Truly, who always catches *everything*. And I know for a fact no-one's following me.' He signalled Gabriel for the same again. 'So I think I'm safe. Your threats ran out of steam a long time ago.'

The Killers were playing now and Dodge slumped back as the first bars of 'Human' washed over him. 'Why are you doing this?'

'Both of us know that. I told you it was about the banks. That's the *what*. Well, now they're going for the big one.' Dodge stared at him as Roscoe nodded. 'Bank of England.'

'When?'

'Tomorrow.'

'What sort of bomb?'

Over by the door the bar suddenly erupted in laughter. 'That's all I have,' said Roscoe when the noise subsided.

'Jesus Christ,' said Dodge, knocking the table again as he hurled himself forward. He grabbed Roscoe's forearm, but this time it was from agitation, not violence. 'You can't just come out with this shit and expect me to walk away.'

'Really?' Roscoe freed himself and stepped over to collect the drinks as Gabriel called from the bar. He paid with a twenty pound note and left the change.

'This is going to totally screw me,' said Dodge.

Roscoe nodded. 'Correct.' The two men sat for a moment staring at each other. Tearing through Dodge's shattered mind was the avalanche of questions he would face the moment he called John Kerr. 'Like I told you before,' said Roscoe eventually, 'they're are not out to hit your ordinary working people.'

'You know I have to report this.' Dodge caught Roscoe's shrug, mocking him. 'And to know how you know.'

'Or you'll look even more stupid, you mean?'

Dodge shifted as his stomach churned, the alcohol's warmth replaced by cold fear as panic climbed into his chest and seized his heart. He found himself gripping the table edge with both hands to avoid keeling over. 'How the fuck am I supposed to sell this back at the Yard?'

Roscoe took another drink and studied Dodge's bloodless knuckles. 'You're the expert.'

White noise filled Dodge's head, wiping out very other sound. 'Bobby, you have to tell me your source.'

Roscoe gave another sloping smile. 'First names now?'

'And a contact number.' Dodge was attempting an ultimatum but the words emerged as a plea. 'We don't react to info from a cold caller.'

'But I'm not, am I?' Roscoe shifted sideways and tapped his inside pocket as another man eased past them for the toilet. 'Fancy a line to go with the whiskey? Cops don't bother us here. Present company accepted.'

Adele's voice now filled the bar with 'Someone Like You' and, behind him, a group was singing with her. Sometimes it lasts in love, but sometimes it hurts instead. 'Why are you doing this to me?'

Roscoe made an upturned fist on the table and uncurled his fingers, the nails grimy and split. 'It puts you right there.' Dodge felt Roscoe's hand slide across his own, strong, the skin of his palm rough and scratchy. 'How do you feel, Dodge, being in here with me, watching all these guys having fun?'

'Go fuck yourself.'

He stood as Dodge pulled his hand away and slumped back in the chair again. 'Things to do,' said Roscoe, draining his whiskey. 'But I'll be in touch.'

'What am I supposed to tell them?' Dodge was looking up at him, sickened by the desperation in his own voice.

'You could always admit the truth about Frankie,' said Roscoe, squeezing Dodge's shoulder as he left. 'And yourself.'

Chapter Twenty-Five

Friday, 14 October, 17.48, The Fishbowl

Mid-afternoon, as soon as Donna called him, John Kerr had dropped by her office to collect the stolen telephone number. 'Did the boss ask for me yesterday?' he said, slipping the tissue into his pocket.

'I winged it for you, as usual. He's all over the place but needs to see you as soon as.'

'Right.'

'I'll give you a call.'

Kerr had swung by 1830 to have the subscriber details and call history identified, then flushed away Donna's note in the men's room, ensuring the mobile number had risen from the Bull's jumbled calendar to Fargo's telephone expert without leaving a trace.

Back in the Fishbowl he played catch-up for a couple of hours before putting in his call to the government's top secret science and technology laboratory at Porton Down, near Salisbury in Wiltshire. Polly Graham was in one of the external stores when he finally got through, her voice echoing around the concrete walls as she prepared for her second trip to London in less than a week. While they spoke Kerr imagined her in her trademark grey combat pants and baseball cap, loading search equipment into her ancient Land Rover Defender.

The widow of Captain Richard Graham, BEM, an Army bomb disposal officer killed in 1987 while defusing a car bomb in Belfast, Polly had developed her own career as a Home Office explosives engineer. She and Kerr had been friends since the nineties, when she had data mined every explosive device planted in London, as well as reviewing IRA bombings in Hyde Park, Harrods and Brighton a decade earlier.

'Did Melanie have a chat with you?'

'Thanks for sparing the time.'

'Hold on.' Kerr heard the familiar squeak of the rear door opening, then something scraping across the floor. 'I know you've got IRA code words and operation names, John, but I'm not pointing a finger at the obvious suspects here.'

'Do you think you'll come up with a single player? Someone we already know?'

'Everything looks a one-off at the moment,' she said, pausing to catch her breath. 'Your afternoon of excitement at Hammersmith, then Victoria. Different explosive. No obvious connection to each other or anything in my database. No evidence of technology transfer. Did you see my reconstruction pictures of Hammersmith?'

'Of course. Brilliant.'

'I'm working on the same for Victoria. Let's see what Cheapside has to offer. I'm meeting the explosives guys at the scene in a couple of hours.'

Gathering bombs around her like others collected antiques, Polly Graham had demonstrated that every bombmaker in the world improvised in a singular way. To Polly, each twist of wire, sliver of circuit board and angle of screw was different; every timer and shred of detonator cord unique. She studied the way the explosive was packed and the container in which it was delivered. Her thesis was simple: every bomb left a signature as exclusive as an artist's monogram or silversmith's hallmark.

'And you've spoken with Derek Finch, right?'

'Why wouldn't I? Everything through your Bomb Data Centre.'

'So why is he telling everyone this is Irish dissident?'

She paused, then gave a little laugh. 'Now you're talking politics. Definitely not my area. Look, I'm saying the IRA have never used Semtex from that Czech consignment. The SA11 batch, as I told Melanie yesterday. Perhaps Finch isn't listening. Maybe he knows something I don't. Ask him.' A couple of doors slammed. 'You know what, John? I never had this crap when I was with the Army.'

In 2006 Polly had been deployed to Camp Bastion in

Afghanistan, profiling booby trap bombs recovered by the Army's engineers. In two long tours of duty, working day and night, she would dismantle every device recovered intact and, where the bomb had detonated, reconstruct mock-ups from the tiniest fragments. Over a career spanning three decades, Polly Graham had emerged from the shadow of her husband's murder to become the UK's expert in the analysis of improvised bombs. She had used her skill to identify dozens of terrorists for prosecution or elimination, scoring each success as a shot of revenge for her husband.

Kerr heard the engine start up. 'I'm saying there may be a new kid on the block who hasn't crossed my radar before. So you have to look further afield than the IRA, whatever Finch and Security Service are saying.'

Kerr frowned. 'MI5? Has Toby Devereux been on to you?'

A sigh of frustration came down the line. 'John, don't let yourself get distracted. Find the intelligence. Let me follow the science.'

'But we are talking different bombmakers here, right?'

'Early days.'

'From different terrorist groups?'

'Patience, my friend.' The diesel surged as Polly accelerated into the open. 'If I come up with a signature you'll be the first to know.'

Donna summoned Kerr just as Polly rang off. He found Bill Ritchie emerging from his personal washroom, shirt cuffs rolled back, shaking his hands dry. 'First chance for a pee in two hours and the cleaner's nicked the towel,' he said, leaning against the conference table and massaging his temples.

'That good, yeah?'

'Commissioner twice, Home Sec, Mayor's office. Non-stop. Everyone windy as hell. COBRAs coming out of my ears. PM and Home Sec racing each other back from their constituencies to take charge.'

'What's new?' said Kerr, lingering by the door, ready to get out of his hair.

'This,' he said, wiping his hands on his trousers before reaching for his yellow legal pad. 'Cabinet Office ordered a Silver Scrum for tomorrow night.'

'Saturday? Really?'

'Key experts only. Out of the limelight.'

'Silver Scrum' was Whitehall jargon for the Current Intelligence Group, a cluster of intelligence experts who prepared briefings for the high level Joint Intelligence Committee and Number Ten.

'To achieve what?' said Kerr. 'Convince ourselves the IRA really have made a comeback?'

Ritchie sat down, slid a chair clear of the table with his foot and beckoned him closer. 'It's going to be a difficult one and I want you there with me.'

'To persuade Toby Devereux of the alternatives, yes?'

Ritchie regarded him. 'How's Polly?'

'On her way to Cheapside.'

'Stay close. She's the only voice of sanity around here.'

'Polly says we should be looking in the other direction.'

'I know. And you're about to tell me you were right all along.' Ritchie fell silent for a moment. 'So can you raise Justin before the CIG?'

'Not contactable,' said Kerr, shaking his head. 'Monday, earliest.'

'Okay,' said Ritchie, rolling down his cuffs with a glance at the clock. 'But he's good, yes?'

Kerr stood, replaced the chair and hunched his shoulders. 'Justin's fine.'

Ritchie checked him by the door. 'Donna reminded me about your promotion board,' he said. 'Want me to push it back?' He slipped into his jacket, grabbed his notepad and followed Kerr out.

'And that's going to make me look better?'

Ritchie chuckled and gave Kerr's arm a squeeze. He swung round to speak to Donna but she was already holding up a couple of clean white towels, neatly folded. He slowly shook his head. 'Have you still got this place bugged, or what?'

Friday, 14 October, 19.36, Hornsey Vale

Kerr arrived at Nancy's Sergeyev's house to the aroma of casserole and the chorus of 'Hotel California'. He had invested half a decade and most of his salary in a classy refurbished top floor apartment five miles away in Islington, with beech hardwood floors, Amode furniture picked out by his daughter, and a balcony with a view of Chapel Market. He enjoyed his flat but loved Nancy, so personal treasures had begun to join his clothes on the journey across north London. On Easter Monday, four days after her decree absolute, Nancy had silently offered him Karl's door key, and from that moment Kerr had embraced Nancy's modest Victorian semi, with its Turkish rugs, log burner and children's chaos, as his true home.

Friday was Nancy's day off from the local GP surgery where she worked to boost the money Karl gave her. Dodging a scooter, green BMX bike and multi-coloured trainers, Kerr found her in the kitchen, flushed from cooking, a glass of Merlot on the table. She was barefoot, in a red stripy top with white leggings, and her dark hair was cut in a new bob. She slid his jacket off as she kissed him, scratching his stubble. 'You look knackered,' she said, waving the remote to switch off the muted wall TV, still looping footage from Cheapside.

'Want me to get a shower?'

'I want you to eat.'

Until her disastrous marriage to Karl Sergeyev, Nancy had maintained the photographic archive in Special Branch Registry, animating sterile reports with deadpan mugshots, stolen personal snaps and blurry surveillance images. Nancy understood better than most the importance of snatching downtime from a terrorist campaign; but the glass she poured Kerr was smaller than her own, as if she knew he would be called out before morning.

The kitchen lay at the end of the hall, next to the small dining room which was home to the ironing board and a perpetual mountain of clean laundry on the armchair, as well as children's laptops rooted to the table. Above the original cast-iron fireplace hung Nancy's latest watercolour of the railway arches on Walthamstow Marsh, a little lopsided. The family invariably squeezed around the stripped pine table in the kitchen and Kerr sat there now, reclaiming space from Amy's half-finished stitching cards and a Spacebot.

He dropped his BlackBerry onto the table as Nancy dished up. 'All quiet up there?'

'They gave up waiting. Tom's building a Lego monster or something.' Nancy's son was six, named after Karl's Russian grandfather, Tomas, and a year younger than Amy. 'Says you promised to help him?'

Joe Walsh was singing 'One Day at a Time' and Kerr turned up the volume. They clinked glasses and he smiled at her. 'What would *you* like me to do?'

Nancy ran her fingers through her hair and frowned, still caught unawares by the change. 'Find a few minutes to read up for that bloody promotion board.' She swallowed some wine and suddenly looked serious, as if Bill Ritchie himself had been on the phone. 'You've got two days, John. That's all.'

'I've been swotting.'

'Rubbish.' She turned the sound down again and waved her fork at him. A piece of carrot fell off and dropped to the table. 'Look, I'm asking you to play the game for once. Tell them what they want to hear.'

Kerr's shoulders lifted. 'Absolutely,' he said, a second before his mobile rang. Robyn's name was showing on the screen but he jabbed Ignore, hoping his hand had been quicker than Nancy's eye.

'I'm serious.' Chewing fast, she leant over to give his nose a tweak. 'Listen to me. Karl was bad enough. I don't need two mavericks in my life.'

Kerr had just bought a new Espresso maker but they skipped

coffee and went straight to bed, avoiding the creaks on the staircase and rolling aside Amy's giant inflatable globe on the landing. They were just getting warmed up when Tom stumbled into the room with a handful of Lego pieces, but past the point of no return as Robyn's name reappeared on his BlackBerry. This time Nancy beat him to the draw, reaching down to swipe it from the bedside table with her book and tube of moisturiser.

'Robyn's an eager beaver,' she said as they recovered, stretching back on the pillows.

'It's nothing. Probably worried today might be connected to Hammersmith.'

'You told me Alan Fargo was handling that side of things.'

Kerr took her in his arms. 'She still believes it may have been meant for her.'

'Was it?'

'Don't think so. Her or me, who knows? But she was the one just back from Belfast. It's a good project.'

'Human rights. Of course. And she couldn't wait to tell you about it.'

'It was a drink.'

Nancy sat up and plumped the pillows. 'On a fucking houseboat? Do me a favour, John. It was a date.'

'It was business. She's Gabi's mother.'

'So if it's so bloody platonic why didn't you take her first call?'

'Because I'm here with you.' Kerr slid out of bed and wandered around the room collecting things; his BlackBerry had almost made it to the door. 'Gabi's dying to meet up. Keeps pestering me to introduce you.'

'So why don't you? Ashamed of me?'

'Nancy, come on.'

'Where were you last night that you couldn't even get a shower and shave?' Kerr was clutching a bundle of clothes and she made a grab for his shirt. 'Or change this?'

'Nowhere.'

Nancy lay back on the pillows, slowly shaking her head. 'Don't insult me with your secret squirrel bullshit, John. I've heard it all before, remember?'

The phone buzzed again and Kerr showed her Dodge's name on the screen before she could react. Still naked, Kerr stood close to the bed, trying to make sense of the Irishman's drunken slur, stock-still for an agonising minute as the dire reality crowded in on him. 'Dodge, I need you to stop right there... Where are you?... Listen to me. Get yourself to the office... No way, take a taxi... Go to the Fishbowl and wait for me... Not a word to anyone... Yeah, half an hour tops.'

He cut the call and bent down to kiss Nancy's forehead. 'Sorry.'

'For what?'

'Look, I'm with you, sweetheart,' he murmured. 'Never been more serious in my life.'

Nancy reached between his thighs and gently pulled him to her. 'You coming back?'

'Of course. Where else would I go?'

Chapter Twenty-Six

Friday, 14 October, 21.17, The Fishbowl

Deeply preoccupied, half-sprinting for his car, Kerr collided in the dark with Nancy's next door neighbour, walking her Jack Russell on a long lead. He apologised, disentangled himself, folded himself into the Alfa and skidded away, flicking the blue light on the dash the second he cleared Nancy's street. Dodge's hot intelligence was grave, but his garbled delivery alarmed Kerr even more. In all their years working together, not once had Dodge sounded so tanked up, anxious and defensive. The message was starkly simple, yet the words had poured down the line in a jumbled rush, like pieces of a jigsaw. In all their critical agent cases, Dodge had never let drink do the talking, especially over something as terrible as this.

However, it was the trickle of wretchedness beneath the news that troubled Kerr most, the despair he had recognised before in operatives depressed by overwork, lonely and unsung, reeling on the brink. Since 9/11 two frontline Special Branch officers had taken their own lives, by rope and shotgun, their voices unheard, every plea for help undetected. Forty-eight hours ago he had rebuffed Melanie's warning about Dodge, and now, because he had learnt to spot the red flags, his carelessness hurt even more.

Dialling as he swung left into Stroud Green Road he caught Melanie in 1830 with Alan Fargo, searching Mercury for the next day's non-Irish surveillance targets. 'Have you seen Dodge?'

'He's sick,' she said.

'He's on his way in by taxi. I want you to call me when he arrives and tell me where he goes.'

A pause. 'How about I just meet him in Back Hall?'

'Without him knowing. He's coming to see me in the Fishbowl but might go to the source unit first.'

'To his own office, you mean,' she said after another gap, her voice flat with sarcasm.

'I want to know if he checks any files.'

'You're asking me to sneak on Dodge?'

Kerr braked hard at the junction with Seven Sisters Road before accelerating through the red and swinging right towards Kings Cross. He was less than a mile from the terrorists' safe house in Finsbury Park.

'Something's wrong. I'm worried about him.'

'Yeah. Finally,' she said, her words laced with 'told you so' recrimination.

'I'm about ten minutes away,' he said, weaving through crawling traffic at the Nag's Head junction.

'I'm not...'

'Hold on.' He swerved to the wrong side of the road and cut a sharp left, racing south for the straight, fast stretch of Caledonian Road.

'...John, I said I'm not happy about this.'

'I want you there with me. In the Fishbowl. He's going to need plenty of black coffee. And can you get hold of Jack? It's going to be an all-nighter.'

Melanie was waiting for him in the underground garage with Styrofoam coffees in a cutout tray. 'He went straight up to see you,' she said, heading for the spiral staircase. 'He's there now.'

Kerr held open the door. 'What's he doing?'

'Sobering up.'

They found Dodge hunched in the darkened Fishbowl, his broad back disturbing the blinds. He sat forward when Kerr walked in, legs wide apart, suit jacket scrunched in his hands. 'I'm sorry, John,' he slurred, suddenly noticing Melanie. 'I couldn't not...I had to tell you.'

'Stay put,' said Kerr, flicking the blinds closed as Dodge began to stand. The tiny room smelt of sweat and sick, so he left the door open.

Melanie eased the lids from the cups. 'I've already tried that,' said Dodge, as Kerr gently pressed a coffee into his chubby hands.

'Drink it,' he said, squeezing behind his desk.

Dodge shifted to make room for Melanie on the chair beside him. He looked a complete mess, his tie trailing from his jacket pocket, his shirt front peppered with specks and stains. As Melanie took his jacket and folded it over the back of her chair he raised his head to look from one to the other. 'Sorry, guys,' he mumbled. 'Couldn't take the risk.'

'It's alright,' said Kerr, sloshing coffee onto the desk as he mishandled his own cup. 'Dodge, you just told me they're going for the Bank of England tomorrow.' He glanced at Melanie, cramped beneath Dodge's hefty shoulder with her hand resting on his arm. 'That's basically it, right?'

'Right.'

Kerr plucked Wednesday's copy of the *Guardian* from the waste bin and laid it over the spill. 'Tell me again. Exactly as you remember it.'

'I only saw him for a wee while, five or six minutes. He says the people who did Victoria and Cheapside are going for the Bank of England tomorrow.'

'Saturday?' frowned Melanie. 'But the City's empty at the weekend.'

'Symbolic,' murmured Dodge. 'That's what he told me.' Dodge took a sip of drink and the surface trembled in his hand, as if someone was blowing on it.

'What about the rest? Time? Place? Type of device?' said Kerr. 'Does he know the attackers?'

Dodge balanced the cup on the floor between his feet with exaggerated care. 'I've only got the target. That's all.'

Kerr regarded him for a moment, dissatisfied. 'So let's have chapter and verse on the source.'

'He gave me a name. Roscoe. Bobby Roscoe. But don't waste your time,' said Dodge, as if expecting one of them immediately to run a check. 'He's no trace in Registry. But it has to be a false ID. A man like this will definitely have a criminal record.'

'Or terrorist. When's the next meet? I want to be there.'

Dodge fell silent, but Kerr could smell his breath from across the desk. 'What does his contact number tell us?'

'Refused.'

Kerr stared in disbelief. 'So why didn't you nick him?'

'I was on my own.' Dodge pulled at his handkerchief and a pile of change clattered to the floor. A couple of pound coins plopped into his coffee.

'Leave it,' he said as Dodge bent down. 'What does he look like?'

'Thirties, about your height. Clean-shaven, no distinguishing marks.' Dodge shrugged. 'Your manual worker type…but educated. English, but not from here. Up north, but don't ask me where.'

'You've just given me Everyman,' said Kerr, unable to keep the sarcasm from his voice.

'I'm doing my best.'

'So let's rewind things,' he said, as Melanie looked daggers at him. 'What do we have? A walk-in?'

'Phone-in.' Dodge breathed deeply, exhaling another stale breeze that ruffled Kerr's face. 'On the landline.'

'A cold caller.' Kerr looked at Melanie again, silently sipping her coffee, her arm still pressed against Dodge. 'But you were sick today.'

'Couldn't sit at home with Cheapside running,' said Dodge, his face sagging lower with each shake of the head. 'It came in a little before seven. Roscoe said he had info about the bombs that we wouldn't get anywhere else and it would cost.'

'Which number?'

'Our confidential hotline.'

'So there'll be a recording.'

'Blank,' mumbled Dodge. He coughed, shakily retrieved his coffee from the floor and took a sip. 'Machine never kicked in.' He sounded dehydrated, from alcohol or lies, and Kerr's look of disbelief sparked another glare from Melanie.

Kerr let his eyes settle on Dodge's shirt. 'Where did you meet?'

'Not a pub. That was afterwards,' said Dodge. 'Seven-thirty on Clapham Common.'

'Your choice?'

'His. Said it had to be in the open.'

'So no CCTV. Who did you take for back-up?'

'Just me. Everyone was out and about.'

'But you let someone know, Dodge?' said Melanie, leaning forward to look him in the face, as if pleading for him to get it right. 'Surely you gave a heads-up before meeting him? That's the rule, isn't it?'

'There wasn't time.'

'Why didn't you grab a body set?' asked Kerr.

Dodge shrugged.

'Jack and I could have covered you,' said Melanie kindly. 'You only had to call.'

'Look, I went straight out without telling a soul, okay? Broke my own code.'

'And that's the bit I don't get,' said Kerr. 'Two attempts on your life and you never suspected it might be a trick? That you were being set up? Ambushed? After all you've been through?'

'It felt okay.'

'From a single phone call?' said Kerr. 'Dodge, how can you say that? Anything could have happened. You had no control over this guy?'

'I'm here, aren't I?' he said, suddenly looking up. It was his first display of the old assertiveness, but his face betrayed him, the lies leaking through his skin like raindrops.

'You put yourself in harm's way when there was no need,' said Kerr. 'Christ, you've sacked people for less.'

Dodge lifted his eyes to Kerr's. 'Well sometimes you have to chuck the codes of fucking practice in the bin, don't you, John? Go with your gut feeling. We're still shovelling bodies and he was ready to cut the call. Was I under threat? Who knows?' he said, suddenly out of breath. 'I turned it into an opportunity. Letting him get away, that was the risk.'

Kerr fell silent for a moment. 'Have you made your calls across the water?'

'No…obviously…not really a good time with me like this… don't think it's Irish.'

'Why not?'

Melanie gripped his arm. 'Is that what he told you, Dodge?'

'How about it's a hoax, or complete bullshit?' said Kerr.

Dodge's outburst had turned his jowls a pallid grey. He stayed silent, leaving a cloud of dead air between them.

Kerr's sigh was of resignation. 'So we have a source with no name, untested and non-contactable. No photographs or voice print, no address, phone, email or motive, and a description that fits Walter Mitty. He's given us a target and a day, intel we have no way of corroborating. Tell me, Dodge. What would you do in my shoes?'

'I think we have to go with it.'

'I mean, you know how the system works,' said Kerr, glancing at his watch again. 'It's getting on for ten. You've presented me with a ticking time bomb that I'm going to plant in Bill Ritchie's lap as soon as we're finished here. And he'll dump it on the Bull tonight. You see my dilemma.'

'John, I had to pass it on.'

'And you still think he's the real deal? That's your professional assessment?'

Dodge shrugged and looked down again, his voice scarcely audible. 'We'll find out tomorrow, won't we?'

When Kerr had finished with him, Dodge insisted on taking a cab home, picking his money from the floor and resisting all Melanie's offers to drive him.

'Do you believe a single word?' said Kerr when they were alone, trying Ritchie's direct line and getting no reply.

'It's what I've been telling you all along,' said Melanie. Her voice sounded sharp, still angry at Kerr's scepticism.

'But you see why I needed you here?'

'Oh, yes,' said Melanie. 'You want me to keep an eye on him.'

'No,' said Kerr, scrolling through his contacts for Ritchie's home number. He dialled and looked straight at her. 'I want you to follow him.'

Chapter Twenty-Seven

Saturday, 15 October, 10.07, A406 North Circular Road, Neasden

For their rendezvous Bobby Roscoe had selected an isolated patch of scrub and woodland between Brent Reservoir and Neasden Junction, less than a mile from where the M1 lost itself in north London's suburban sprawl and petered out at Staples Corner. Neglected by day, even by the birdlife from the local nature reserve, the area came to life after dark as one of the capital's premier dogging venues.

Access from the A406 North Circular Road lay at the end of a long terrace of rundown 1930s housing with concreted gardens and drooping net curtains, just before New Delhi Delight Curry House and Gusto Kebabs and Pizza. The entrance was wide enough for medium-sized rigid lorries, and deep furrows in the dried mud testified to its night time popularity with London's swingers.

With Fin on the pillion, Kenny had ridden the Honda motorcycle from Roscoe's yard in Willesden, where the brothers had finished the roof under Roscoe's direction, warmed chicken soup on his camping stove and spent a restless night catnapping on a mattress in the cold workshop. Roscoe had brought the brothers here weeks earlier, on the Sunday of their initial target recce, but the turning was so inconspicuous that Kenny almost rode past. Behind the main road lay a parcel of waste ground with seeded conifers and three old wooden picnic tables in a waist high thicket of brambles. A strip of dried mud ran through the middle to a wooded area at the far end and Kenny bumped along this now, edging between the ruts and potholes.

Lorry drivers had to abandon their vehicles at the edge of the scrub, for the wood was accessible only to cars or small vans. It was cooler in here, gloomy and lifeless beneath a thick blanket of cloud, with the track forcing a narrow circle through the untended trees and bushes. Every few metres they came upon a van-sized clearing, where men pimped their wives to strangers. Kenny made a complete circuit to check they were alone, but the only sign of life was muffled gunfire from the local shooting range. They parked the motorcycle and perched on a tree trunk to wait, still protected by their crash helmets. Scattered around them was the detritus of used condoms, tissues and mashed underwear. They sat in silence, blind to the dregs of voyeurism and quick-fire sex, minds fixed on their most dangerous mission yet.

Bobby Roscoe arrived at ten-fifteen, dead on time. They heard the whine of the Citroen Jumper van in low gear, then its tall white body appeared through the undergrowth, lurching heavily from side to side. It sat low on the ground as Roscoe reversed into the clearing, the strengthened tyres creating their own ruts. He left the engine running and jumped from the cab. 'Are we clear?'

Pulling at his latex gloves, Roscoe waited for Fin's nod before swinging the rear doors open and standing aside, like a mobile trader showing off his merchandise. The brothers crowded round, still in their helmets, trying to avoid the exhaust fumes. Fixed to the launch frame was the bomb, a battered orange metal sheath the length of two calor gas canisters. At the base was a diagonal metal plate bolted to the reinforced floor and wired to a sealed electronic container the size of a shoe box. More cables trailed from the box through a rough hole into the driver's cab.

'Neat, yeah?' said Roscoe proudly, smiling between them as if he had designed and fitted the contraption himself. This morning he was Mister Jocularity, friend and comrade-at-arms, not the maniac who had threatened Fin with his own gun the day before.

'Did it drive alright on the way down?' said Fin, unimpressed. Roscoe had always insulated the brothers from the actual bombmaker: all they knew was that he had taken the van to Luton the night before and just returned down the M1.

'She's heavy, alright,' said Roscoe, giving the casing a cold slap. 'And a full tank for extra fireworks, so keep the speed down.'

Fin peered into the cylinder to study the bomb. Buried deep beneath the rim was a rough silver cone, like the dented lid of a round biscuit tin. He looked sceptical. 'And this is going to fly?'

'She's the fucking Bankbuster,' smiled Roscoe.

In the cab he showed them another metal box on the passenger seat, smaller than the first. It had a single metal switch and a black button beneath an illuminated red light. 'It's already charged. You keep the engine on at all times. Flick the switch, wait till the light turns green and press the button hard.'

'How much time do we have?' said Fin.

Roscoe shrugged.

'What the fuck does that mean?'

'Enough,' said Roscoe, 'if you move quick.'

•••

Saturday, 15 October, 10.19, Arbeider Brokerage, Threadneedle Street

Command and control for the operation to protect the Bank of England was managed from the City of London Police Headquarters in Wood Street, half a mile to the west, but the real hub was Langton's confined observation post above Cigar Haven in Threadneedle Street. The premises were leased to Lars Arbeider, a Dutch PE teacher turned shipping broker and Jack Langton's friend from Loughborough College, where both had studied sports science. Langton's sourcing officer had located a second base, an empty apartment on the corner of Bartholomew Lane and Lothbury, offering perfect line of sight along the bank's eastern and northern perimeters.

Kerr, Langton and Melanie were crammed into an office designed for two, helping themselves to cappuccinos from Arbeider's flashy Senseo coffee maker as Melanie trained their cameras on the street below. Against the back wall, a principal from the City of London Tactical Firearms Group had set up shop alongside a liaison officer from the Met's SCO19 Specialist Firearms Command. Their heavily armed teams of Trojans were hidden nearby in unmarked black Range Rovers, primed to arrest any suspects identified by Langton's surveillance teams.

Langton had two lookouts inside the entrance hall of the Underground station, with six pairs of armed operatives melting around the perimeter of the Bank. Because the devices at Victoria, Cheapside and Canary Wharf had been delivered by hand, Langton's focus was pedestrians, possibly arriving by public transport. Kerr peered up and down Threadneedle Street: the City was quiet, with only a fraction of the normal weekday traffic. He accepted another cappuccino from Langton, perched on Arbeider's solid hardwood desk and tried to relax.

•••

Kerr felt anxious, for the operation unfolding beneath him was secret and risky, and had not been won without a fight. After his curious meeting with Dodge, Kerr had deployed Jack Langton and Melanie to stake out the Bank of England, then called Bill Ritchie, who had immediately driven to the office for a word by word briefing. By midnight, Ritchie had notified Derek Finch and the two others who needed to know about an imminent attack against one of London's most iconic buildings.

The Bull had been suspicious, the City of London Commissioner jittery and Avril Knight, the Home Secretary, opportunistic. Energised from beating the Prime Minister to the COBRA chair, still fixated upon IRA culpability, she had personally called Ritchie twice to extract every detail.

The collective reaction had been truculence about the lack of specifics and demands for every scrap about Dodge's informant. Briefing through the night, Kerr had been disingenuous to everyone, yet utterly loyal to his friend. In describing the source as 'secret and reliable' he had been grading Dodge, the troubled messenger, not his peculiar new asset; and the clichés about 'unique access' and 'uncorroborated but credible intelligence' were straight lifts from the agent runners' playbook. Kerr had broken as many rules as Dodge in the flurry of tense calls and frosty meetings, but the purpose of his dissembling had been to shield his trusted comrade, not to immunise the untested stranger in the park.

It had taken an hour to raise Toby Devereux through Thames House. The MI5 duty officer had claimed he was working in London, but when Devereux finally called back he had sounded sleepy and distant. Finch had arranged a conference call for two o'clock, at which they skirmished over disruption versus discreet, covert surveillance, what Ritchie called the 'Elephants or Chameleons' debate. Devereux, swiftly tailed by Finch, had insisted on safety-first deterrence rather than red-handed capture; Ritchie and Kerr had countered that a heavy police presence on a Saturday morning would blow the source and leave the terrorists free to strike again. The end had been swift, with Devereux invoking the lead and Ritchie trumping him as protector of the agent.

Within the hour, Jack Langton had called in his favour from Lars Arbeider; by dawn, every camera in the Ring of Steel had been checked, explosives officers warned, and armed response vehicle crews placed on standby for a briefing from Derek Finch.

Kerr had returned to Nancy just after four and slept deeply for three hours, his first decent rest since the dash to Washington. He had showered, given Nancy breakfast in bed while the children overslept, and returned Robyn's call from the Alfa on the way back to the Fishbowl. She had been on the move, too, driving to the Saturday Farmers' Market at Tor San Giovanni, and berated him for ignoring her calls. Her responses to the lack of progress on Hammersmith, his denial of any link to the week's other attacks, and promise to visit Rome soon, had been impatience, suspicion and disbelief.

'I called you last night, John, because it's exactly three weeks since some bastard tried to fucking vaporise me...'

'Not you, Robyn. Me.'

'Wonderful, except whose name's on the rental agreement? Who's been pissing off nutjobs who think human rights means an Armalite under the bed?'

'Robyn, this not connected to your Belfast project. Whoever did this was trying to get me. I'm certain. They most likely attached the bomb while we were on the boat.'

'Really?' Robyn had murmured, eventually. 'Jesus, that was one hell of a costly shag.'

The car door had opened to the bustle of the market as Kerr recalled their afternoon together. 'Have you finished the report yet?'

'No. Third draft. I'm waiting on some more stats, and for you to tell me I'm not about to get bumped off. And I still might not let them publish.'

Kerr had tried to sound reassuring. 'Robyn, you're safe. Finish it, and I swear I'll be out next week.'

'I'll believe that when I see the taxi. Thank Christ for Gabi,' Robyn had said, just before the line died.

•••

Alan Fargo called as Kerr was speaking with the SCO19 leader.

'Can you come back now, John?'

'What is it?'

'Urgent, but not for the phone,' said Fargo, then rang off, as abruptly as Robyn. Kerr took no offence as he raced downstairs: the two men had dispensed with elaboration a long time ago.

Chapter Twenty-Eight

Saturday, 15 October, 10.32, Room 1830, New Scotland Yard

Kerr reached the Yard in ten minutes and went straight to 1830. It was a full house, buzzing with energy, the blinds still drawn against the early morning sun.

Fargo was working Mercury but minimised the screen as Kerr entered. 'I think we've got something, John,' he said, almost before Kerr sat down. Fargo was unshaven, in a crumpled shirt with the sleeves unevenly rolled, his glasses and contact lens case half buried beneath a bundle of pink Registry files. He rubbed his eyes, as if still undecided about which to wear.

'You were sitting there when I left last night,' said Kerr, regarding him carefully. 'Have you had any sleep?'

Fargo ignored him and went for the glasses, vigorously polishing the lenses on his shirt. 'You asked me to touch base with our European partners,' he said. 'For any group wild enough to hit the banks in London.'

'So what did you come up with?'

'Well there's only one runner, isn't there?' Fargo's tone was almost chiding as he reached for the top file. The cover was marked Secret, with a reference, RF300/08/187, and the subject, Anti-Capitalist Insurrection. He riffled through the pages, sending a draught over Kerr's face. 'I imagine it's ACI you're interested in, seeing as your writing's all over it and there's a monthly RBF flag.' RBF was shorthand for 'report bring forward,' the routine marker for a subject of special interest.

'Only since June.'

'Quite. Anything 1830 needs to know about?'

Kerr crossed his legs, brushed his nose and dodged the question. 'What did the guys have to say?'

'A lot. Gilbert confirmed the theft of the Semtex in Marseilles. Paris thinks ACI could well be up for this. Globalisation, austerity, bank bailouts, trickle down wealth, they're pan-European and anti-everything. The Greeks call them "Hydra." Demitri says it's time we slashed off a few of the heads.'

'But they think ACI are organised enough to have done this?'

Fargo nodded. 'ACI call themselves anarcho-syndicalist but the Germans say that's bollocks,' he said, flicking through his scribbles. 'Hierarchical with strong funding…leaders extremely secretive…tight cell structure…' He looked up. 'Yeah, like the IRA, and just as secure. Plus they're paranoid, with no permanent base, so difficult to track and penetrate. And because they're morphing all over Europe no single country has taken ownership and investigated them.'

'Until now.'

'So I see,' said Fargo drily, flipping through Kerr's minutes on the file. 'They use social media to communicate, mostly on Skype because it's difficult to intercept.'

'Anything new on the tactics?'

'Rabid statements against IMF, G7 and EU Finance meetings, but it's their actions that speak loudest. They take over a regular protest movement like Occupy and inject it with violence. They deal in agitation and entryism, you know…they're an insane version of the old revolutionary left, except they call it TDA.'

'Transformative direct action, yeah. I think we already had most of that?' said Kerr, tapping the file.

'The facts, but not the intensity. It's the sheer scale of the mayhem that everyone's talking about. The worst of the anti-austerity violence in Greece was down to ACI. Same with *Los Indignados* in Spain. Paolo Ibarro says we're up against political Ebola. The overnight consensus is that ACI is spreading across Europe like a virus, and no-one's doing anything to stop it.' Fargo took back the file and found a note from Kerr. 'It's like you say here, back in July. "Through its ability to infiltrate and hijack peaceful protest movements ACI has evolved into a significant international threat…increasing numbers of UK activists and possible access to weaponry. Through its TDA strategy…da de da…capacity to escalate violence suddenly and without warning." No-one we spoke to overnight would disagree with any of that. But we've all underestimated them. I don't think anyone realised their utter destructiveness until this year. And leaving the EU is not going to reduce the UK threat.'

'Quite. There's something further back about an ACI cell involved in the UK riots,' said Kerr, flipping through the file. 'That was from the Germans, wasn't it?'

Fargo nodded. 'BKA forwarded their intel to us and MI5 but it was never verified. None of the arrests were confirmed ACI.'

Kerr sat quietly for a moment. 'So does anyone have evidence of expertise around explosives?'

Fargo shook his head. 'But we can't prove a negative because our combined oversight is so limited. Steffi Hoffnung is offering a scrum down in Berlin to share our product. But if you ask me whether ACI *could* have done Victoria and Cheapside? Do they have the motivation and capacity? The access?' Fargo shrugged. 'The readout overnight is a definite yes, and everyone's worried they're next on the list. We're all distracted by the jihadi threat across Europe. Ignoring the menace in our own back yard.'

'Which may be why MI5 have rejected every surveillance request against activists visiting the UK.'

'Didn't know they had.'

Kerr handed back the file. 'It's in there. Check the tasking and co-ordinating group log,' he said, dialling Langton and putting the BlackBerry on speaker. 'Jack, can you think back to your ACI surveillance requests with Willie Duncan?'

Langton came back immediately. 'A4 have blanked us every time.'

'Reason?'

'More pressing G Branch priorities, according to Willie. You know, British lowlifes with a Syria fetish and name change. They score higher, apparently. When I press him he shelters behind the management.'

'Does Willie actually mention Devereux?'

A chuckle filtered down the line. 'Doesn't need to.'

'Okay. Thanks.' Kerr could hear radio static in the background, then Melanie's calm voice. 'Anything doing?'

'Zilch,' said Langton. 'We'll be on the ground in about thirty minutes.'

'I'll join you soon.'

'MI5 may have agent coverage,' said Fargo, as Kerr rang off.

'If there is, they're not sharing.' Kerr folded his arms and blew his cheeks. 'So where does this leave us, Al? The warning calls, the known code words, method of delivery, etcetera. Everything harking back to the last Real IRA campaign? Then we find ACI willing and able, but not a shred of evidence to put them in the frame. Is ACI another false trail?'

'They're connected by hatred of the banks.'

'And that's the best we can do?' said Kerr, retrieving the file. 'You called me back for this?'

'No. Let's just say for a moment ACI are responsible. Why would they put it on Irish dissidents? What's their motive in framing them? I mean, why not claim the credit for themselves?' Fargo pushed back in his chair. 'Have you considered there may be another common thread? Apart from anti-capitalism?'

Kerr looked at him steadily, in wait.

'Paolo threw me a few dots overnight and I think I've managed to join them up,' said Fargo, brushing crumbs from the desk as he took an atlas of Europe from his drawer, already open at Spain. 'A French ACI activist Skyped a business associate from north-west Spain. Galicia. That's what Paolo tells me. Somewhere just outside the town of Marin,' he said, finding the location with his finger. 'Here, on the coast. The call was to the IRA.'

'The IRA where?'

'Don't know. It was after four am local on a Tuesday in

September. That's all Paolo had. He apologised, but, actually, it was more than enough.' Fargo discarded the atlas, swung round to Mercury and logged in. An unintelligible list of numbers immediately flooded the screen. 'This is GCHQ data, intercepted signals traffic provided by the National Security Agency under our bilateral agreement.'

Startled, Kerr jerked forward and peered at the screen. 'You've accessed CRUCIBLE?'

'The Skype intercepts, yes.'

'Jesus, how did you get in?'

'This is Skype data leaked earlier this month in the US. The Janner case,' he said, isolating a single line of numbers. 'And this is an outgoing from Marin in the early hours of Tuesday, September twentieth. Seven minutes after four in the morning, to be precise.'

'Three days before Hammersmith.'

'The IRA associate he called was in Columbia. Bogota.'

Kerr managed to remain impassive as lightning flashed inside his head. In an instant he was back with Rich Malone in Washington, strolling beside the Reflecting Pool.

'Do we have a name for the IRA contact?' said Kerr.

Fargo shook his head. 'Paolo says the call was to finalise a drugs consignment into Europe. ACI are probably doing the lot, buying, selling and laundering, but you can bet your life this is how they fund themselves. Here's what connects them, John. They're bound together by cocaine.'

'Narco-terrorism,' murmured Kerr.

'...*Mister Brogan has reinvented himself as...link man for their cocaine smuggling operations into Europe...money launderers in Western Europe...it's still narco-terrorism.*'

'Find the IRA go-between and we crack the case,' said Fargo.

'Good work, Al,' said Kerr, looking round the room. 'Everyone. Brilliant.'

'We need an operation name for this, but not from the regular list. I think Broker would be good, under the circs.'

Kerr sat quietly for a moment, holding back on Brogan, stitching the information together. 'What's the latest on Gina Costello?' he said, eventually.

Fargo immediately reached into the bundle for a second secret pink file marked Secret, in Costello's name, with the reference RF450/08/172. 'Amsterdam,' he said. 'And John, is there anything else you want to tell me?'

Kerr slowly shook his head, opened the file and studied Costello's photograph. 'Let's call it Javelin,' he said, quietly.

Chapter Twenty-Nine

Saturday, 15 October, 10.32, Edgware Road, London, NW9

Bobby Roscoe's tutorial in the clearing took less than five minutes, including repetition of the priming instructions. When he slapped the cold metal of the bomb for a second time to demonstrate its integrity, Fin could tell he was in a hurry, anxious to be clear of the danger zone. Roscoe's bravado was not reassuring, for the brothers had been told nothing of the bombmaker or his pedigree, and this contraption belonged in a different league from Semtex packed into a child's lunchbox and vindaloo carton.

Roscoe oversold his mortar like some marvel from science fiction, but to Fin it looked a lethal pile of junk with oversized bolts and dodgy welding. For a few moments they stood arguing by the rear doors while the van's exhaust fumes washed over them. When Fin rapped his knuckles against the casing it reverberated like a giant tuning fork, and his instincts told him it would never leave the ground. As Roscoe closed the rear doors and climbed into the passenger seat, Fin exchanged a glance with his brother, already sitting astride the motorcycle. He saw white fear in Kenny's eyes, framed by his helmet, and guessed his thoughts; high as kites on Roscoe's cocaine, neither was under any illusion about the hazard.

Fin removed his own helmet, tossed it to Roscoe and jumped behind the wheel. Sliding his Glock into the door storage pocket, he stretched the neck warmer over his chin and put on a pair of wrap around X-Loop sunglasses. The massive load pulled at him like a sea anchor as they lurched over the ruts in first gear, a swamped boat on the verge of capsizing. With Kenny at a safe distance he swung left onto the North Circular Road, heading alongside the reservoir on the short drive back to Staples Corner. Roscoe's warning voice was constantly in his ear as he struggled with the most cumbersome vehicle he had ever driven, the brakes heavy but the steering light as a feather. Roscoe was still chiding

Fin about his speed as they joined the slip road for the sprawling roundabout, swaying south round the long curve into Edgware Road.

The drop-off point was a modest retail park bordering a stretch of dual carriageway, its landmark a yellow and green pagoda that could have been lifted straight from Peking. Fin recognised it straight away, gingerly swinging left beneath the yellow metal height restriction to park between RC Hobbies and Tile and Stone.

Roscoe took a mini *London A to Z* from his pocket and laid it beside Fin's helmet.

'I won't be needing that,' said Fin.

'Page seventy-seven. If you do I'll be seriously pissed off.' In the wing mirror, Roscoe watched Kenny ride to the far end of the park and swing round to face them, engine running. 'Is the kid gonna be okay?'

Fin felt a surge of irritation. 'Why wouldn't he?'

'This is gonna work, guaranteed,' said Roscoe, laying his gloved hand on the control box for the last time. His door clicked open. 'If there's a screw up, I'll be putting it down to you.'

'Where will you be?'

'Waiting,' he said, then the door slammed shut.

Fin watched Roscoe hurry from the car park to walk back the way they had come. He reversed slowly, waited for Kenny to gun the Honda, and rejoined Edgware Road. The map was an insult, for Roscoe had chosen the most direct route into central London and spent hours in the safe house testing them every inch of the way. Fin ramped up Magic FM and settled into his seat as the sun broke through the cloud and he rocked south east through Cricklewood, Kilburn and Maida Vale. The further he penetrated the capital the more relaxed he became without Bobby Roscoe's relentless nagging.

He tested the brakes behind an old maroon Volvo with children giggling and bobbing on the rear seat, then gently moved off, watching the red glow on the control box deepen with the acceleration. He waved a police patrol car from a side turning, checking the Glock as the young woman behind the wheel smiled her thanks. Behind, a loaded scaffolding lorry and double decker bus separated him from Kenny. The lorry driver was on his tail but Fin stayed cool, holding back from the cops as he drifted past the Lebanese restaurants, shisha cafés and kebab shops on the approach to Marble Arch.

Then the police car accelerated away and everything changed as he fed into Park Lane and a fantastic world of grand façades, limousines and opulent hotels he had only ever seen on TV in Belfast. Even the autumn sun shone more brightly here and the central reservation, with its freshly mown grass, flower beds and towering plane trees, looked wide as a park. The scene shifted again as he whirred around Hyde Park Corner towards Buckingham Palace, circling the Victoria Memorial into Birdcage Walk for the Houses of Parliament. From the barracks to his right, the blare and thump of a marching band drowned out Sam Smith on Magic, each soldier in scarlet, everything a show of swank and swagger.

Fin flipped the door lock and shook his head in disgust. He had never seen himself as a political animal: the republicanism flowing through his body was an accident of birth rather than a creed. He was more hired hand than zealot, driven by cocaine not idealism, yet the statues and symbols of Empire revolted him. Another police car raced from Parliament Square, its siren isolating him in the wide, straight thoroughfares until Big Ben loomed straight ahead. 'Stay With Me' was still playing and, in the wing mirror, Kenny's gloved thumbs up told him they had made it to the killing zone, the most target-rich seam in the country. Fin glanced down at the steady red glow, then felt for the pistol again. All the police here seemed to be armed, but he settled and breathed deeply: everything had fallen within striking distance.

Filtering into Parliament Square he kept to the middle lane, tracing the northern edge to the junction with Whitehall.

Traffic was heavier now and bile rose in his throat as he slowed beneath Churchill's glower. Roscoe had warned that cops would be scouring the City from first light, so he continued across Westminster Bridge, watching for Kenny to peel left along Victoria Embankment. Their separation in Parliament's shadow was the point of no return, but this time, so close to the onslaught, neither risked any secret sign.

On the south bank Fin followed the road signs east, tracking the wide arc of the Thames past Waterloo and Blackfriars Bridges, then pitching left into Southwark Bridge Road for the river and his final destination. On the approach he pulled into a motorcycle bay with a clear view to the opposite bank, killed the radio and waited for Kenny.

Roscoe had chosen Southwark Bridge because it carried the least traffic of London's river crossings and barred direct vehicle access from the Ring of Steel. Intended to protect the City from attack, the restriction also raised Fin's odds of escape. The blue and green arch bridge was narrower than the others, too, with a footway, cycle path and single traffic lanes just wide enough for lorries to pass.

Three minutes. Fin rolled the neck warmer high over his face, lay the Glock on the seat beside him and put on his crash helmet. Kenny appeared over the low rise of the bridge at eleven-thirty exactly, startling a couple of pedestrians as he raced up the cycle path. The bridge was lined with high, ornate lanterns and he came to a halt by the fifth, just short of the mid-point, swerving in a half circle and waving his brother on. Fin snapped his gloves, gunned the engine and checked his mirrors. Traffic was light, even better than they had hoped. With a deep breath he rammed the engine into first and pulled up the gentle slope.

The bridge was still clear when he reached Kenny, the van's engine labouring in second gear. He steered into the opposite lane then swung hard left, bumping over the kerbs separating the road, cycle path and footway to position the bomb parallel with the motorcycle. He manoeuvred three times until Kenny gave a nod, then drove forward hard against the iron balustrade.

As he leapt from the van and wrenched open the rear doors a white Ford Transit van was approaching from the south, followed by a black taxi. Fin looked over his shoulder to the north bank. The target was the City Dealer bar three hundred metres away. He spotted the wooden furniture and umbrellas, just as he remembered them from the recce and Roscoe's photographs. Traffic was building from both directions now, blocked by the van and its open doors. Its position suggested an accident, though Fin's aggression and crash helmet implied something more sinister, a heist or hijack. Evidently neither possibility had occurred to the Transit driver, honking and shouting as Fin disappeared behind the wheel. As Fin revved the engine, the man's shaven head filled the passenger window, its fleshy face contorted with rage. Three gold chains lashed around his mottled throat as he wrenched at the locked door, seemingly undeterred by the gun on the seat and Fin's hand on the switch, or fatally unaware. *Click*. He raged against the glass until Fin saw the red light turn green, raised the Glock and shot him through the left eye.

His thumb over the black detonator button, Fin saw that Kenny had drawn his weapon, too. Astride the Honda, covering him with the Glock raised in both hands, his kid brother looked able-bodied and threatening. Fin pressed the black button hard, shoved the door open and ran for the motorcycle. Horns blared from a long way off, but vehicles trapped on the south side were being abandoned in panic, their drivers scurrying with arms raised from the corpse on the road and the gunman in the van.

From the north side a cyclist ran at them with fists clenched, bravado and sweat wrapped in red lycra, so Fin executed him with another headshot. Only the taxi driver behind the Transit van had stayed with his vehicle. From a bus length away Fin heard the surge of diesel and saw him sideways on, licence swinging against his chest as he bumped over the kerbs to escape. He was craning forward against the steering wheel to clock them both. Fin saw him yelling into the radio as he reversed again, so he bent his knees and loosed a couple of shots through the passenger window.

The only silence came from Bobby Roscoe's bomb, telling Fin he had been right all along as they raced down the cycle path. The explosion came a second later with a *crump* that convulsed the bridge in a shock that made Kenny swerve and brake to a halt. They both looked back, mesmerised by a white flash that turned the van luminous before erupting into an orange furnace shooting flames in every direction.

Then the air erupted with a different sound, a proper, recognisable detonation as the front of the van smashed into the balustrade and its strengthened suspension collapsed onto the road, the whole vehicle pulverised by an invisible crusher. Instantaneously the roof split in two as the junk that Fin had told himself would never fly shot into the air and soared for the target, its silver cone sparkling in the sunshine as it turned and revolved in slow motion, a lost moon craft tumbling through space. The brothers stared, rooted to the spot, as Roscoe's Bankbuster found its arc before crashing into a giant barge moored alongside the City Dealer.

The final shockwave came not from the bomb, but the exploding fuel tank. It almost lifted them from the Honda, engulfing the van in a multi-coloured fireball that blasted shrapnel into the sky, set both corpses alight and produced the firework display Roscoe had always promised them.

Chapter Thirty

Saturday, 15 October, 11.36, Upper Thames Street, EC4

Jack Langton's Suzuki motorcycle was being repaired after his narrow escape in Victoria, so he was working with Melanie out of a silver VW Golf. They had spent the past forty minutes refining the surveillance operation around the City, including a dash to the Yard for any new leads from Alan Fargo in Room 1830.

The alarm sounded as they were returning to link up with the fourteen units on the ground.

'Red Nine to Red One, urgent message.'

'Go.'

'Correction, this is no longer an RTA…Repeat, not RTA. We have a Talisman… Receiving, over?'

Talisman was surveillance code for a live terrorist attack. 'Did I get that right?' said Langton, with an anxious glance at Melanie. Red Nine was on Tetra Five, the protected channel his units used for surveillance operations, and they could hear raised voices with a lot of engine noise in the air. Langton screwed his face, turned up the volume and leant close to the speaker. 'Pete? Talisman where?'

Red Nine's voice had risen a couple of notches since his initial message reporting a road traffic accident, RTA, blocking Southwark Bridge, and he continued as if no-one was listening. 'I'm caught in a Talisman right now…Southwark Bridge. Multiple shots fired…I'm not carrying. Jack? Jack…you getting this? All units urgent assistance, Southwark Bridge.' Langton heard the engine racing, as if Red Nine's foot was trapped on the accelerator, then it dropped and surged again. There was a thud as he bumped over something, then the crunch of a collision.

'Ninety seconds,' said Langton, forced back in his seat as Melanie rammed her foot to the floor. 'Red Three do you copy this?' he continued, calling the young female comms operative managing Lars Arbeider's office.

'All received,' she replied instantly, as a burst of orders crackled from the tactical firearms cell behind her. 'And Trojans deploying now.'

'From Red Nine, we have a white van. Citroen. Think they're trying a mortar to the north side and we fucking missed it… There's two down at least, handgun. Maybe more.'

Red Nine's name was Peter Webb. He should never have been there, but had fallen victim to the coincidence that trapped so many front line operators, the jeopardy that held life and death in its grasp. Webb was the Red Team's trained black taxi driver. Alone and unarmed, Langton had redeployed him from a jihadi plot in Streatham to provide mobile cover outside the Ring of Steel.

A second later came two unmistakable cracks of a firearm and Pete Webb screaming his Mayday. 'Jesus, I'm hit. He's fucking shot me.' The diesel surged again, a tractor racing out of control. 'Neck or shoulder. I'm bleeding. Shit. Fuck.' They heard a screech of brakes and the sound of Red Nine yelling into the street – 'Get in! Don't argue. Now!' – then a scrabbling and other voices, male and female, a door slamming and someone sobbing hysterically as Webb accelerated again.

Charging east along the Embankment, the speedometer hovering above eighty, Melanie was already clearing Victoria Embankment as Langton responded, his Newcastle voice low and calm. 'It's okay, Pete. Get to the south bank and we'll pick you up.'

The Golf shot into the Blackfriars Underpass to a whooshing sound over the radio followed by a loud explosion, then Red Nine again, crystal clear above the tunnel's echo. 'It's gone. The van's gone up right in front of me. Fucking fireball…Bomb gone! We have a bomb gone. Mortar into the City.'

'Hold on. We're coming for you.'

'You won't get through. Wait one.' Voices from the taxi, more screams as Melanie shot out of the tunnel into Upper Thames Street. People were crying in the back and then Pete again, shouting at someone. 'Press the pad down there…doesn't matter. Hold it firm so I can drive.'

Traffic was light and the noise from a motorcycle racing from the opposite direction almost drowned out Webb's order. His voice had risen again, anxiety seeping through the information. 'Bleeding buckets here…two males to the north side. It's a blue motorbike, both with Glocks…I'm going to…Listen, I'm gonna get to Southwark Street…need the paramedics. You getting this, Jack? Feeling shit…have to know you're with me.'

'Yes, yes. Hang in there.' Langton swung his head round but the motorcycle had already disappeared, swallowed up by the tunnel. 'That was blue, right, Mel? With two up?'

But Melanie was already reacting, slewing into a handbrake turn at the junction with Southwark Bridge. She spun them into a neat arc between a double decker and low loader, rammed into first while they were still sliding and accelerated hard the way they had come. Braced against the door, Langton's voice never wavered. 'Red Three from Red One, officer down. Did you get Pete's location, over?'

The voice bounced straight back from the observation post – 'Medics on way' – just audible above the urgent voices behind her.

'You hear that, Pete?' said Langton. 'Couple of minutes. We're going for the bike.'

'What's the plan?' said Melanie as they reached chasing speed again. 'Surprise or interception?'

Langton's response was to slap the blue light on the dash as they shot back into the tunnel mouth.

'They're armed,' she persisted, accelerating hard past a traffic tailback, her voice still measured and cautious. 'We're just going to find and follow, right?' The underpass was about eight hundred metres long but they emerged into the sunshine in less than twenty seconds, swerving between a coach and a bus, Langton still silent as they flashed into a second tunnel beneath the Blackfriars Bridge approach.

They spotted the motorcycle a quarter of a mile ahead on a tree-lined stretch of Victoria Embankment, the last in a line of cars and coaches slowing for the junction by Temple Underground station.

Melanie braked and flicked off the blue light, holding back. They listened to Red Three in the observation post, coolly juggling messages from the City's fast response vehicles, Trojan units and paramedic teams as they searched for Pete Webb in his bullet-holed taxi. Langton understood how these crises played out. From now, with the bomb gone, others high in the command chain would be giving the orders. But in these vital first moments, with Red Nine's distress electrifying the airwaves, the critical judgments about his survival lay with Langton's newest recruit, and she was not going to relinquish her grip until Pete Webb had been saved.

Up ahead, they watched the motorcycle gently increase speed with the other traffic as the lights changed. 'Everyone's on it, Jack,' said Melanie, nodding at the radio. 'We should lead the Trojans to them.'

They had traced a giant left curve alongside the river and the pall of black smoke over Southwark was clearly visible through the rear passenger window. 'They just shot Pete,' said Langton, then leaned forward to laser on the assailants. 'Red Three from Jack, we have the targets travelling west along Victoria Embankment, towards Waterloo and Charing Cross. Stand by.'

Melanie threw him a quick glance sideways. 'You want me to go for them?'

Langton was already reaching for his Glock. 'They'll do it again if we don't stop them now,' he said, vainly searching the mirror for other blue lights.

'Okay,' said Melanie simply as she charged forward.

'Red Three, we're in pursuit,' said Langton, levelly.

'West on Victoria Embankment, all understood,' responded Red Three. 'Please change to Three Zero and maintain commentary for Zulu.' Zulu was the main City control room call sign, and

Three Zero the designated radio channel for its live operation and back-up for Langton.

The motorcycle took off a second later by Waterloo Bridge, just as Langton was leaning forward to flick through the channels. The bombers may have been spooked by suspicion of the Golf steaming onto their tail, the swirl of sirens from unseen units racing to the bomb scene, or the blue light from a solitary cop car racing along the opposite bank. Whatever the reason, they suddenly veered wildly between the two lanes of crawling traffic as they closed on Embankment station, roaring through a red light to swerve away from the river for Trafalgar Square.

'Right, right into Northumberland Avenue,' reported Langton calmly, flicking on the emergency light again.

Caught in the tailback, Melanie crashed over the central reservation onto the opposite lane and charged after them. The bombers snaked between a batch of cars and tourist buses as they raced crazily onwards, with Melanie gaining ground in the oncoming lane. Dead ahead was a raised triangular island, a refuge for pedestrians waiting to enter Trafalgar Square. It was crowded with a party of about twenty children, none more than seven years old, all in bright yellow baseball caps, their bobbing heads vivid as a field of flowering rapeseed.

Langton watched the bombers hurtle down the centre of the road and lose control as they flipped round a street lamp. The bike slewed straight for the island, mounted the kerb and took off. To Langton's horror, the bike scythed through the children before careering across the street to collide hard with the square's perimeter wall.

The block of colour instantly dispersed into separate yellow dots as terrified children ran for their lives into three lanes of traffic, screaming in shock. Four or five children were lying to each side as Melanie eased the Golf through the clearance, a couple of women teachers with rucksacks racing from one child to another. To the right, a little girl was crushed against a road sign with her leg twisted at an impossible angle, a jagged shard of bone protruding through her tights.

'We have to help them, Jack.'

Langton stared straight ahead as the bombers remounted the motorcycle. A gun appeared in the hand of the pillion passenger, probably a Glock, like his own, just as a wild man leapt from nowhere and blocked his view, raving and banging on the windscreen, laying the carnage on them, too. Then the body fell aside and Langton's luck ran out as the windscreen shattered, something punched him hard in the left shoulder and the air snapped twice more as the motorcycle raced away.

'Zulu from Red One, Trafalgar Square, east side. Shots fired. Urgent assistance. Eight, nine children down.' Langton was finally having to raise his voice, for desperate screams obliterated every other sound as Melanie followed the Honda onto the pavement, her fist staining red as she punched out the remains of the windscreen and weaved through startled bystanders impotent with shock.

'Jack, you injured?'

'Drive on,' was all he said, his voice low again, the Glock suddenly in his lap. 'I'm ordering you.'

She chased the motorcycle into the square, where it shot through a close row of concrete bollards and tore diagonally across the pedestrian concourse, swerving to avoid a cleansing vehicle. Unable to squeeze through the gap, Melanie screeched to a halt, reversed hard into a J-turn and stormed along the base of Nelson's Column. 'They're cleaning. I know a way,' was all she said as Langton pressed a blood-soaked hand to his shoulder.

At the opposite corner a removable iron post took the place of the last concrete bollard, and she slid sideways through the gap at forty, scattering tourists as they tore past the fountains. At the far end, the bombers had already reached the long flight of steps leading to the upper terrace.

Langton wanted to say something but the words dried in his

throat. He tried for the radio, but Melanie was doing the speaking for him, too. 'Zulu from Red Two, officer down, officer down.'

'Location.'

'Still the Square. They have a hostage.'

'What?' whispered Langton, straining ahead, fighting unconsciousness.

Four or five steps up the first flight, the gunman had his arm round the throat of a young woman in jeans and denim jacket. Beneath her, at ground level, a buggy gently sailed away on the breeze as she begged for her baby. Behind them, the rider was walking the damaged bike up the stairs, throttling the engine over each step. Melanie skidded sideways in another precision handbrake turn as one bullet spat through the roof and another skittered along the water.

As they rocked to a halt Langton realised that she had positioned the Golf perfectly behind the square's famous empty plinth, sheltering him from the gunman's elevated advantage. He wanted to thank her for saving his life but she was already out of the vehicle.

Fading fast, Langton was just in time to see her drop to the ground, weapon forward in locked arms as she rolled to the base of the plinth. He saw her crawl forward to neutralise the threat and keep him safe. He pushed his injured shoulder against the door to join her but the pain was too great, his blood sticky against the window as everything started to slip away. Fingers closed around the Glock, his focus finally abandoned him and he sank beneath the revving of the killer motorcycle, the tornado of sirens and Melanie's voice, yelling at the bombers to let the hostage go.

Chapter Thirty-One

Saturday, 15 October, 19.06, Cabinet Office, 70 Whitehall

Kerr spent the afternoon at St Thomas's Hospital just across the Thames from Westminster, watching over Peter Webb and Langton. Webb required immediate surgery and Kerr had hung around intensive care, restless and wary until the nurses convinced him that both were out of danger. Mobiles were banned but he took a call from Alan Fargo while coaxing a few words from a drowsy Langton, reacting so sharply that he almost dislodged the intravenous drip. The revelation from 1830 was concise but startling, a vindication of his judgment five months earlier.

Bill Ritchie had his driver on standby at the Yard but decided to walk with Kerr for their meeting at the Cabinet Office. The evening air was cool and clear, their constitutional through Parliament Square a chance to speak face to face, agree a game plan for the Current Intelligence Group and digest Fargo's information.

Global panics excepted, the Silver Scrum was rarely allowed to interrupt the weekends of Westminster's securocrats. Number 70 Whitehall looked deserted and even bleaker than usual as they approached along the darkened street, its brass name plates glinting in the light of a passing bus. Inside, a group in their twenties and thirties huddled in the anteroom, uncomfortable in their work clothes. Most were texting on their iPhones, probably hoping for a quick policy decision and race home to the country.

The custodian looked blindsided behind his security screen as the committee secretary leaned in, tapping his pass on the counter with each repetition of the date, time and room booking. Eventually, balancing his apple core on the mouse pad, the jobsworth licked his fingers and reached for the phone. There was another hiatus as the Bull arrived with Toby Devereux, each making a show of 'after you' deference before cramming through the doorway together, like a couple of party gatecrashers. With the lift out of order and their usual room closed for redecoration, they scrummed down in B3, a bleak subterranean meeting space with a horseshoe of oak tables beneath a portrait of the Queen on a horse and, by the door, a forgotten vacuum cleaner, mop and bucket.

The chairperson was Ruth Horbury. Wearing her trademark black pumps, she bustled in with an 'Evening all' while the group was getting settled, taking her seat in front of the fireplace. Jacket on the back of the chair, she scribbled on the agenda while the secretary set up his laptop. 'Chop, chop, Tim,' she muttered, running a hand through her hair.

She flashed a quick smile at Kerr, perched with Ritchie at the end of the spur nearest the door. Devereux always sat on the horseshoe's curve, just outside Horbury's personal space, but this evening Finch upset the pecking order by squeezing between them. When he tried to engage Horbury in terror talk she excused herself and sought Kerr out again. 'John, so sorry to hear about your officers this afternoon. How are they doing?'

'Hoping for a full recovery. We were lucky.'

'That's good to hear.'

'Thanks for asking.'

Ruth Horbury was another core member of the nation's intelligence family. Before joining the Cabinet Office Assessments Staff she had been a career GCHQ officer, a fluent Russian speaker rising from the ashes of the Cold War. She and Kerr had become friends since 9/11, as part of a scratch task force working with the Americans. Afterwards, she had re-trained in Arabic to analyse signals intelligence in Baghdad and Kabul, before returning to head all language analysis at Cheltenham.

Occupying the other seats were a secondee Kerr recognised from MI5's Joint Terrorism Analysis Centre, JTAC, the usual quartet of players from Home Office and Foreign Office, and a stubbled Ministry of Defence analyst Kerr had not seen before. Sitting opposite was Lisa Jordan from the Northern Ireland Office, the woman Ritchie had mentioned at Monday's COBRA meeting. Kerr knew she was the NIO lead on human rights policy, because Robyn had interviewed her in Belfast. Beside her was a small wheelie bag, suggesting she would be flying home that evening.

'Right everybody, order, order,' said Horbury, briskly. 'Apologies for the Saturday callout but it's our worst week of mainland attacks since…well, I don't know,' she said, without leaving airtime for an answer. 'Victoria, Cheapside and Southwark Bridge in six days. The dud at Canary Wharf, plus Hammersmith a month ago…'

'Twenty-third of September,' interrupted Finch.

'…three weeks, but we still don't know if it's linked.' She glanced at her papers. 'Government. COBRA meets again at nine in the morning and the PM's called an emergency NSC at Chequers for noon before he leaves for Berlin and the Article Fifty prelims.' NSC was the National Security Council. 'Home Sec will make a statement in the House on Monday afternoon. This evening's readout will go to the JIC on…Tim?'

'Monday at three.'

'Everyone alright with that?' she said, eyes lowering again. 'Media. The Sundays are about to drop doo-doo all over us, and not much of what I'm hearing makes sense. I want a coherent narrative so Number Ten can draw up Lines To Take. Stringent LTTs are crucial. We need ministers to speak with a single voice. Avril Knight has interviews first thing, correct?' she said, waiting for the Home Office nod.

'Andrew Marr and Sky.'

'And we don't want anyone going off piste.' She twisted her upper body to address the Bull, attending CIG as a one-time invitee. 'Thanks for coming, Mr Finch. All very grateful. I have the casualty readout for Victoria and Cheapside as eleven and seventeen respectively?'

Finch shook his head. 'Twenty-nine. Another female passed last night,' he said, solemnly. 'And the two on the bridge, of course.'

'So thirty-one murders?' said Horbury.

'And many with life-changing injuries.'

Finch had omitted to mention that the dead included a police officer. He was sounding like an undertaker, sending a chill hush over the room as people bowed their heads to digest the news.

'How ghastly for them and their families,' said Horbury after a pause, covering her cheek.

Kerr understood their awkwardness. The job of CIG officials was to make an unstable world intelligible to their political masters. Brutality, suffering and degradation belonged in another country, so nothing touched them personally. They dealt in policy, not empathy, sanitising nuclear threats, spilt blood and cyberspying with a dry assessment of the threat to British interests. Horbury's quiet condolence for lives destroyed a couple of miles away laced an intellectual exercise with compassion, and no-one broke the silence. A floor polisher whirred somewhere deep in the building.

'So where do things stand this evening?' asked Horbury, eventually.

Finch took his cue. 'This is a dynamic and fast moving series of interconnected operations,' he began, shifting from pious to pompous. 'Highly complex, unprecedented in my three decades of service. I have over three hundred specialist officers working for me. We recovered the abandoned motorcycle near Charing Cross and CCTV of the bomb vehicle as well as…'

Finch may not have heard Horbury's impatient sigh, but the clink of bracelet against wristwatch stopped him in his tracks.

'You want an update, right?' he said.

'I want to know who did it, Mr Finch.'

The Bull cleared his throat. 'The two men today probably did all the attacks. They won't get far.'

'I mean "who" as in "which organisation",' said Horbury evenly.

'We're talking Real IRA. That's my professional opinion. The bomb warnings with known code words, the method of delivery, the use of Semtex, etcetera. We've recovered today's bomb intact. It's a mortar, same type as the IRA used against Number Ten and

Heathrow in the nineties. The intelligence today was faulty,' he said, with a hostile look at Kerr, 'but other channels are available to me. All credible and true. Military. Everything fits the dissident profile. I'm afraid remnants from the past have returned,' he said, ominously.

Kerr caught Horbury's glance in his direction but stayed silent: this evening, his commander would do the talking.

'Whenever we suffered an IRA attack on the mainland in the past,' said Horbury, 'the RUC Special Branch were able to tell us if paramilitary suspects were away from home. Has that happened here?'

'We've moved on from those days,' said Finch. 'Everything's community based now.'

Horbury made a face. 'How about MI5?' she said, turning to Toby Devereux. 'Anyone playing hooky?'

'As outlined at Monday's COBRA,' said Devereux with a shake of the head, 'we have no intelligence of travel to the mainland, or other illicit activity. Is this the work of dissident paramilitaries? We raised the mainland threat level in May, as you know.' He indicated a pile of papers beside the secretary. 'It's in our draft submission, T6D, in your bundle. I find myself agreeing with the police on this.'

'And whose idea was it to sacrifice Mark Bannerman?'

Horbury's bluntness seemed to catch Devereux by surprise. 'It was a joint decision with MI6,' he said, carefully. 'We had to confront them…'

'By sending Mark into the lion's den? What were you hoping for? An IRA confession?'

'…and give them the opportunity to hand over the perpetrators.'

Horbury looked at him in disbelief. 'You seriously expected the IRA to grass up their own volunteers?'

'Or confirm they were not responsible.' Devereux wore round, steel framed glasses, which Kerr often saw him polish at moments of stress. This evening he used his tie. 'The mission did not turn out as we hoped, obviously.'

'The humiliation and torture of one of our finest Arabists, you mean?' said Horbury, her voice flat with sorrow. 'You wasted Mark to prove a negative?'

'This was agreed at top level, Ruth.'

'And is Philippa available this weekend?'

'DG's on a bilateral in France.'

'Yes, I already tried her in Paris.'

'Antibes, actually,' said Devereux. 'Back tonight.'

Horbury muttered something inaudible as she returned to the agenda.

With every painful exchange, Kerr had watched Lisa Jordan's face grow more flushed, either from anger or dismay. When her turn came for the Northern Ireland Office assessment, she pushed her glasses up against her tortoiseshell hairband, revealing a deeply furrowed brow. 'Our reaction to all this, Ruth? God, where do I start? You'll know about last night's shooting spree, a Loyalist gang invading a fish and chip shop in the Ardoyne. Five Catholics murdered. We're bracing for a bunch of tit for tat killings spiralling out of control, just when we dared to think those days had gone. Unless we resolve London quickly, expect firebombings, shootings, marches and general rampaging.'

With fifteen years at the Northern Ireland Office, Lisa Jordan was a seasoned political operator in a crowded field, a pragmatist under no illusions about her homeland. As an A level student at Belfast's Freshland High, she had rhapsodised about peace as a shrub with infinite possibilities, until a professional life grappling with the legacy of sectarian war took its toll. Early release of killers, comfort to terrorists and denial of justice to victims; rows over law and order, parades and flying the Union Jack: all had toughened her. With hope tempered by experience, a cactus was the only desk plant she tended these days.

'It comes down to this. If we prove that extreme nationalist elements are responsible, unionists will pull back from power-sharing. But they'll walk even if there's reasonable doubt. People have seen the devastation on TV and drawn their own conclusions. They *believe* the Real IRA have just bombed London. And as soon as the secret code words leak, all bets are off. Politically, we've slipped back a lifetime in just six days.'

'So how do we stop the rot, Lisa?'

'We're getting an avalanche of denials from Stormont and the police, but that won't cut it. Ambiguity abhors a vacuum in Northern Ireland, so we need crystal clarity from London. A rebuttal to match Stormont's, removing any scintilla of doubt. And after the uncertainty around Brexit, any whiff of anti-republican bias from Westminster will create a firestorm. I'd say we have a week to get this sorted.'

Home Office was next on the agenda, but Ritchie's hand was in the air. 'Bill?' said Horbury regarding him over her spectacles.

'Lisa is spot on about urgency. May help if I dive in here?'

'Of course.'

'To be absolutely clear, we believe these bombings are *not* dissident republican.' Across the table, Kerr watched the Bull shift in his chair. 'The IRA always claims its attacks. A mainland campaign is a massive propaganda coup, so why not own it? I think Government should be declaring that, in the LTTs.' Horbury was already scribbling. 'Second, nothing stacks up. Our counterparts across the water tell me the dissidents are incapable of mounting a campaign in London. I know the IRA, Ruth, and this doesn't feel right.'

'Twaddle,' interrupted Finch.

'Not a word we recognise, Mr Finch,' said Horbury.

'My people have just recovered fragments from a Memopark timer. Used routinely by the IRA.'

'During the seventies, Derek,' said Ritchie calmly, 'but not this version. Memoparks are made in Zurich, which draws us to

Europe. Same with the Semtex. We have to look east, not west, to resolve this.'

'Any specifics?' said Horbury.

'Yes. We've been working flat out with our intelligence liaison experts across Europe. The London targets are all financial institutions and our profiling suggests this is anti-capitalist extremism. We believe one group in particular satisfies the capability test.'

'Toby?' said Horbury, sharply, but Devereux was polishing again.

'We'll be developing this with MI5, naturally,' said Ritchie.

Finch's voice rose in another breach of protocol. 'And why am I hearing about this for the first time now?'

'Because it's happening now.' said Ritchie. 'Our agent was partially right today and I think we can crack this.'

'On what balance of probabilities?' said Horbury. 'Scale of one to ten?'

'I'm looking for certainty.'

'Proof positive,' said Kerr, unable to restrain himself.

•••

The Bull charged from the meeting early, making 'ring me at once' gestures across the room. Forty minutes later, Kerr and Ritchie were already outside by the time an angry Devereux caught up with them.

'Working through us? Since when? We have the lead here, in case you've forgotten.'

Ritchie stayed in the lee of the building, his voice low. 'Toby, does the name Gina Costello mean anything to you?'

'Why do you want to know?'

'Because we've sponsored her three times at our surveillance tasking meetings and keep getting turned down.'

'Who by?'

'A4, who else? Willie Duncan says it's down to you. You know, Anti-Capitalist Insurrection? Costello's a leading player.'

'Possibly,' he said, slipping behind his 'need to know' mask.

'And John just discovered something extremely interesting. Did you know one of the chiefs at Dolphin and Drew Bank was Costello's stepfather? She hates him, apparently.'

Devereux studied his watch, which might have been a diversion or fear of missing his train. 'We should diarise a meeting,' he mumbled, making Kerr wince.

'How about now?' said Ritchie, nodding to the blue Audi A6 waiting in the bus lane.

Devereux shook his head. 'I have to get to Paddington and call Philippa.'

'So I'll tell Donna to expect you Monday,' he called, as Devereux darted away.

Kerr stood for a moment, watching him cross Whitehall. 'Now that's a man running for cover.'

'Maybe,' said Ritchie, returning Lisa Jordan's wave as she hurried down the steps with her wheelie bag. 'Let's see if Lisa needs a lift to London City.'

Chapter Thirty-Two

Sunday, 16 October, 10.07, Vanessa Gavron's Apartment, City of London

Two decades of exclusives had brought Vanessa Gavron admiration, professional envy and the occasional death threat. Her reputation and unique access had generated a series of luxury cars, business class travel and a City condominium with bespoke Poggenpohl kitchen, mood lighting and a gym facing the river.

Wrapping her hair in a turban, she stepped from the shower, reached for a fluffy white bath robe and brushed her teeth for a full three minutes to clear the aftertaste of last night's whiskey. She padded barefoot into the living room and searched the cluttered table for the TV remote and an e-cigarette, still missing her Rothmans after almost a year. On the concave screen the meteorologist was describing a weather system building from the south-east, so she lingered by the picture window, watching the clouds advance from Kent in real time.

Through a gap in the buildings she could see the rise of Southwark Bridge, still dotted with figures in white forensic suits. Because Gavron travelled relentlessly, she loved spending a moment here at the start of every day in London, gazing at the Shard and the Gherkin, relishing the permanence of Shakespeare's Globe Theatre across the river.

Gavron flicked through the channels in search of the Home Secretary. Andrew Marr had already signed off on BBC1 and Sky was following another shooting rampage in the States. Avril Knight's interview was shown for 10.40 in the running order, after the Sunday papers review. She flicked to BBC24 as she collected the whiskey glasses, then wandered into the open plan kitchen and inserted a capsule into the Dolce Gusto coffee machine.

Knight's scolding rhetoric caught up with her by the toaster, with an admonition that she was 'not going to speculate.' Gavron turned up the volume and perched on a bar stool. 'The police have a job to do and we must wait for their investigation. If these attacks are connected – and I'm obviously not going to be drawn on that – then we have entered a dangerous new era, as menacing as the threat from Islamist extremism.'

'So you don't believe Islamist jihadis are responsible?'

'I'm not saying that, either.' In a navy trouser suit, hair styled into a tight auburn bun, Knight reddened as the hack sifted the papers strewn on the table between them.

'So who, then? A lot of the headlines are carrying the same message,' he persisted, holding up broadsheets and a couple of tabloids for the camera. *'Over Thirty Dead: The Real IRA Just Came Back.' 'Loyalist Gun Rampage in Retaliation for IRA Attacks on Capital.' 'Mortar over London: They Never Went Away.' 'Stormont in Meltdown as the IRA Returns to the Mainland.'* 'These will resonate with voters who remember the IRA bombings on the mainland decades ago, won't they? Are you saying they're all wrong?'

'I'm saying it's not helpful for the media or politicians to try and do the police's job for them. As Home Secretary I have to be open to every possibility. Of course I do. That's why I shall be making a statement in the House tomorrow. We are in this together. *All* of us. Look at Belfast now, then remember how it used to be. Nothing must be allowed to jeopardise that.'

'Especially an attack on London by republican dissidents?'

'Look, no-one is under any illusion about the difficulties here. A just and lasting peace comes at a price. These cold-blooded murderers must be brought to justice, whoever they are. But that is for Derek Finch and his team to determine. We have to wait for the evidence.'

Gavron gave a little shake of the head as the presenter moved on and the toast popped up. She had waylaid Avril Knight twice, in London and Belfast, and still felt the sting of rebuke in every answer, even to questions she had not asked. As a newly elected MP to the Northern Ireland Affairs Committee, Knight had discredited IRA promises on decommissioning and denounced the Good Friday Agreement; these days, she picked at the scab of devolved powers, unsolved murders and concessions to convicted terrorists.

As she buttered the toast and poured the coffee, Gavron allowed herself a wry smile. She had just witnessed a classic 'nudge and a wink' denial, an IRA stitch-up to rival Iraq and the 'dodgy dossier.' 'Christ, Avril,' she murmured, putting the e-cig to her lips, 'might as well have tossed a balaclava onto the table.'

Gavron had to be in Haringey by noon. She checked the sound recorder in her tote bag and dressed quickly in a blue striped cotton shirt with denim jacket, skinny jeans and Skechers, applying minimal make-up, just moisturiser and a dab of lipstick. On the way out she checked the spare bedroom, a fug of dog breath and stinky feet that reminded Gavron of her brother's bedroom in their Galway cottage. Donal Quinn was fast asleep, knocked out by Jamesons and jet lag, strands of hair sticking to his glistening forehead. Disturbed in the early hours, she had crept in to find him shouting at someone and thrashing in the bed. He was mumbling now as Gavron picked his Yankees shirt and jeans from the floor, so she paused to stroke his head, sensing his whole body relax beneath her. When he was quiet she left the room and scribbled him a note in the kitchen before grabbing her camera and taking the lift to the underground car park.

Many of the streets around the City were still closed following the bombings, so she drove to Aldgate before swinging north up the Commercial Road. The capital seemed to be having a lie-in except for a few joggers, dog walkers and immaculate ladies in wide hats on their way from church.

She found herself in Ducketts Road earlier than anticipated, lowering the window to check for signs of life from the presbytery as she cruised past. This time she continued to the junction, turned right into Green Lanes and parked outside Seventh Heaven acupuncture clinic, her white Saab hidden among the parishioners' hatchbacks. She calculated she could reach the church entrance in about seven seconds at a racing walk, and saw that one of the double oak doors had been left ajar.

Gavron had deliberately chosen the eleven o'clock Mass for families and young people, 'God's Hope for the World,' according to the blurb on St Jude's website. Music floated beneath the drone of a distant leaf blower, uncertain voices trailing the organ's wheeze, and Gavron recognised the third verse of 'Come Down O Love Divine.' She hummed the refrain, aimed her Nikon D3200 and fired a couple of test shots.

After a stretch of silence the service ended with a fortissimo organ voluntary that blew both doors open and rolled across the street. Father Michael was first to appear, in full ecclesiastical rig, sausage fingers linked above the lace embroidery of his surplice, body perfectly still, red face benign. *Satan dressed as the fucking Man of God*, Donal had said, his young body still trapped in a nightmare sweat after all these years. Now it was Gavron's turn to capture the shepherd as he lay in wait for his flock, evidently oblivious to the gentle snap of the Nikon across the street.

It took several minutes for the church to empty, with the congregation filing out in a steady line and everyone wanting a piece of Father Michael. In return, he spared each of them a precious, beaming moment, blessing infants, chucking their siblings under the chin and back-slapping some of the dads. The families dispersed quickly, leaving a gaggle of teens that soon reduced to a core of seven, four boys and three girls, as their priest demoted himself from reverend Father to worldly uncle. Gavron watched the arm encircle young shoulders, the hand touching and squeezing, the stooping, in-your-face smile, with laughter spilling across the street and everything caught on the Nikon's video.

Father Michael's behaviour was the blend of solicitude, blarney and showbiz that Gavron had seen in so many abusive priests. He was still playing the Vatican's favoured son, tactile but untouchable, and his recklessness left her stunned. She replayed her video, a groomer's masterclass in ninety seconds, and thought of the survivor in her spare room.

A grey-faced woman in black suddenly appeared at the church door, thin hair stretched beneath a plain hat. Father Michael's housekeeper squeezed sideways through the group, probably scurrying home to prepare his lunch. Head darting like a bird's, she clocked Gavron's white Saab as she drew level across the street and immediately spun back, tugging at the priest's sleeve, leaning into his ear and pointing. Gavron was out of the car before either could react, dodging between a skip lorry and cyclist, holding their eyes. 'Good morning, Father,' she said, checking in her bag for the recorder's green light.

His smile melted into unease before hubris took over. 'As you can see, I'm busy right now,' he said, spreading his palms in a flourish, though they both knew the pastoral gig was over.

'Only take a moment,' said Gavron, camera in hand as she smiled at a couple of his young disciples. 'We can do it right here.'

Father Michael sent the kids away, warning them not to be late on Thursday evening, then led Gavron into the church porch.

'What happens on Thursdays?'

'Instruction in the Catechism,' he said, curtly.

The housekeeper tried to squeeze inside but he dismissed her, too. 'I won't be long, Mary.'

'I should stay, Father,' she said, with a glare.

'Why don't you go back and uncork the Rioja?' said Gavron, looking away to study the service and duty rosters.

'Go on, Mary. I'll be alright.'

'She knows about Belfast, then?' said Gavron, as Father Michael scraped the heavy door shut and flicked on the light.

He turned and squared up to her, his voice intimidating in the cramped space. 'There's nothing to know.'

'About the children's home. The Olive Tree. You didn't ring me back, Father.'

'What the hell are you doing here?'

She held up the camera. 'And I see you haven't stopped the inappropriate touching.'

'Don't give me that Channel Four guff.'

'Do you still get a stiffy from ministering to the young?'

'You're disgusting.'

'No, I'm sickened. Donal has told me everything you did to him.'

The priest's derisive laugh echoed off the stone walls. 'The word of one ungrateful, sinful boy? You've got to be kidding me. Priests get this shit all the time.' Gavron saw that belligerence had displaced Wednesday's shock, his eyes glimmering with relief that young Donny, immature, confused and troubled, was her only weapon. The door grated again as Father Michael tugged at the iron ring and a sliver of daylight found his surplice. 'Go to hell. Fuck off out of my church.'

'I know where you sent them.'

The door was suddenly still. 'What?'

'The other boys from the Olive Tree. I know the place where you took them in the black taxis every week. I have the lot, Father.'

The priest's mouth gaped but no sound came as the colour drained from his cheeks. 'What is this?' he muttered finally, Adam's apple wobbling against his dog collar.

'The road and the number of the house. I've checked everything. The names of the rapists you delivered them to. I recognise all their faces. Well known, weren't they, in that closed world, and threatened to kill the boys if anyone breathed a word. That's why no-one ever came forward, isn't it, Father?'

'Every word a filthy lie.' He had found his voice, but Gavron could almost hear the bombast deflating. 'All garbage.'

'It's a scandal that's going to rock Stormont and put you in jail.'

'If you had a shred of proof you'd have gone to the police.'

'Like I said, I'm giving you the chance to give me your story first.'

'There is no fucking story,' he said. 'I've told you.'

'You think I'm bluffing?' said Gavron, incredulous.

'And even if there was, it's in the past, like the IRA. Lies from damaged kids about things dead and buried. You can't write about any of this.'

Gavron shrugged and eased round him. 'Suit yourself.'

'No. I have…can give you something better,' he said, the words almost lost. 'About the present.'

'You what?'

'The bombs.'

'Go on.'

'I want to stop this,' he murmured.

'Tell me.'

'Things I heard about…who is doing these wicked things.'

'Heard when?'

'Secrets I am forbidden to repeat.'

'*When?*'

'Friday.'

'Secrets,' repeated Gavron, tracing a finger down the church roster. 'Confession, Friday afternoon? You're saying someone *confessed* to you?'

'It's more complicated,' said the priest, jowls shaking. 'He was in distress. Look, I can't do this here, not in church. You have to give me space.'

'You know I'm recording every word, don't you?'

'Yes, I assumed…I will call you. I just need another day, to reflect and to pray.'

'Alright, Father, make your peace with God,' said Gavron, regarding him shrewdly. 'Then unburden yourself to me.'

Chapter Thirty-Three

Monday, 17 October, 06.32, Bayswater

Naked beneath the satin sheets, limbs entwined, the lovers embraced and kissed deeply, oblivious to the alarm clock coming out of snooze mode. On Friday and Saturday nights the Home Secretary slept with her husband at their constituency home in Sussex, but Sundays belonged to Benita.

Avril Knight pressed the button and checked the time: less than an hour to get ready. She dragged herself from the bed, walked round to Benita's side and peeked through a gap in the curtains, looking for her official car. The overnight rain had faded to a drizzle, glistening on the copper beech tree in the tiny front garden. It was still dark, the raindrops orange in the distant street light, and the only Toyota Prius in the narrow cul-de-sac belonged to Benita's neighbour. At the start of her affair the car had turned up very early, but now she forbade her security team to arrive before seven-thirty. Knight felt a pulse of gratitude for the extra moments of privacy as she felt Benita's hand gently take hers, tugging her back to bed. Squeezing her fingers, she bent to kiss her lips and tiptoed for the bathroom.

Knight had been driven by political ambition since attaining a First in PPE at Oxford, followed by her shoo-in as a special adviser at Westminster. After a lifetime's plotting and manoeuvring she had scaled the pinnacle, one of the four great Offices of State, just as this stronger passion engulfed her. The two women had been introduced at a diplomatic drinks party before the summer recess, where Benita was seeking British government support for her Anglo-Spanish cultural endowment. Knight had found pretexts to see her again, first for a post-Referendum Home Office meeting including officials, then dinner for two at a discreet tapas restaurant in Notting Hill, with her protection officers ordered to wait in the car.

It was their first and only public outing. The Home Secretary's London home was a heavily alarmed apartment in Pimlico, close to Dolphin Square, but she soon came to cherish every hour at Benita's eclectic, cluttered flat on the top floor of a villa behind Portobello Road market. A professional artist thirteen years younger than Knight, Benita worked from home in the bright, airy studio she had converted from the second bedroom. Trained in watercolour landscapes, these days she used oils in primary colours and her hands instead of brushes, creating a dynamic, swirling style the critics loved. To Avril Knight, she was a tangle of paradoxes, the messy, earthy peasant in the studio, then elegant and quiet as they relaxed with red wine and planned their future together.

During these stolen hours they would talk constantly, exploring anything but politics. Benita had scarcely mentioned the bombings or Knight's TV appearances, not because she was heartless, but to give her lover a break. 'The sun still shines over her abundant earth,' Benita would say, whenever things looked bleak, and Knight found her optimistic love of life and indifference to Westminster's intrigues utterly liberating.

Knight had two sons, lawyer clones of their father she scarcely knew in a conventional family unit that appealed to the party chiefs and voters. For the woman with high ambition, an uncomplicated personal life was the whips' Rule Number One. Over two decades she had assiduously built her image, only for it to collapse beneath love at first sight.

Her professional life was a churn of secrets and risk. Weighing the odds of her own political survival, she placed adultery a long way beneath same-sex prejudice, which made privacy essential. She confided in no-one from her private office, and had been brutally intransigent with her security detail.

On Sunday afternoons, the protection team would collect Knight from the family home in West Sussex and drive her to London. For her first sleepover she had waited until they were halfway up the A3, then looked up from her red box and abruptly diverted them to Benita's address, with the order to collect her in the morning. 'Rejig the satnav or find another assignment,' she had snapped when the team leader remonstrated about security checks. Her attitude came as no surprise. Secretaries of State endured 24/7 protection through friendly co-operation or grumpy intolerance, and Knight had been bloody-minded from day one.

'And you don't tell a soul,' she had said, stepping from the car with her overnight bag.

•••

Monday, 17 October, 06.59, Portobello Community Garden

Directly across the street from Benita's flat was a narrow patch of open land between two terraces, fronted by a mesh wire fence staggered to deter cyclists. A pitted asphalt path disappeared through an arch of overgrown trees into a wild plot half the size of a football pitch, screened on all sides by oaks, limes and *leylandii*. A sign in faded green italics said 'Welcome to Portobello Community Garden,' with an outdated 0171 phone number for 'Jenno, Project Co-ordinator.'

Permanently shrouded from the sun, the garden smelt dank, with tracts of moss encroaching everywhere. A maze of red block footways led Fin through a jungle of willows, firs and holly, forcing him to stoop low as he searched for potential witnesses. The overgrown paths meandered beside uncultivated vegetable patches, tiled mosaic abstracts and an ancient brick barbecue, its grill rust red. Here and there smooth burrows had been moulded into the undergrowth by rough sleepers, every pitch marked by a crumpled tin of Strong Brew or empty vodka bottle, and all abandoned during the night's downpour. A rustic bench faced a choked pond and a copper sculpture of a heron with a fish in its bill.

Bobby Roscoe was waiting by the garden's shed, hands cupping his face as he peered through the mouldy glass window. The padlock on the rickety door gave easily under Fin's chisel. It was damp inside, with the rotting timber floor holed in several places. A workbench stood against the far wall beneath a blanket of cobwebs, peppered with corpses and sagging from the roof like a hammock. The only other contents were a plastic bucket, a rusting hoe and a fork with a shattered handle. There were no signs of occupation, the shed too decrepit even for the neighbourhood's homeless.

Hoods raised against the dripping roof, they hid and waited, neither saying a word as they checked their weapons. Kenny should have been there, too, but had injured his leg in the motorcycle crash during the getaway from Southwark. Shattered and fearful when they finally made it to the safe house after their narrow escape, Roscoe had shown only cold anger, as if Kenny had screwed up. Late on Saturday night Fin and Roscoe had almost come to blows again; now, minutes away from another risky attack, their mutual resentment was palpable.

Seven minutes passed before Roscoe's mobile vibrated twice, then cut out. Roscoe heaved the door open. 'Let's go,' he ordered, stepping back into the rain.

•••

Monday, 17 October, 07.11, Bayswater

Knight had her shower while a sleepy Benita prepared breakfast of espresso, churros and tostadas. Sitting in Benita's bathrobe at the tiny kitchen table she tried some new Spanish phrases, waiting for her lover to chide her again. 'Still so posh and touristy,' she laughed, cupping Knight's face, a thumb across her lips. 'You must stay with me always and I will teach you everything.'

Knight's phone rang twice as she hurriedly applied her make-up, followed by the agreed signal at the door, a single ring followed by a double knock. The car was early again, and Knight felt the familiar sadness as they embraced at the top of the stairs. With Benita in her life it was not political oblivion that unnerved her, but a dread that their romance would fall into the same black hole.

Monday, 17 October, 07.13, Bayswater

From her regular TV appearances, Fin had all he needed to know about Avril Knight's height, weight and build. The front door had two stained glass panels and he could see her coming down the last few stairs. She flung the door open so sharply that the heavy black knocker gave a double thud. In the hallway's gloom she looked taller but slighter, her eyes immediately wide with shock at the two hooded strangers. Fin took stock of the black heels and pleated cream skirt beneath a belted navy raincoat. Easily manageable.

'Oh God.' Knight's face turned to fear as Roscoe's Glock levelled with her face.

'You're to come with us,' said Roscoe, quietly, making it sound like an invitation, as Fin grabbed the raincoat and dragged her over the threshold. Knight's voice returned as Roscoe snatched away her bag, so he rammed the gun beneath her chin. 'And shut the fuck up.' From the cover of the beech tree they checked the street, then hurried her across the road, one at each arm, Fin's gun concealed against her waist.

By the time they reached the cover of the garden her voice had sunk to a groan, a plea to be saved from her fatal error. Fin wanted to say something back but was under orders to stay silent. They sat her on the bench by the pond while Roscoe taped her mouth and hooded her. Further along the path she twisted her ankle, then lost a shoe as she blundered through the drenched foliage. By the end, her upper body was soaked, the white cotton hood sticking to her face.

A section of floor gave way as they pulled her inside the shed, igniting a final spark of resistance. She thrashed about as they lifted her onto the bench, groaning and tossing her head from side to side. Roscoe lent on her shoulders while Fin ripped the belt from her coat and used it to bind her legs. She tried to say something as Roscoe took the hoe and pressed it against her throat until she was perfectly still. Then Fin aimed his weapon, waited for Roscoe's nod, and fired a single shot through the side of her skull.

Diluted blood was radiating through the hood as Fin took a folded length of cardboard from his coat and placed it on her chest. TRAITOR, it said, in bold computer print. Then he used the hoe to hack at the cobwebs until they collapsed across Knight's body, hiding her beneath a second skin, a dead spider curled over her mouth.

The exit to the garden was an arched brick tunnel leading to a maze of side streets, only a brisk four minute walk from Ladbroke Grove tube station. 'Thanks For Visiting!' said another sign on the wall. 'Come Again Soon!'

Chapter Thirty-Four

Monday, 17 October, 08.03, Room 807, New Scotland Yard

'So it's alright for undercover officers to have sex with activists? In your professional opinion?'

'Not at all.' Kerr took a deep breath, choosing his words with care. 'I'm saying a false friendship can evolve into a true relationship.'

'Intimacy, yes. And you're implying that's a *virtue*?'

Paula Weatherall, former boss to Ritchie and Kerr in the SO15 Intelligence Unit, now carried even more braid as deputy assistant commissioner and 'Director of Equality and Diversity, People Development and Local Engagement Programmes,' according to her updated résumé. She wore her hair piled in a bun, speared by a tortoiseshell clip that seemed to aim at Kerr's heart whenever she turned her head.

'The operative may fall in love,' said Kerr. 'It's a reality. A risk of long-term undercover work.'

Weatherall's eyes widened. 'And that's your excuse?'

'No. An explanation.'

Fifteen minutes into his promotion board for detective superintendent, Kerr's prospects were sinking fast as his three interrogators fidgeted behind a row of metal tables, their backs to the windows. Someone had raised the blinds, and the early daylight threw their faces into shadow. The evening before, Nancy had switched off *House of Cards* to help him research the Total Policing online blurb for any last minute eye-catching initiatives. Just before ten Melanie had called, still anxious about Dodge, but Kerr had cut her short to take an incoming from Bill Ritchie. The boss had made his own enquiries about the interview panel and was ringing to wish him luck. 'Watch out for the torpedo attack,' he had warned, ominously.

To Kerr's left was a uniformed commander, a bulked up gym

fanatic with a buzz cut and hairless forearms nick-named Steroids. He covered 'Well-Being and Performance Betterment,' and had a serious man-spreading problem, his left thigh constantly encroaching against Weatherall's. To her other side was a thirtyish civilian with old acne scars, chewed fingernails and tinted glasses whom Kerr had never set eyes on before. He introduced himself as 'Assistant-Director of Business Continuity slash Compliance and Risk,' a title that required three lines on his name badge. 'But everyone calls me Bizcon,' he said, amiably.

The interview had started promptly at 07.45, with Kerr the opening bat in a field of seven, and they had already sought his views on police station closures, efficiency savings and the perils of stop and search. Kerr's rare encounters with policy nerds always had a dusting of make-believe as they sailed through a blue sky of stats, trends and impact assessments. The brutal reality of street wars, savage cuts and stalled careers lay far beneath them, dark smudges on the landscape. Despite the tragedies of the past week, the panel had not posed a single question about covert policing, until Weatherall's ambush about illicit sex.

'A licence for deceit,' she said, inching away from Steroids. 'How dreadfully cynical.'

'The macho side of intelligence work,' said Steroids with a sneer.

'Both wrong.' Kerr took another deep breath, mentally erasing the 'with respect' preface. 'But grasping undercover work is difficult territory for senior officers who have never been there.'

Kerr had ignored the warning about switching off mobiles and, in his breast pocket, the BlackBerry started vibrating. He felt them all staring, as if challenging him to answer it.

'Sorry,' he murmured, lifting his palm to cover the noise.

Steroids was about to say something but Weatherall checked him, then paused to look at Kerr over her glasses. 'And you have, haven't you?' she said. '*Been there?*'

Each panel member had a copy of Kerr's service record and

application, but Weatherall suddenly produced an original pair of pale yellow A4 sheets with the Home Office logo, a rabbit out of the hat. Kerr immediately recognised the summary of his annual security interview, known as the DVR, the 'developed vetting refresher.' DV status gave access to classified material; for an intelligence officer, its withdrawal was game over.

'You were an undercover operative, weren't you?'

'I don't think that's relevant…'

'…and you had a…you duped an activist into having an intimate relationship with you…'

'This is a personal thing,' said Kerr, sitting forward in his chair, Ritchie's tip-off ringing in his ears.

'…and she gave birth to a daughter.'

'Not for discussion here.'

'Really?' said Weatherall, covering the papers with her hand. 'And what does that tell us about transparency? Your personal integrity? You deceived this woman, yet now you invite us to promote you.'

Kerr looked to the others, but they were fiddling with their notes, avoiding him. 'Actually, I don't think Robyn has ever regarded herself as a victim.'

Weatherall was giving him the look again. 'But I take it you regret what you did to her?'

Kerr shook his head. 'We're very proud of our daughter. Her name is Gabrielle, by the way, and the three of us speak all the time. Robyn is a highly respected human rights campaigner, just back from a tough assignment in Belfast. For what it's worth, we think the Hammersmith car bomb may have been targeted against her.'

'That's awful,' said Bizcon, making Robyn's brush with death sound like a compliance failure. 'But in terms of personal morality, professional ethics, probity, whatever, you accept that you are compromised, right?'

Through the window an airliner crossed Kerr's line of vision, descending on its final approach into Heathrow. He sat back, crossed his legs and looked between them. 'I think you should move on from this line of questioning. We all know it's completely inappropriate,' he said, just as the mobile came back to life.

Steroids was glaring again. 'You want to turn that thing off?'

'It's alright,' said Weatherall, clearing her throat. 'Mr Kerr, this is a competitive process, with a number of highly experienced candidates. You've served many years in the Special Branch arena. Useful work, some of it, but we've moved on. Intelligence is MI5's remit now.'

'And you're saying that's an improvement?'

She closed the file, sending Kerr another pulse of alarm. 'I think we should pause to take stock. A moment while I consult.' The hairclip skewered him again as she looked to each side, drawing them into a *University Challenge* huddle. Kerr used the time to check his BlackBerry. There was a repeat text from Alan Fargo: 'prot msg hs missing call in urgent.'

'I'm going to propose an interim measure we can review in, say, twelve months,' said Weatherall, sounding almost apologetic. 'You seem to us a classic candidate for SkillShare.'

Kerr heard the whoosh of the torpedo. Bomb gone. Derided in the Twittersphere as #ShoeHorn, Weatherall's signature programme was a rehashed system for uprooting specialists for dispersal around the Met. Already discredited, its most recent high profile victim was Detective Inspector Kirsty Jakes, mother of three and one of the Met's finest homicide investigators. A friend of Melanie, she had been transferred overnight to co-ordinate Neighbourhood Watch, then sacked because of a mildly satirical post on her Facebook page.

Kerr could tell that Weatherall had just been confirming, not taking counsel, and his future had been stitched up even before the introductions. She managed a smile. 'That alright with you?'

'Why would a mathematician want to teach geography? Check

the blogs. Everyone knows it's counter-productive.' The mobile was tickling Kerr's palm. 'I need to check this.'

'We're not done here,' snapped Steroids, looking angry enough to leap over the table. 'Show the chair some respect.'

Kerr ignored him. This time Fargo had sent an email, backed by a text to call in immediately. Kerr scanned the gist, then studied the detail. He faced them again. 'I'm sorry,' he said, expressionless. 'What more is there to say?'

'You'll know we've been advertising for professionals from other walks of life to join us,' said Steroids.

'Direct entry superintendents, yes. Fast food retail to crack house bust in a week. I thought that fantasy had been quietly dropped?'

'I'm looking for leaders who can bring freshness to the Service, a business-oriented perspective. Why should we select you over one of them?'

'Why not?' said Kerr.

'The Home Secretary wants an entirely new approach,' said Weatherall.

'Not any more,' said Kerr flatly, holding up his BlackBerry. 'Someone just executed Avril Knight with a single shot to the head. The protection team found her body in a garden shed in west London. We believe it's linked to the bombing campaign, so I have to leave right now.' He stood and buttoned his jacket. 'Unless you want to send one of your takeaway stars?'

Chapter Thirty-Five

Monday, 17 October, 11.17, Holyhead Ferry Terminal, Isle of Anglesey

Gina Costello suspected they were being followed within minutes of clanking off the ferry at Holyhead on the Isle of Anglesey, just after her boyfriend had mock saluted the freshly painted Croeso y Gymru sign, 'Welcome to Wales.'

To hide beneath the security radar, Costello had taken her usual circuitous route from Amsterdam to London: a cheap Aer Lingus flight from Schiphol into Dublin, a drop by her mother's seaside home in Killiney to collect the British registered car, and then by sea to Holyhead. Because of an engine fault, the ferry had been over two hours late leaving Dublin. Traipsing below deck as they bumped against the dock, Costello had felt a weary frustration as the articulated lorries disembarked in a noisy procession of late deliveries, missed pick-ups and bad-tempered calls to depots on the English mainland. Though tired, she was absolutely certain that the ship's assortment of cars, towed caravans and motorcycles had not included the brown Volvo estate and silver Honda Accord that drifted into her vision as she crossed the railway bridge and joined the A55 Expressway.

Costello rarely tested her ageing maroon Fiat Uno above sixty-five these days, and the traffic soon dispersed ahead of her like mist. But these two cars stayed with her, the Honda in front, the estate holding back behind a Dutch container lorry. There seemed to be a third player, too, a motorcyclist who joined from the old Holyhead Road, both rider and Suzuki featureless in black, speeding away only to reappear on the slip road from Llangefni.

'What do you think, Jay?' she said, stroking her boyfriend's thigh.

They had reached a raised stretch of road and Jay was looking across the Menai Strait towards Snowdonia. It was a beautiful autumn day, with rain not expected until late evening, and the distant mountain range was a rich texture of deep shadowed valleys beneath snow-capped peaks.

'Absolutely bloody beautiful.'

Costello flipped his visor for the vanity mirror. 'Shit coloured Volvo behind the truck with the foreign plates.'

Jay peered into the tiny glass for a second, then swung round to check through the rear window. 'And?'

Her finger flicked up from the steering wheel. 'Silver Accord up ahead. Two on board and I'm pretty sure they weren't on the ferry.'

'Isn't it a bit old hat now, following that close?' he said, returning to the mountains. 'I thought Plod uses trackers these days.'

'That's his third pass,' she said as the motorcycle flashed by, doing seventy plus. 'Fucking police state.'

He tugged at her shirt. 'Or Gina being paranoid.'

'Fuck off, you,' she said, pinching his leg.

Jay pointed at the next exit sign. 'So let's find out.'

Costello pulled off at the village of Llanfair PG, a truncation of Europe's longest place name. Abbreviated out of pity to signwriters and the English, its full fifty-eight characters stretched the length of the platform at the train station. Checking her mirrors, she turned off the high street and bumped over the railway crossing beside the signal box, enhanced by neat flower beds and window boxes. She continued down the single track lane away from the village and stopped at the first passing place while they wound down the windows and listened. Silence, except for cows and birdsong.

Deeply pitted and bordered by tall hedgerows, the lane was evidently intended for local drivers who conceded nothing to oncoming strangers, and Costello had to give way twice before reaching the Farmers Arms, a pub so old and sunken it seemed to have emerged from the undergrowth. The lane continued across a stone bridge before swinging left to rejoin the main road but

Costello pulled into the muddy car park packed with spattered flatbeds, pick-ups and quad bikes.

The clock above the door showed ten minutes before noon but farmers were already crowding the bar with pints and crisps, everyone speaking Welsh. The men stooped beneath the blackened oak beams, taller and bulkier than their nineteenth century ancestors, and fell silent to register the two foreigners. Costello ordered pints of lager and led Jay through a low arch into the stone flagged snug.

They sat beside a trestle table loaded with coffee mugs over a scattering of leaflets (Gas From Shale? No Sale!) and Costello realised they must have arrived at the end of a protest meeting. The snug was empty except for an elderly woman in comfortable trainers and a yellow sweater with an embroidered red dragon breathing the words 'Frack Off!' The campaign organiser, guessed Costello, waiting for her lift home. Sipping cider, she peered through lopsided glasses at *The Times*, marked in newsagent's pencil with the name 'Rhiannon.' The completed crossword lay abandoned on the floor with a Sudoku book. 'Are you press?' she enquired in English, stooping to toss a couple of logs into the grate.

Jay finished his drink in four or five gulps, just as the Volvo appeared from the other end of the lane. It crossed the bridge, visor down, and continued slowly past the pub. A couple of minutes later they saw the Honda lurch into the car park from the narrow lane they had just driven, squeezing into the only remaining space beside the stream.

Then the pub fell quiet again apart from the crackling of the logs as a skinny Asian man in his late twenties eased a path to the bar. A stocky white woman in jeans and T-shirt followed him, an ex-military type with the smudge of a tattoo on her forearm. She leaned in to order two Diet Cokes, slice, no ice, then hovered with her partner outside the snug as the hubbub revived around them. They stood sideways to each other and drank without relish, looking nowhere while the locals stared at them, the world's most unlikely lovers a long way from home.

'No way are those two legit,' said Costello, drinking up. 'Let's go.'

The Expressway took them across the Britannia Bridge, then raced towards Chester. To flush out her followers Costello chose the old A5, the original historic route through the mountains, with sharp bends, fierce climbs and plenty of stopping places. Traffic here was light and they pulled in to goof around with selfies, Jay pretending to support the mountain with one hand, Costello working through her ironic sex worker routine. The Honda cruised past as they loitered by a lake, and they found the motorcycle at a lay-by three miles further down the road. To their right, a ribbon of water traced the bottom of a glacial valley dotted with farmhouses, then they were driving beneath a slope of scree and rocks, an avalanche waiting to happen. Nearing the high point, Costello suddenly swerved onto a stony track that disappeared behind a screen of bushes. She switched off the engine, ramped back her seat and smiled at him.

Jay peered up at a towering mass of smooth grey slate, slickened by mountain springwater. 'Here?'

'Why not?' she said, untucking his T-shirt and sliding her hand down his belly. 'You frightened of the sheep?'

Up ahead, a farm gate had been hooked open. 'What if he comes back?'

'He'll wait.' Through a gap in the bushes she registered a flash of brown as the Volvo cruised past on the main drag. Jay was already hard as she unzipped his fly and released him. Wriggling out of her jeans and pants, she slithered into his space. 'Let's give them something to talk about.'

There was no hesitation. In the middle of the night, tipsy and bored by the ferry's delay, they had managed to sneak below deck for sex in the car, and knew the logistics of penetration in a Fiat Uno. Jay reclined his seat, shuffled down and arched his hips as Costello unbuttoned her shirt and lowered herself onto him. From the main road came the throb of a passing motor cycle, then Costello caught the glint of a distant camera lens through the offside window, and the Englishwoman from the pub, perched on a drystone wall thirty paces below them.

Towards the end Costello's head kept banging against the swaying roof. 'Alright?' mumbled Jay as she squirmed to wedge her left knee against the gear stick. 'No, it's beautiful,' she said, accelerating the rhythm again. 'Awesome, absolutely fucking awesome,' she laughed as his mouth found her breast, and even managed a smile for the camera.

•••

Monday, 17 October, 12.48, The Fishbowl

Despite the heavy maintenance payments and high rent, Karl Sergeyev appeared to be wearing another new suit, a light grey two piece with faint red stripe. Elegant and coolly handsome in a crisp white shirt and powder blue tie, Nancy's former husband paused by the open door waiting for Kerr to wave him in, respectful as ever. For years the two Special Branch men had counted each other as friends, and Kerr greeted him warmly as he cleared a pile of books and a DVD from the visitor's chair. Tieless after the morning's eighth floor fiasco, his own jacket hanging from the back of the door, Kerr waited for Sergeyev to adjust his holster before picking an imaginary speck from his trouser leg, like a talk show host playing for time. Or the Foreign Secretary's close protection officer, slumming it in the Fishbowl.

'So how are the kids?' said Karl.

'Fine,' said Kerr. Both were still coming to terms with the reversal in roles. The court had granted Sergeyev regular access to his children but it was Kerr, the substitute dad, who read them *Horrid Henry* most evenings.

Sergeyev shook his head as Kerr held up the coffee pot. 'And Nancy?'

'Everything going well. I'd call you otherwise.'

'Very good, John. Thank you.' Sergeyev looked genuinely relieved. Kerr had hooked up with Nancy several months before her divorce, yet Sergeyev had never openly resented Kerr for taking his place in her bed. In fact, their domestic triangle rarely featured when they bumped into each other, except to ask about the children. Since August Sergeyev had been seeing a Russian model and actress with money and a wine bar in Chelsea, so Kerr guessed he was too distracted for jealousy. For Nancy, victim of his countless extra-marital affairs, it was a bad conscience that kept her ex silent. 'Guilt hangs around Karl like aftershave,' she had insisted to Kerr in the early days of their romance. 'Believe me, John, I can still smell the cologne.'

'Thanks for dropping by,' said Kerr, easing behind his desk. Since the transfer of ministerial protection from Bill Ritchie's intelligence unit, Sergeyev had become his primary source for the secrets, tricks and frailties of the people they safeguarded. With Kerr detained on his promotion board, Alan Fargo had tracked Sergeyev down to the VIP lounge at Heathrow Terminal Five, just arrived from Tehran.

'No problem. I made a few calls, dropped the man at King Charles Street and came straight here.'

'Anything? Such as, you know, how the fuck could they have allowed this to happen?'

Sergeyev gave a shrug. 'Sorry, boss, can't get anywhere near Avril Knight's team.' His stamina was always a source of amazement to Kerr: despite the overnight flight, Karl looked as if he had spent a lazy weekend at the beach. 'Finch has them practically under lock and key, like they're the ones who killed her. Everyone strictly incommunicado. Long story short, we have protection command in meltdown and Number Ten scapegoating like crazy. Losing a principal never looks good, does it? Careless.' He shot Kerr a look of injured professional pride. 'Especially like this. Very stupid.'

'How about Ted?' Kerr often found civilian ministerial drivers to be the most productive sources of all.

The shake of the head again. 'In the frame, with the others.'

'Alright, Karl. Well, thanks for trying,' said Kerr, raising his hand in a telephone mime. 'And, you know, if you manage to pick up anything…'

'Actually, I used to know someone in the private office. Sara, one of the diary secretaries? She remembers you?' he said, waiting for Kerr's nod. 'Anyway, Knight sacked her last month for something totally rubbish…time-keeping, I think. Tell me, John, should someone lose her job for wanting a personal life?'

'And you stayed in touch?'

'She's the person I called from the airport, actually.' Sergeyev smoothed his trouser leg, flashing double cuffs and a Breitling watch with multiple time zones. 'Listen, Avril Knight was absent from her HA because she was seriously over the side.'

'With a woman called Consuela,' said Kerr, glancing at his pad. 'I already have that from Alan. Maria Benita Consuela.'

'It was all round the office, a love job, according to Sara. She was married with two sons but this was definitely your classic suitcase in the hall, leave home scenario.'

Kerr regarded Sergeyev in vain for any hint of embarrassment. He even managed to inject disappointment into his voice, as if Knight's adultery had smashed the mould of cabinet politics.

'I get all that,' said Kerr, 'but since when did we allow principals to wander the streets unprotected?'

'Since the day ministers began to talk about their entitlement to privacy and family life. Human rights, John. Everyone's equal now. Even secretaries of state.'

'Pathetic. Did the team report this back to anyone?'

'Unlikely. Avril Knight was a Rottweiler. She would have vetoed anything official.'

'So they should have got their commander involved. Can you imagine Bill Ritchie letting her get away with this?'

'That's the Branch, John.' Sergeyev shrugged and shifted in his seat, like a man who had to be somewhere else. 'New world now.'

'You're the second person to tell me that today.'

'I'm thinking the team probably dealt with this as a SPEC,' said Sergeyev. 'That's often the way these days.'

'A what?'

'Sensitive Personal Consideration. Basically, it means flexible protection around ministers cheating on their partners.'

'Jesus.'

'Unofficial, of course, but they would have kept everything secret from people outside the loop.'

'Yeah, right,' said Kerr, reaching for the phone. 'Except the people who killed her.' He was already dialling 1830 as Sergeyev paused by the door.

'John, I was wondering…would it help you to have Knight's personal phone records?'

Kerr replaced the phone and looked up in surprise. 'You can do that?'

'They kept a trace of every number. You know, for insurance. Perhaps revenge, also.'

'Who?'

'The people closest to her, of course. Sara. The other young women she bullied and intimidated.'

'That's fantastic.'

'Yes. They belong to the new world, too, don't you think?'

Chapter Thirty-Six

Clearing the mountains, they pressed through a gentler landscape as dark rain clouds chased them from the west, with Costello giving a running commentary about suspicious vehicles and Jay, calm as ever, telling her to relax.

'Who's to say they're even British? The Dutch do a lot of collaborating with the English police. That's what I heard,' she said, eyes flickering between the mirrors. 'Perhaps they flew over, you know, bloody waiting for us. You think they've got guns?'

'For what? They can't show out, so what are they going to do? It's probably the cops updating their files, I dunno, taking a break from jihadis. It happens.'

In fact, to Gina Costello, it did not. This was new. She was expert in the dark arts of intrusive surveillance by Europe's secret states and had long ago sacrificed privacy for direct action. Radicalism extinguished free speech, as Jay and her other comrades in Anti-Capitalist Insurrection were always reminding themselves, shrouding their phone calls, emails and texts with doublespeak and paranoia. For militants living beneath the radar, there was no safe place for social media.

These were the invisible perils of cyberspace and Costello had learned to live with them. Avoiding Facebook was no big deal. But the drive from the ferry terminal had brought something new, the first tangible evidence of physical surveillance, of real people actually following her. She had found it unnerving, then provocative. Sex in the mountains had been an impulse, a retro, hippy protest. The real fight back, what Jay called the 'ultimate revenge strike,' had been conceived while held in a bottleneck at Llangollen, and fully planned by the time they crossed the English border.

Whirring down the slipway onto the M6, Costello could

feel the adrenaline pumping again. 'Whoever they are,' she said, filtering into the nearside lane, 'we're about to seriously piss them off.' She waited for Jay to say something back, but he simply gave her thigh a squeeze and gazed out at the fields.

Costello breathed deeply and scanned the mirrors. The motorcycle and Honda were nowhere to be seen, but she located the Volvo six cars behind. Caught behind a lorry trailing a Wide Load sign, she had her finger on the indicator, impatiently waiting for a gap in the middle lane. 'How can you always be so...so fucking *cool* about everything? These jerks are watching every move we make and it's like you're in the sack with Zen. I mean... how?' she said, losing patience and forcing a way out.

'Because they've got nothing on us,' said Jay quietly, craning his neck to the wing mirror, reminding Costello how much he had already suffered for his zealotry. 'If they did, we'd be in jail.'

Their destination was Corley Services, a Welcome Break facility in Warwickshire with fast food bars, shops and toilets on each carriageway, linked by a covered footbridge. They found a place in the busy car park just as it started to rain. Costello stayed a long way from the entrance, concealing the Fiat between a motorhome and a self-hire Transit, and they sat in silence, ignoring the squeak of the windscreen wipers.

The Honda arrived first, followed by the Volvo and motorcycle together, the only vehicles without lights against the rain and thickening cloud. They memorised their parking places, plotting the number of rows from the Fiat in each direction. In the glove compartment was the six inch Phillips screwdriver Costello had used to repair the engine's water hose on her last visit to Dublin. She laid it next to the cup holder and took Jay's hand. 'Okay?'

They watched the female motorcyclist remove her helmet and walk to the service area, followed by the Honda crew, all of them hurrying through the drizzle with heads lowered. The Volvo driver went last, losing himself among a couple of families in bright summer clothes as the rain suddenly intensified. He was in his late fifties, stocky and grey haired in a North Face waterproof. Easily identifiable. 'Come on,' said Costello as soon as they had disappeared, ramming her door open against the Transit and making herself tall to double-check the Honda.

They strolled into the entrance hall past a bank of slot machines before separating for the toilets. By the time Jay re-emerged, Costello was dawdling by the row of burger bars, checking out the menus beneath a muted TV screen showing the latest on the Home Secretary's murder. The hall was noisy, with clumps of new arrivals escaping the dangerous traffic conditions. As soon as Jay joined her they raced for the footbridge, taking the steps two at a time and jogging across the motorway.

On the other side they disappeared into the toilets again, locking themselves into cubicles for exactly three minutes. As she left, Costello managed to collide with the female watcher from the pub, hurrying down the corridor. Costello apologised and backtracked a couple of paces to hold the toilet door open for her, forcing eye contact.

The food outlets and shops here were even more crowded than those on the opposite side, but they easily located Volvo Man in the open-plan seating area, then his Asian partner perusing newspapers in WH Smith.

'Ready?' murmured Costello, squeezing Jay's arm and waiting for his nod. They dashed up the staircase and sprinted back over the footbridge, deserted except for a mother with a child in a buggy, the rain now driving against the glass. Beneath them every vehicle was showing headlights in the spray and gloom, and the bridge itself had become a brightly lit shaft, with no hiding places. At the far end Jay stopped to make an imaginary mobile call, looking back along the footway to maroon the watchers while Costello scampered down the stairs.

The Suzuki rider had evidently remained on the southbound side and Costello caught her loitering in the queue for coffee, bumping the helmet against her leg and apparently murmuring to herself. Avoiding a wheelchair and a couple of lads in Liverpool shirts, Costello hurried through the giant revolving door into the open, enjoying the rain on her face as she sprinted for the car.

By the time Jay appeared she was already on the move, wheel-spinning towards him across the glistening tarmac. She slowed for him to clamber aboard, then raced for the Volvo as he grabbed the screwdriver. 'Go!' she screamed, slewing sideways as he leapt out and stabbed the two front tyres, then skidding around the perimeter as he dodged between parked cars to reach the Honda. He had already spiked one of the front tyres by the time Costello reached him, and paused to skewer the rear offside as she shoved the passenger door open for him.

They attacked the Suzuki last, on the sprint for the Exit. Braking hard, she looked around for witnesses, but everyone was hurrying to and from the entrance with hoods and umbrellas raised, oblivious to them. As Jay destroyed the front tyre she acted on impulse for the second time that day, leaping from the Fiat to kick the heavy bike until it crashed from its stand.

Their acts of sabotage had taken less than three minutes.

'How fucking great was *that*?' yelled Costello above the racing engine, as they charged back onto the motorway with wipers at full speed.

Jay was using his shirt to dry his head. 'Feel better now?' he said, his voice muffled.

'Sex is great, but, hey, the serious stuff is even better,' she laughed, accelerating into the blinding spray.

Chapter Thirty-Seven

Jack Langton returned to duty within forty-eight hours of being shot. When he broke the news to John Kerr from his home in Mill Hill, north London, he was acting against the advice of his doctor at St Thomas' Hospital, where the paramedics had rushed him from Trafalgar Square. He listened impatiently while Kerr ran through the obligatory guidance on health and wellbeing, officer safety and return to work, interrupting him in the middle of work-life balance. 'Save it, John. See you later,' he said, then rang off and speed-dialled Melanie.

By the time she arrived he was in the kitchen deflecting half-hearted dissuasion from his wife, Katy, the second Mrs Langton. A Geordie, like Jack, she taught sports technology three mornings a week and had just collected their three year old daughter from nursery. 'You know Jack's trouble?' she said, pouring Melanie's coffee. 'Testosterone and bravado outgun reason every time.' Langton, silently adjusting his sling while the little girl fetched his shoes, may as well not have been there. 'I mean, don't you think getting blown up in Victoria is enough excitement for one week?'

'Yeah, we'd rather he stayed home for a while. It's probably the Home Sec thing,' said Melanie, brushing away a stray hair. She was wearing a sleeveless navy smock with jeans and cheap silvery trainers, hair scrappily tied back and no make-up. 'Thinks he's indispensable.'

'That's what you're working on now, is it?' said Katy, tugging at a yellow duster poking from the smock. 'Playing Mrs Mop?'

'Trust me,' said Melanie, with a laugh. 'I'll make sure he behaves.'

Katy shook her head in resignation. 'You're all as bad as each other, really,' she said, dispensing two sweeteners into her coffee.

Mindful of her own domestic situation, Melanie genuinely sympathised with Katy, tossing a few disparaging comments across the worktop while Langton looked sheepishly between them. In truth, Melanie *was* just as guilty, for both had declined the Yard's offer of stress counselling, an HR tick in the box following a COLT, or 'Critical Officer Life-Threatening Trauma,' the latest fancy euphemism for attempted murder via handgun.

Langton pulled a face as soon as they reached the street. 'Is that all you could get?'

Melanie had booked out a green Vauxhall Astra from Langton's covert vehicle pool in Wandsworth, a high mileage, non-operational vehicle used for ferrying operatives between surveillance plots. When she clicked him into his seat belt, Langton's grimace was from distaste as much as pain.

'You're on light duties, Jack,' she said as she drove away. 'That's what the boss told me.'

'Did he get promoted? It's obvious he's been cramming.'

'Guess.'

Langton studied Melanie's domestic cleaner outfit. 'We're going to the office?'

'Eventually.'

Kerr had given Melanie strict instructions to keep Langton away from the surveillance around the Avril Knight investigation. Instead, as Melanie joined the A41 Watford Way for London, they talked about Saturday's near-death experience, Langton masking his discomfort every time Melanie braked, turned or accelerated. This was their first contact since the paramedics had rushed them to St Thomas', the conversation Kerr had encouraged Melanie to trigger, mutual counselling masquerading as operational debrief.

They worked through the chronology, from Pete Webb's distress calls to the explosion on Southwark Bridge, the chase and the terrifying climax in Trafalgar Square. Langton talked at length about Webb, his core team player and friend, whom he had sat with late into Saturday night, despite his own suffering. According to the duty staff nurse, the bullet had shattered Webb's right collar bone and ricocheted into his chest, passing through the lung before shredding the lumbar muscles and exiting his lower back. After two days of intensive care in a private room off the male surgical ward, his condition remained serious but stable.

Langton, on the other hand, knew he had been extremely lucky. Slowed by the angle of the windscreen, the bullet had travelled cleanly through the soft tissue of his left shoulder to bury itself in the rear head rest. Langton had suffered trauma and blood loss, but a few weeks of intensive physio would return him to full strength. 'Should be me in there, Mel,' he said grimly, looking away through the side window.

'Survivor guilt?'

'No, not that. I'm younger than Pete. Fitter. Should've been me.'

They drove in silence for a while, half-listening to LBC's blanket coverage of the Home Secretary's murder. Melanie's tasking from Kerr was to check out the phone number Donna had lifted from Finch's diary on Friday afternoon, and she could sense Langton reviving as she briefed him. According to research by 1830, the mobile was listed to Philip Deering, a retired major general, now CEO of Wymark Corporate Solutions, a private limited company registered at 23 Chapel Row, Mayfair, W1K. Incorporated in 2007, accounts filed with Companies House the previous December showed a net worth of £3.2 million and liabilities of £367 thousand.

Melanie turned off Park Lane into Mount Street and took another left as Berkeley Square came into view. 'Should be up here on the right.'

Both were familiar with the myriad private security companies thrown up by the wars in Iraq and Afghanistan. All ravenous for lucrative government contracts, they based themselves as close as possible to prestigious Mayfair, as if W1's high octane wealth and access would rub off on them. The majority specialised in guns for hire, special forces veterans retooled as bodyguards to oil engineers, construction workers and other contractors at risk of murder or kidnap. A few were more shadowy, specialists in threat assessment and intelligence gathering with dubious links to foreign intelligence agencies, as well as MI6.

'So which is Wymark?' said Langton, 'Psycho or spook?'

'Bit of both, so far as Alan can make out…there it is,' said Melanie as they cruised past a long row of tall, red-brick mansion blocks, each with a black oak doorway and multiple bell pushes. 'No marketing, nothing showy. Looks like business by word of mouth only.'

Langton adjusted his arm. 'What's Deering?'

'Your bog standard career soldier. Sandhurst, staff officer jobs and a glide upwards without firing a shot in anger, apparently. But he lost a son in Northern Ireland.'

'And why the secret trysts with the Bull?'

'Big beasts comparing their willies, probably,' said Melanie, turning into a cobbled street of white mews houses and parking away from the corner. 'But you never know.'

She cut the engine, opened the boot and took out a battered vacuum cleaner. 'No, Jack,' she called inside, as Langton's seat belt clicked open. 'Don't move. Back in a mo.'

Melanie sauntered into Chapel Row, climbed the steps to the entrance and studied the bell panel. Wymark was shown on the third floor, one down from the top, with the company name handwritten on a piece of card in a yellowing plastic sheath. Melanie selected the classy looking Glencore Finance for access, on the basis that it covered the whole of the fourth floor and probably received the most visitors. Sure enough, the door buzzed open the moment she pressed the button.

The vintage lift at the core of the building was out of order, its concertina grill jammed open, so she took the stairs, pausing to activate the camera concealed in the vacuum extension before reaching Wymark. Without knocking she eased the door open with her shoulder, entering a small reception area. Facing her was a chest high counter with a brass bell push. There was a camera high in the right corner, but no receptionist or other security. To the right was a dark conference room with leather chairs around an oval table, with faded prints in cheap frames crowding the walls. Above the fire place hung a modern painting at odds with the general mood of faded grandeur.

The door directly in front of Melanie was also open, and a convex mirror reflected a cluttered office to the left with a leather inlaid desk in the far corner, presumably Deering's workplace. Behind the door, a middle-aged woman sat by her computer eating a sandwich. She looked up, startled, when Melanie pressed the brass bell.

'Brightmore Cleaners for Glencore.'

It took the woman only a single, bad-tempered glance in the mirror. 'Next floor,' she called at Melanie's distorted image, pointing her finger upwards.

Retreating without a word, Melanie padded down the stairs into the street.

'Anything?' said Langton as she rejoined him in the car.

Melanie shook her head, reaching into the glove compartment for an iPhone. 'No-one home, but the place looks pretty standard,' she said, then checked the video and uploaded the file to 1830. Turning around at the end of the mews, she frowned. 'Alan says the net worth is over £3 million. That's a lot of equity for a tinpot outfit showing two directors.'

Langton was the first to spot Dodge. Tieless, unbuttoned suit jacket flapping around his stomach, he emerged from Piccadilly Circus Underground while they were held in traffic on the way back to the Yard. 'Look who's here,' he said, flipping their sun visors as the lights changed to green and Dodge veered across the street two cars ahead. He looked grey and sweaty, breaking into a trot as he hurried across Regent Street and headed up Shaftesbury Avenue.

'Slow down, Dodge,' murmured Melanie as she changed course after him. 'You'll give yourself a heart attack.'

'What do you think?' said Langton, his free hand already on the door.

'About what? John wants us back at the Yard,' said Melanie, held behind a double-decker outside the Apollo Theatre.

'No,' said Langton. 'He asked us to keep an eye on Dodge.'

They watched him rush down the pavement just in front of them, barrelling through a group of French students as he crossed Great Windmill Street.

'And I told him I'm not happy about it.'

'Yeah. I heard,' said Langton. 'Why do you think Dodge took the wrong exit from the tube? Cock-up or counter-surveillance?'

'Spying on Finch is one thing. But this? Snooping on our friend? No way. God, he looks terrible.'

With a sharp look behind him, Dodge made a left into Wardour Street.

'Soho,' said Langton, simply.

'He's probably meeting an agent.'

'So it'll be in the source unit log, won't it? Except he isn't, and it won't. Something's wrong.' Langton's seat belt clicked for the second time, then the door. 'I'll cover him on foot.'

Before Langton could move, Melanie reached across and pulled the door shut, knocking against his injured arm. 'No, Jack,' she said, 'and he'll spot you in a heartbeat looking like that.'

'You go then,' he said as they reached the junction and caught a flash of Dodge swerving right into Old Compton Street, on the way to Soho's heart.

'You can't drive, either,' she said, forcing a U-turn at Dean Street and accelerating back towards the Circus. 'And I'm boss today.'

'Who says?'

'John Kerr. It's the upside of you getting shot.'

Chapter Thirty-Eight

Checking his BlackBerry as he swiped into Room 1830, Kerr almost collided with a wall of large black plastic crates piled between the door and the reading room. New Scotland Yard was on the move. Within weeks its key personnel would be uprooted to a new building on Victoria Embankment, close to the original Scotland Yard that now provided office space for MPs.

Commander Bill Ritchie had different plans for his intelligence unit. Alarmed by press leaks, corruption and other integrity breaches swirling around the Met, he had tasked John Kerr to look for a secret base south of the Thames, within easy reach of the Secret Intelligence Service headquarters at Vauxhall Cross. Before its dissolution in 2006, Special Branch had been sole occupants of the top three floors at New Scotland Yard; now, Ritchie was determined to a rebuild the Chinese wall between usable evidence and secret intelligence, saving his highly vetted officers from the clutches of Derek Finch.

Kerr looked around for the displaced cybercrime team and found them doubling up in the overheated space behind Mercury. 'When are we escaping?' he said, pulling a chair alongside Fargo's desk.

'It's in the pipeline,' said Fargo, 'if you believe the intranet.'

Kerr scanned the files and readouts from Mercury. 'So what have we got?'

'First pictures of the crime scene and the flat,' said Fargo, handing Kerr an A4 plastic wallet.

Exactly a week after the murder of his mother and sister Fargo sounded upbeat but looked tired, his eyes red and watery behind the contact lenses. Kerr had kept tabs on his state of mind indirectly through Gemma, though anyone in 1830 could have told him Fargo was using work to hold grief at bay. He sifted through the colour stills. 'Does Finch have any suspects yet?'

'No,' said Fargo, nodding at the wall TV. 'But that lot have already made up their minds.'

They paused to watch the news rolling through the screen. Within minutes of the Cheapside attacks, standard BBC and Sky footage had been overtaken by shaky iPhone video of people fleeing the scene, streaming carnage to rival anything from Baghdad, Kabul or Bangkok. In the past hour, tape of Avril Knight on *The Andrew Marr Show* had been spliced into the loop to convey a single message: the Home Secretary had just become victim number thirty-two in a single terrorist campaign.

'So they're looking at serial killers,' said Kerr. 'What do you think, Al?'

'It's a similar MO to Mark Bannerman's murder.'

'The message round the neck, you mean, or the brutality?'

'Both, plus the arrangement of the bodies. It's the *exhibitionism*, John. Bannerman's scapegoating, Knight's betrayal.'

'Drawing us back to the IRA.'

'Knight was spouting anti-IRA rhetoric all her political life. It's a pretty raw history,' shrugged Fargo. 'Then the "non-denial denial" about IRA guilt in her interviews yesterday.'

'Which gets her murdered...executed, less than twenty-four hours later.' Kerr looked again at the photographs of Knight's body in the shed. 'She spends the night with her secret lover. Who knew about that? The private office and her prot team, according to Karl Sergeyev. No-one else.' He peered at the head wound. 'So how did the killers get to her?'

Suddenly there were two loud raps on the door, then Melanie swiped herself in, followed by Langton and a porter wheeling more crates. In search of privacy, Kerr edged past the trolley for the reading room, avoiding Langton's shoulder as they squeezed together around the cramped table. 'Good to see you, Jack.'

'Nice to be here,' said Langton, waggling the fingers of his injured arm.

Kerr looked between Langton and Melanie as she shoved the ill-fitting door shut. 'So how was Wymark? Anything to worry us?'

Melanie shook her head. 'Frugal offices in a posh location with loads of equity. I sent you the pictures, Al?' Fargo nodded. 'This has to be Derek Finch on job search. He's greedy for a consultancy and they want a name to draw high roller clients.'

'But why meet them the day after Victoria? What was so urgent?' Kerr frowned. 'I mean, London's burning and the Bull's out for brunch?'

'It's the celebrity terrorist catcher feeding his vanity,' said Langton.

'Yeah, right,' murmured Fargo, squeezing his eyes with his thumb and forefinger. 'All those victims must be sending his market value through the roof.'

Melanie, squashed beside him, laid a hand over his.

'Jesus, Al...' said Langton.

'I'm fine.' Fargo slid Kerr the wallet of photographs. 'Avril Knight?'

'Tell us about the girlfriend,' said Kerr.

'It's only a pen picture so far.' Fargo produced a passport photograph from his bunch of papers. 'This is Maria Benita Consuela, Spanish citizen, forty-three years, born in Barcelona. Married in 2003 to Maximo Leon Salvatella. Max. Second time round for both, and they moved to Madrid to set up an art dealership. Resettled in London three years ago with their two young daughters, but she divorced him and hooked up with Avril Knight around July last year. Max got custody and took the girls back to Spain.'

'Registry?'

'No adverse traces on either.'

'So how did Consuela and Avril Knight get together?'

'Benita. Everyone calls her Benita. Karl's looking into it. The

Spanish embassy says she worked with its office for cultural and scientific affairs, a mover and shaker on women's projects in media development, audiovisual education and film festivals. Recently she's been fundraising for international co-productions with Italy and Greece, and Anglo-Spanish projects for disadvantaged kids.'

'So where is she now?'

'Under doctor's orders and heavily sedated, apparently. Distraught, like she and Avril were the real deal.'

'Do you think they were?'

'I'm working on it,' said Fargo.

'Who's the doctor?'

'Local GP. She's staying with friends in Notting Hill while the murder team search her flat, but no-one's in a rush to interview her. Unless something drastic turns up, Benita is definitely in the category of grieving lover.'

'But central to the murder investigation,' said Langton. 'What if she was blackmailing Knight?'

'We've got multiple traces of her phone number in Knight's call log, obviously, but it's almost entirely outgoing from Knight. The victim was making the running here.'

'When was the last call?' said Langton.

'From the constituency house on Sunday afternoon, presumably to confirm she was coming.'

'Anything from the flat while Knight was there?'

'Did our Benita tip the killers off, you mean?' Fargo shook his head. 'Both phones were switched off.'

'What about suspicious activity around the address ? Any signs they were being watched?' said Kerr.

'There's no CCTV in that street, and house to house will take time,' said Fargo. 'On the face of it, nothing unusual here.'

'Hold on,' said Melanie, peering at the photographs. 'Have you run Benita's telephone log through Mercury?'

'Next on the list.'

Melanie pulled out a still of Benita's flat, slid Fargo's notes aside and laid it squarely on the table. 'Did you watch my video from Wymark?'

'Not personally, no,' he said, nodding at his team through the glass.

'Don't bother.' She rapidly scrolled through her iPhone, enlarged an image and laid it beside the photograph. 'Philip Deering's conference room, if you can call it that. Look at the picture above the fireplace.' She paused as they all craned in, then picked up the photograph of Benita's cluttered studio. 'And then just here, leaning against the wall, next to the red snake thing.'

'Same picture,' said Kerr.

'Benita's original oil painting. Which tells me she's linked to Wymark.'

Langton leaned in for a closer comparison. 'Or Deering's an art lover?'

'But he's not. Look,' she said, scrolling through the video, 'the other walls are full of waiting room crap, prints of ships, fields and battles. Then he hangs this weird…I dunno, orange and green abstract…sunrise, sunset?…right there in pride of place.' Melanie looked between them. 'Derek Finch, Philip Deering, Maria Benita Consuela. All connected.'

Fargo gave a low whistle. 'That's one hell of a triangle.'

'With Finch sucking up to Deering and soft-pedalling on the girlfriend. Take it from me, guys,' said Melanie. 'Benita's call history is going to be v interesting.'

Fargo was already pushing his chair back. 'I'll go and run the numbers.'

Chapter Thirty-Nine

Monday, 17 October, 16.33, Paquito's Tapas, Old Compton Street, Soho

For his third shaming, Dodge arrived before Bobby Roscoe. Breathless from the race along Old Compton Street to arrive on the dot of four-thirty, as ordered, Dodge could find no sign of his nemesis. Perhaps it was as well. Since Saturday, overwhelmed by the near deaths of Langton and Peter Webb, he had been beside himself with anxiety, unsleeping and murderous.

Paquito's was an arty, stylish bar and eatery a few doors away from the Admiral Duncan pub, target of a homophobic nail bomb attack in 1999, and a short walk from the Groucho Club in Dean Street. Dodge wondered if Roscoe was hiding somewhere in the street, holding back and checking for surveillance. He lingered for a moment in the doorway, suddenly worried that he might be in the wrong location, though Paquito's bright red and yellow striped awning lifted it from the neighbourhood's older haunts. Alert to a trap against himself, Dodge snatched a final glance up and down the pavement before entering the crowded bar and easing his way to the toilet.

Opened three years earlier, Paquito's had quickly become the go-to place for writers and media types to network, pitch and play. Upstairs were rooms for the night and a quiet area for study and research, but the real action was on the ground floor, with hot staff in scarlet aprons serving rioja, tapas and bowl food. Drinkers socialised at the bar or worked their tablets at pine tables along the far walls, though Dodge could tell from the hubbub that the real movers and shakers occupied the brown leather sofas in the centre, scripts on knees, heads up close, hands doing the talking. The lunchtime crowd was still busy, big shots hearing out nobodies and hipsters coaxing chic women for an advance on royalties, every voice schmoozing, promoting or dealing. Searching for Bobby

Roscoe, Dodge was thrown by a scattering of people he vaguely recognised, TV faces or tabloid fodder whose names he had never pinned down.

Roscoe appeared as he was heading back through the bar. This time he was wearing an old black donkey jacket with jeans and work boots, and waved at Dodge as if he were a lifelong friend. In the far left corner, separated from the main bar by a slatted partition, was a carpeted area signed The Retreat, with a couple of armchairs and the day's newspapers. Roscoe checked it was empty and led Dodge inside. They stood facing each other for a moment, Dodge suddenly feeling breathless. 'Shall we talk here?' said Roscoe, spreading his hands.

'Not where we can't be seen,' said Dodge. 'I'd probably kill you.' He spotted a couple vacating one of the sofas in the bar and moved to stake his claim, glaring at a young man in round glasses shifting from one of the side tables.

'Want some rioja?' said Roscoe, sinking into the leather cushions. 'Tapas?'

'You've got to be fucking joking.' Dodge dragged over a matching armchair, sat forward and leaned in, his voice a growl. 'Two of my friends nearly died because of you.'

Roscoe wiped a trace of spittle from his cheek. 'You think none of the blame lies with *you*?' Dead calm, he shuffled out of his heavy jacket and laid it beside him on the sofa. 'How about a carajillo, then? With whiskey?'

'Cut the crap. Why am I here?'

Roscoe gave the slow, taunting smile Dodge remembered from before. 'We've known each other nearly a week. It's time to confess, Mr Dodge.'

'What the hell are you talking about?'

'Frankie. I want to know what happened,' said Roscoe, maintaining the smile. 'Who gave the order?'

'There was no fucking order. I already told you,' said Dodge angrily, then the chair rocked noisily on the wooden floor as he lunged forward. 'Stop laying that shit on me.'

Roscoe looked down, unflinching, as Dodge's fingers turned white on his forearm. 'You gonna move your fat pig's trotter? You want everyone staring, like you're some hissy old queen?'

Dodge released his hold and slumped back. 'You've got this wrong.'

'I've brought you some more info.' He stood up and slid a twenty pound note from his back pocket. 'Let's order a couple of long blacks and talk about it.'

'No,' said Dodge, pulling him back. 'Tell me now.'

Roscoe shot his eyebrows at an inquisitive couple nearby, then perched on the arm of the sofa, his splayed thigh touching Dodge's arm. 'You go first.'

'There's nothing to say.'

Roscoe shrugged. 'Okay, here's what I heard.' He bent in, so close that Dodge could feel his lips brush against his earlobe. 'If you see a truck parked up with its hazards flashing, run the other way.'

'An IED? You're handing me a fucking lorry bomb?' Dodge threw himself back in the chair, struggling to make eye contact. He wiped his brow with the back of his hand. Sweat was soaking into his shirt, but his mouth felt dry as the desert. 'Jesus Christ. How do you live with yourself?'

'It's you should be taking a look in the mirror,' said Roscoe, harshly. 'I'm giving you an early warning, big man. You should be thanking me.'

Dodge sat forward again. 'What else?'

'When, you mean? Who?' Roscoe gave a short laugh, like before, and Dodge felt a powerful arm encircle his shoulder. 'You know the drill, my friend.'

'So you're doing it…passing me this…this fucking nightmare that's a little bit true, three parts shit, just so you can destroy me,' said Dodge, flatly.

Roscoe slowly shook his head, like a chiding parent. 'This is about Frankie, not you or me.'

Dodge wanted to shift again, but Roscoe's hold was too strong. To the people nearby they must have appeared as friends comforting one another, Dodge speaking quietly into Roscoe's lap. 'Do you have any idea…I can't just let this…'

'Yes. Until you come clean, the pain goes on.'

'Bobby, I'm asking you,' murmured Dodge, the first name wrapping everything else in a plea.

'No. You're begging,' said Roscoe, then leant into his ear again. 'How's your daughter by the way? Still out all night, sleeping with that boy? And the missus? Nicola, right? She has a secret, too, doesn't she? Two legal eagles in one family, and both misbehaving.'

'Bastard,' croaked Dodge, his voice full of sand.

'This is about us both doing the right thing.' Roscoe clapped Dodge on the back and stood again, suddenly looking expansive. 'A deal, like everything else in here. Think about it while I get the coffee.'

Dodge acted quickly as Roscoe threaded his way to the bar. Heaving his bulk across to the sofa he checked no-one was watching, grabbed Roscoe's heavy jacket and searched the side pockets. Roscoe was left-handed, so he checked there first. It was heavy with a ring of three Yale keys and a couple of Banhams, plus the usual work detritus of chewing gum, screws, allen keys and a small clasp knife. No phone or car key. At the bar, Roscoe drifted out of sight behind a clutch of drinkers. The right pocket was empty, with a hole in the fabric. Dodge forced his hand inside the lining and widened the tear, exploring the space below the pocket. He pricked his finger on a sharp piece of metal and pulled out a receipt stamped FOR CASH, badly stapled to an old fashioned invoice headed 'Thomas Roache and Sons, Building Supplies,' in block print. Blood was seeping onto the paper, so Dodge slipped it into his pocket, straightened Roscoe's jacket and made for the bar.

Roscoe was turning with the coffees when Dodge reached

him. He looked surprised, then flashed his mocking smile again. 'Something I said?'

Dodge beckoned him away from the bar, towards the window, as Roscoe held out his cup and saucer. This time it was Dodge who moved in close. He grabbed his arm, slopping coffee over Roscoe's T-shirt. 'Be sure to ring me before anything goes down, you prick,' he growled. 'And leave my family alone, or I swear I'll kill you.'

Shaftesbury Avenue was unusually light when he reached the junction, the traffic held up by a pair of female Mounted Branch officers making their way into Piccadilly Circus. Dodge crossed the road and watched them trot past, sliding into single file to make way for a tipper lorry. He caught up with them again outside the Trocadero, posing for a bunch of Japanese tourists, then saw them continue left into the narrowness of Great Windmill Street, breaking into a canter on the way to Haymarket.

The clapping of the hooves off the high walls stirred something in Dodge's fevered brain that made him change gear, too. Loping down the centre of the road he reached them at the junction, where they were held at a stop light. 'Engaging locally' was the Met's name of the game these days, so the officers were using the time to chat with passers-by. His grey suit jacket patchy with sweat, tie over his shoulder and shirt tail flapping in the breeze, Dodge panted past, then turned to look up at them, his face puce, gasping for air as his eyes shifted between them, watching caution temper their smiles. Even the horses, trained against feral humans, seemed puzzled, pricking their ears forward as they fixed on him. The lights changed to amber but Dodge stood blocking their path, rubbing away a heart attack as he rummaged for his phone and punched the number for Reserve at the Yard.

'Walk on,' said one of the officers, and Dodge bounced aside as Gemma Riley picked up.

'Dodge. Where are you?'

'Do you still have the voice recording from Victoria?'

'It went to the lab ages ago. I've got a rough copy. Hey, you know we're worried about you?'

'You heard horses, right? On the tape. That's what you told John. Clippety-clop, clippety-clop?'

'Have you been drinking?'

'I'll be there in ten. It would be our guys, right? Or army?'

'In the middle of London? Well, it certainly wasn't the Jockey Club.'

Chapter Forty

Kerr's selection panel broke the news by text. He was driving to a safe house in Kentish Town, north London, caught in the perpetual traffic jam on the approach to the station when his BlackBerry pinged. He continued until the bus lane petered out, then paused the Alfa outside a vegetable shop to read the message, as curt and uncompromising as a tweet. 'Thanks for your participation,' it read. 'Regret unsuccessful on this occasion. Feedback to follow by email.'

He flicked on the hazard lights, dashed into the shop to buy a couple of bananas with a carton of milk, and drove towards Highgate Hill, thinking ahead to the clandestine meeting he hoped would be a game changer. Yesterday had been Kerr's second attempt at detective superintendent, and this result surprised him no more than the first. Parking around the corner from the safe house, he rang Nancy to let her know, downplaying the negatives. 'There's always next year.'

'Really?' Nancy had just dropped the children at school and was on the hands-free, driving to the surgery for a nine o'clock start. She sounded miffed, a reminder of how hard she had worked to prep him. 'And how many more "occasions" is Bill Ritchie going to offer you?'

'Honestly, darling, I'm happy doing what I'm doing,' he said.

'I don't suppose that shimmy between you and Robyn helped,' she said, drily, 'with all this hoo-ha about undercover officers having sex.'

'Ancient history, Nance. Didn't come up. You know what they're like.'

'But you are seeing her tomorrow?'

Kerr reached inside his jacket for the crumpled easyJet boarding pass from Donna's printer. 'Nine-thirty from Luton. Lunch in

Rome with her and Gabi, then straight back. I'll be home in time to see the kids.'

The safe house was in the roof of a three-storey Victorian terraced house in a tree-lined side street off Kentish Town Road. It was one of three hideaways maintained by Dodge's source unit, each cheaply furnished, with a single bedroom, bathroom, living room and kitchen, plus rations in the freezer. They were used to debrief agents or, on the rare occasions when an asset was compromised, as boltholes before permanent resettlement. The others were buried in Streatham and Ilford, though Kerr favoured the north London base for private meetings or a refuge to study the latest *Blue Global* from 1830 away from the distractions of the Yard.

The meeting was scheduled for nine o'clock but it was nearer half past when the intercom buzzed, with Kerr on his second cup of coffee.

He could hear Justin Hine taking the stairs two at a time, though the willowy young man who slid inside the safe house looked pale and tired. As usual at these sessions, Justin's face was obscured with a beanie pulled low beneath a dark grey hoodie, a double layer of protection to augment the wispy beard he had grown since his deployment. In the living room Kerr faced him squarely and gripped his shoulders, more like a welcoming father than a boss with a hundred questions. 'You've lost weight,' he said, though Justin's tensed muscles told him the slenderness was deceptive.

'I'm telling you, boss, it's been non-stop,' said Justin, whipping off the beanie and stuffing it into his pocket.

'But nothing to worry about?'

'Just that I shouldn't be away too long.' Justin darted into the kitchen, tested the kettle, flicked the switch and searched the cupboard for the chipped ceramic mug he always used. He threw Kerr a savage smile as he spooned the coffee and sugar. 'Not every day a Home Sec gets herself topped.'

Kerr slid his mug along the counter. 'Let's do the admin first.'

Justin tugged a clump of ragged papers from his back pocket and palmed them smooth. 'Sorry about the mess.'

Since the third week in June, Justin Hine had been living undercover, tasked with a top secret mission shared only inside Kerr's immediate circle. With western intelligence agencies distracted by the threat from Islamic State, Kerr had never lost his focus on the fallout from the global banking crisis in 2008. Alert to the political turbulence and extremist activity from anti-capitalist groups throughout Europe, Kerr had pressed Bill Ritchie for an aggressive operation to warn of any terrorist overspill into the UK. The young Special Branch officer who now slouched by the kettle, mild-mannered, soft-spoken and atypical, was the result: four months into his mission, Justin Hine's infiltration of Anti-Capitalist Insurrection had surpassed expectations.

They covered the paperwork in the time it took the water to boil, leaning against the kitchen units. Justin had brought petrol receipts, a couple of intelligence reports and a crumpled diary sheet showing his overtime hours: black biro for weekday working, red for weekends. In exchange, Kerr handed over a bundle of fifty pound notes, the rent for Justin's studio flat off Ladbroke Grove in west London.

'So what is the reaction to Avril Knight?'

'Pissing themselves laughing, mostly,' said Justin.

'Costello?'

'Gina's been pretty quiet about it, actually.'

'So let's keep working on her.'

'Like MI5, you mean?'

The kitchen fell silent as the kettle clicked off.

'You what?' said Kerr.

Justin took a few gulps of milk direct from the carton, like a student lining his stomach. 'You have to realise Gina Costello is sharp as a razor, John,' he said, wiping his mouth with the back of his hand. 'Netherlands to Dublin, no sign of surveillance. All clear to the ferry terminal.' He poured the coffee and a splash of milk. 'Then the moment we drive off at Holyhead, bingo! Welcome to bloody Wales. I spotted them at the first roundabout but she was only a few seconds behind. I'm telling you, she's quality.'

'But mistaken,' said Kerr, mentally replaying the CIG meeting on Saturday evening and the reaction from Toby Devereux. 'A4 have turned down every request to cover Anti-Capitalist Insurrection.'

'Too busy fighting jihad, you mean? Well, I'm telling you it happened,' he said, his pale blue eyes signalling the hypersensitivity of every deep cover officer Kerr had known. 'Two cars and a motorbike, certainly not locals and they stayed with us till halfway down the M6.'

'You managed to lose them?'

Justin shrugged. 'We think they dropped off at the services, but that's not the point, boss. All that dry cleaning shit via Dublin for nothing and Gina's wondering how they knew. Of course she is.'

Kerr frowned. 'Commander and I met Toby Devereux on Saturday. Maybe he had a rethink…'

'…a U-turn.'

'…without telling us. I'll call Willie Duncan in A4. It's no problem.'

'You really think that?' said Justin, his voice leaking anxiety. 'Look at it from ACI's point of view. Until now, Gina Costello has always stayed beneath the radar. MI5 only starts tracking her after I appear on the scene.'

'Has Costello said anything you're unhappy with?'

'To let me think she's suspicious, you mean?' Justin shook his head.

'So you're in the clear.'

'No, I'm thinking that's the last thing Gina would do. She's too clever for that.' Justin blew on his coffee and peered sideways at Kerr. 'You've not picked up anything?' Stooped in his tan skinny jeans and green, V-neck T-shirt, forehead still red from the hat, he looked vulnerable again, a sapling swaying in the breeze.

Kerr stepped past Justin to rinse his mug. 'No. Justin, you can relax. Your cover is rock solid,' he said, flagrantly understating Justin's exposure. The day before, Alan Fargo had reported a Legend Alarm, a tip-off that someone had searched the birth date of Justin's pseudonym in public records: in all likelihood, Kerr's operative had just been checked out by Anti-Capitalist Insurrection. Kerr turned to face him, drying his hands on the only tea towel. 'Come on, let's get started.'

Squeezing past Justin into the living room, Kerr felt no discomfort about his deception. He understood the existential stresses of life undercover, the surreal flipping between identities, the toxic drip-drip of deceit. Lesser men than Kerr described their human sources as 'assets', as commodities to be valued, exchanged and discarded. As a former operative himself, Kerr saw only their humanity, the hunger for encouragement and praise. Sometimes it was nobler to deceive than weigh them down with the truth.

Justin loitered in the doorframe. 'You haven't declared me to MI5, have you, boss? Devereux doesn't know, right?'

Kerr shook his head. 'No-one.'

'But A4 will have me on their surveillance log. "Male unknown," whatever? Photographs, too.'

'So what?' said Kerr, quizzical. 'I've said I'll deal with it.'

Justin's mobile rang before he could reply. Nervously tugging at his beard, he checked at the screen. 'Shit, I have to take this,' he said, darting past Kerr for the privacy of the bedroom.

'Costello?'

'Worse.'

Chapter Forty-One

Tuesday, 18 October, 09.53, Great Scotland Yard, Whitehall

Dodge had never visited the stables of the Met's Mounted Branch before. They were tucked away in Great Scotland Yard, approached beneath a massive white arch spanning Whitehall Place. The exterior shared the gravitas of London's Victorian police stations, most long closed, its upper floor distinguished by a line of traditional round and half moon windows swung open to take in the morning air. With hardly any passing vehicles or city noise, it belonged to policing's temperate era of bobbies on the beat and cat burglars, a world apart from the misery of suicide bombers, stabbing epidemics, acid attacks and cybercrime.

The animal heat struck Dodge the moment he pushed at the doors. There was an echo of hooves scraping on concrete, with humid, comforting smells spiriting him back to his childhood holidays in Castlereagh. He counted six or seven horse stalls in an area little larger than a couple of squash courts, and three horses in residence, their blankets slung over the side walls. Everywhere he looked were saddles, bridles and riding capes.

A man and woman in blue overalls were sweeping the floor and laying down fresh straw, while a third rubbed her horse down with soapy water from a yellow bucket. Laughing and joshing each other as they worked, no-one paid Dodge any attention, and he had to walk right inside to make himself heard.

'Good morning…morning! Hello?' Eventually the horses became restless and one of the officers swung round with her broom. Dodge recognised the rider from the street the day before, with her hair in a ponytail. 'I'm looking for Jane?' said Dodge, flashing his warrant card. 'Admin?'

Dodge looked and felt calmer today, businesslike in a light grey suit Nicola had made him buy from M&S. If the officer had any recollection of Dodge, she chose to hide it, shouting to make herself heard above the others. 'Day off.'

'No. That was yesterday,' said Dodge. 'I just spoke with her on the phone.'

'Physio, then, later on.' She indicated a wide concrete slope tracing two walls to the upper level and more stabling. 'Next floor.'

A hooter interrupted them from the landing and Dodge looked up to see a wheelchair wedged against the railings. 'Sir, I'm up here,' called another woman's voice, as a hand emerged beneath the banister, fingers wagging. 'Fire escape by the tack room. Just over there, next to the toilets.'

The odour of urine, leather and sweat followed him upstairs to a mezzanine of four horse stalls off a wide corridor bedded with fresh straw. Jane Hemming was waiting for him in her office, adjacent to a store piled with riot gear on racks identified by the names of horse and rider. The whole space had been adapted to accommodate her state of the art power chair, with accessories from NASA and tyres caked in manure. Around the walls curved a continuous shelf, replacing the conventional desk and chairs, and a framed Press Association photograph showed Hemming with horses being mucked out in the corridor behind her and the in-house caption 'Jane Hemming Still in the S H One T.'

'Welcome to the penthouse,' said Hemming as they shook hands. She looked slimmer and sharper than in the photograph, with neatly cut brown hair, pale blue sweater over a white blouse and navy cotton trousers.

'I hope I'm not holding you up, Jane?' said Dodge. 'They told me you have a medical?'

Hemming shook her head. 'My workout at Imber Court this afternoon. They strap me to the saddle and Daniel takes me for a couple of training circuits, so long as I behave myself.'

The two had never met before, but Dodge knew her background. An experienced Mounted Branch officer, Jane Hemming had been thrown by her horse, Daniel, at an anti-austerity riot in central London when a homemade firecracker exploded directly in his path. With her back, career and marriage broken, Hemming had returned to the stables as the administrative officer within eighteen months; six years on, while the perpetrator stayed low, Jane Hemming was celebrated throughout the Met for her courage, tenacity and lack of rancour.

'You said on the phone you think the call was made in the centre, yes?' said Hemming. 'Heavy traffic and so on?'

Dodge nodded.

She pulled open a drawer. 'So let's see what we can do.' The workstation was close to the doorway, giving her a partial view of any horses in their stalls. Beside the desktop a more recent photograph showed Hemming in a wedding dress with a little boy holding the train. She was upright, supporting herself on a crutch, arm in arm with her new husband, and Dodge could see the strain behind her smile.

Hemming took two cameras and held them out to Dodge. 'Body Worn Video. BWV. You know about this, right? The Job's rolling them out to all street officers?'

Dodge nodded, though his grasp of the Met's policy on body cameras was sketchy, at best.

'I've been managing our own pilot for the past month. With Tim, over at West Hampstead.' She took the larger of the cameras and held it against her right shoulder. 'This is the one they clip to the uniform when they go out on patrol.' She pointed to another terminal along the desk. 'And they can't go home till they upload the video at the end of the shift.'

'They must love you.'

'I do it for them, if I'm around.'

'But they're not recording the whole time, right?'

Hemming shook her head. 'They only activate for things like stop and search or an arrest. Anything that might be contested.'

Dodge felt a stab of disappointment. 'Okay. Thanks, anyway.'

Hemming made a face. 'You think I invited you here for

nothing?' She picked up the second camera, the size of a large marble. 'We've just started testing the helmet cam. It sits higher above the horse, so better pictures. Steadier, too, except when they're on the gallop.'

'But still discretionary?'

'Are you familiar with Met Cloud, sir?' she asked, then laughed at his expression. 'Of course not. She held the camera between forefinger and thumb. 'This is the baby you saw Jen wearing yesterday. It's different because it uploads automatically.'

'And constantly?'

Hemming rolled to a desktop beneath a large wall screen. 'You're interested in last Monday, right? The bombs? Which is also the first day of the trial.' A satellite map appeared on the screen with a blue arc tracing westwards from Covent Garden through Piccadilly Circus, Green Park and Hyde Park Corner, returning to the stables via the Embankment. 'This is our thin blue line. Each patrol lasts about three hours, with every step plotted as shown.' She indicated a box at the bottom right of the screen. 'Date and patrol reference here. Last Monday we have PC38 and PC29 on patrol, riding Victor and Phoebe, and they deployed from there at twenty past ten. It's day one, so only Trish is cammed up.'

Dodge felt a surge of excitement as his eyes scanned the map.

'What time are we talking, sir? Roughly?'

'Twelve thirty-eight and seventeen seconds,' replied Dodge in a pulse.

'Let's give ourselves some leeway and say twelve thirty-six.' Time flags popped up as she moved the cursor around the route. 'So they reach Hyde Park Corner at twelve twenty-one.'

'Jesus, they're coming into Victoria,' he said, straining forward. 'Right on top of the bombs.'

'Back home by the time of the explosions, thank God,' she said, slowing the cursor and double clicking. 'We've arrived. Take as long as you need, sir.'

The screen suddenly changed to high definition video, giving

Dodge his first horseback ride in over three decades. He was suddenly high above the street, the horse's mane dipping and rising as they walked, its ears twitching, everything instantly recognisable as they entered the bomb zone.

'Hell of a vantage point.' Dodge could hear radio traffic and snatches of conversation between the two officers above the rain pattering on their waterproofs. Traffic was heavy, with the larger vehicles sending up clouds of spray as they eased past the horses. From up here, the pavements were a kaleidoscope of umbrellas as workers hurried back to their offices, unaware of the terrorism about to engulf them.

Everyone he could see was texting, calling or scrolling, yet Dodge identified Bobby Roscoe in a pulse, as if one of Jane Hemming's magic flags had attached itself to his Trapper hat.

Dodge's persecutor was waiting outside a wine bar, dressed for the weather. Standing in the middle of the pavement, he forced the crowd to part around him, the static loner in a fast forward video. He had made no effort at disguise, yet it was the body language that betrayed him to Dodge, the manifest physical power and arrogance he had wielded each time they met.

'Gotcha, you bastard,' murmured Dodge, as a burst of raindrops smeared the lens. He saw Roscoe peering across the road towards a patch of green, mostly outside the frame, and willed the horsewoman to move her head. Then he caught a nod, almost imperceptible, and a phone appeared in Roscoe's left hand. Dodge checked the rolling clock on the screen: twelve thirty-eight and three seconds as Roscoe began dialling, turning away from the traffic noise, a finger blocking his other ear. Drawing closer, he watched Roscoe bend forward in concentration, the sides of the hat folding over his cheeks, and imagined Gemma picking up the call. Then Roscoe began to emphasise each word with his free arm and the horse looked left, its ears fluttering again.

Dodge's lips moved in concert with Roscoe, revising every word from the recording he had played over and over the night before, and he wanted to reach inside the screen and throttle him. Heart thumping in his chest, he could sense Jane Hemming's eyes on him as Roscoe drifted out of sight and the station entrance came into view. 'Can you replay it, Jane? Freeze-frame?'

'Anything you want.'

Dodge stood back, agitated and sweaty again as Hemming worked the keys. He suddenly felt short of breath. 'Have you shown this to the investigators?'

'We told them we had a patrol in the area but they never called back.' She shrugged, tripping frame by frame for the clearest shot of Roscoe. 'We assumed...'

'It's alright. We'll keep this between ourselves.' Dodge produced his iPhone. 'Does your camera do email, as well?'

'I'll forward it now,' said Hemming, rolling back to her workstation to scan Dodge's address. 'What are you going to do?'

Dodge sucked lungfuls of air. 'Take him out.'

Hemming sat back in surprise. 'As in "revenge"?' Dodge nodded. She whirred back to the screen and stared at Roscoe's frozen image. 'The way you were caught up in that just now...I mean...it was like you know him?'

'This is a bad man, Jane. And yes, it *is* personal. Private.'

'A vendetta?' she said, rolling back to her workstation. 'An Irishman turning Sicilian on me?'

Dodge suddenly looked at Hemming's withered legs, strapped tightly to the chair, and checked himself. 'Jane, I'm so sorry. I didn't mean to...'

'Upset the forgiving paraplegic, you mean?' She gave a harsh laugh. 'Don't believe the Met propaganda, sir. I lost my life to the bastard who exploded that firecracker. How do I feel about it, all these years down the road? For me,' she said quietly, pointing at Bobby Roscoe's face frozen on the screen, 'he's as evil as your guy.'

'But I should never have...'

'Yes, you should. Don't be embarrassed,' she said, powering back to Dodge and holding out her hand. 'It's always been personal for me, too. We both want the same.'

Chapter Forty-Two

Tuesday, 18 October, 09.57, Special Branch Safe House,
Kentish Town

Justin's call lasted less than three minutes. When he returned, Kerr was settled at the round oak table by the window, studying the bulky pink Registry file on Gina Costello. 'Everything okay?'

Justin grabbed one of the bananas from the kitchen and sat opposite Kerr. 'Bloke called Paco in Amsterdam. Wants a meet.'

'What for?'

Justin shrugged. 'Probably something about the trip.'

Kerr paused to review Justin's latest telephoned report on Costello. 'How did Amsterdam go? Did they talk about London?'

'They actually changed it to The Hague at the last minute. Top floor flat off Spekstraat, a walk from the train station. It was a big deal. I could tell from the way Gina was talking.'

'How many?'

'Eight activists from all over Europe. Hardcore.'

'Any Brits?'

'That was *moi*, but they didn't let me in. Sorry, boss.' Justin held up his phone. 'They kept me and Paco down in the street as lookouts.'

'To cover them,' said Kerr. 'Which is good, right?'

'I'm still being tested, basically. Not pushing anything. Especially with her,' he said, nodding at the file.

'Fine.' Kerr produced one of Bill Ritchie's yellow legal pads from his secure briefcase and started scribbling. 'Okay. We had the emergency CIG on Saturday evening and everyone in the room put the attacks down to the IRA…'

'…except you and the commander?'

'Correct. With the jury out on Avril Knight. Then European liaison tell us this is anti-capitalism. ACI or a new terrorist cell no-one's ever heard of.' Kerr flipped through the reports. 'Gina

Costello's stepfather was head honcho of leveraged finance at Dolphin and Drew...'

'...who Gina can't stand.'

'...and sacked last year for dodgy dealing?'

'Except I wouldn't know that, would I?' said Justin, tapping the file. 'Because she hasn't told me.'

'What does it amount to, from Costello's point of view?'

'As a motive for the bombing, you mean?' Justin made a face. 'Coincidence?'

'Okay,' said Kerr, twiddling his pen and regarding Justin across the table. 'The attacks last week have the hallmarks of Irish republican dissidents. Agreed?'

'The warnings, the code words, the delivery, the complete works. Yup.'

'And the Real IRA have previous for hitting banks.'

'In Ireland.'

'True, with Dodge's police contacts saying no dissident targets have been away from home. And none of the explosives came from an IRA cache, according to Porton Down.'

Justin leant forward across the table. 'So you want me to tell you the London series is down to ACI?'

'With Irish dissidents. A joint venture.'

'A pan-European conspiracy against the banksters?' Justin unzipped the banana and devoured it in three bites. 'Like I said, boss, I don't know what they talked about in The Hague.'

'But is Gina Costello capable of pulling that together?'

Justin darted to the kitchen and tossed the skin into the sink. 'I'm not that close to her.'

Kerr paused, studying Justin's reaction. 'You've been cultivating her for...how many months?'

'I don't think she fits the security profile,' said Justin, carefully.

'Of a radical, or a terrorist?'

He looked perplexed for a moment, as if the question had

never occurred to him. 'Gina fights social injustice. That's what drives her.'

'Really?' Kerr flipped through Costello's file to the comprehensive report he had commissioned a year earlier. 'We have Politics and International Relations at Manchester University. A good start, followed by the BBC internship at Salford Quays.' Kerr riffled through the papers. 'All I see in here so far is a bog standard media junkie.'

'Which is rubbish,' said Justin, reddening. 'There's a lot more to Gina Costello than the crap in there.'

Kerr slid the file aside and spread his palms. 'So tell me.'

'The financial crash triggered social inequality right across Europe. That's the core of the ACI campaign. The poor seizing justice from the undeserving.' Justin ran a hand through his hair. 'Want to know what makes her angry? Banker criminals still in full flow, ripping off ordinary people and fucking the world up.'

'Enough to bomb them?'

'Being zealous doesn't make you a terrorist.' Justin suddenly sounded arch, as if Kerr should have known better. 'Gina's passion is socioeconomics, not Semtex.'

'Neat.' Kerr grabbed the file and flipped it open at one of several red markers. 'Quote. "The front runner for ACI in Europe by a long way. The woman all other activists defer to, the target with the greatest potential for extremist activity, including violent direct action." Close quote.' He regarded Justin carefully. 'That's your report from August, Justin. What changed?'

Justin looked uncomfortable, as if Kerr was using his own words to trick him. 'I understand them better now.'

'Let's stick with Costello. Gina.'

'Well, I'm getting to know what makes her tick,' he said. 'Obviously.'

The defensiveness made Kerr smile. 'Justin, I'm not trying to provoke you. I just need you to tell me what radicalised her. Was it Ireland? Did everything change when she went across the water?'

A couple of pigeons were cooing in the eaves just above their heads, their feet scratching across the roof tiles. Justin looked through the window to the trees opposite and took a couple of deep breaths. 'Tintack poached her from the Beeb, certainly. But we're talking a small-time Belfast production company here, your standard leftie outfit making indie films. She researched Tintack's projects on sectarianism and the harassment of Catholics. The media's conspiracy of silence around Northern Ireland, all that shit.'

'So that's a yes?'

'Is Gina a Republican, you mean?' Justin's shoulders lifted. 'Definitely not pro-terrorism.'

'Has she ever mentioned a guy called Bobby Roscoe?'

'Who is he?'

'Someone Dodge put up. Possibly linked to dissidents.'

'No way. Gina's always slagging off the IRA. Says they're authoritarian and chauvinistic.'

'But not shy about copying their language,' said Kerr, selecting another tab. 'Irish bankers financing Britain's colonial and capitalist system, for example.'

'That would be when she worked for Tintack,' said Justin, his voice laced with irritation. 'It's just rhetoric.'

'How about Avril Knight's predecessor as "the British overlord"?' Kerr paused to search Justin's face. 'So could the London attacks be a conspiracy between ACI and Irish dissidents?'

Justin looked crestfallen, as if he had just failed a test. 'I'd have picked something up by now.'

'Why did Tintack sack her?'

'They didn't. Gina came to London because the drugs charity invited her.'

'Solstizio, yes,' said Kerr. 'Has she told you who recruited her?'

'I'll work on it.'

'It's okay.'

'She's always wanted to work with drug victims,' said Justin, his lips twitching.

'You alright?'

'Jesus, so many questions.'

'Nearly there.' Kerr flipped to another tab. 'You've already described her flat in Hackney. Do you spend much time there?'

'A few of us visit once, twice a week,' said Justin, indicating the file again. 'It's in there.'

'Costello owns it outright, according to the 1830 financial profile. Do you know how she paid for it?'

Justin looked nonplussed. 'Bank of Mum?'

'Plus a euro savings account outside the UK. Know about that?'

'I'd have reported it, wouldn't I?' he said, quickly.

Kerr sat back while the hot air rose between them. 'Justin, I'm waiting for you to tell me why this doesn't sound right.'

'Okay, it's a bit bloody ironic,' said Justin, lamely. 'For an anti-capitalist.'

'Hypocritical, you mean. Costello's salary as a case worker is twenty-three thousand sterling but Solstizio have been paying additional euro deposits into her account since October. Caja Rural de Galicia. Different amounts each month. Current balance nudging half a million. So I have to assume Gina Costello is using Tintack and Solstizio as covers for something else?'

'Terrorism? No way.'

'Well I want you to imagine it is. A possibility.'

Justin blew out his cheeks. 'Boss, it's just not credible.'

'It means I have to look at technical coverage as well, Justin. To take the heat off you.'

'Pointless,' he shot back. 'Gina uses pay-as-you-go, a new phone every week, sometimes each day. They all do. After this surveillance cock-up she's even more freaked out. And she never emails ACI activists.'

'You've had a look, then?'

'Everything online is charity business or domestic garbage. She uses Facebook and Twitter for cover. It's word of mouth. You want access, boss?' he said, stiffening. 'You've got me.'

'Which means you can get into her computer, right?'

Justin stared at Kerr in disbelief. 'You want me to mess with her PC?'

'I'm thinking of an EC op, to hoover stuff you won't know about.'

'So Gina's computer catches a cold just after she's spotted surveillance, with me hanging around like her new best friend? Too risky, boss. And a waste of time.'

The previous year Justin's technical team had developed the EC, or Echo Chip, in the Camberwell workshop. Attached to a laptop's system board, it combined real time interception with limited microphone coverage; the downside was a temporary loss of processing power.

'I've watched you. It'll take, what, two minutes?'

Justin's face jagged in distaste. 'You're ordering me?'

Kerr reached into his pocket for a grey plastic shard, the size of a thumbnail. He waited for Justin to pick it up and secrete it in his shoe. 'How about Skype?' he murmured.

Justin looked up in surprise. 'You what?'

'Has Costello ever Skyped a member of the IRA?'

'We already covered that.'

Kerr regarded him carefully. 'A few days before the Hammersmith bomb someone from ACI contacted an IRA business associate.'

Justin shrugged. 'I told you, she never calls Ireland.'

'The IRA guy was in South America. Bogota, Columbia. The Skype was to finalise a cocaine deal into Europe.'

'Haven't you been listening, boss? Gina is not into that.' For the first time, Justin's voice held real anger. 'She works for Solstizia, for Christ's sake. Detoxing addicts, not supplying them. No way would she be dealing that shit.'

'The ACI caller was a French male, calling from Spain.'

'So what's the big deal?' said Justin, sweeping his hair back again. 'Why are you putting all this crap on me?'

Kerr flipped to the end of the file. 'Because Alan Fargo tracked the origin of the call to a village called Marin, on the north-west coast.'

'Gina hasn't been to Spain for…well, not since I've known her.'

'But her money has. We followed it there.'

'What?'

'Costello's bank account is registered at Pontevedra, which is less than ten kilometres from Marin. That's where Solstizia pays her the money. It's a twenty minute drive from the coast, Justin. So you can see why I'm pressing you, why I have to follow this up.'

'And you're suggesting…what, that Gina's some kind of fucking narco-terrorist?'

'That the London bombings are funded by drugs money, with Costello as the go-between.'

'Incon-fucking-ceivable.'

'Can you think of anything better?'

Justin's face clouded. 'Why didn't you tell me this at the start?'

'I was hoping I'd hear it from you.'

Kerr's rebuke seemed to ignite something in Justin. 'You've just upgraded Gina Costello from a person of interest to the prime suspect for London. For the bomb that almost killed you and Robyn,' he said, wiping his mouth with his sleeve. His voice leaked anxiety. 'Can you guess how that makes me feel?'

'Gina Costello is good at what she does,' said Kerr. 'So are you, my friend, and she trusts you. Relax. You're in a good place.'

'I thought I was, until you told me all this.'

'Anomalies,' said Kerr, swatting away an invisible fly. 'Anyway, how are you two getting along?'

Justin looked across in surprise. 'Sorry?'

'Well, do you like each other?' said Kerr, studying him keenly. 'You know, is she friendly, or do you have to make all the running?'

Somewhere in the street a car alarm sounded and Justin craned his neck, inquisitive, suspicious, always the street cop. 'You've been there, boss,' he said. 'You know what it's like.'

Kerr kept his smile switched on. 'Compatible, you two? For a long term infiltration?'

Justin's shoulders lifted again.

Kerr pushed the chair back and crossed his legs. 'And how about things at home?'

For the first time, Justin managed a laugh. 'The welfare tick in the box.'

'I was going to drop by and say hi to Louise, if that's okay? It's been six months.'

Justin nodded.

'Anything I need to know?'

'Lou's fine. We're good, thanks.'

Kerr paused, giving Justin the opportunity to open up. Downstairs, a door slammed. They heard a woman's voice calling, then the welcoming yap of a dog. 'You know you can come off at any time, don't you?'

Justin looked surprised. 'Do you want me to?'

Kerr shook his head. He slid Costello's file into his secure briefcase with his yellow notepad and turned the key. 'I believe no-one in the country can work this target better.'

They stood and faced each other. 'You leave first,' said Kerr, holding out his hand. As his operative made for the door Kerr was suddenly back in Washington, listening to Rich Malone's secret warning of another attack in London. 'Have you ever come across the word "Corona"?'

Justin turned, pulling on his beanie. 'As what?'

'A target. It may have come up in the call to Bogota.'

'I'll listen out.'

'And be sure to call me. For anything.'

Chapter Forty-Three

Wednesday, 19 October, 15.54, Piazza di Spagna, Rome

Luggage free, Kerr cleared the body scanner at Luton Airport to find the Departures Lounge smelling of breakfast, though a herd of stags was already downing pints of lager at the circular bar. With his flight to Rome delayed for at least an hour by 'passenger action', he felt a fleeting urge to join them. Instead, he walked closer to the gate to purchase an egg and bacon baguette with scalding black coffee. He found a seat overlooking the runway and caught Robyn's voicemail twice before trying Gabi.

'But you are coming, Dad, aren't you?'

'Where's Mum?'

'Taking a shower. We're really looking forward to seeing you.'

'Me, too, but I have to come back to London tonight.'

A pause. 'Don't think Mum's going to like that.'

Most of the travellers were reading the *Daily Mail* and *Daily Mirror*, but Kerr found an abandoned *Guardian* stripped of its sports pages on top of a trash bin. He skimmed the news, speed-dialling Melanie Fleming. 'How's it going?'

'All good. On a plot in Barking.'

'Jack behaving himself?'

'Insufferable.'

Kerr smiled. 'I take it he's in the passenger seat?'

'Dreaming about his Suzuki.'

'Say hi. And I need a private word about you know who.'

'Today?'

'Asap. I'm on a flight.'

Sipping his coffee while he waited for Melanie to call back, Kerr spoke with Alan Fargo for his morning update. Melanie rang as he was finishing the *Guardian* analysis on the previous week's attacks ('Feel Safe Under the Snooper's Charter? Clueless Yard Fumbles in the Dark While the Bombers Roam Free').

'I saw Jay yesterday.'

'How is he?' This time Melanie was obviously on foot, her voice raised above the traffic noise.

'He's got himself very close to Gina C.'

'Very good.'

'But not in the way I want. Can you call his girlfriend to fix a meet?'

'Sure,' said Melanie. 'Did he mention that she's pregnant?'

'No. Just that everything's wonderful.'

'Which isn't what Louise told me. What are you going to do?'

'I've tasked him to Echo Chip the target. If we get technical coverage, I'm going to pull him off.'

'That drastic? After all his effort?'

'Some of his responses worried me, Mel.'

'Defensive, you mean? Covering up?'

'All that.'

'Telling lies? Arsy? In denial?' A pair of emergency vehicles howled by, but Kerr picked up the sarcasm of the woman who had already endured the perilous front line of undercover work.

'Loss of objectivity.'

Melanie made a noise in her throat, a harsh laugh or cough, smothered by the sirens' wail. 'Doesn't that go with the job?' she shouted.

The stags had disappeared, bound for Rome, long before Kerr reached the gate and boarded his flight. He was in the back row, with the two adjacent seats unoccupied, and Justin Hine's name flashed onto his silenced BlackBerry as the aircraft began to push back. He leant forward and murmured into the phone. 'Can it wait?'

'Urgent, boss.' Justin sounded breathless and anxious. 'I just met the guy who called me yesterday. The one I told you about?'

A middle-aged woman across the aisle was staring at him. 'Make it quick.'

'They want me to fly to the place where we had the meeting last week. There's an airfield nearby.'

'Fly as in "pilot"?'

'It's to collect a package.'

Kerr leaned low towards the window, a finger in his free ear, as the cabin crew pointed out the exits. 'Has your friend told you what for?'

'I'm guessing it may be connected to the merchandise you told me about? The last leg in the transaction?'

'Brilliant.'

'What do I tell him?'

The flight attendant was approaching on the final seatbelt check; she looked even younger than Gabi. 'Let's speak again later.'

'The man wants to know now.'

'When's the pick-up?'

'Forty-eight hours. Maybe sooner.'

Kerr concealed his phone for a moment as the attendant came alongside. 'Can you do it?'

'Of course I can bloody do it,' said Justin, sounding irritated again.

'I mean, does your licence cover it?'

'Boss, is it a yes or no?'

Suddenly the flight attendant was leaning into him. She sounded annoyed, too. 'You have to switch that off now.'

'Tell him yes. Nice work,' said Kerr, then cut the call.

It was after three in Rome by the time Kerr changed his return ticket at Fiumicino airport for a late evening departure and found a taxi. It took another forty-five minutes to crawl into the city centre and walk the narrow cobbled streets behind Piazza di Spagna, searching for the wine bar Gabi had recommended. He came across the intimate Vinoteca Reggio, dark, woody and tourist free, just beyond an ancient tenement choked by dense ivy that dangled across the street to the opposite wall. Adjusting his eyes to the gloom, he spotted Gabi and Robyn sitting at stools deep inside the tiny bar, laughing over gelato amarena with bottles of Peroni. They must have seen the shadow in the doorway, for both turned to him at the same time, Gabi going to him with a shriek of delight ('Dad, you made it!'), Robyn waiting to copy her daughter's hug and three kisses of welcome. Both wore tight jeans and cork wedge heels, Gabi in a white rollneck sweater, Robyn in a silk blouse and the same cream, tailored jacket she had worn outside the pub in Hammersmith. Robyn gave him a look as Gabi turned to order a bottle of Orvieto and joshed him about his rubbish time management. As they chatted over him, Kerr remembered his brunch with Gabi in Victoria nine days earlier, where she had pleaded with him to visit Rome so they could be a 'proper family,' even for a few hours. Now, with the two women in his life perched each side of him, vivacious and chic in their bright red lipstick, Gucci sunshades pushed back, he felt a surge of happiness.

Gabi wanted to talk about Hammersmith but Kerr kept the focus on her career, the orchestra's Russian tour and life in London. 'This is exactly what he did at brunch last week,' she complained to Robyn after the third attempt. 'Diversionary tactics. I'm not too young to hear about this stuff, you know.'

'Drop it, Gabi,' she said, pouring more wine. 'We almost got ourselves blown up.'

'Come off it, *Mother*. You've been banging on about your flipping near-death experience ever since I got here.' She held up her glass. 'I'm perfectly capable of handling it.'

Kerr began to say something, then caught Robyn's warning glare. Later. Not in front of our child.

Thwarted, Gabi bounced the conversation back to Kerr and his relationship with Nancy Sergeyev, starting with her separation from Karl. She made it sound like retaliation.

'Living together?' said Robyn, after a couple of minutes. 'So "good friends" doesn't really cover it, right?' She leant forward until she found Kerr's eyes, signalling the gaps in the tale he had floated past her at Hammersmith. 'And how does Nancy feel about you seeing me again? After your latest brush with the Grim Reaper?'

'Not moved in, exactly,' said Kerr, awkwardly. 'We can cover this later.'

'I think she's a bit jealous of you, actually, Mum,' said Gabi, poking Kerr in the ribs.

'Me? The wicked witch from Glasgow? Don't be insane,' said Robyn. 'And when you get to meet this Nancy, tell her she's welcome to him.'

Gabi's phone rang as she was about to order another bottle. 'Sorry, guys, Angelo's early.' She made a face and slid from the stool, downing her wine. 'Catch up with you in the restaurant.'

Kerr looked quizzical as Gabi scampered into the street.

'String player on the tour. A poet, too. If you believe a word she says.' Robyn wriggled on the stool and straightened her back. 'Right. What do you want to know?'

'Here?' Kerr checked for the barman, just visible in the back room through the rack of bottles. 'You sure?'

'Isn't that why you came? To interrogate me?'

'Okay.' Kerr drank some more wine. 'This is how I see it. Belfast was a specific project for Spirito e l'Anima, right? I get that. But you never really explained it.'

'Because we were busy getting pissed, remember?'

'So what happened over there?'

Robyn eased down from the stool and rapidly waggled her legs to adjust her jeans. It was a slinky move he remembered from over two decades ago, when they had shuffled into their clothes after sex in the back of his van. She caught him watching and gave a little smile, as if she, too, was casting her mind back. 'Let's walk,' she said, smoothing her jacket.

They strolled to the Piazza heading for the Scalinata di Trinita dei Monti, Rome's famous Spanish Steps, the widest staircase in Europe. The air was warmer than forecast, and Kerr slung his jacket over his shoulder as they weaved through the knots of visitors.

'Let's suppose you're right about Hammersmith. You were the target, not me,' said Kerr as they began to climb. 'They took a massive risk snatching your bag.'

'My laptop. And stop talking about "they." This is the Real IRA, John. They followed me and put that bomb under my car.'

'And I'm waiting for you to tell me why?'

She gave a harsh laugh. 'Do you have any idea what it's like across the water? For people trapped in those estates around Belfast? The despair and deprivation, even now?' Kerr began to speak but Robyn ignored him. 'You should try it. Take a look beneath the hype about prosperity and paradise. Christ, you spy on everybody else.' Robyn spoke slowly and deliberately as they climbed, using the steps to punctuate each phrase. 'Belfast has more so-called peace walls now than during the worst of the Troubles. Did you know that?'

'Everyone does.'

'I don't think so. Belfast is a city of apartheid, John, and no-one want to know. Human rights for people living in ghettos? Forget it. Do you really understand the sheer bloody hatred that still divides them?'

'The scandal of sectarianism, yeah,' said Kerr.

'Which everyone shrugs off, just like you are, now. And the real outrage is the refusal to go public. So that was the mission they gave me. Research, record and expose the truth.'

'For instance?'

'How about the actual cost of the long-term unemployment and lost opportunities for Catholics? The scale of the grinding poverty and inequality? Well, it's far worse than anyone is prepared to admit. Belfast hides more sleeping dogs than Battersea.' She laughed again. 'But why should we be surprised when the media is so fucking tongue-tied?'

'So we're back to "the press as instruments of government" pitch?'

'Don't mock it, John. The peace process is a sham, propped up by a conspiracy of subjectivity, selectivity and silence, take your pick. Even the bloggers have fallen into line. So much for the precious Fifth Estate.'

Breathless, they turned and sat on the steps, with the Trinità dei Monti church towering at their backs. Robyn flipped down her shades to face the lowering sun and they sat in silence for a few moments, gazing down into the Piazza as tourists advanced towards them.

Kerr glanced at her. 'Did you come across a company called Tintack? They make documentaries. Strongly pro-republican?'

Robyn shook her head. 'But there are dozens of outfits like that. And you know what I think of reporters.'

'So you spoke out against discrimination. Important, fundamental social stuff.' Kerr waited for an overweight couple with backpacks to wheeze past. 'But where's the lethal part?'

'You what?'

'Come on, Robyn. What did you uncover that made the dissidents want to kill you?'

'Look, I drove this project straight down the line,' she said, sharply. 'I've supported Irish republicanism all my political life. You know that. A Glaswegian Catholic, what else? But when I work for Spirito I'm strictly lapsed. Neutral. Every interview audio-recorded and streamed to the laptop. From Loyalists, too. They didn't like it.'

'They?'

'No-one, from either side.' She took a deep breath. 'Nothing's changed. The paramilitary hierarchies are still in place at both extremes. After Brexit, Brussels threatens to turn off the magic money tap early at the slightest hint of violence, so Stormont doesn't want to hear this stuff, either. John, you won't believe how much hostility I faced over there. This is the Mafia breaking bread with the Freemasons. I'm telling you, a lot of people were warning me off.'

'So why didn't you mention this when I called?'

'I already told Finch's officers, you know, when Dumb and Dumber came out here to take my statement?' She stared at him. 'Jesus, don't you people speak to each other?'

'What did you tell them?'

'The Real IRA sent those two kids to get me. What else? Then last week they call me to say Hammersmith was first in the series of dissident attacks. How lucky am I?'

'Which is nonsense.'

'Thanks.'

'Different explosive.' Suddenly Kerr's BlackBerry was buzzing. 'I'll explain later,' he said, twisting upright from the step as Justin's name lit up the screen.

Robyn patted his backside. 'Send Nancy my love.'

Kerr took a couple of steps sideways and dropped his voice again. 'How's it going?'

'I just took a call from Gina,' said Justin, abruptly. 'The package is a person. A male.' He sounded as stressed as before.

'Know who?'

'Not yet.'

'What's it about?'

'Everything's tight but Gina must have organised this when we were over there.'

'And never mentioned it.'

'She had to be sure about me, like I told you,' said Justin, his voice quavery. 'I'll have three up on the flight back, so it'll be a Cessna 172.'

'Okay, let's speak tomorrow.'

'I'll probably have to fly out of Clacton,' he said, his voice floating down the line in a whisper. 'There'll be masses of paperwork, boss.'

'I'll handle it.'

'And back-up.'

'We'll cover you on the other side.' Kerr could tell that Justin was calling from some temporary refuge close to his targets. 'You sound worried.'

'I'm in a rush. They'll be wondering.'

'Sure you're up for this?'

'Gotta go,' he said, then the line went dead.

Chapter Forty-Four

The young driver's work name was Maxine. She was German with near perfect English, but hoped to complete her mission without speaking a word. Tired from the long drive to the Hook of Holland, she needed to catch up on lost sleep during the ferry crossing to Harwich, building energy for the return as a foot passenger with a different passport. Her vehicle was an old, high mileage horsebox mounted on a Renault chassis, registered in Paris. With its dark grey bodywork, stylish silver logo of a horse at full stretch and, inside, racks for saddles and bridles over clumps of straw, the vehicle was unremarkable. Only in England would its true purpose be realised.

In black sleeveless puffer jacket over a fawn roll neck sweater, woollen hat and jeans with knee length boots, its driver, too, passed unnoticed. Maxine planned to sleep in the horsebox but was spotted by a deckhand, pillow and rolled blanket under her arm, and ordered upstairs to the commotion of the passenger lounges.

As soon as they reached open sea she realised that her exclusion from the car deck, with its fug of oil, diesel and rubber, had been fortunate. Squalls rising to force eight had turned the ship into a rollercoaster, pitching and wallowing over the roiling North Sea as passengers searched the windows for a fix on the horizon. Avoiding a knot of drinkers toughing it out in the bar, Maxine zipped her jacket and followed a couple of smokers into the storm, sucking lungfuls of air as she peeled aft to face down the churning waters. She thought she had found shelter in the lee of a machine room until the wind howled around the bulkhead to snatch at her, pitiless as the blast from her comrade's bombs. Back inside, she dodged slicks of vomit to play a couple of fruit machines, then found refuge in the cinema, dozing in the back row while James Bond saved the world.

After almost eight hours the ferry approached Harwich in a calm sea, light winds and watery sunshine. Maxine returned to the horsebox and trailed ashore behind the assorted caravans, saloons and pick-ups. At the first layby on the A120 she switched on her mobile, pinged a prearranged text, and waited.

•••

Wednesday, 19 October, 16.11 GMT, safe house, Finsbury Park

Minutes after his return to the safe house, shoes thrown across the floor, Fin slumped in one of the camping chairs and devoured a Thai green chicken curry. He held the plastic bowl just beneath his chin, together with a slab of naan bread, watching the news break on Sky. Balanced on one of the builders' trestles was a paint spattered radio and CD player, tuned to LBC. Fin's Glock occupied its usual place in the cup holder, so the mug of tea sat beside him on the floor.

The TV was showing looped video of another evacuation in the City, with a live radio report from the scene streaming behind him. Fin had walked half a mile to place his hoax call on one of Roscoe's prepaid mobiles, then hurried back to enjoy the fallout. According to Sky sources 'close to last week's investigation,' the male caller had spoken with a 'strong, Northern Irish accent,' which was the reaction Roscoe had wanted.

Loitering outside the safe house, a mangy black cat had padded between a terracotta pot and the recycling bin to rub itself against Fin's calf as he inserted his key. Bending down to stroke the bony, half-starved body, Fin had resisted an urge to bring it inside for a dish of milk and sliver of chicken.

Now he heard movement again, ten minutes earlier than scheduled, the sound of Bobby Roscoe lugging his old wheelie bag down the cracked basement steps. The key turned in the mortice lock, then there was a squeal and a scuffling, clearly audible above the radio. He imagined the cat escaping, hurt, into the street, and hated Roscoe even more.

The ill-fitting door shuddered from the heft of a powerful shoulder, then Roscoe was inside the safe house, lifting his bag onto the rickety pine table in the front room. Fin stabbed a piece of chicken and saw a wave of anxiety flood Roscoe's face as he searched for Kenny.

Roscoe dipped his head into the bathroom. 'Where's the kid?'

Fin kept his eyes fixed on the screen, a slap of disrespect. 'Come and see the bastards running for their lives.' He held out the mobile for Roscoe to take and destroy, as instructed. 'Scared as rabbits.'

Roscoe snatched the mobile, kicked the plug from the TV and stood over him, waiting.

'Well, obviously, your man's out, isn't he?' said Fin, evenly, without meeting his eyes.

'What the fuck are you boys playing at?' growled Roscoe.

Fin kept his voice calm as he took the last mouthful. 'You know how bad Kenny's leg is. I warned you about it from the start.' He heaved himself from the chair, tossed the bowl and fork into the sink and turned down the radio. 'Can't you feel the damp and chill in here? It seizes the muscles, gets so bad he can hardly walk. You really expect us to stay banged up here all the time?'

'That's the deal,' said Roscoe.

In truth, his brother's sudden disappearance had alarmed Fin as much as Roscoe. Fin had been away from the safe house for less than forty minutes making the bomb call; Kenny, resting on the bed, had vanished by the time he returned. He turned away to the wheelie bag, feeling Roscoe's eyes bore into his back as the truth hit home. 'Oh, shit,' said Roscoe. 'You haven't got a clue, either?'

'He'll have gone for a walk,' said Fin, casually, unzipping the bag. 'You know, to stretch his legs. Loosen up. Get fit to deliver this little bag of tricks tomorrow. You should be grateful.' He eased open the supermarket bag to peer at the bomb in its plastic carton, then turned to look at Roscoe for the first time. 'Anything different here I need to tell him?'

'The little shit deserves a bullet.'

'Going to shoot his other leg, are you?' He gave a mocking laugh. 'Who else would do your dirty work?'

They stood over the bomb, facing each other in silence. Both knew that their flickering comradeship had died with the failed mortar attack. Only necessity bound them now, and Fin could see fear as well as anger in Roscoe, the weakness of the school bully channelling violence at home. It made him wonder again who was pulling Roscoe's strings. 'We're not the enemy here, pal,' he said, quietly. 'Not me, nor Kenny. You want someone to punish? Find the boys over there who kneecapped my brother.'

Before Roscoe could answer, his mobile beeped. 'I have to be at the workshop,' he said, without glancing at the screen.

'So relax,' said Fin, keeping his voice low. 'Everything's going to be fine. Kenny is sound as a bell.'

'Find him. I'm giving you two hours.'

Fin kept him there, facing him down. 'Haven't you forgotten something?'

'When I come back,' said Roscoe, turning away to the door. 'And the kid had better be here.'

'No, you bastard. Now.' Roscoe swung around, eyes widening as Fin raised the Glock into his face. '*That's* the deal.'

Carefully, Roscoe took a packet of cocaine from his coat. He tossed it beside the bomb but the barrel stayed jammed against his forehead. 'What else?' he murmured.

'Hurt the cat again,' said Fin, quietly, 'and I'll blow your fucking brains out.'

Chapter Forty-Five

Kerr and Robyn took their time to reach the top of the Scalinate. Warmed by the exertion and late afternoon sunshine, they ambled left along the quiet Viale Gabriele d'Annunzio, keeping a look-out for Gabi.

'Why did you ask about that Belfast film company?' said Robyn when they had caught their breath.

'Tintack. I'm investigating a European activist with links there.'

'Which group?'

'Anti-Capitalist Insurrection.'

'You're telling me ACI could be involved?' Robyn looked astonished. 'In London?'

Kerr shrugged. 'All the targets have been banks.'

'You seriously believe they have capacity on that scale?'

'What do you think?'

'Jesus. You got to me just in time.'

Kerr smiled. 'You've always been there for me, right?'

'Your leftie deep throat in Europe.' She paused by the low stone wall and faced him. 'That's why you're here isn't it?'

Kerr shook his head. 'To find out what happened in Belfast.'

'And play happy families, for Gabi's sake?' said Robyn, laughing at his straight face.

They traced the top of the ridge in silence for a few moments, enjoying the red domes and towers of the churches stretching to the west, starkly beautiful in the fading light. Beyond a group of trees they came across an outlook point carved into the hilltop, lined with wooden benches cemented into the stone. The nearest carried a small brass plate in English: 'Guido, who Fought with the British Army but found Peace in This Place, In Memoriam, 1921 – 2008.' They were early for dinner so Robyn sat and stretched out, crossing her legs at the ankles. 'I could have saved you a lot of time, if you'd come to me earlier. The London bombs are absolutely not down to Anti-Capitalist Insurrection. Nor anyone in Europe, for that matter. That's what I think.'

Kerr was sitting forward, elbows on his thighs. 'How about a joint enterprise?' he said, turning.

'Educated European activists taking orders from Irish paramilitaries? Or subcontracting to someone else? Why the hell would they do that?'

'Because they hate the same people.'

'Nice try, but inconceivable. I've known a lot of European radicals in my time and they're self-obsessed. Most, anyway. High octane, take no shit and always snatch the credit. Remind you of anyone?' she said, giving Kerr a look. 'The IRA belongs to yesterday, John. That's the message in Europe, and everyone in Belfast is tuned in except the failed old fucks clinging to the past. Which is the reason they're doing London, with their stupid code words and harum-scarum bombs.'

'So why is everyone in Belfast denying it?'

'Stormont politics?' she said, throwing up her hands. 'You can figure that out back home. I'm giving you the worm's eye view. Everyone saw the bodies at the station and that bank in the City. Passers-by, trapped in the wrong place and time. What about their human rights? This was random violence, which makes them no better than Islamist psychos shooting up beaches and concert halls. Marauders with bomb belts, obsessed with death. Savages.' She paused to let a couple of walkers pass behind them. 'Okay. Look, at Spirito we rub along with security gurus, analysts and know-nothing spin doctors who never see eye to eye. Most say that, yes, ACI has the capacity for violent direct action...'

'Which is what our liaison guys tell us.'

'...but the blood on its hands will belong to some dead bankster, not a bunch of yuppies out for lunch or mum with kids waiting for a bus. No shoppers in body bags, right?' The words had poured out in a torrent and she paused to draw breath. 'Right?'

'No collateral damage. I've got it,' said Kerr, as his BlackBerry buzzed. It was a message from Gemma with another bomb threat notification. Kerr held up his hand and scanned the text: 'Livebait rec'd 15.46. Bomb at Stock X. 30 mins warning, code Emerald. Evac, area searched, no trace. Best, G.' He frowned. 'We just had another bomb threat in London.'

'A bank?'

'Stock Exchange. Nothing found, so looks like a false alarm.'

'And you're going to tell me they used the IRA code word for a hoax, aren't you?'

Kerr sat back on the bench, folded his arms and looked left to the towers of the Trinita dei Monti, just visible through the trees. 'Yet the Semtex was sourced in Europe.'

Robyn tapped his forehead. 'Did you listen to anything I said? Let's try again. Spirito has been working on the migrant crisis. Free movement across Europe? Forget it. We're looking at a security lock-down. Wherever your explosives came from, any cross-border co-operation is a no-go. The London campaign is being driven from Belfast.' Kerr looked sceptical as Robyn pulled him to his feet. 'Yes, John. Just like the old days.'

Gabi had made their reservation at Ristorante Edoardo, as intimate as the bar below but with crisp linen table cloths and napkins. Edoardo served Italian and Spanish dishes and was favoured by the locals because it lay beyond the range of tourists climbing the Scalinate. The evening was still unseasonably warm, so Robyn changed their place to a table in a corner of the open-sided conservatory, with a sheer drop down the hillside and an uninterrupted view of the Piazza del Popolo.

Robyn texted Gabi before ordering a bottle of Amarone with spaghetti for them both.

'When I called on Saturday you said your report might be delayed,' said Kerr as they clinked glasses.

'This is very delicate. Our project was commissioned by the EU before the Referendum, so we have real influence here. Forget Brexit and the two years from Article Fifty. A thumbs down from Spirito stifles the EU grant allocation for Northern Ireland peace projects *right now*.'

'Such as?'

'A sharp spike in violence, especially sectarian attacks. That's a biggie, obviously. Spirito can seriously rock the boat, basically, so I have to double-check every element.'

Kerr tucked the napkin into his shirt. 'And if the IRA returns to war?'

'The EU pulls the plug immediately.'

'To be replaced by Westminster.'

'With the Home Secretary assassinated?' Robyn's face jagged. 'Yeah, like that's going to happen. Still puzzled about those denials from Stormont?'

'I'm wondering which "element" nearly got us killed?' he said, just as Gabi appeared, beaming at them as she hurried through the restaurant.

Gabi kissed Kerr, flung herself into the chair and poured herself a glass of wine. 'So how do you like Edoardo, Dad?' She looked hot, with strands of hair sticking to her temples as she checked her face on her iPhone camera. 'Yuk.' She glanced at their dishes, smiled at their waiter and signalled for the same.

Robyn poured her a glass of water. 'Give us a couple of minutes, will you?'

Gabi looked between them. 'You're arguing? Already?'

Kerr looked at Robyn. 'Later?'

'Has to be now,' said Robyn sharply, sliding her make-up bag towards her daughter. 'Cool down. Freshen up.'

Gabi downed the water in one gulp. 'Okay, I'll give you five minutes, max,' she said, splaying her fingers as she made for the toilet on the far side of the bar.

Robyn regarded Kerr carefully, as if trying to convince herself of something. 'What I'm going to tell you is completely secret,' she said, turning her spaghetti. 'No-one knows except our director, and I wasn't going to tell you. Any leak comes straight back to me. Understood?'

Kerr nodded.

Robyn drank some wine, then took a deep breath. 'Before I left Rome for Belfast I got a call from another charity worker. Thirtyish, same work, different outfit. He was in Greece, then Hungary and Germany, always on the move. But he's Irish, born in Belfast to a single mother who pissed off to America.' The conservatory was empty, local early birds having taken tables indoors, but Robyn took a moment to double-check. 'He grew up in a children's home.'

'Oh, God. Where?'

Robyn shook her head. 'Outside the city, not one of the places already investigated. This is different. Scary. He says there are at least twenty-three names.'

'Poor kids.'

Robyn shook her head. 'Not the victims.'

Kerr put down his fork. 'These are the abusers?'

'The clients.' She leaned in and dropped her voice. 'Staff at the home were pimping out these children to paramilitaries. Exclusively,' she said, before Kerr could interrupt. 'He's named some already. Says he'll give me the others when he knows he can trust me.'

'The stats you mentioned on the phone?'

She nodded. 'Grunts, mostly. But some big shots, too. From both sides.'

'They're *sharing*?'

'No bigotry in child abuse, I guess.'

'Are you going to tell me his name?'

Another shake of the head. 'I call him Nick. And yes, I *do* think the man is credible.' She sat forward, her body language mirroring Kerr's, a couple making love. 'The things he's telling me are true, John, so don't bloody look at me like that.'

'Can you prove it?'

Robyn finally started eating again. 'Another boy from the circle tried to speak out a wee while back and got himself murdered. Executed, more like. So Nick decided to take it from there.'

'How many years is "a wee while"?'

Robyn threw Kerr another look of refusal. 'You'll be trawling through the bloody archives. Anyway, Nick's been secretly building the case. The catalogue, as he calls it. Dates and details of the abuse. Names and descriptions of the attackers. Physical peculiarities. Distinguishing marks.'

'Nick showed this to you?'

A breeze wafted through the open sides of the conservatory, disturbing the table cloth and distracting them. The sunset was suddenly painting the sky deep red and she turned to admire the darkening cityscape. Kerr sipped some wine, silent, waiting, as Gabi reappeared in the corner of his eye, flirting with their waiter.

'All that beauty and I'm talking about blemishes, birthmarks and tattoos,' murmured Robyn. 'Pimples, scars and circumcisions. It's disgusting.'

'It's hearsay. You know the risks, Robyn.'

She swung back to face him. 'He's got high quality video.'

Kerr craned forward, as if he had misheard. 'Of terrorists torturing children?'

Robyn's nod was almost imperceptible and, when she spoke, her voice so quiet that Kerr strained to hear the words. 'Thugs with beer bellies and baseball caps raping little boys. The faces are visible.'

'How did Nick get hold of this stuff?'

'He hacked into the main abuser and raided other accounts from there. They saved everything in six folders. The hurt that keeps on giving. Forget your English rockers, DJs and parliamentary pricks, John. This is going to be earth shattering.'

Kerr sat quietly for a moment. 'So how is Spirito going to handle it?'

'After the attack on me?' She gave a shrug and gazed at the last slice of sun sinking beneath the distant spires and domes. 'I'm looking for another way.'

'Robyn, we can't let this go.'

'We?' She looked at him steadily, as if reading his thoughts, and there were tears in her eyes. 'Further down the road,' she murmured, as Gabi reached them.

'So tell me about Angelo,' said Kerr, watching Gabi's eyes scan their half-eaten dishes.

'There you go again, Dad,' said Gabi, as her spaghetti arrived.

'I mean his poetry.'

'You wouldn't get it.' She nodded sideways. 'You do remember it's Mum's birthday tomorrow?'

'For God's sake, Gabi,' said Robyn, as Kerr reached for his glass.

Gabi studied Robyn's face for a moment and looked sceptical. 'You *are* staying over, Dad?'

'I'm booked on the last flight.'

'Miss it.' She swallowed some pasta and pointed her fork at him. 'You can have my bed if you're that fussed. I'm sleeping at Angelo's.'

Chapter Forty-Six

As Gabi wolfed down her spaghetti, brushed away talk about a taxi home ('Mum, we're celebrating!') and showed the waiter their empty bottle, journalist Vanessa Gavron sat in the cocktail lounge of the Hotel Jasmine with New Scotland Yard's head of counter-terrorism.

The hotel lay in the quiet streets behind Paddington mainline station and Derek Finch had secured his favourite spot, a softly-lit alcove invisible to business travellers and mid-range hookers lingering in the foyer. Ten days into the terrorist campaign, with multiple victims and no credible suspects, the deputy assistant commissioner looked unruffled as he settled into the chintz armchair, unbuttoned his jacket and smoothed his powder blue tie. 'So, Vanessa. What are you going to do for me?'

Gavron's chair was at right angles to his, the arms almost touching. 'I'm going to tell you who's putting the bombs down.'

This was a reversal of the usual information stream. In the previous century, Detective Superintendent Finch had been Gavron's contact in the National Crime Squad, and his chauvinism still needled her. She had changed into a charcoal trouser suit for their meeting and instinctively shifted her knees as he leaned closer. 'What makes you think I don't already know?'

They paused as the waiter arrived with Martinis on a silver tray. Finch was an infrequent visitor, yet the barman indulged him as if he were a celebrity living in the penthouse, reaching for the vodka as soon as he entered the lounge. It was the deference that flowed from generosity or fear; and, knowing Finch to be a mean tipper, Gavron sensed pressure around his shaky immigration status.

'Well, you're buying, aren't you?' she said. 'Cheers.'

Finch brushed an imaginary speck from his thigh. He had acquired another expensive looking watch since their last encounter and a couple of charity wristbands she did not recognise. 'Perhaps I just enjoy your company,' he said, holding her eye.

Gavron laughed. 'Come on, Derek. Have you seen what the hacks are writing about you? On the telly more than Jon Snow and they still say your investigation's shit.'

'So you've come here to save my skin?'

'You're a busy man with the mortuaries full, the cells empty and a dead Home Secretary draped around your neck. I guess you'll be getting a lot of phone calls right now, and none as friendly as mine.' She checked her iPhone, stirred her drink and popped the olive into her mouth. 'I called your office, what, less than one hour ago? And here you are, practically out in the sticks. Which tells me you've got sweet FA.'

'I'm staying the night, as a matter of fact. Usual room,' said Finch, shifting in the armchair. 'And now you're making me impatient.'

Gavron smiled. Usually, she agreed to meet at a location chosen by her contact, or a quiet coffee bar behind Charing Cross Road. The Bull always insisted on the Jasmine, for daytime meetings and discreet overnight stays. At times of high activity, a reservation on the Met's corporate card saved the late night drive home to Bromley. It also offered a haven for illicit sex and escape from the second Mrs Finch, a cut-throat health professional with a hatred of bed-blockers. Gavron knew all this because Finch had confided in her. Recently, in a straight trade-off for sensitive information about a corruption scam in South America, she had agreed to join him in Room 806. The sex had been unprotected, stifling and short. Afterwards, collapsed on his back, chest hair glistening with sweat, he had slapped her bottom as she slipped from the bed and joked about a 'Fairtrade fuck'; locked in the bathroom, showering away every trace, Gavron had reproached herself for a joyless connection she vowed never to repeat.

She searched her tote bag for a plain notebook and flipped

the pages. 'Someone just passed me information you need to have urgently. A Catholic priest.'

'Another paedophile,' said Finch, flatly.

'A source. I was expecting the call but not the content.'

'So what's the big deal?'

'Something he heard from a young man in church.'

'As in "confession"?'

Gavron nodded. 'A walk-in last week.'

'About the bombs? And you left it till now?'

'He came back this afternoon. The priest rang me straight away and here we are.'

Finch looked sceptical. 'I'm all ears.'

'My source is obviously bound by the seal of the confessional.'

Finch smirked and sipped his drink. 'How long have you been blackmailing him?'

Gavron took a moment to scan her notes. 'The guy claims he put down the devices.'

'Irish?'

'Belfast accent, according to the priest.'

'And he would know, right? Because he's from there, too?' Finch loomed close again and dropped his voice. 'Bollocks to the priest, penitent thing, Vanessa. I want names.'

'Irish, but not IRA,' she said, evading him again. 'That's the point. The boy hates them. The Real IRA kneecapped him for dealing drugs then rode him out of town, told him to get lost and never return. Exiled, basically, and that's how he ended up in London.'

'So I'm looking for a bomber on crutches?'

'No,' said Gavron, shaking her head. 'But worth another look at the CCTV?'

'Who's he working with, this druggie?'

'He was picked up a few weeks back and hidden away in a safe house, apparently.'

'Where?'

'Somewhere in London.'

'Brilliant.'

'Then they ordered him to place the bombs at Victoria and Cheapside.'

'Just like that,' said Finch, unimpressed. 'And the mortar attack?'

'He hasn't mentioned that. Or any accomplices.'

'When was the first meeting?'

'Friday.'

'After he watched the bombs on TV?' he said, as Gavron shrugged. 'So you're giving me a fantasist on dope.'

'Or an arsonist who claims his fire.'

'And why would he do that?'

'He was acting under duress and feels remorse about the people he's murdered, I suppose.' Her shoulders lifted again. 'The boy wants forgiveness. Aren't you going to ask me who's pulling his strings?'

'Are you going to stop wasting my time?'

'I'll tell you, anyway. He's an Englishman, the voice of the bomb warnings. Other people make the devices but the whole thing is being run from London.'

Finch suddenly looked shrewd. A couple of rogue nasal hairs quivered in her direction, like antennae. 'This is hearsay, Vanessa. No, it's less than that, because you haven't even convinced me your boy exists. I'm investigating complex, high-end terrorism, well planned and executed. Have some facts. The orders are coming from west Belfast. The bombs are being made and put down by Real IRA paramilitaries.'

'Really? You have forensics to prove it? Confessions? Criminal charges? Paddington Green isn't exactly overflowing with suspects, is it?'

Finch took another drink and checked his watch. 'This is what the intelligence community is telling me.'

'Ah.' Over the years Gavron had cultivated a senior contact in MI5, always willing to brief on success, real or imagined. As she shook her head, a cartoon image popped into her head of Toby Devereux leading the Bull by the nose. 'Well, they're wrong. Don't you see? The people doing this are making it *look* like the IRA.'

'And you offer me, what? Damaged goods. A boy on drugs and a priest teetering on the brink.'

'Who risks excommunication for disclosing this.'

'And public humiliation by you if he doesn't,' said Finch, curtly. 'Your reverend father has been weighing his options, right? Kicked out of the church or thrown into prison. That's his angle. What's yours?'

'Doing the right thing. Being a good citizen.'

'Very nice,' smiled Finch, nastily. 'And hoping I'll give you a story.'

'You already have. I'm unravelling a conspiracy to stitch up the IRA and drag us back to war but Scotland Yard refuses to listen. Readers love a cover-up. This one practically writes itself.'

'Vanessa, there's nothing in this for you, or me. It's a distraction.' Suddenly, he rested his hand on her thigh and nodded at the bar. 'Let's have another drink. I'll give you more about the thing in Brazil.'

'How can you be so dismissive? And so sure?' The waiter was hovering but Gavron swung round to wave him away, dislodging Finch's grasp. 'With so many unanswered questions swirling around? I mean, you've got masses of denials from across the water, no suspect in sight and not a shred of evidence. With a hundred detectives working on each attack, give or take? That's just weird,' she said, slipping the notebook into her bag. She stood over him, frowning. 'And you also look extremely pissed off, which intrigues me even more.'

'You can't write any of this,' he growled.

Gavron bent down to look him in the eye. 'What's your angle, Derek?' she murmured. 'That's what I really want to know.'

•••

Cooking fish fingers and fries for her children, Nancy Sergeyev did not hear the iPhone because she had taken it through to the living room to arrange a babysitter and forgotten to retrieve it. The voicemail must have been beeping while she coaxed Tom and Amy to bed, checking hands, faces and brushed teeth before picking up the stories John Kerr had promised to read them.

She did not check her emails and pick up Kerr's message until an hour after lights out. It was brief and affectionate, from somewhere in the open, the words suffused with drink and contrition. He must have thought he had covered all the bases, his voice full of assurance about an early morning flight and promises to the future; Nancy poured a glass of Sancerre, paused *The Good Wife* and called him back, anyway, stirred by feelings of disappointment, indignation and curiosity.

Perversely, listening to the international dialling tone, she half expected Robyn to answer. When Kerr's voicemail cut in, she rang off and dialled again. This time, he picked up almost immediately.

'Nance? Everything okay?' He was inside, now, somewhere quiet, and sounded croaky, as if she had woken him up.

She checked the time: just after ten in Rome. 'Fine. Guessed you'd be late but wasn't expecting a no-show. I made a casserole.'

'Look, I'm really sorry.'

'You didn't say where you were staying.'

'I'm on the early bird. Coming straight home.'

Kerr was keeping his voice low, which answered her question. She heard other sounds, too, the creak of an old bed frame, the swish of a duvet being kicked away as Kerr stepped onto the tiled floor, then a second voice, smaller, sleepy, a woman murmuring to him.

Nancy took a slug of wine. 'How did it go?'

'Good. We covered a lot of ground. Not just Hammersmith. The whole shebang.'

'What, from the Italian liaison officer?'

'We kept it low key, actually. Unofficial.'

'So just you and Robyn, in the sunshine all day?' she said.

'Gabi was there, too.'

'Not all work, then?'

'Okay, we had a nice lunch. Gabi reminded me about Robyn's birthday.'

'And I bet you've given her a present to remember,' said Nancy, wincing at her own crassness.

Silence at the other end. 'Nancy, she's the mother of my child.'

'But you're staying with her, right? Spending the night there?'

'It's not like that.'

'You've already got a girlfriend.' Above her, she could hear Tom scampering along the landing. She leaned across the sofa to peer up the stairs and spotted a flash of pyjamas heading for Amy's room. 'Bed! Now!'

'Kids alright?'

'Not really. Don't change the subject.'

'Nancy, that bomb on the bridge almost killed her. Me too.'

'And what? It's brought you closer?'

'This is ridiculous. You need to…'

'Don't bloody give me all that crap. I went through years of two-timing with Karl, remember? I was stupid then and it's not going to happen again.' He was quiet at the other end, so she drank some more wine. 'You hear me?'

'Nancy, this is not what you think.'

'Stop it. Just bloody stop it,' she said.

Another phone rang from somewhere close by, the bedroom. She heard a woman's voice answer quietly in Italian, then English, removing all doubt.

'Listen,' said Kerr. 'We can do this tomorrow.'

'No,' said Nancy, draining her glass. 'We can't. So. Here's what *you* need to do. Catch the flight in the morning and drive home. I mean, to your place, not mine. Decide what you want. Don't ever call me again unless you're absolutely sure.'

He had started to speak again as Nancy rang off. She paused at the foot of the stairs to listen for a moment, on her way to the kitchen. All quiet, everyone settled. She loaded the dishwasher, lit a flame under the casserole and poured herself a large glass of Merlot.

'*Ciao,*' she said, winking at her reflection in the oven door.

Chapter Forty-Seven

Wednesday, 19 October, 21.18, Vanessa Gavron's Apartment,
City of London

Anticipating cocktails with the Bull, Vanessa Gavron had left her Saab in the undergound car park of her apartment block near Bank station, changed and taken the tube to Paddington. Rush hour was in full flow by the time she escaped the Jasmine and it took over forty minutes to reach home, balancing against a handrail in the packed carriage as she scribbled Finch's exact words into her tiny notebook. In Reception she smiled at the concierge and took the lift to the sixth floor, making a face at her reflection in the full-length mirror: Gavron's long day had begun with an early morning drive to Heathrow, delivering a nervy Donal Quinn to Virgin for his flight back to New Jersey. Double-locking the front door behind her, she unbuttoned her jacket, kicked off her shoes and stripped his bed, relishing the return to normality.

Stuffing the sheets into the washing-machine, she added her white blouse and underwear to the load, then padded into the bathroom. In a career of lifting stones, chasing contacts and avoiding enemies, home was a haven where she could roam naked and do whatever she pleased. Gavron cherished her privacy, and young Donal was one of the few men invited to share her space. There had been only two longish-term relationships in her life, with a sports writer in Dublin and a married professor of political history. Both had been ill-starred, the men unreliable, jealous and needy, the academic fleeing as her fertility reached the cliff edge. Now, time-poor, at the threshold of middle age, she managed her sex life through pornography and an upmarket dating site, no-strings-attached. One-nighters with rogues like Derek Finch she discounted: stories for sex were a necessary evil.

She took a long shower, refreshing herself for the night's work. Lifting her face to the gentle rain, she tried to make sense of her conversation with the Bull. A credible senior detective would have welcomed a fresh lead to re-boot his stalled inquiry; Derek Finch, the highest of them all, had been dismissive, and his shadiness intrigued her. Evasive, stubborn or stupid, the Bull's response goaded her, flooding her mind with possibilities. Towelling herself, she hurried into the bedroom, chasing the story. In silk pyjamas, leaving her hair damp, she searched the fridge for last night's sushi, poured herself a large glass of Chardonnay and flopped onto the sofa for her evening news fix. She flicked through the channels to settle on Al Jazeera, staring at the screen while her own exclusive took shape.

When she was ready, she moved to her workspace at the dining table beside the picture window, with a clear view of the river. Late evening found Gavron at her most creative, immersed in a ritual of e-cigarettes, Bushmills on the rocks and Enya's *Paint the Sky with Stars* on the surround sound. She fired up her ancient laptop and gazed over the Thames, a languid, inky blackness studded with lights, swirling away to the sea. An email popped up as she was about to start, a line in the Subject box from the private office of Charles Brandon, editor-in-chief of news agency CBB. 'Free for a call from Charles?'

Gavron frowned. The Father Michael investigation was her third CBB sponsored project, but this would be the first out of hours call from Charles in person. Dialling, she glanced at the clock on her phone: after nine, well into Brandon drinking time. 'Hi, Trace. What's up?'

'Sorry to gatecrash your evening. Charles wanted to be sure you can speak in private.'

'I'm at home. Christ, don't tell me he's still got you in the office?' said Gavron, mischievously. Tracey's affair with her thrice married boss was the worst kept secret among staffers in the CBB greenhouse, a cliché of stolen looks, snatched phone calls and synchronised departures. Gavron concluded she must be calling from his flat in Canary Wharf.

'Hold on,' said Tracey. There was a hiatus at the other end as she handed over the phone, a muttered 'Ta,' then Brandon's voice slid down the line, fruity and lubricated. 'Vanessa, thanks for touching base. I wanted to share the feedback on today's session.'

'You're firing me.'

A chortle down the line. Charles Brandon, OBE, was an Irish Unionist, born and educated in North Down, though in drink his voice slurred into South Ken, as if scared of being found out. 'Everyone on the team is *very* happy with your exposure of this… recalcitrant man of God,' he drawled.

'That's good to hear,' said Gavron, cautiously. 'But?'

Another chuckle, then silence, as if he was reading something.

Gavron filled the gap. 'Actually, there's been a development,' she said. 'The man's looking for a deal. I called Nisha about it.'

'And Nisha rang me, which is why I need a word. What does your reverend father have to trade?'

'He claims to have spoken to one of the bombers.'

'Yes. In the confessional. And in return?'

'I back away from the sex abuse.'

'The mechanics create difficulties for us,' said Brandon. 'Ethically.'

'But not the essence. The source claims the bombing campaign is being organised within England to frame the IRA. That's our exclusive, Charles.'

'And you intend to pass this new evidence to the police?'

Gavron suppressed a laugh. She had spent a lifetime exposing liars, and Charlie Brandon's bluff floated across on a sea of red wine. The Bull must have called him from the Jasmine the moment she left.

'I already have,' she said.

'Like any good citizen.'

'Except they completely blanked me. Still fixated on the Irish dissident bullshit.'

'So you propose to do…what, exactly?'

'Ask the obvious questions. The Yard are always boasting about going where the evidence leads them. Well, the investigation is flagging and I've just offered them the way out of the maze. Why would they wilfully reject it?'

'They may have other tricks up their sleeve.'

'After ten days with no arrests? No, they don't want any new evidence to undermine their foregone conclusion.'

'Which is?'

'That the Real IRA have come back to bomb the mainland.'

'Perhaps they have.'

'Okay. But why not take a moment to follow this up?'

'Too busy hunting actual terrorists?'

'Or playing politics. Which is it, Charles? Incompetence, cover-up or conspiracy? What are they hiding? Those are the questions I need to ask, because no-one else will.'

Another silence. 'Finished?'

Gavron took a sip of whiskey. 'That's the story I'm going to write.'

'In which case, I've caught you just in time. I don't think the public interest is served by shovelling excrement on the boys in blue. And OJ advises that a piece along those lines would be unwise. Counter-productive, even.'

Gavron groaned. Everyone knew the intervention of Ollie Jacobs, Brandon's shit of a lawyer, spelt sudden death. 'What's the problem?'

'Where to start? Your priest will say anything to save himself from humiliation and jail, even if that means betraying the confessional. And if he exists, his mysterious young penitent is uncheckable, the allegations impossible to corroborate. Shall I go on? Vanessa, this is not a story I can take to market.'

'So you're spiking it? You and Ollie?'

'Too many legal flies to swat. You're proposing to interfere in a national security investigation, and that leaves us open to litigation, or even criminal proceedings. Do I need to spell it out?'

'Is that Ollie's opinion, or a threat from Scotland Yard?'

'Vanessa, you offered me a scoop about a priest raping young boys…'

'Who got to you?'

'…not a…some deep throat in a clerical collar.'

'You don't really like us, do you, Charles?'

'I hold you in the highest professional…'

'Catholics, I mean.'

'Please, no more insults. You have a contract with CBB.' The voice was suddenly harsh, as if the Irishman had found himself again. 'So keep to your side of the bargain.'

'Stuff the bloody bargain. I'll find a blogger.'

'That would be unrealistic.' A deep sigh blew down the line. 'Look, it's good that we work together. Take the evening off and let's speak tomorrow. Lunch.'

The line died before she could reply. 'Screw you, Charles.' She watched a pleasure boat drift beneath Southwark Bridge, its deck fired by red and blue strobing lights, and wondered how many more would die if she kept silent.

She knew Brandon would not be fazed by her threat to work with a blogger. Gavron was famously elusive, resisting the lure of Facebook likes, Twitter feeds, prizes and celebrity. She always traced her leads from the shadows, letting the exclusive speak for itself.

She went into the kitchen, clattered ice into her tumbler and poured more Bushmills. Two powerful men had leaned on her in less than six hours, as if she suddenly posed some kind of threat, and the challenge gripped her. A new plan edged alongside the story as she sat by the window, energised and fearless.

Gavron kept her valuables in the bedroom, hidden inside a small safe in her wardrobe. She hurried there now, took out her contacts book and flicked through the crowded pages. It took a while, for she was searching for someone she had met recently, first name only.

She took a sip of whiskey, wriggled back into her chair and dialled.

•••

Wednesday, 19 October, 22.19, Robyn's Apartment, Tor Cervara, Rome

Robyn had forgotten to mute her phone when they collapsed onto the bed. Later, shaken awake by Kerr's call from his girlfriend, she had been aware of him pushing the duvet back and pattering across the cold tiles into the soggiorno, his voice and body language quickened by guilt. Inquisitive, she had strained to eavesdrop on the conversation, until his murmuring faded to a whisper and she dozed off again. One of them must have knocked her own phone to the floor, where it lay hidden beneath her jeans. It took her a moment to track the ring tone and feel beneath the pile of clothes. 'Pronto.'

'*Buona sera*. Can I speak to Robyn? It's Vanessa.'

'Oh…Hi. Hello.'

'I'm sorry. Did I wake you?'

'No,' said Robyn, sitting up in bed. 'It's fine.'

'You don't remember me, do you?'

Robyn checked the screen, relieved to see the name there. 'Of course,' she said, as memories popped into her brain: Guinness and cocktails in a teeming hotel bar, her round, my round, both shouting to make themselves heard. 'How are you?'

'Good, thanks. Did you get back okay?'

'Usual security alert. You?'

'Robyn, I know it's late but I need your help.'

'For the project?'

'The London bombs, and it's very urgent. Look, when we were in the bar you told me you had a boyfriend in Special Branch.'

'Confessions?' said Robyn, rubbing her eyes. 'God, was I that pissed?'

'I was wondering…you know…if you're still in touch?'

'Off and on. But he's secret squirrel, and they don't talk to reporters. Sorry.'

'This isn't for a story. I'm trying to *pass* information, not buy it. One of the good guys, for a change. And you trust him, right?'

'Your little black book must be full of real coppers?'

'For this, I need an outsider.'

'Well, he's certainly that.'

'Someone to listen to what I have to say, then do something with it. Will you give him my number?'

'I'll ring him.' She watched Kerr finish his call and stand quietly for a moment, slowly shaking his head. 'But I can't promise anything, love. You know what they're like.'

'Cops?'

'Men.'

Chapter Forty-Eight

With grey beanie pulled low on his forehead, Kenny watched the little girl hop onto the crowded carriage at Caledonian Road station. Her teenage mother gripped the hood of her coat in one hand and, with the other, a pushchair and green Bag for Life identical to the one resting between Kenny's legs. In bobble hat and woollen tights, dummy clamped in her mouth, the child clambered onto a priority seat opposite Kenny while Mum scrolled through a technicolour smartphone, probably clinging to her own vanishing childhood. Too young to spot stranger danger, the toddler threw Kenny such an open smile that her dummy dropped to the floor, tumbling against his bag. 'Ta,' said Mum as Kenny reached a gloved hand to retrieve it, her spare thumb never leaving the phone.

Operating solo for the first time, Kenny had taken the secure route beside the railway track to Finsbury Park tube, and his right leg ached painfully, even through the mist of cocaine. He looked along the carriage. Apart from a few oldies leafing through the *Metro*, everyone was streaming music or locked onto a screen: girls in headscarves jolting against eastern Europeans and bearded men wearing turbans; suits beside trackies; heels, trainers and muddy work boots; everyone thrown together underground, isolated by social media. This morning Kenny took a special interest in London's melting pot, for the bomb at his feet was already ticking.

Beneath Holborn the train remained at the platform. The delay sent Kenny a pulse of alarm, for his device no longer carried a priming switch, reducing him to a mule smuggling a cache of drugs. An angry Bobby Roscoe had removed the bomb from the safe house to be 're-engineered overnight' with a long-delay timer to detonate the kilo of Semtex at eleven o'clock precisely. 'It's a whizzy smart bomb we have now,' Roscoe had growled that morning when he and Fin returned with his wheelie bag. 'Thinks for itself. Even you can't fuck this one up.'

Fear had been pricking Kenny's skin since whirring into the tunnel at Finsbury Park, passing the point of no return. Ten days ago Roscoe had bragged about the Victoria bomb, too, and his timing had been way off, catching passers-by with no connection to Rafal Eisner Capital Bank. Sickened by the thought of the same nightmare below ground, Kenny stole another glance at his fellow travellers, trapped in the wrong place and time. 'What if it goes off early?' he had asked Roscoe, unthinking. 'On the tube, I mean. We're not aiming at them, are we?' To his dismay, Fin had joined in Roscoe's laugh, both of them mocking the weak link, the thin-skinned kid who had bottled it at Canary Wharf and fretted about 'collateral damage.'

At last, the driver explained that they were being held 'to regulate the service.' Kenny fidgeted as more passengers boarded the train and angled past him, wincing as a woman's boot kicked against the bag. After an age, the doors swept shut and the train continued west towards Covent Garden. His cramped leg gave another spasm as he looked around at the new intake: different people, same diversity, isolation and fate. He glanced at his watch, a reflex action since leaving the safe house: forty-seven minutes to detonation. The toddler, half-hidden behind a woman's flapping raincoat, crammed crisps into her mouth with a chubby hand and flashed him another rosy smile.

On the approach to Hyde Park Corner the train came to a sharp halt. The operator's microphone clicked open, then the voice, barely audible, crackling something about a stalled train ahead. They had stopped deep inside the tunnel, sending Kenny another stab of alarm: forty-four minutes, provided the timer was as smart as Roscoe said. In the restless silence he lifted the bag onto his lap and leaned forward, as if protecting it from a rain shower. Droplets of sweat plopped onto the plastic as he stared at the black woollen scarf folded over the bomb, convinced he must be signalling fear or threat. To his left, a middle-aged woman sat with a book that might have been a Bible or the Koran; above him, the woman in the raincoat stood engrossed in an oversize Kindle. The stillness of the carriage magnified every sound and movement, but only the child seemed to notice he was special.

The watch beckoned again: thirty-eight minutes. With a deep breath, he folded back a corner of the scarf to glimpse Roscoe's newfangled timer attachment. It was a silver metal sphere, about the size of a golf ball, fixed to the plastic carton, and he narrowed his eyes into lasers, as if will power alone could make time stand still.

His target was Caja Soller Direct, a Spanish finance house in Gloucester Road, and he closed his eyes to visualise every step of the recce. Four minutes from the station to the bank, two to slip down the service road behind Harry's Handishop, dodge the CCTV camera at each end of the street and conceal the bomb in one of three giant black wheelie bins. Four minutes to get clear. Gloucester Road station was two stations away from Hyde Park Corner, say, seven minutes, even if they started now. Another message from the driver, irritable and terse, a non-apology for a lack of information, somebody else's fault. People were making faces at each other now, shrugs of commuter camaraderie: 'all in this together, what can you do?' He knew from TV that broken down tube trains caused long delays. Jesus, he had seen passengers on the track, stumbling by torchlight.

Thirty-six minutes. Kenny had to plant the bomb and get clear before Bobby Roscoe's coded warning brought hundreds of cops wailing to the scene. He folded back the scarf and held the bag closer. Think. Think. His brain froze, refusing to do the maths, while the bomb in his lap ticked down with split second accuracy.

•••

Thursday, 20 October, 10.23, Betta Tyre and Exhaust, Old Oak

Common Lane, Willesden

Reversed against the workshop entrance, the horsebox fitted snugly beneath Bobby Roscoe's new roof. He had collected it from Luton early that morning, before sunrise. Fin had trailed him down the M1 in the battered Ford van he used for work, with Kenny's reconfigured bomb, already primed, wedged against the spare wheel in the back. They had delivered the shopping bag bomb to the safe house, Fin helping Kenny strap his leg as he talked him through every detail of his mission. Roscoe had silently produced a couple of twenty pound notes and waited impatiently while the brothers snorted cocaine together, too angry to speak to Kenny. 'Screw up again and you're dead,' was all he had grunted as they left, once Fin was out of earshot.

Leaving Kenny to walk the circuitous route to the station with his Bag for Life, they had driven back to Willesden to prepare the horsebox for its final journey. While Roscoe made coffee and breakfast on the gas ring in the workshop, Fin sponged the bodywork and hosed it down before the heat of the sun could smear the soap. The Englishman had been silent on the run to Luton, making Fin park in a side street and stay in the van while he met the bombmaker in secret. Only now did he vent about Kenny's disappearance the previous afternoon, a breach of operational discipline that remained a mystery to them both.

Roscoe checked the oil, tyres and brake lights to minimise the risk of breaking down or being pulled over by the cops. Even with a near empty fuel tank, the horsebox weighed three kilograms heavier since being driven off the ferry at Harwich, due to the Semtex carefully kneaded into the narrow space secreted behind the driver's compartment. The exact time of detonation was known only to the Luton bombmaker, Bobby Roscoe and whoever lay behind them.

Roscoe's Topaz warning calls aside, both bombs would resonate with deadly IRA history, a neat frame-up of precedent and pedigree. The golf balls attached overnight to the horsebox and Kenny's plastic carton were bespoke, digital variants of the long-delay timing device used in the 1984 bombing of Brighton's Grand Hotel, when the IRA had attempted to assassinate Margaret Thatcher and her Cabinet. The vehicle was also highly symbolic: in 2000, Special Branch had foiled an IRA plot to explode a horsebox bomb in central London.

When everything was ready, Roscoe collected another pay-as-you-go phone from his office. He paused to admire his handiwork while Fin emptied the bucket and rolled the hosepipe.

'Has to be there by now,' said Roscoe. 'Is the kid going to come through?'

Fin shrugged into his denim jacket, impatient to return to the safe house. 'Did you give him any choice?'

'Bollocks. Would you have risked it? Trusted him to flick the switch?' Roscoe used his sleeve to rub the driver's wing mirror. 'This time it'll blow, one way or the other. Let me know if he gets back.'

'If?'

'Unless we see him spattered all over the news.' Roscoe gave a sour laugh, filling Fin with an overwhelming urge to break his neck there and then. Instead, he checked the watch he had synchronised with Kenny's just before they separated.

'Haven't you got a call to make?'

'You should have kept a closer watch on that kid.' He shoved past, powering up the phone, and Fin let him go.

•••

Thursday, 20 October, 10.42, Piccadilly Line

Several minutes into a news blackout from the driver, Kenny's train crawled a few metres along the tunnel and promptly gave up. Peering inside the bag again, he could just make out the detonator through the opaque plastic, a silver cylinder the size of an AA battery. It narrowed at one end, reminding him of the rifle round a drugs dealer had once used to threaten him in Belfast. Against the opposite edge were two fatter batteries, bound together with black tape. Kenny glanced down the carriage, seeing the faces of people who would die here with him, hundreds of feet underground. The watch again: twenty-seven minutes. He closed his eyes. Too late.

Bless me, Father, for I have sinned. Suddenly he was back in St Jude's Church, kneeling before the lattice screen, beneath the wooden crucifix. Veins tracing the old priest's cheek, the lips fleshy, his voice probing, inquisitive.

Hand shaking, he pressed his thumb against the lid of the carton. It clicked open and he froze again, waiting for the explosion. Nothing. Just Father Michael's voice in his head again. Turn back from sin. He felt cling film wrapped around the Semtex, the explosive soft and malleable, like the modelling clay he had played with at school. Then the train whirred off again, brushing his fingers against the detonator and sending his heart into his mouth. He wiped his face, slithery with sweat. The priest again. When was his last confession? Kenny had wandered into St Jude's Church after his failure at Canary Wharf, and returned yesterday afternoon, at the priest's injunction. Across the carriage, the little girl was studying him carefully. Harm no more.

They crept into Knightsbridge station and the whooshing of the opening doors pulled Kenny back, the platform's cool air drawing him to freedom. He could run away, abandoning the bomb on the train, or carry it up to the street and dump it somewhere close. Shamed, he listened to the voice through the screen again, sonorous, calm, with a kind of absolution. *Make satisfaction for your sins.* The words rooted him to the spot as more innocents pushed on board. This would be his act of penance: to stay with them, hold the bag close, own the atrocity. The watch: twenty-two minutes.

He was staring at the platform advertisements when the doors closed, his eyes chasing movies, books and exhibitions as the train moved off. Inside the bag again, he found two wires trailing from the battery pack, pulled them loose, and felt for the golf ball. *Whizzy. Thinks for itself*, Roscoe had said, convincing Kenny he had not done enough. A timer so advanced must have its own power source, the old-fashioned batteries no more than a back-up. The bomb was still live.

The train slowed for Gloucester Road station. This would be how he redeemed himself, expiated his sins. Bobby Roscoe had threated to kill him if he turned back, but the priest held out the possibility of eternal life.

He stood with his bomb as the doors parted, his conscience racing ahead as he made for the street.

Chapter Forty-Nine

It was revenge, not contrition, that spurred Dodge into action. Since meeting Jane Hemming at the Mounted Branch stables in Whitehall he had spent two sleepless nights at home agonising over what to do next. Jane's video had positively identified Bobby Roscoe making the bomb call at Victoria, and his obligation was to share this discovery with Derek Finch's investigators. Instead, in the stillness before dawn, Dodge decided to hunt down his nemesis in secret, lifting vengeance above duty.

He knew that either course spelt disaster. Crouched on the sofa in his old dressing gown, Dodge sipped whiskey while Nicola called from the bedroom. The charge sheet was long: he had repeatedly met with the prime suspect in the London bombing campaign, the terrorist who was blackmailing him and making threats against his wife and daughter. Ripping apart his own rule book, he had withheld intelligence that could have prevented Cheapside, passed false information about the Bank of England, and concealed the threat of a lorry bomb. By his own exacting standards, Dodge's conduct had been disloyal and unprincipled. Only John Kerr would speak for him, and even his defence would not be enough.

Nicola's sleepy voice again. 'Darling, come back to bed.'

'Be right there,' he called, draining the tumbler. He moved to the window and held one of the curtains back to gaze over the park, startled by his exhausted reflection. Game over. Soon, Roscoe would use their guilty secret to strike Dodge down. His future lay in prison, or some darker place.

He lay quietly for a couple of hours while Nicola stirred beside him, then wandered into the kitchen to bring her breakfast in bed: tea, cereal and a croissant. She was in no rush to leave for the office, for today was the partners' annual lunch, a day out for everyone. He encouraged her to wear the new green and white dress they had chosen at Brent Cross, with her silver charm bracelet and earrings. If she thought he was being over-attentive, or sensed his looming personal crisis, she never let on: Dodge's working life had always been a book of mysteries and secrets, a family album with whole pages torn out. 'Don't be late, big man,' she said, giving him a hug as she left, then a wave from the front gate. He responded with a thumbs up and wide smile from the living room window, wondering how many more shared days were left to them.

Dodge, too, had scheduled another awayday. When he was showered and dressed he took out the bloodstained invoice he had filched from Roscoe's pocket in Paquito's, charged his phone and checked the news while he made fresh coffee, chain-smoking on the balcony to steel himself.

Builders' merchant Thomas Roache operated out of a rundown Victorian terrace in Harlesden High Street, just north of the railway line. According to its monochrome website, the firm traded 'exclusively with construction professionals,' offering discounts for bulk purchases 'unrivalled north of the Thames.' The drive from Harrow was slow because Dodge had reverted to the counter-surveillance techniques that had saved him during the final, terrible months in Belfast. Racked by Roscoe's mocking threats, he had started covering his tracks again, each pause at the newsagent, superstore or pub an imagined game of cat and mouse. Three hundred metres from home, he swerved the Audi into his local BP petrol station to refuel, buy cigarettes and test the eyes in the back of his head.

He found Roache's narrow shop front between Dev's Auto Sales and Bethel Pentecostal Church, their giant placards shouting cheap credit and salvation. The shop to the left of the terrace was boarded up, and the pair at the far end permanently shuttered. Apart from Chi-Chi Hair and Beauty, the other shops supported the plumbing, electrical and building trades, with 'Thomas Roache and Sons, Estd 1957,' evidently a cut above the rest.

Dodge found a parking space in a side road and watched a man in overalls load paint cans onto a flatbed truck. As soon as he drove away, Dodge locked the car, checked around him and hurried across the street.

Inside the shop, an open set of double doors led to a back yard. The man behind the counter was a larger, less photogenic version of the website mugshot and wore a headset, presumably to communicate with the yard. Dodge waited while he served a roofer in steel capped boots, then unfolded the invoice on the counter, peering at the name tag on his sweatshirt. 'Tommy. You recently sold this stuff for cash.'

Tommy's face wrinkled as he took in Dodge's suit and accent, sensing trouble. 'So?'

'I want to know who to. And the address.'

Tommy glanced down. 'And you are?'

Dodge tapped the invoice. 'Looks like timber posts and sheets of plastic, if I'm reading your scribble? I need to know where they went.'

'You a copper, or what?' said Tommy, shuffling through his options, his right hand drifting to the headset.

'It's like this, pal,' said Dodge, leaning close. 'I'm in a hurry and you've got bricks to sell. Let's not waste anyone's time.'

'Haven't you heard of data protection?'

'In a dump like this?'

'We don't have it. Cash sale. No record.'

'But the address will be in your ledger, computer?'

'We don't give out private information.'

Dodge's mobile was buzzing in his jacket pocket. On the screen was a group text from Gemma, with another bomb threat: 'Livebait rec'd 10.43. Bomb at Caja Soller Direct, Gloucester Road. 20 mins warning, code Topaz. Evac under way. Best, G.'

Dodge suddenly felt his whole chest on fire and, when he regarded Tommy again, he was scarcely able to speak.

Sensing danger, Tommy swung round to escape into the yard but Dodge grabbed his sweatshirt, pulling him so close that their faces almost touched. The younger man must have weighed over two hundred pounds but Dodge hauled him over the counter as if he were a child, ripping away the headset and hurling him against the far wall. His own body spinning out of control with rage and guilt, Dodge took a giant spirit level from the counter and rammed it across Tommy's throat, 'Where is it, you useless lump of lard?'

The younger man was trying to say something, so Dodge dropped him in a headlock, dragging him back to his post behind the counter and bolting the yard doors. Tommy slumped in the corner, clutching his throat and pointing at a row of ring binders on a shelf beneath the counter. 'Orange one,' he croaked.

It took Dodge less than two minutes to find Roscoe's order. There was no address, simply a mobile number scrawled across the top, with the words 'Cust. to collect.'

Someone was banging on the yard doors as Dodge copied the number and photographed the order on his mobile. He patted Tommy on the cheek. 'Thanks, pal,' he said, then hurried into the street.

•••

Thursday, 20 October, 10.46, Thomas Roache and Sons, Building Supplies, Harlesden

Because Jack Langton was still out of action following his brush with death five days earlier, Melanie had collected him from home in the green Astra just after seven and driven straight to Harrow for their continued surveillance of Dodge. Late the previous night, frustrated, he had freed his injured arm from its sling, and was already talking about his Suzuki. This morning, both had brought the overnight bags every surveillance officer kept close by, for Kerr had warned he might need them in the Netherlands the following day.

They found a vantage point by the park, with a clear view of the entrance to Suffolk Hall. Nicola had emerged first. They watched her hurry to the bus stop, just out of sight from their apartment, let the 183 bus for Pinner go, then cross the road and climb into a waiting black Mercedes.

'Poor Dodge,' Melanie had murmured, as Nicola leant across to kiss the driver.

'Not our business.'

Dodge's dirty Audi had appeared just after ten, his paranoia immediately apparent as he pulled into the petrol station and loitered by the pump, clocking the traffic in both directions. 'So what's making him scared?' Langton had said, as they left Dodge to swing into his third side road in less than twenty minutes.

'Perhaps it's us.'

They accelerated away as Dodge reappeared on the main drag, almost out of sight. 'Be much easier if I had the bloody bike,' Langton had said, massaging his injured arm.

They watched Dodge park in Harlesden, cross the street and enter Thomas Roache, then found an unmade slope beside the railway bridge with a diagonal line of sight into the shop doorway. Langton looked irritated. 'What the hell is he doing at a builder's yard?' he said, watching Dodge show a piece of paper to the shopkeeper.

'God knows.'

They saw him reach into his jacket pocket, just as their own mobiles buzzed, seconds apart. 'What do we do now? About Dodge?' said Melanie, reading Gemma's bomb warning.

She had Langton's answer instantly. 'Red Three, Red Three, from Red One, receiving over?'

'Go ahead.'

'I'm calling a Starburst from Gloucester Road.'

'I already pressed the button. We have you at Harrow?'

'Stand by,' he said, drawn by Melanie's intense gaze across the street. 'What's up?'

'Dodge just flipped. Bloody hell, Jack. Look at this.'

Langton unclicked his seat belt and craned across Melanie's space in time to see Dodge drag the shopkeeper across the counter and punch him, before both men stumbled out of sight. 'So fatso sold him some duff taps or something.'

'No. It's Gemma's warning that's driven him crazy. Has to be.' Melanie shouldered her door. 'I have to sort this, before he gets nicked.'

'We have a Topaz,' said Langton, restraining her. 'We cover the bomb warning. That's our job. Dodge looks after himself…Red Three from Red One, RV in fifteen.' He leant across again and turned the ignition, wincing in discomfort. 'Drive.'

•••

Thursday, 20 October, 10.47, Gloucester Road

Loping across the ticket hall for the street exit, the bomb live by his side, Kenny realised Roscoe must have made his warning call while he was still underground. The mayhem roared in from the street as he touched out his Oyster card on the yellow reader, a clamour of sirens and shouted orders as terrified pedestrians crowded past the station entrance to safety. The police evacuation was in full swing, with stressed officers unrolling cordon tape as they struggled to clear the area, straining into their radios for updates and new instructions. Shirt tail flapping, an overweight cop occupied the station entrance, yelling orders at the staff to send people back underground. Face red with frustration, he lurched inside the hall and held his palms high, as if he, alone, could turn back the tide of passengers.

Weaving past him into the street, Kenny glanced to his right and saw that his planned approach was blocked. He swung left along Gloucester Road, losing himself in the crowd being herded north, away from Caja Soller Direct. His watch: twelve minutes to detonation. Kenny pulled the hood over his beanie and swung the bag by his side, scanning the tumult for a place to lie low and make his bomb safe. He saw only hi-vis cops ahead of him, their vehicles abandoned across the road, doors left open, blue lights flashing. They waved at oncoming motorists to turn around and get clear, harsh with anyone who hesitated or questioned them.

Just beyond the station, shoppers hurried from Gloucester Arcade to swell the stream, buffeting him as they elbowed their way from danger, and he flinched as a folded bike bumped hard against the bag. So many victims, packed even tighter here than on the train, stoking his anguish. Frantic in the crush, Kenny lifted the bag as though it were a child, and the Semtex warmed him through.

Shuffling forward, he realised the crowd was being evacuated to the crossing with Cromwell Road, lined with stucco mansion blocks set back from the pavement. No place to lie low. Beyond the junction lay buildings with flags flying from their upper floors: hotels, perhaps, or embassies, with security cameras and guards. The watch summoned him again: seven minutes. He tracked the road to his right and spotted a coffee house, Shelley, with a raised pavement terrace, empty now, abandoned cups of coffee still cooling on the table. Between the terrace and an adjacent fast food joint was a wedge of empty space. He crabbed his way through the crush and slid down the wall beside an old supermarket trolley and dirty blanket, with the bomb cradled in his lap. The commotion was easing now as people funnelled into the safety of Cromwell Road and he saw a line of four cops advancing with a length of tape stretched between them, like stewards at the end of a parade.

Head lowered, Kenny enveloped his upper body in the reeking blanket and searched inside the bag, working from memory, not daring to look. The carton clicked open, then his hand closed around the detonator, the metal smooth, his fingers shaking, slippery with sweat.

'Everybody keep moving!' The cops had drawn level with

Shelley and he recognised the nearest as the shouter in the station, still panicky, belligerent. He spotted Kenny at the last moment, the only still life in Gloucester Road, and hesitated, calculating whether the normal rules of humanity applied, as Kenny's fingers slithered free. 'You. Get away!'

Kenny stayed motionless as his hand found the detonator again. The cop was striding over as he gripped the narrow cylinder, then a boot connected with Kenny's bad leg, making him cry out. The officer stumbled forward onto the trolley, his foot tangling in the blanket, dislodging the bag and separating the detonator from the Semtex as cleanly as a cork from a bottle.

Above the hubbub, Kenny heard only silence. 'My stuff,' he mumbled, as the officer dragged him upright, shoved him away and reached for his yellow tape.

'Get lost now,' growled the cop. 'You're in grave danger here.'

Nearby, a church clock was striking eleven, but the broken bomb lay dormant beneath the blanket. Kenny shuffled away, resisting an impulse to tell the cop he was wrong.

Chapter Fifty

The first flight from Rome was fully booked, but Kerr managed to secure a standby seat just before the gate closed. Arriving at Luton shortly after eight, his Blackberry buzzed with a text from Justin Hine the moment the seat belt sign pinged off: 'need 2 speak will call at 10 exact.' As Nancy had insisted, he drove back to his apartment, rather than her house, to shower and change. He made coffee and an omelette, and picked up Justin's call on the first ring.

'Boss, I've only got a couple of minutes. Are we still go for tomorrow, or do I need a Plan B?' He seemed to be in the open somewhere, a busy street, and the wind whipped at his words.

'Are you alright with it? You know, flying solo?'

A vehicle began reversing nearby and he heard Justin curse over the beeps. 'You think I'd take that chance if I wasn't ready?'

'I didn't mean it like that,' said Kerr.

'It's a hundred and forty miles in a Cessna, not a bloody moon shot. The course is a cinch and the forecast looks good. It'll be fine.' His voice was high-pitched, the stress leaking over the traffic noise, and Kerr strained to hear him. 'I know you've been away, on the road.'

'In the air. And it was a bumpy landing. That's the only reason…'

'It'll die down, no worries.'

'Let's have another call last thing.'

'Sorry, boss, won't be at mine tonight. I'm staying over.'

'At Costello's?'

'We have to be away first thing and Hackney's closer to the airfield.'

'Do you often do that? Spend the night with Gina?'

The wind tugged at his words again. 'It's not like that.'

'Can't you get out of it?'

'I'm a single guy, remember?' Justin managed a nervous laugh. 'No life outside the group.'

'But you're not, are you?'

A pause. 'Boss, I'm a bit pushed right now. Just want to be sure I'm covered your end?'

'We're running through everything right now.'

'I'll have Gina alongside,' he said, lifting his voice above the street noise. 'This is a test, boss, so no screw-ups. It's just…I can't afford to get pulled at Rotterdam.'

'You'll walk straight through. Anything else?'

'Like, what?'

'Like, who are you bringing back?'

Justin's voice rose a notch. 'If I knew that, don't you think I'd report it?' For a moment Kerr thought Justin had cut the call. 'Right now I'm just thinking about the weather over the fucking North Sea.'

'It's okay. You're doing…'

'Better go. They'll be waiting…see you.'

'Stay safe,' said Kerr, but the line was already dead.

Kerr had intended to check on Nancy; instead, he made a quick call to Alan Fargo before driving to the Yard. Justin was trying to disguise his relationship with Gina Costello and downplay the flight to the Netherlands, chipping away at Kerr's unease. The pilot as cover had been Kerr's idea, but now his bravado left him anxious.

Gemma's notification of the bomb threat came through as he drove into the underground car park. 'Anything?' he said as he swiped into Room 1830.

'Still waiting,' said Fargo. 'The Reds are on Starburst from Gloucester Road tube.'

Fargo led him away from the hubbub into the reading room, where a giant chart of the English and Netherlands coasts was spread over the table. They sat side by side, in sight of the breaking news from Sky visible through the glass partition. 'How was the trip?' said Fargo, watching for the live TV pictures from Gloucester Road.

'Later. Do I need to speak with air support?'

Fargo flattened the chart, shaking his head. 'It's cleared as a planned aerial surveillance operation.'

'National security or drugs?'

'I kept it vague, and haven't notified MI5 or the National. If they keep their mouths shut downstairs, no-one's going to know. Mel and Jack fly to Rotterdam tonight. Henk's providing an unmarked hatchback from KMar.'

Kerr nodded. KMar were the Dutch Royal Military police, responsible for security at Holland's main airports, and Henk Jansen was their principal contact.

Fargo was studying the chart again. 'Clacton's showing a crosswind first thing, eight or nine knots, but Justin tells me a Cessna can handle that.'

'So why is he so nervous?'

'Wouldn't you be?' said Fargo, prodding the North Sea. 'He's done less than twenty hours solo. A rookie.'

Kerr looked rueful. 'Not for much longer.'

'Who can blame him?'

Whatever the outcome of his undercover mission, both feared Justin's days in the Met were drawing to a close. Disenchanted by narrowing career opportunities, skewed priorities and bullying top brass, many talented detectives of his generation were hovering around the exit. For Kerr's young technical guru, the alternative was a no-brainer. With a private pilot's licence under his belt and his eyes on multi-jet training, they guessed Justin would soon be trading shifts at Camberwell for stopovers in the Caribbean.

'Let's just get through the next couple of days,' said Kerr. 'Get him back in one piece.'

One of Fargo's cybercrime experts put her head round the door. 'Nothing recovered at the bank. They're holding the area in lockdown and extending the search radius.'

'Thanks, Rosie.'

Kerr stood up, BlackBerry in hand. 'And I have to be somewhere else.'

•••

Thursday, 20 October, 11.34, The Headsail, St Katherine's Docks

For his meeting with journalist Vanessa Gavron, Kerr chose St Katherine's Docks in the shadow of Tower Bridge, a square of restaurants, bars and apartments developed from abandoned warehouses around a smart marina. The brickwork and oak beams of The Headsail marked it out as one of the few original structures to have survived. It was a traditional London pub, with framed prints of the original docks, overlooking a permanently moored barge, Celestine. In the past, Kerr had occasionally used the quiet upper room for debriefing James Thompson, his secret source within MI5.

He made his way there now and sat at his favourite corner, with the top of the Gherkin just visible through the open terrace doors. Gavron arrived in less than five minutes, easily recognisable from her byline picture in grey skirt, black jacket and patent leather flats. It was too early for the lunchtime crowd and her hand was already outstretched as she hurried across the empty bar. 'John?'

Kerr stood to greet her.

'I know you've got a lot on,' she said, nodding outside, as if the next bomb was ticking below in the marina. 'Thanks for sparing the time.'

They ordered drinks, a glass of Merlot for Gavron, Bloody Mary for Kerr, and settled beneath a sepia photograph of Celestine plying the Thames.

'So how do you know Robyn?' said Kerr.

'What did she tell you?'

Kerr bit his celery. 'Not much.'

Gavron shrugged out of her jacket. 'Have you heard about my work on child abuse?'

'Of course. Priests in Northern Ireland.'

'Not just there, actually.'

'But today we're off the record?'

'Oh, I already have my exclusive.' Kerr looked quizzical, so she laughed and held up her glass. 'Yesterday afternoon I gave information about the man I believe is planting these bombs and got blanked. As in "talk to the hand." Which is weird, right? When I'm trying to be a good citizen?'

'Who did you speak to?'

'Top man.'

'Finch?'

Gavron nodded, then talked him through her investigation and Father Michael's disclosure of the bomber's confession in return for her silence. Speaking rapidly and succinctly, she recounted the bomber's kneecapping in Belfast, his exile to the mainland and his claim that the terrorist campaign was being organised in London.

Kerr listened carefully, without interruption. 'Interested?' she said, taking a sip of wine. 'Or are you going to disappoint me, too?'

'A full name would be nice. Obviously. And the church.'

'Sorry,' she said. 'He's a source.'

'A witness,' said Kerr, shaking his head. 'A bad man with critical information about the bombing campaign.'

'And I've passed on everything he knows. As my good deed.'

Kerr leant forward. 'Vanessa, you know how it works. I'll find out, anyway.'

'Special Branch spying on journalists?' Gavron laughed. 'Jesus Christ. Robyn was so right about you. He'll deny everything.'

'Who says I'm going to speak to him?'

'If he's telling the truth and you're so eager, why did Finch practically laugh in my face?'

Kerr shrugged. 'He wants to lay this on the Real IRA. Like most of the Whitehall establishment.'

'MI5?'

Kerr nodded.

'Politicians?' she said, studying Kerr's face.

Kerr's shoulders lifted. 'You don't have to be reporter of the year to see where Avril Knight was coming from.'

'But you're unconvinced?'

'The intelligence is not guiding me to Belfast.'

'And I'm offering the best lead. So why do they ignore us both and go with a lie?'

Kerr raised his eyebrows. 'That's your story?'

Loud laughter spilled from the staircase across the room as a couple of middle-aged men in waterproofs breezed in and ordered gin and tonics, bankers posing as yachties.

Gavron lowered her voice, though the bragging from the bar made it unnecessary. 'Finch rang my editor the moment I left.'

'You *told* him you were going to write this?'

'As soon as I reached home Charles called to spike it.'

'Charles Brandon?' said Kerr. 'Are you going to tell me why?'

Gavron smiled. 'Are you familiar with Charlie's military background? He's on record as a liaison officer with the Parachute Regiment, but that's a cover. During the seventies he was an intelligence officer in Northern Ireland. Special Reconnaissance Unit, then Fourteen Intell. Same business as you guys, stuffing the IRA. But he left suddenly after three years. Kicked out, resigned, and no-one seems to know why.'

'And?'

'Things didn't come to an end with the peace process and power-sharing. The IRA never put their weapons beyond reach and people like Charlie never stopped hating them.' She looked away. 'It's a get out of jail card for IRA murderers, arrest at dawn for retired British soldiers, and all to keep the bloody peace process on its legs. A lot of people on the right feel very resentful. Betrayed, actually.'

'Tell me something I don't know.'

'Including intelligence officers and politicians like Avril Knight. Christ, I'm a republican and even I think it's unfair.' She paused to take a sip of wine. 'I believe the London bombings are the strike back, to frame the Real IRA.'

'A criminal conspiracy, you mean? That's your exclusive?'

'Are you going to talk me out of it?'

'I'm asking myself how much you're holding back,' said Kerr.

Gavron tilted her head. 'And I'm wondering how much of this you already know?' They regarded each other in silence for a moment, then Kerr's BlackBerry was buzzing with a flagged email from Alan Fargo. 'Give me a minute while I deal with this.'

'It's okay,' she said, draining her wine. 'I've done my duty.'

'Not completely.' Kerr scribbled his number on a beer mat. 'I need evidence. And names.'

'Start with Derek Finch.' Gavron gave him her business card and shook hands. 'Take a closer look at your boss.'

Stepping onto the terrace, Kerr scrolled through his contacts for Polly Graham. She was evidently on the road from Porton Down, shouting to make herself heard above the Land Rover's diesel.

'Polly, you got the info about the device?'

'Something about a rough sleeper?'

'Looks like he picked up the bag from the bank without realising, then dumped it. Photographs to come. But it's intact, so may give us the bomber's signature, right?'

'What are we dealing with?' shouted Polly. 'Cock-up or malfunction?'

'Sabotage. Looks like the bomber disabled it.'

'Which is not so brilliant for me if he's buggered the mechanism.'

Kerr could hear classical music and the crackle of an intercom. 'I've got a lead on the man who planted it.'

'So let's hope we both get lucky.'

As soon as she rang off, Kerr dialled Fargo. 'Alan, I want you to search Mercury for Charles Brandon. Military in NI, then journalism. Focus on recent associates.' Below, he watched Gavron hurry across the footbridge, smoking an e-cigarette, mobile to her ear. 'And I'll need an urgent satnav audit.'

'Index number?'

'Give me a couple of hours.'

Chapter Fifty-One

Eyes hidden behind the aviator shades that Gina Costello called his 'Jay-Bans,' jacket wrapped around him in the pale October sun, Justin slumped in the corner of the bar's rickety wooden couch and pretended to doze. Drained by a night of anxiety sex and broken sleep, shattered after the adrenaline rush of the early morning flight, he glimpsed the vast tract of sand stretching to the grey shoreline. Beside him, lips flecked with foam from her second draught beer, Costello toyed with a phone he had never seen before, fidgeting like a child on a sugar high. She had brought with her an unexplained holdall, now tightly wedged between her feet, and her eyes constantly scanned for watchers as the minutes ticked away to their pick-up.

Rustic and quirkily retro, the Hendrix stood alone in the shadow of an elevated disused water tower at Scheveningen's northern edge, well clear of the main promenade with its strip of pop-up restaurants catering for the summer rush. Isolated between the featureless beach and shifting sand dunes, the only vehicle access a narrow track winding from a distant trailer park, the bar's remoteness was perfect for their illicit rendezvous.

They had travelled the twenty kilometres from Rotterdam by taxi and, in the half hour since their arrival, Justin had seen only dog walkers and seagulls. Beyond the vast beach, windsurfers in wet suits scudded to and fro in a swirling panorama of bright sails, the smack of their boards carried inland on the breeze: perfect flying conditions. The Cessna had performed beautifully, picking up a tailwind as they reached cruising altitude and locating Rotterdam without deviating from the course, responding to Justin's hands and brain, pilot and aircraft working in harmony. Pressed beside him in the right hand seat, Costello had studied the instruments and bombarded him with questions, even persuading him to hand her the controls for a couple of minutes mid-flight, then falling silent as he locked into Dutch air traffic control for the descent.

The bar was empty except for a couple of locals in deep conversation with the manager. Through narrowed eyes, Justin watched a thirtyish couple in shades and beanies drift outside with draught beers and take the opposite couch, lounging with their legs stretched across the low table. Intimate and intense, they were just visible through a tangle of creepers around a crooked pergola, eyes only for each other as they embraced and shared a joint, the man's left arm resting on a cushion. Justin took in Melanie's jeans and brown calf length boots with sleeveless puffer jacket, Jack's light waterproof and man bag. Everything was a potential hide for the tiny cameras, mikes and tracking devices the Reds routinely deployed from the Camberwell workshop. It occurred to him that Jack had travelled here less than a week after cheating death, an act of loyalty that touched him. The smoke from his friends' marijuana drifted to him across the terrace, sweet, musky, comforting. No longer alone, Justin felt his heart subside as he pressed the button-sized transmitter sewn into his jacket, an instinctive signal of thanks.

•••

Friday, 21 October, 11.15, Thames House, London

On Friday mornings, Jack Langton would bike over to the MI5 headquarters at Thames House to agree surveillance targets for the coming week with his Security Service counterparts. He and Willie Duncan, de facto head of the watchers in A4, spent their lives disrupting radicalised thugs, lone wolves and insane zealots, though neither had ever paused to calculate the number of thwarted attacks. The grandiose Surveillance Tasking and Co-Ordinating Group propagated a myth of transparency that regularly imploded, and was known to the Reds as the Seven Up, a sardonic nod to the communication lapses around 7/7.

Today, with Langton occupied in the Netherlands, Kerr had taken his place, arriving fifteen minutes early for a private chat. Shaking hands in Reception, Duncan seemed taken aback, evidently assuming Melanie or another of Langton's deputies would have filled in. He was solicitous about Langton's injury. 'Poor sod,' he said in the lift, stabbing the third floor.

'He appreciated your call.'

'I told him to shift his arse quicker next time.'

Fiftyish and overweight, with crinkly hair and a ragged moustache, Willie Duncan was one of many second career veterans disparaged by Whitehall's élite as 'army retreads.' A warrant officer in Saudi and Yemen, with rusty Arabic but razor sharp insights, Duncan had recently been credited with broadening the ethnic profile of MI5's watchers to meet the Islamist threat. Kerr had never known him wear anything but jumbo cords with brown shoes.

Duncan led the way through the silent open plan offices to their usual spot, a bare corner room with a clear view across the river to MI6, the Security Service's flashier, insubordinate sister service. 'What's on your mind?' he said, dropping his thick bundle of papers on the table and pulling up a couple of chairs.

'Gina Costello.'

Duncan groaned. 'Again?'

'We raised her with Toby on Saturday evening.'

'You're kidding me, right?' said Duncan, fanning through his papers. He pinched a folio at the top of the bundle. 'You've seen the Belfast taskings?'

'Costello will be a lot more productive.'

Duncan shook his head. 'Word from the Sanctuary is to concentrate on Real IRA suspects.'

'But we don't have any of those,' said Kerr, lightly. 'Do we?'

'Targets, then. Dissidents. Extremists.'

'A wish list, you mean?'

'Persons of interest. The loyalists are kicking up, Brexit's bubbling and Stormont's in meltdown. NI want this sorted before it gets out of hand.'

'So let's take a look at Costello. She's involved, Willie. This is ACI.'

Duncan shook his head. 'Give us some evidence with the complete network and we'll reconsider. Right now we can't waste time on European leftists.'

Kerr's voice dropped as he leaned in. 'So why did A4 put a team on her?'

Duncan looked up from his bundle. 'Who told you that?'

'It's true, isn't it?'

'Nothing came from the desk.'

'No. Toby Devereux must have ordered it, after our chat at the Silver Scrum?'

'I'm not responsible for what they do upstairs,' said Duncan, tugging at his moustache.

'All received. I'll ask Bill Ritchie to give Devereux a call.' Kerr felt a pang of sympathy. From his first day in MI5, Willie Duncan had set his sights on a desk officer post in G Branch, eager to exercise his skills honed as an army intelligence officer embedded in the Middle East. Each year he had been rejected, a non-com disqualified by age and background for a senior grade that should have been a shoo-in. 'Thing is, Willie, I put some coverage on her.'

Duncan looked up, startled.

'Seeing as no-one else wants to play. And Jack gets blanked every time he brings her to Seven Up.'

'What type of coverage?'

'Limited.' A group of A4 team leaders were loitering by the door, giving their boss space. Kerr smiled and threw them a wave. 'She's been making herself busy in The Hague, back tomorrow. Can you lend me half a team for back-up? See where she goes next?' This was a bluff: concerned about the risk of another surveillance compromise, Kerr had no intention of covering Justin's arrival at Clacton.

Duncan glowered as Kerr's mobile buzzed deep in his pocket. 'Didn't you hand it in?'

Kerr's shoulders lifted in apology as he glanced at the screen. 'Yes or no?'

Duncan beckoned his troops to the table. 'What do you think?'

'That Toby Devereux will be seriously pissed off.'

An hour later, escorting Kerr down in the lift with a couple of strangers, Duncan began humming a phrase of religious music Kerr recognised from his schooldays. Willie Duncan sang as a tenor in the combined choir of MI5 and MI6, which practised in a church near Dolphin Square: insiders said St Bede's was the only place where the spooks truly worked in harmony.

'Isn't that from *Messiah*?' said Kerr, handing over his visitor pass.

Duncan looked surprised again as they paused by the security pods, then embarrassed. 'Christmas programme. *Glory to God in the Highest.*'

'And peace on earth, right? Goodwill towards men?' Kerr held out his hand. 'Very nice.'

'So don't grass me up to Toby.'

•••

Friday, 21 October, 12.21, Hendrix Beach Bar, Scheveningen, The Netherlands

Melanie relit the joint for Langton, nestled deeper beneath his good shoulder and checked the tiny screen sewn into her puffer jacket. They had three cameras between them, in their jackets and Langton's bag, and directional microphones grafted into their shades were capable of collecting speech at forty metres. To keep tabs on Justin, a tiny tracker was built into Langton's iPhone. Beside a prostrate Justin, his face turned away from them towards the beach, Gina Costello seemed trapped in a state of constant movement, a cycle of sipping beer, checking her phone and peering inside the bar, the holdall never moving from her feet. From the pier half a mile away came the faint scream of another bungee jumper, then the gulls again above the sounds of the sea and murmured conversation from the inside bar. Melanie understood why they had chosen this spot, away from prying eyes in The Hague; but its privacy worked in her favour, too, leaving a clear field for the targets to be photographed and recorded without distraction.

She felt Langton stir as a man appeared in the doorway. He stood checking the terrace, flinty eyes probing them for a second, as Costello slipped the phone into her denim jacket and leapt from the couch. 'Luca! Hey!' He held her shoulders and bent to greet her, three kisses, then they hugged for several seconds as Justin pretended to wake up and the watchers made themselves smaller. Tanned and neatly bearded, he wore a tawny polo neck with slim trousers and tidy canvas pumps, no socks. To Melanie, who years ago had learnt to distinguish true militants from the parasites who clung to them, he appeared mean and threatening, and she guessed Langton was thinking the same. He was probably a generation above Costello, yet possibly her lover, and their intimacy sent Melanie a pulse of alarm: how the hell could Justin not know about this guy?

'This is Jay.' Justin lazily got to his feet as Costello introduced them. Justin would have bumped fists but Melanie watched the new arrival grab his hand and pull him close, a powerful move that could have been comradely affection or a discreet pat-down. She saw Justin surrender his place on the couch for a single chair at right angles, allowing the cameras a clear line to both targets, and caught Langton's murmur of approval. When the barman appeared Costello signalled for more drinks, chiding Justin for not drinking beer with them, until Luca restrained her and tapped Justin's Diet Coke for a replacement.

For almost fifteen minutes they talked, while Melanie eavesdropped. Costello included Justin in the preamble, only to ignore him as Luca slipped into French, leaning in so close that their heads touched. Abruptly, Luca stood with his beer and walked into the dark interior. 'Look after my stuff, Jay,' said Costello, grabbing the holdall and following him. Through the pergola, Melanie saw Justin immediately remove his watch and lay it on the table. She shifted against Langton's shoulder for a discreet view inside the bar, watching them move beyond the cluster of locals before disappearing to a deeper spot near the toilets. 'Lost,' she murmured to Langton, immediately easing forward as he got to his feet and ambled inside with their empty glasses: so long as Langton stayed in the bar, the plot was clear.

She looked across at Justin, tense, upright, poised for her nod. The moment she gently dipped her head Justin moved with lightning speed, dodging back to the couch to search Costello's jacket for her new mobile. In one smooth movement, his long fingers never fumbling, he unclicked the back panel, took out the Sim card, pressed it against the metal watch strap for five seconds, replaced it and returned the phone to the jacket.

When Costello returned seven minutes later, smoking a joint and spilling beer, she found Justin stretched out on the couch, shades lowered against the strengthening sun, her jacket clutched over his chest. By the time Luca reappeared with a different bag, she was kneeling beside him, unsteady, blowing marijuana into his nostrils. Melanie watched her stroke his brow and kiss him on the mouth, teasing him with her tongue, gently scolding him until Luca nudged her with his foot. 'Is he good to fly?' He was speaking French, but Melanie caught the gist. 'Wake him. I want to leave now.'

Luca's eyes were scanning again as Melanie looked away to the beach, and this time it was jealousy, not vigilance, that animated his face. She watched them leave for their taxi back to Rotterdam, Costello holding on to Luca, Justin trailing behind, sidelined, isolated, vulnerable. She knew about the loneliness of the spy and felt especially close as he disappeared without a glance. Sitting quietly while Langton checked the tracker, she also thought about

Justin's girlfriend. *I'm getting near the end of the road...has he got someone else?*

'They're in the taxi,' said Langton, watching the blip slide along the screen. 'You alright?' he said, peering at her.

Melanie shook her head. 'Let's move.' She led him the long way round to the car park, her anxiety for Justin sharpened by sorrow for Louise. And pity for their unborn child.

Chapter Fifty-Two

Cherry-picking his emails, Kerr saw Gemma approaching through the main office, a loaded Waitrose bag in each hand. She stood in the doorway, stray hairs wafting as she blew out her cheeks. 'Spare a minute?'

Kerr could not recall the last time Gemma had visited the Fishbowl. 'For you to slum it upstairs? You bet,' he said, weaving round the desk to take the bags from her.

'It's Alan's turn,' she said, 'but I'll be waiting for ever. And he gets the wrong stuff.'

'Sounds comfortable.'

She made a face, gave him a pretend slap and sat down. 'Do you know how long it is since I last shared?'

'I wouldn't dream…'

'Eight years.'

'So this is a big deal.'

'Tell me about it,' she said, wiping her forehead. 'Alan's coping. Not brilliant on the food front, but improving.'

'So you're good?'

'We're good.'

He smiled. 'Lovely man, right?'

'Stop prying.'

Kerr held his hands in surrender.

'Actually, I've been poking my nose in, too. Which is really why I'm here, and hope you don't mind. I've been moonlighting from home. Just open source stuff, Google, etcetera, which makes it alright, yes?'

'About what?'

'Who. Avril Knight's girlfriend.'

'Maria Benita Consuela. Don't waste your time,' said Kerr,

searching his screen. 'Already logged to Finch's urgent inquiry team.'

'Who immediately boshed her as no further action, which Alan says is, quote, utter bollocks, pardon my French, so I've been doing my own research, which you may find interesting. Or not.'

Kerr regarded her for a moment. 'Gemma, you've got enough on with managing the comms. Plus the other things in your life right now.'

Gemma was wearing a charm bracelet, which she kept sliding up her wrist. 'This is personal, kind of, because it's connected to the bombing campaign…and the way it's affected Alan? He asked me, sort of subcontracted me, and I'm perfectly okay with it, honestly.'

Kerr nodded at the shopping. 'Do you want to park that in the fridge?'

Gemma shook her head. 'Won't take long.' She slapped her hands on her thighs, making the bracelet jangle, then searched her bag for a crumpled sheet of A4 and held it up. 'Late night scribble. So. Avril Knight's beloved. Bereaved victim, arty, floaty, earthy. Charitable projects through the embassy, saviour of deprived kids, heart of gold, etcetera, etcetera. Get the picture? But we think there's something suspect about her, don't we? The clandestine sex, the killers getting to Avril Knight on Benita's doorstep, the only place she wasn't protected. Benita's painting hanging in pride of place in the Wymark office. And we know Deering's lot are dodgy. No website, secret clients stashing their lucre offshore to evade tax, and goodness knows what else. All very shady.'

'But circumstantial.'

'John, forget the unworldly-painter-naked-beneath-the-kimono spiel. I found a window to Benita through her ex, Maximo, and she was heavily into the big bucks. As soon as they moved here from Madrid they set up shop in High Street Ken.' Gemma checked her scrawl. 'Manera Ceramics and Fine Art. Incorporated three years ago, according to Companies House.'

'Where did the money come from?'

'Two tics. Within weeks of trading they had a major burglary. Practically everything lifted. Old Bill were useless, of course, couldn't give a monkey's, so guess who they employed to do a private investigation?'

Kerr's eyebrows lifted. 'How did you find that out?'

'Hubby's FB.'

Kerr started. 'You hacked into his Facebook?'

'Alan searched it, through Mercury. Maximo Leon Salvatella is an unusual name, practically jumped out at us.' Gemma stared back in mock surprise. 'John, I hope you're not going to *chastise* me? Anyway, Deering's finance guy befriended Max,' she said, checking her notes again. 'James Walker. Sunny Jim, ecstatically divorced, dating a Spanish babe he met online, the full midlife crisis bit. There's even a picture, the lech and the gold digger heading for the cliff, though the buddies mostly text each other on Skype. Alan's got the screengrabs but, reading between the lines, Wymark's investigation got nowhere, then the insurance refused to cough up because Max's alarm system was rubbish. Point is, Benita and Max borrowed massively for the start-up and the banks called in the loans. Pulled up the drawbridge overnight and ruined them, basically. Alan's terrorist finance women are going to identify the lenders.'

'And the collapse broke their marriage?'

'That's the story they put about, only it turns out the saintly Benita was already having it off with the chap at the kids' charity. Xavier. That's what the junior man on the Home Sec's protection team told Karl Sergeyev. Basically, Xavier fixed the first meeting with Avril Knight, and Benita made the play. Then Benita followed up with a twosome at the Notting Hill bistro, almost like she was, you know, grooming her. I've been on a date there, and it's nice. Tapas, red wine and mood music. Bingo. They're in love.'

'So is Karl suggesting it was a set-up? They targeted her?'

'Junior thinks so, but no-one's listening.' Gemma shrugged. 'Perhaps someone told them Avril was susceptible, or Benita just got lucky. Her phone log shows a series of very brief outgoing calls on Monday mornings where no-one picks up. Which is suspicious, right?'

Kerr gave a low whistle. 'Why didn't protection warn her off? Flag it up with us?'

'Cross a secretary of state? Can you remember the last time anyone did that?'

'You've just been speaking with him.'

'Karl is Special Branch, doesn't count,' said Gemma, with a short laugh. 'We're talking bodyguards now, not intelligence officers. Want to hold on to your job? Keep your mouth shut and submit to the principal. Karl's words, but anyone can see. And Avril Knight was an intimidating bitch. Apparently.'

Kerr thought for a moment. 'So what happened to Max Salvatella?'

'Not much on FB, though his Twitter's interesting. That was Alan, again, not me. I checked the Spanish Companies House – *Registro Mercantil* something or other – apologies for dodgy pronunciation, and Max pops up as sole director of a company called *Puente Importaciones*. It's on the west coast, miles from Madrid, almost like he's dropped out,' said Gemma, turning her notes over and over. 'Town called Ponty something. Similar name to his firm.'

Kerr darted forward, remembering. 'Pontevedra?'

'Sounds about right,' she said, peering closer. 'If I can read my jottings. Max is seriously vexed about the bank foreclosure thing. Masses of tweets about filthy capitalists, secret Panama papers, offshore tax evasion, greedy bankers, criminal bastardos, etcetera etcetera. And all spiced up with a stream of re-tweets from something called *Podemos*, which bangs on about corruption, austerity, inequality, and miscellaneous money people who should be shot for causing the banking crash.'

'Gemma, this is brilliant.'

'And just a bit relevant, yeah?'

'Are you kidding?' Kerr was already scrolling through his folders for the latest intelligence on Gina Costello as a low voice floated from the doorway.

'She told you, then?'

They both swung round to see Alan Fargo leaning there, a couple of secret pink files under his arm, beaming down at Gemma. 'Yes,' said Kerr, 'and it's gold.'

Fargo squeezed inside and tossed Costello's file onto Kerr's desk. 'Pontevedra's at folio fifty-seven,' he said, flipping the reports. He looked warm, and smelt of soap and dusty paper. 'Gina's cash deposits are with the Caja Rural de Galicia, in the old town.' There was also a slim folder for Maria Benita Consuela. 'The grieving lover took a call twelve minutes ago. From Rotterdam.'

Kerr looked up sharply. 'Costello?'

Fargo shrugged. 'Twenty-three seconds, from an unregistered number. We're looking at Mel's pictures now. The new guy is called Luca and Jack just rang to say the three of them walked straight to the aircraft. Justin's doing the pre-flight checks now.'

Kerr checked the time, grabbed his car keys and came round the desk. 'Thanks, you two,' he said, by the door, but Fargo was already probing the shopping, muttering about the fridge.

•••

Friday, 21 October, 12.31, Bill Ritchie's office

Bill Ritchie was finishing a call from his MI6 contact in Karachi when Donna entered without knocking. She stood by the door. 'Barbara just called. Mr Finch is on his way up and he's not happy.'

'Is he ever?'

'That MI5 geek with the Harry Potter glasses came over and it's really freaked him out…' Before Donna could say more the door flew open, pitching her a couple of paces into the room. His face a livid maroon, the Bull looked breathless and distressed, as if he had raced up the fire escape. Jacket collar awry, perspiration radiating across his shirt, he glared for a second at Donna, as if she were responsible.

'You alright?' he grunted, holding the door for her to leave.

Ritchie nodded Finch to the conference table. 'What's going on?'

The Bull was clutching a brown envelope, smudged with sweat. 'I'm supposed to be your fucking boss,' he panted, emptying a sheaf of photographs onto the table. 'What else are you keeping from me?'

Ritchie crossed the room and put his head round the door to check on Donna. 'No harm done, fortunately,' he said, settling at the table. While Finch palmed his jet black hair and caught his breath, Ritchie scanned surveillance photographs of Gina Costello driving through Wales with a scarcely recognisable Justin Hine. 'This is the woman I raised on Saturday as a person of interest, isn't it? When everyone was obsessing about the return of the IRA?'

'I've just been schmoozing a very pissed off Toby Devereux.'

Ritchie's eyebrows lifted. 'What does that look like?'

'According to that fucker Kerr, you put coverage on this woman without telling the Service.'

'These are from A4?' said Ritchie, holding up an image of Costello in the car park of the Farmers Arms in Anglesey. 'We've been nominating Gina Costello at the Seven Up for months and the A4 bloke has consistently rejected her.' He tapped the photograph. 'This is the Security Service not sharing, Derek.'

'It's not for you to question the MI5 lead.'

Ritchie gave a short laugh. 'So much for transparency.'

'What are you doing against Costello?'

Ritchie regarded him for a moment. 'Who says we are?'

'Kerr told A4 this morning.'

'I'll ask him.'

'Do it now.'

'He's on the road.' Ritchie peered at a long shot of Costello's car on the farm track. 'Sex in a Fiat Uno? They could sue for invasion of privacy, right?'

Ritchie's flippancy seemed to inflame Finch's rage. He jabbed Justin's head. 'What do you know about this man?'

'Why?'

'He trashed their surveillance vehicles.'

'Embarrassing.' Ritchie shuffled through the photographs again, studying Justin, dissembling.

'Devereux is demanding to know if we've deployed an agent into Costello's group?'

'Dodge manages recruitments for me, but I would know, obviously,' said Ritchie, slowly shaking his head. 'But this is a good call. Belatedly. We *should* be looking seriously at Gina Costello and Anti-Capitalist Insurrection. That was my case to Ruth at the Silver Scrum.'

'Which fell on deaf ears. Toby's interested in terrorist networks, not a middle-class European leftie you have a bad feeling about.'

'Yet he had her followed.'

'MI5 have their reasons.'

'A government agenda, you mean? Is Toby going to share that, too?'

'Listen to me,' said Finch, leaning across the table. 'My job is to stop jihadis blowing themselves up and the IRA putting bombs down. I'm fighting a war on two fronts and don't need a third. If you don't get that, it's time to move on.'

'So where are these IRA suspects?'

'You're supposed to be the intelligence expert.'

'What if there aren't any? Here or across the water?'

'So find some.'

'Like Iraq, you mean? Make the intelligence fit the prejudice?' Ritchie laughed. 'Is that what Toby's doing for you?'

'No. This is your failure,' said Finch, his voice suddenly low. 'When the reckoning comes, we'll be holding you responsible.'

'I'm sure you will.' Ritchie had rarely seen the Bull so

dishevelled. The unbuttoned shirt collar and loosened tie seemed to have released Jack the Lad, the last century's racist, sexist, corruptible detective still lurking just beneath the surface. Finch was already warming up for the blame game, and it made Ritchie smile. 'Anyway, it's not all bad news, is it? I mean, a device recovered intact is always a forensic treasure trove.' He watched Finch collecting the photographs together. 'Will you be disappointed if Polly Graham finds the bomber isn't Irish?'

Finch stood to leave, shoving his chair back so violently that it almost toppled over. 'Just do your fucking job.'

'What if he turns out to be an anti-capitalist? Or she? You know, a *leftie*? That's the great thing about science. You can't argue with it.'

Finch stood to face him and handed over the envelope. 'I want to know who that man is. And if I find Kerr has been pulling stunts behind my back, you're both fired.'

'Unless we're right, of course,' said Ritchie, quietly, walking away to the door.

There were so many questions he wanted to level at Derek Finch: the connection to Wymark and Philip Deering, his aborted inquiry into Maria Benita Consuela. Why had he so blatantly dismissed Vanessa Gavron's information?

Instead, he opened the door and called into the outer office. 'Donna. Mr Finch has something he wants to say to you.'

Chapter Fifty-Three

Friday, 21 October, 13.43, Clacton Airfield

Racing east along the A12 towards the Essex coast, Kerr flashed past a stream of foreign trucks bound for the Harwich ferry. With Justin's safety on his conscience, Kerr had decided to rely on the tracker sewn into his operative's coat, rather than deploy the Reds to follow him away from the aircraft. Reliance on technology rather than feet on the ground was a calculated risk, though he guessed that Justin, wary of a foreign activist being sharp-eyed as a hawk, would also prefer things this way.

Such decisions were pieces in the game of chance Kerr had played all his working life and yet, for this operation, he needed to see Justin's safe landing with his own eyes. It was professional duty bound with personal obligation, a mark of the nagging, 24/7 worry about the young man he had deliberately sent into harm's way. He slowed to seventy as a sudden gust of wind buffeted the Alfa, pestering him with self-doubt. Did spying on Gina Costello justify a rookie pilot risking his life over the North Sea? Undercover deployments were about symmetry, balancing hoped-for revelations with real physical hazard, and he felt the scales tip as the wind struck again and rain streaked the windscreen. He slowed for the A120 slip road, scowling at the rolling clouds.

The airfield and Aero Club lay west of Clacton-on-Sea, opposite the golf course and a short stroll from the beach. Popular with townie pilots seeking a day at the coast, its only drawbacks, according to Justin, were the offshore wind farm and right of way for dog walkers crossing the grass landing strip. Surrounded by fields, the airfield stretched at right angles from the coastal road. Only two vehicles occupied the gravel car park, a VW Golf with a Clacton Airshow sticker beside a battered two door Fiat Uno.

Looking for a hiding place, Kerr drove past the modest clubhouse and reversed along a potholed, overgrown track to conceal the Alfa behind a screen of brambles. He ducked through a jungle of bushes and saplings to higher ground, searching the horizon for Justin's aircraft. Like an outgoing tide, a sea of blue sky over the town was receding before a grey blanket of cloud from the north, heralding the next batch of showers. The breeze freshened as he crested the slope, quickening the wind turbines out to sea and filling the airfield's orange windsock.

He had been there less than three minutes when Alan Fargo called to confirm that Justin's call sign had been picked up, closing on the Essex coast.

'Brilliant,' said Kerr, sweeping the sky.

'There's something else,' said Fargo before Kerr could ring off. 'Did you authorise a Trig deployment?'

A 'Trig,' 'or 'Triangulator,' was a handheld unit capable of tracking a mobile phone anywhere in Europe, even when it was switched off. The devices were retained in a safe in Room 1830, and their deployment required written authorisation.

Kerr put a finger in his other ear. 'Come again?'

'Dodge dropped by, waiting for me when I got back from the the Fishbowl.'

'Dodge? He doesn't do gadgets.'

'Says you okayed it last night.'

'How did he look?'

'Terrible.'

'What's the reason?'

'Testing a new source he's not happy about.'

'In that case,' said Kerr, 'it must be down to me.'

Seconds later he spotted the Cessna far out to sea, a white dot flying into the wind from the west, then forming and droning as it tilted left to line up with the grass strip. He glimpsed Justin over the dipping wing, flaps down as he throttled back for the glide, crabbing right into the crosswind, then straightening to float in a near perfect touchdown. The Cessna gave a little skid on the damp grass and bounced once, twice, before slowing gently to a halt with a hundred metres to spare.

Kerr breathed easily again as they taxied to the right of the airstrip and parked alongside an identical aircraft. He could make out the three occupants as they jumped down onto the grass, then strolled towards the car park and climbed into the Fiat. Bumping back along the track, Kerr was just in time to see Costello pull onto the main toad and take the route into town.

Keeping five vehicles behind in the slow-moving traffic, Kerr followed them along Marine Drive, lined by Victorian villas, apartment blocks and pastel hotels. Beyond the pier they swung left, heading out of town for London, and Kerr prepared to break away as the traffic thinned, leaving nothing to chance.

To his surprise, they turned into the mainline station and parked in the drop-off bay. Costello's door was already open as Kerr swerved to the far side of a green facing the Victorian entrance. Costello released the driver's seat, then Justin unfolded himself from the back, flipped his sunglasses down and stretched. Kerr saw Costello press something into his hand, then hug him close. By the time she rejoined the road, Justin had disappeared into the station and Kerr was texting him a letter S, the signal for 'area safe, urgent contact.' Window shopping outside an estate agent, he found Justin in the reflection and strolled back to the Alfa. 'What's going on?' he said, driving off before Justin could pull his door shut.

'They kicked me out. Gina gave me money for the train.'

'But they're friendly?'

'I got them down in one piece,' said Justin, buckling up. 'Why wouldn't they be?'

Kerr turned left, retracing the route to the seafront. 'Couldn't you have just sat tight?'

'It wasn't Gina. Perhaps they want to talk personal. Whatever.' He was speaking rapidly, still pumped up from the flight. 'You don't argue with this guy.'

'Don't know where they're going, either.'

'I left the coat on the floor, scrunched beneath the seat. The tracker wakes up when they reach London and you'll have their location within a couple of metres.' He glanced sideways, drawn by Kerr's look of scepticism. 'Boss, I should know. Camberwell designed the software.'

Kerr laughed. 'Hungry?'

They drove into town, settling for fish and chips at the Cheeky Chappie Chippy by the pier entrance. The place had capacity for about thirty diners but was less than half full, with most customers ordering takeaway. Kerr found them a corner table overlooking the seafront.

'So how did it go?' he said, as Justin unstrapped his watch and removed the link housing the Sim card reader.

'Well, I greased it down, didn't I?'

Kerr's eyes followed the queue snaking out of the door. 'I watched you.'

Justin chuckled. Evidently shattered from the flight, he had stayed silent in the car while Kerr contacted the office and terminated Bill Ritchie's urgent call about the Bull's visit; now, the mug of sweet builder's tea re-energised him. 'Side wind, six knots and gusting, practically a full load.'

'Not bad,' said Kerr.

'Good solo experience for the log.'

'Cool. How about the passenger?'

'Gina calls him Luca. Speaks French but doesn't look it. Understands English but doesn't let on.'

'How close to Costello?'

'They're acquainted.'

Kerr blew on his tea. 'Friends or lovers?'

'Activists.'

'Not drugs, then?'

Justin shook his head. 'It's the political cause every time. Anti-cap, like me.'

'Yet Gina's never mentioned him before, which must be disappointing.'

'She trusted me to bloody fly him here, didn't she?' said Justin, reddening. The food arrived before he could say more, and he seemed to check himself. 'These people live in silos. Same as us.'

Framed on the wall facing Kerr was a review featuring the patron with a fresh cod and wide smile ('Five Stars for Clacton's Triple C'). He shifted his chair. 'So what have you brought us? A hashtag warrior or the real deal?'

'Well, we're certainly not talking your radical chic, piss and wind revolutionary.' Justin ripped a couple of sachets of sauce with his teeth and squeezed them over the chips. 'Luca is the genuine article. Been there, done it, didn't hang around for the T-shirt.' He began eating hungrily. 'Remember, back in the day, when European militants actually relished taking on the state? Well, I've just delivered a nine carat zealot, a mean, partisan bastard who needs to stay beneath the radar.'

'You managed all that from his French?'

'His silence.' Justin shook his head, sucking air to cool the batter. 'Which is why I'm supposed to be on the train right now, not exchanging life stories in the back seat of the Fiat.' He swirled a piece of cod in brown sauce. 'So. That's my initial readout. Luca in a nutshell. Quality.'

'So not big on email?'

'Or phone, or social media,' said Justin, chewing fast. 'But you don't need a Twitter account. I've got Gina.'

'Later,' murmured Kerr, hesitating as fairground noise suddenly blasted through the open door.

'You what?'

'Has she ever talked about a woman called Benita?'

'Spanish?' Justin looked out to sea, frowning. 'Who is she?'

'Maria Benita Consuela. We think she's involved in the Home Sec's murder.'

'And why would Gina know her?'

While Justin cleared his plate, Kerr briefly talked him through Gemma Riley's raw information on Benita and her divorced husband, Maximo. By the end, Justin wore the look of a student who had just won the argument. 'Terrific. She has to be the missing link here. The connection to everything,' he said, the moment Kerr picked up his fork again. 'Al told me the op name?'

'Javelin.'

'Right. So Benita takes the heat off Gina, right? And me? Why hasn't she been nicked?'

'Hold on. Max moved to Pontevedra. Doesn't that ring any bells?'

Justin looked through the window at a couple of fishermen ambling along the seashore. 'The claim about euros being deposited in Gina's name?'

'Not claim. Fact.'

'Coincidence. Like her stepfather being a director at Dolphin and Drew.'

'The bank is in the old town,' said Kerr, 'and someone just paid in twenty-three thousand euros.'

'When?'

'Yesterday.'

Justin left Kerr waiting as he gazed over the grey sea again. 'Okay, so the money could be for, I dunno, our political justice campaign.'

'Or terrorism.'

'Or a scam. A hundred things unconnected to the murder of Avril Knight.'

'We also talked about a call to an IRA man in Bogota, remember? From Marin, only a few miles down the coast?'

Justin nodded.

'The caller was a Frenchman. Luca?'

Justin groaned. 'Or a million others.'

'Until we get voice recognition. But I'm going to lift them in the next few days. Costello and Luca.'

Justin stared at him. 'Which will cause me a massive problem.'

'No, Justin,' said Kerr, quietly. 'You're not in the equation.'

The fryer suddenly hissed and crackled as someone threw in a fresh batch of chips. Justin sat back in disbelief. 'Boss, did you just *fire* me?'

'You told me the man is dangerous. I can't let them run. It's unsafe.'

'Bollocks. And I've already said Gina's not into terrorism. Or drugs.'

'She organised Luca's infiltration. That's your own info.'

'No. At the very most, she's being used, same as me.'

'But I can't take that risk.'

'So is this it? Six months work down the pan?'

Kerr paused to watch a dinghy tacking from the pier. 'The problem is, I don't have the Echo Chip on her computer. Without cover, I can't let them run.'

'It's too risky…I already told you…especially now. Jesus, you've gotta be fucking kidding me.' His voice had risen above the buzz of conversation around them, drawing a sharp glance from a young mother in a Barbour with a buggy the size of a small car. Kerr nodded an apology and, when he turned back, Justin's shades had dropped over his eyes again. 'I just gave you her bloody phone log.'

'Not enough. Can you do it this weekend? For real time, three sixty monitoring I need the EC in her laptop. Key strikes and audio.'

'Why can't we do a technical on the flat?'

'No time.'

'And if I say yes?'

'I'll make a case to the commander to keep your op running.'

'So now it's an ultimatum. He's agreed to this?'

'That's the deal. In the meantime, work on an exit strategy. Come up with a reason not to be around them.'

'Boss, I asked if Mr Ritchie knows.'

'Prepare to disappear. Family emergency, whatever, while we think of something plausible for the long term.'

'This is so unfair.'

'You need a rest,' said Kerr, dropping cash on the table.

Justin gave a harsh laugh. 'Now I've done your dirty work.'

It was drizzling again as they walked to the car park and sat in silence, staring out to sea through the crescents left by the wipers. 'Where to? Safe house or Louise?' said Kerr, eventually.

'Gina's.' In the shade, Justin's eyes had disappeared behind the glasses, and the straggly beard left his face unreadable. 'I have to recover your tracker, remember?'

Kerr started the engine, then studied him for a moment. This was Justin in disguise and denial, hiding his anger from Kerr and the truth about Costello from himself.

'Justin, it's not personal,' said Kerr. 'You've done a fantastic job. Nothing changes that.'

'No. It's over,' he said flatly, clunking his door open. 'I'll take the train.'

Chapter Fifty-Four

Saturday, 22 October, 07.46, Dodge's Apartment, Harrow

Trig, the cellphone triangulator that Dodge had lifted on false pretences from 1830, was smaller than his ageing Samsung Galaxy with the idiot's-guide screen commands, yet it still left Dodge perplexed, as if Fargo had asked him to babysit Mercury for a couple of hours. The device enabled real-time tracking by locking onto an agent's mobile phone, and the source unit regularly 'Trigged' new prospects or recent signings whose conduct was suspicious. His four agent runners were experienced millennials who treated HUMINT like any other business, except that the best clients were idealists or extremists, and the cash inducement was often laced with coercion. Such integrity tests were the secret world's version of commercial due diligence, and Trig data often showed the client to be cheating, betraying or double-dealing. Dodge, a leftover from the analogue generation, had never used Trig or its earlier, less reliable versions. In a lifetime pitching bad people on both sides of the Irish Sea, agent-running's heaviest hitter had trusted instinct over technology, right up until the day Bobby Roscoe ransacked his life and blitzed his self-respect.

He had spent most of Friday afternoon in his hidey-hole at the Yard, fiddling with the device in baffled isolation before calling his most experienced handler for help. Helen Farr, already concerned about her boss's erratic behaviour, had scooted from the main office to give him a rapid tutorial with black coffee on the side. 'Thanks,' he had grunted, feeding in Roscoe's mobile number. 'And sorry for being a grumpy bastard.'

'We've been worried about you.'

'Tell them I'm better now.'

'Sure about that?'

'Helen, I mean it,' he had said as she reached the door. 'Everything's going to be fine.'

Fifteen hours later, taking more caffeine at home after a sleepless night, Dodge fixed on the white dot that was Bobby Roscoe, still motionless over Old Oak Common Lane in Willesden. Home address or safe house? Conflicted, he took a shower, tilting the jets to pressure wash his face and flush his mind. Roscoe's threat of a lorry bomb was as real as the cardinal rule of terrorism: never let an attack go to waste. Last Saturday's mortar had been a mark of defiance to dominate the weekend news; but why explode a lorry bomb in the City outside banking hours? Sweating through Friday's rush hour, eyes fixed on Trig, Dodge had felt his panic slowly recede. He had a respite of two days to plan, act, and close down the nightmare. He could capture Roscoe, drawing the spotlight onto his secret guilt, or save himself, jeopardising innocent lives. He had to choose between duty and self-preservation. The band tightened around his chest again as a third option sparked in his brain. Resolved, he dressed for confrontation, made breakfast in bed for his wife, and waited.

Shortly after eight, smoking on the balcony, he saw the dot shimmer and pulse. It faded, then glowed steadily again and turned right, a tiny star leading him north. He hurried into the kitchen, grabbed his car keys and kissed Nicola. She was already showered, wearing a powder blue sweater and the light perfume that reminded him of Fridays. 'Have to go out, love,' he said.

Nicola was making more toast. 'When are you back?'

'Not long,' said Dodge, his face creasing into the look she had seen a thousand times.

'Doesn't matter. I'll be in all day,' she said, absorbing his lie into her own.

Three minutes later, Dodge was edging through Suffolk Hall's electric gates, Trig jammed on the dashboard. The lack of TomTom satellite navigation or blue lights on his high mileage Audi A4 did not impede him for a second. Dodge knew his way around London and split the light Saturday morning traffic with a repertoire of flashing headlights and expeditious hooting.

Accelerating through another red light along Harrow Road, he raced to the A40, shamelessly goading the speed cameras, knowing that, one way or another, today would mark the end of his torment.

The travelling white dot had reached the M1 but Dodge kept speeding east, his destination the place Roscoe had just left, the screen marker seared into his brain. Driving up Old Oak Common Lane he had to brake hard as a stream of oncoming vehicles snaked into his lane to pass a stationary bus. Dodge's angry headlights lit up the tail-ender, a grey horsebox with French registration. He caught the lowered sun visor, the stubbled driver's raised finger and, as it swerved past, the image of a silver racehorse at full stretch.

Dodge had expected Bobby Roscoe's home base to be a flat or terraced house, but Trig's overnight marker pulsed insistently as he lurched across the pitted yard of Betta Tyre and Exhaust, parked across the entrance and spent a moment studying the new roof. It was evident at once that Trig had brought him to the right place, for its timber spars and corrugated plastic sheets matched the order he had extracted from Tommy Roache. Wisps of straw blew around his legs as he made a rapid survey of the grim, deserted building and snapped on a pair of latex gloves. The only access was beneath a rusting roll top door secured by a single padlock. From the boot of the Audi he took a crowbar, the professional prop he always carried for protection against double-cross or compromise. The padlock gave at the second attempt, and a single shove from Dodge sent the door screeching up to the roof. Adjusting to the gloom, he took in the dark inspection pit and the piles of exhausts and tyres, wrinkling his nose at the reek of oil, rubber and dankness as he made for Roscoe's jumbled workplace in the far corner. No sign of a desktop or telephone. A set of grimy blue overalls lay across the rickety captain's chair, but the pockets were empty. The paper strewn oak desk had two drawers on the side, one crammed with fuses and light bulbs, the other with gay porn mags and emergency kit of mouthwash, Vaseline and Trojan condoms.

He tipped the contents onto the concrete floor, searching through the piles of business letterheads for phone numbers, emails, a diary, anything that might offer a window into Bobby Roscoe. Trig left him in no doubt that Roscoe had spent the night here, yet there was no space to sleep, wash or change, and no toilet. Out of frustration as much as curiosity he overturned the chair, ripped into the upholstery and smashed open the Roberts radio. He stole another look around the grim interior, then back into the daylight at the inexplicable new roof. Nothing anywhere, except a workshop empty of vehicles and an office incapable of generating business. A cover.

Another glance at Trig: the light still pulsing north. Along the rear wall, brand new tyres and exhausts were stored in racks according to their make and specification. They were based on the ground except for three piles of remoulds stacked on a heavy duty steel platform trolley by Roscoe's office. It was the symmetry of used tyres rising in neat silos that drew his attention. Flexing the crowbar between the rubber, he saw they were supported from the inside by three vertical iron rods. The trolley implied mobility, but these tyres were going nowhere. Something was wrong. He pulled hard on the trolley handle. The platform rolled on its castors away from the wall to reveal a plywood door built into the breeze block wall, secured by another padlock that gave as easily as the first. Beyond was a windowless, rectangular cell the size of a large garden shed, dark as night, with the dog breath of recent occupation. Fiddling to find the torch on his mobile, he located a wash basin, roughly plumbed toilet and wooden chair squeezed against a futon. Dirty underwear lay scattered over a crumpled sleeping bag, with a reading lamp beside it on the floor. He pocketed his mobile, checked Trig again, then used the lamp to scan every inch of Bobby Roscoe's hideout. Squeezed into the left corner was a wheelie bag on top of a rigid motorcycle pannier, but it was the opposite wall that grabbed Dodge's immediate attention. Hanging from a nail was a blue Trapper hat over a long black coat that instantly spirited him back to the stables at Great Scotland Yard and Jane Hemming's startling video, with every detail unrolling inside his head: Bobby Roscoe standing in the rain, phone to his ear, the side flaps of the hat folding as he bent forward, hand chopping the air to emphasise the short, lethal speech Dodge knew by heart.

The wheelie bag was empty, the pannier locked. He smashed the lid, glanced inside, retreated to the relative light of Roscoe's office and tipped the contents onto the desk. There were yellowing cuttings from the *Belfast Recorder*, each carefully annotated in fading pencil, and letters with other personal effects: keys, a small wooden crucifix and a Letts diary among fading colour photographs of a smiling young man in his early twenties. Frankie, photographed on his own, now with another man, as Dodge peered close and found himself staring into the eyes of a younger, leaner Bobby Roscoe.

Hands trembling, suffocating in the workshop's rank air, Dodge uprighted Roscoe's chair as the iron fist squeezed his heart again. He propped Trig on the desk and began to read.

Chapter Fifty-Five

Saturday, 22 October, 09.03, New Scotland Yard

Kerr's last contact with Nancy Sergeyev had been her phone call to Rome late on Wednesday evening. Since then, the texts and calls from his Islington apartment had loitered in the ether, Nancy's invitation to leave a message seeming to become terser with each attempt. When at last she did pick up, in the middle of his toast and cereal, he found the bar set low for small talk. They sparred for ten minutes, Kerr trying to justify himself, Nancy frustratingly noncommittal, finishing the call before he could suggest dinner. A couple of minutes later he was in the bedroom, pulling on his navy chinos and polo shirt, when the BlackBerry rang again. He was hoping for a change of heart, then saw Melanie's name on the screen.

'Welcome back. Where are you?'

'1830. Jack wanted to brief the Reds, so I dropped him in Brixton. Al tells me you saw Justin.'

'Yup, all good. Waiting for him to surface again.'

'Are you coming in, John?'

'Why?'

'We've been taking another look at the readout from his tracker.'

Kerr left a pause, disconcerted. 'And?'

'There's some odd data.'

Kerr slipped into an old pair of loafers, intuition telling him Saturday was going to be a long stretch. 'Does it affect Justin?'

Another pause. 'Depends what he's been telling you.'

Kerr grabbed a cotton jacket. 'On my way.'

Twelve minutes later, free-wheeling down the ramp into the Yard's underground garage, Kerr immediately spotted Polly Graham's mud spattered green Land Rover Defender among the assorted hatchbacks, squeezed beside a spare armoured Jaguar.

He parked, already speed-dialling, and left a brief message on her voicemail. Polly bumped into him at the top of the spiral staircase as she backed through the door with a rucksack and canvas tote bag, mobile clamped between ear and shoulder.

They exchanged a hug on the metal platform as a couple of Finch's officers edged past, then stood for a moment, indecisive. 'Up or down?' said Kerr.

'I already did the Fishbowl.'

'So come back. I'll make you a coffee.'

'I have to be at Porton Down by noon,' she said, shaking her head. 'Let's talk here.'

The Land Rover was parked hard against a pillar, but Kerr managed to angle himself inside as Polly cleared a couple of loaded box files from the passenger seat. She leaned over to dump them in the back on a platform of four bespoke metal containers that filled the rear compartment. 'Unclassified research stuff, in case you're wondering,' she said, making a face.

Kerr chuckled. 'The last place to leave secrets lying around, right?'

The interior was littered with pens, three crushed Red Bull cans, a couple of tiny notebooks, a box of tissues and a pair of dressmaking scissors. Polly's overalls hung from a hook on the side pillar, and a smell of leather and grease evoked his dad's old car and the shooting range at Lippitts Hill. 'So, did you find our bombmaker?'

Polly shook her head. 'But I can tell you a lot about him. Or her. And I've already briefed Derek Finch, before you ask.' She lifted her baseball cap to run a hand through her hair. 'When the bomber made it safe he didn't damage any of the components, so the device is more or less intact, except for a few pulled wires. We were able to dismantle it ourselves and test each element.'

They faced the garage wall through clear crescents left by the windscreen wipers. The rest of the glass was streaked with dirt and dead insects. Kerr turned to her. 'We?'

'Bomb Data Centre. The Bull wanted a pair of tame tecs alongside me, so we used the lab at Lambeth.'

'To make sure you came up with the right answer?'

'Fat chance.' Polly traced a finger along the dashboard. A layer of dust covered every surface, as if no-one had driven the vehicle for months. 'For starters, the Semtex is from the Czech SA11 consignment stolen from Marseilles.'

'Same batch as the earlier devices?'

'And never used by the IRA, which tells me this is not Irish dissident, obviously,' she said, studying her fingertip. 'Needs a clean. Anyway, that's what I just told Finch.'

Kerr raised an eyebrow. 'Not the result he's looking for.'

'That's the trouble with science,' said Polly, drily. 'Doesn't follow orders.'

'Completely insubordinate.'

'But keeps on giving and never tells lies, so listen up. Your bombmaker is meticulous, installing a very neat plywood circuit board with matching brass screws, brand new. Soldering, wire chasing and fixing, you name it, everything perfect, even the way the explosive was weighed and packaged. I'm giving this guy an A star.'

'But?'

'The construction is too precise. For a signature I need idiosyncrasies. The *way* the bombmaker operates is art, not science, and this baby is picture perfect, straight out of the engineering manual.'

'Looking for a creative and finding a robot,' said Kerr. 'That's tough.'

'It is, a bit. I've found nothing singular enough to ping our bombmaker profiles at Porton Down. Sorry to disappoint you, John.'

'But if we find the screwdriver?'

'Even the fretsaw,' shrugged Polly. 'In the meantime, if you come across a left-handed suspect, give me a call.'

Kerr stared at the wall for a moment, then turned to her, as if he had misheard.

Polly was smiling. 'He slipped up. Finished making the perfect bomb, then took out the circuit switch to fit a Memopark timer. Why? It was obviously done very quickly, a bodge-job completely out of character, which is great, because cock-up means more unique tool markings. And in the rush he must have ripped his glove, because I lifted a partial print hidden behind the Memopark.'

'You what?'

'Well, hardly even that, really. A smear of a dab of a smudge. A whorl and a loop. Couple of bifurcations, some dots and ridges.'

'Enough to put through the scanner?' Kerr was referring to AFIS, the Automated Fingerprint Identification System, designed to compare suspect marks against a database of known and unknown prints.

Polly started the engine. 'Enough to promise you it's the middle finger of his right hand where he held the timer to screw it on.' The diesel rattled through the garage and the sound of Elgar flooded the inside. She lowered the volume and crunched into reverse. 'Sooner I get back…'

Kerr eased the door open against the pillar. 'Thanks so much for sharing, Polly.'

'It's hardly anything, so keep it close.'

'Have you told Finch?'

'Not yet,' she said, with a sly wink. 'The Bull only deals in certainties.'

•••

Saturday, 22 October, 09.17, Room 1830

Kerr found Melanie sitting beside Fargo, surfing Mercury. They immediately led him into the reading room. 'Justin was fabulous,' she said, as they jockeyed around the cramped table. 'Cloning Costello's Sim at the beach bar was seriously fraught. He had a tiny window when they disappeared inside. Class act.'

'Why did they kick him out at Clacton?'

'Sexual jealousy,' said Melanie, immediately. 'From what I saw, this guy Luca and Gina Costello have a history that goes way back. They were shimmying around the second he arrived, snogging in the bar, then she's trying to stick her tongue down Justin's throat. We're talking male possessiveness, not suspicion. Sex always outshines the mission. Jesus,' she murmured, 'I should know.'

'Justin rates Luca as the real deal,' said Kerr.

'And I'd say our Justin is right on the button.' She nodded through the glass to Mercury in the main office. 'We snatched masses of photographs. See for yourself.'

'In a moment. Which is Luca's dominant hand?'

'Left-hander,' answered Melanie in a flash: for a surveillance officer, such detail was as routine as height or hair colour. 'Why?'

'Any concerns at all about Justin's cover?'

Melanie shook her head. 'He's trusted, but that doesn't make him less vulnerable. It's the nature of this thing with Costello that worries me, not the quality.' She glanced at Fargo for support. 'John, we talked about this.'

'Are you happy he's giving you everything he knows?' Fargo had paused from scrolling through Melanie's tracker reader, a bespoke street map on an eight inch tablet.

'Why do you say that?' Kerr looked from one to the other, forced on the defensive for the second time that morning. 'Does Justin show bias towards his closest associate, you mean? Is he protecting her? Of course, and I've factored in all of that stuff. But he stole her Sim and he's bugging her laptop this weekend. So is he delivering what I want? Yes, again.'

'Yet he told you Costello had never heard of Maria Benita Consuela, didn't he?' said Melanie.

'No.' Kerr felt a spark of irritation, the boss having his judgment questioned. 'He said Costello had never mentioned her.'

'Which is why you need to see this,' said Fargo, swivelling the reader to Kerr. The screen showed satellite imagery of London, with a green line tracing the Fiat's route from east to west and a grey time marker against key locations. 'Obviously we couldn't live monitor Costello's drive from the airfield, because we were hanging around Schiphol,' said Melanie. 'So this is historical.'

'But I'm guessing the tracker ended up at Costello's flat?'

'Yes,' said Fargo. 'We're hoping Justin retrieved it from the car and stayed over.'

'That was the plan. Where's the problem?'

'I've been retracing the route back to London,' said Fargo. 'She didn't go straight home to Hackney. Overshot, see? Took the Mile End Road, as you'd expect, then diverted along the Westway to Bayswater.' He scrolled through the map and double-clicked. 'Then I find a pause, just here, see? Woodfield Crescent, back of Portobello Road Market. Stationary for just over three minutes, then straight back home.'

'Benita?'

'Not to her front door, but close enough. Luca's drop-off point. No diversions, no backtracking. Gina Costello knows exactly where to find Maria Benita Consuela.'

'Costello is playing Justin,' said Melanie, 'or Justin is lying to you. Either way, it's not good.'

Kerr's BlackBerry rang. 'I need to deploy the Reds…'

'Jack's already on it,' said Melanie. 'Look, this is dangerous. You promised you were going to pull him out.'

'I said I'm thinking about it.' Kerr glanced at the screen and drew a hand across his throat for silence. He began to say something, then gave up, craning his head to concentrate. 'Where are you now?' he managed after a couple of attempts, waving for Fargo's pen and notebook. 'That's a complete no-no, understand? Where, exactly?' he said, scribbling furiously. 'It's alright, I'm coming now. Don't move from there.'

Melanie and Fargo must have heard enough to recognise

Dodge's voice. When Kerr rang off, both were looking anxious. 'He doesn't sound okay,' said Fargo.

'He's crying,' said Kerr, flatly, looking between them.

'Where is he?'

'I need my Glock.' Kerr stood so abruptly that the chair tipped back and left a dent in the partition wall. 'Al, check any activity from his Trig and phone it through.'

'Sure.'

He paused by the door, having second thoughts. 'Mel, I need you with me, too.'

Chapter Fifty-Six

It took just eighteen minutes of hard driving to find Dodge, tearing west through Marble Arch and Hyde Park Corner, the speed rarely below sixty. As they careered along the Westway, Melanie took a short update from Jack Langton, then paused while Kerr squirted the siren to clear roadworks on the approach to Ladbroke Grove. 'The Reds say Benita's place is empty. Luca must be on the move.'

The sign for Betta Tyre and Exhaust Services was so dilapidated that Kerr almost missed the turning. Pulling into the rutted yard, they passed Dodge's Audi and parked behind a screen of brambles. The workshop door had been rolled within a metre of the ground, and the only sound came from traffic and the distant thump of a Crossrail pile driver. They sat in silence for a moment, watching for threats.

'Let's go.' Kerr got out of the car, drew his Glock and jogged to the side wall. He crouched to glance through the gap, then hoisted the door open. He spotted Dodge through the gloom, slumped by the desk. 'Dodge, is it safe?' he called.

Dodge peered at him, as if resenting the intrusion and the light of day.

'Just me,' he grunted, beckoning Kerr inside.

Kerr perched on the desk while Melanie watched from the door. Photographs were scattered around and Dodge was reading newspaper cuttings by torchlight, an older, lonelier figure than the friend Kerr knew so well. 'Where are we?'

Dodge held up a photograph. It showed two young men in swimming trunks, arms around each other, smiling and squinting into the sun. 'That's Bobby Roscoe on the right,' he said, then nodded at the opening behind the trolley of tyres. 'Hideout's in there.'

Hands in pockets, Kerr peered inside. 'And a crime scene. Where is Roscoe now?'

Dodge screwed his eyes at Trig, propped on the desk. 'Retail park in Luton.'

'Is he planning another attack? Is that why you're in such a state?'

'We're safe, I swear. Bear with me a while.' Dodge looked up at him, distraught. 'Please, John.'

Kerr grabbed a couple of plastic crates for a makeshift seat but Dodge gripped his arm. 'No. Mel can't hear this. I'm begging you.'

He beckoned to Melanie. 'Too late.'

Melanie came over and stood by him, taking in the crowded desk. She squeezed his arm and pointed a finger at Trig. 'Do we need to get people up there?'

'Not if Dodge is being upfront with us,' said Kerr. In the dim light, Dodge's tear smudged cheeks had turned grey and blotchy, the skin saggy around his jaw. A dark vein throbbed down the centre of his forehead and his whole face seemed to have dropped, weighted by sadness. Kerr felt an overwhelming urge to rescue him.

'Boss, this feels bad,' said Melanie, seeming to read his thoughts. 'We need to be out of here.'

'No,' said Dodge, swinging round in Roscoe's battered chair. 'Has to be here and now, or I'll never manage it.' He slapped the crates for Melanie to sit down, then fell silent, wringing his gloved hands.

Kerr helped him out, studying the other man in the photograph. 'Is he involved, too?'

Dodge took a deep breath. 'I told you I'd never lost an agent, right? Well, that's another lie. This is Frankie Magill. Belfast kid, raised in a boys' home.'

'Which one?'

'Not the place all the fuss was about,' said Dodge. 'The Olive Tree, outside Springfield.'

Kerr adjusted the shoulder holster beneath his jacket. 'And he was working for you?'

Dodge nodded. 'Around the millennium, Frankie gets arrested for rioting and firebombing. Before they can charge him I get myself into Andersonstown, have a chat in the cell and sign him in time for breakfast.'

'What did he offer?'

'When he's nine years old, Frankie and a couple of the other boys in the Olive Tree are being treated special. "Low-hanging fruit," the fathers call them.'

'Abused, you mean?' said Melanie.

Dodge nodded. 'Inside the home, but pimped out, too. And sometimes the clients are paramilitaries.'

Melanie glanced at Kerr. 'You exploited that? Isn't the first call to child protection?'

'Hey, I pass all this stuff up the chain. Anyway, that was then, this is now. The boy is going on nineteen. So, Frankie is still seeing a very bad man we have a powerful interest in, one of the commanders, inside track and all. Frankie services his terrorist uncle twice a month. Soon, the Belfast office has enough for an approach. Code name Nighthawk and the Branch keeps it tight as a duck's arse.'

'Who is he?'

'Sorry.' Dodge shook his head. 'He's still active. It's peace in our time, remember. Politicians turning somersaults to appease terrorists, so the op gets binned. The RUC receives a George medal, the Branch gets shafted and Nighthawk runs free.'

Kerr was thinking back to Robyn's disclosures in Rome, just five days earlier. He glanced at a couple more photographs. 'Did Frankie ever mention a boy at the Olive Tree called Nick?'

'No.'

'So what's freaking you out?'

Dodge fell silent again, looking at his hands. 'I have to meet

Frankie away from the city, so we end up in Capanagh Forest, near Larne.'

'That's a long way. Whose choice?'

'Frankie has a van and we drive there separately. After dark, no-one about, low risk.' Something seemed to catch in Dodge's throat, dust from the newsprint, or craving for a cigarette. He broke into a hacking cough and turned away, a podgy hand covering his mouth. 'I'm sorry.'

Melanie spoke first, understanding. 'When did you cross the line?'

Dodge swung back to the desk and lowered his head so that they had to strain to hear. 'One night he brings a drop of whiskey and things get out of hand. The instant Frankie touches me I'm completely out of control. He takes me into the van.' He fell quiet again, struggling to control himself. 'I'm supposed to be the controller and he's leading me through the trees like a wee lamb. It's our secret for a couple of hours.' He began sobbing, then something escaped from deep inside, like the sound after a yawn. Kerr waited for Melanie to comfort him but she stayed on the crates, her face unreadable as Dodge wiped his tears. 'Anyway, after a couple of months he says we have to stay in the car. He's got photographs of me and him together. Had the van wired, or someone. Frankie's been playing me all along. This is a honeytrap in reverse, him and whoever he's working for.'

'So is it money?'

'Secrets. He tells me they want everything we have on dissident targets.'

They let the silence hang until Dodge raised his head, eyes glinting through the tears. 'Now you're thinking, did I report it?' He gave a harsh laugh. 'We're talking the dog days of the RUC here and I'm a married man. Do I confess to being gay? Christ, are you out of your minds?'

Kerr shrugged. 'It would have stopped them.'

'John, we're talking Ulster in the fucking dark ages.'

'But not as bad as the alternative,' said Melanie, quietly.

'And *you* are out of order. I didn't give away any frigging secrets.' This was Dodge pulling rank but it came out tired, half-hearted. He found Kerr one of the press cuttings. 'Within a week, Frankie's dead from a headshot.'

Dated February 2001 and headed 'This Is Belfast At Peace?' the yellowing extract reported the murder of nineteen year old Francis Magill, speculating he had been an informer for the RUC. Kerr handed it to Melanie and reached for a longer extract: 'For God's Sake, Bury The Past.' This included a blurry photograph of the victim, spinning the murder into a denunciation of the RUC Special Branch against the new Police Service of Northern Ireland.

'Shallow grave in the Capanagh Forest,' said Kerr. 'Coincidence?'

'The IRA nutting squad got him for being a tout. End of.'

'Except it's not, is it?' said Melanie.

'No. The following year Nicola and I escape to the mainland.'

'Because of the death threats, yeah,' said Kerr.

'And by now, PSNI are working to MI5 and Sinn Fein. The new brooms don't want us blocking the gutter, so most of us jump ship. The new "Disappeared".'

Melanie nodded at Trig. 'Bobby Roscoe?'

Dodge took a deep breath. 'For fifteen years I hear nothing and start to think this has gone away. Then I get a call out of the blue. He knows my name and tells me he got the number from Frankie, which is bollocks, like, the boy just rose from the grave. Orders me to Covent Garden. Bobby Roscoe made the warning call for Victoria and is totally involved in the bombings. I can prove it with video, even the clothes he wore.'

'How many times have you seen him?' said Kerr.

Wheezing, Dodge held up three fingers. 'He feeds me half-truths, knowing I have to take action, that I'll be shown to be wrong and people will die because of me. It's driving me mad, and it has to end today.'

Melanie looked around. 'How did you find this place?'

'Builder's merchant who sold him the roofing stuff,' he said, making sense of the fight Melanie and Jack Langton had witnessed in Harlesden.

'So tell us why he needs a new roof,' said Kerr.

'I met him again in Soho, Monday afternoon. They're planning a lorry bomb, but it won't fit in here. He needs the roof to hide it from the air. That's what I think.'

'So where is it?'

Dodge shrugged. 'But they won't do it on a weekend.'

'Dodge, they already did,' said Melanie. 'The mortar? Jack and I were there, remember?'

'That was symbolic, to make the news. The lorry bomb is to leave bankers dead in the street.'

'So why now?' said Kerr.

'I don't know.' Dodge stabbed the photograph. 'Bobby Roscoe was Frankie's lover and he's taking his revenge.'

'Against the IRA, or you?'

Dodge suddenly sounded exhausted. 'John, isn't it obvious?'

'So he holds you responsible?'

'Frankie Magill was an informer.'

'A blackmailer, too,' said Melanie. 'Roscoe believes you killed Frankie, doesn't he? To save your own skin?'

Melanie sounded harsh, her insubordination catching Dodge off guard. 'Is that what you think?'

Kerr's BlackBerry broke the silence. He listened for a moment and rang off. 'Did Roscoe ever mention his accomplices? Hints about Ireland? Anywhere in Europe?'

Dodge shook his head. 'He refused everything.'

'Well, we just got the readout from Gina Costello's Sim. There are only three items,' he said, 'and number two is the mobile you fed into Trig. They know each other, Dodge. In it together.'

'And Roscoe's on the move again,' said Melanie, rotating the screen to show the star pulsing south.

'It's like I told you. He's coming back here. For this,' said

Dodge, scuffing at his life's detritus on the desk. He looked at Kerr, pleading.

'It's alright,' said Kerr, adjusting the Glock against his ribs. 'I'm not calling Finch.'

'John, this can't be about Dodge,' frowned Melanie. 'We have to get an arrest team here, now.'

'That's you and me.' He looked at Dodge's hands. 'Gloves the whole time?'

'Since crowbarring the door.'

'And is the garbage all here? All the photographs from the van?' Dodge held up a torn A4 envelope and nodded. 'Okay, here's what you do. Collect your demons and disappear. You were never here, and we haven't seen you. Where's Nicola?'

'At home.'

'Do what you have to do, then join her. Speak only with us. Understood?'

Dodge nodded. 'What happens to Roscoe?'

'What you should have done from the start…Mel?'

'M1 southbound.'

He gripped Dodge's shoulder. 'Drive.'

Chapter Fifty-Seven

Kerr and Melanie kept watch at the door while Dodge collected every incriminating document into the pannier and carried it to the Audi. The boot kept sticking and he had to kick the lid three times to release the catch. Breathless from the exertion, he bent to insert the key in the ignition, then stood upright, sucking in lungfuls of fresh air. Overwrought and ashen-faced, he lingered awkwardly by the driver's door, his mouth working silently. Melanie stepped forward before he could find his voice and hugged him tight, while Kerr held the door, waiting for him to get behind the wheel. Dodge finally stripped off the gloves and held out his hand. 'John...I...'

'It's not necessary,' said Kerr, gripping his hand. He pointed at the boot. 'Just be sure not to leave a trace.'

'Will you let me...you know...'

'Yes. I'll call you at home, when we're done.'

They watched him drive away, then Kerr shifted the Alfa across the street to a slip road bordering the canal, reaching into the glove compartment for a set of plastic handcuffs. When he returned, Melanie was cautiously exploring the hideout, with a close watch on Trig.

'Where's Roscoe?'

'Still the M1, just north of Hendon. The speed he's going, Saturday traffic, I'd say we have less than fifteen minutes to get our act together.'

'Good.'

'So, do I call for back-up?' Melanie stared at him. 'John, how are we going to play this?'

'Anyone tell you how many lives Dodge saved across the water? I'm going to protect him.'

Melanie looked exasperated. 'But this is about more than looking after our friend. There's a bigger picture here.'

Kerr looked around the dismal workshop. 'And I guess we're standing in it.' He picked Dodge's crowbar from the floor and handed it to Melanie. 'So let's not screw up.'

They spent the next three minutes planning their ambush, working on the element of surprise. If Roscoe arrived alone, or with a conspirator, they would contain the situation inside the workshop; two or more others, and they would steal away from the yard, call from the Alfa for urgent assistance, and keep watch.

Roscoe would find the workshop unlocked, for Dodge had smashed the padlock and hasp beyond repair, suggesting burglary or vandalism rather than a covert police search. Melanie lowered the door to waist level, a little higher than Dodge had left it but low enough to compromise Roscoe as he ducked inside or rolled it open.

They concealed themselves behind a thicket of brambles with a clear view of the entrance and an escape route across a low, wire mesh fence. They had less than seven minutes to wait before a dirty silver Ford Courier van pulled into the pitted yard, slowed in front of the half-open door and swung in a wide arc to stop less than a couple of car lengths from their hiding place. Kerr silently drew his Glock as they sank into the scrub. Silence settled with the dust as the driver remained in the car, watching and waiting, as cautious as Kerr and Melanie when they had come for Dodge. Then the door clicked open and heavy footsteps crunched across the gravel within touching distance of the brambles. Finger against the trigger guard, Kerr stole a look at the figure loping past and recognised Bobby Roscoe immediately. In jeans, work boots and white T-shirt, he was taller than Kerr had imagined, stronger and nastier than the fresh-faced, barechested boy with a slender arm around Frankie Magill.

At the workshop Roscoe shifted to the left, watching for the slightest movement as the sun sneaked from behind a cloud to flood the yard with light. Shading his eyes, Kerr snatched a look back to the van but Melanie had already ensured Roscoe was alone. The crowbar appeared in her hands as they exchanged a nod and eased to their feet. The swish of the traffic and distant thump of the pile driver offered low background noise but they needed the screech of the rusting door to mask their ten metre charge across the open scrub and gravel. They saw Roscoe bend low, squint through the gap and jerk the door hard. Kerr broke cover first but Melanie overtook him, reaching Roscoe at full stretch with the door still rolling. On high alert for threats within, not behind, Roscoe was too slow to pick up the danger as Melanie smashed the crowbar across his upper back. Her direct hit threw him off balance, propelling him into the dark interior, and his howl of pain echoed around the walls as he collapsed onto the greasy concrete floor at the edge of the inspection pit. Melanie leapt at him, spinning him onto his injured back with the crowbar hard across his throat. Half-blinded from the sunlight, Roscoe struggled to focus. 'What the fuck...' he croaked. 'Who...?'

Kerr, taking his time, walked up to him, tapped Melanie on the shoulder to roll clear and kicked Roscoe into the pit. He used such force that Roscoe's head crashed against the far wall before he collapsed into a mess of oil and hydraulic fluid, yelping like a trapped animal. Kerr took up the firing position, the Glock aimed for a head shot as Roscoe struggled to his knees and squinted up at them. 'Where's the vehicle?' he said, calmly.

Roscoe looked terrified. 'What vehicle? Who sent you?'

Kerr took a pace back. 'Get out.'

Roscoe slowly stood, bringing his head level with the floor, then climbed the short metal ladder. He was evidently in pain, with blood oozing from his temple, scarcely able to lift his arms for support. After a few seconds Melanie lost patience, grabbing his shirt to haul him up the last three steps. She manhandled him into the office, made a rapid body search and shoved him back into the chair Dodge had just vacated. Roscoe massaged his throat, taking in the upturned drawers and the opened hideout.

'The lorry bomb,' said Kerr, covering him with the Glock again. 'Where is it?'

Stunned by the brutality of attackers apparently intent on murder, the demand sparked a complete change in Roscoe. 'You're cops? Counter-terrorism?' He looked like a gangster reprieved from the mob, fear of execution suddenly banished by hard arrest. Now, arrogance stiffened his voice. 'So you've been listening to the queer Mister Dodge? Where's your fucking ID? Search warrant? This is how cops treat the public these days? You think you can get away with attacking a businessman in his place of work?'

'A rat living in a hole,' said Melanie.

'I demand to see a lawyer, now.'

'Answer the question.'

Roscoe tried to cross his arms but the pain was too raw. 'The fat bastard has been feeding you lies.'

Melanie thrust the cold steel against his face, jerking his head back so violently that his boots kicked the underside of the desk. When she let go, Roscoe twisted painfully in the chair. 'Don't stop now. Look, I'm turning the other cheek,' he grunted. 'I want it all black and blue. Come on, make me rich. You are *so* going to jail.'

'We know about you,' said Kerr.

'You know nothing.' Roscoe let out a hoarse laugh. 'Your friend is a sexual predator, and you're protecting him.'

'That's a lie.'

'An animal. Ask him about Gabriel's Bar, the room upstairs, where he tried to rape me and offered me a payoff to keep quiet. Thousands.'

'To get you on the books.'

'To be a spy. He forced me to be a grass and demanded sex. Payment for services. Hush money. Take your pick.'

'Because you're a bad person with good connections.'

'Totally wrong. He told you that?'

'That's his job. We know you made the bomb call at Victoria.'

'So arrest me, or get off my property.'

'And now you're going to confess to us for free. Your least worst option is to die in prison.'

Roscoe's smile mocked them. 'He really did a good job on you.' He rubbed his throat again and glared at Melanie. 'When I told your man where to stick his bribe he threatened to stitch me up. Fact. And here you are, doing his dirty work. Same stunt he pulled in Belfast, raped a lad then murdered him to keep it secret.' He glanced at the smashed door to his hideout. 'He was here, right? Yes. Well, tell him I've got a lot more than the stuff in there, too much for you to cover up. Looking for a lorry bomb? Go and beat the shit out of him, not me, then tell your bosses what he's really like. Show his wife and daughter what a fucking fraud he really is.'

'You scumbag,' said Kerr, stirred by the man's coolness. With the Glock never wavering from his head, Roscoe had spun a semiplausible attack against Dodge to instil suspicion and buy time. In pain, his voice weakened from Melanie's assault, Roscoe's presence of mind was chilling.

'If you don't, I will, right now,' said Roscoe. Ignoring Kerr, he fixed on Melanie again, his petrol grey eyes fully open in the shadows, and shuffled forward in the chair until Melanie shoved him back again. Then Kerr's BlackBerry vibrated in his jacket, Gemma's text quelling any doubts about Dodge's corruption or Roscoe's victimhood. 'Livebait rec'd 11.06. Bomb at Greenwich, no further pars or time frame. Code Topaz. Caller male with Northern Irish accent. Search underway of borough core target premises annex. Banks prioritised. Best G.'

Eyes never leaving Roscoe, Kerr held the screen up for Melanie, just as her own mobile beeped with Gemma's group message.

Kerr raised the Glock to Roscoe's temple again. 'That's your bomb warning.' He spoke slowly and deliberately, clocking a bright yellow hose reel tucked away in the far corner. 'And your time just ran out,' he said, speed-dialling Alan Fargo in Room

1830. 'We have to do whatever is necessary, so I'm giving you one more chance. Where is the lorry now?'

Roscoe looked up at him, grinning. 'And I'm still telling you to piss off.'

Fargo picked up immediately. 'Alan, on the Livebait, tell them they should be looking for a vehicle. I'll have more info very soon, so stay where I can get hold of you.'

Roscoe chuckled as Kerr rang off. 'Don't *bank* on it.'

'Which one?'

'You're too late.'

'Who made the call just now?'

'Go fuck yourself.'

Kerr reached into his pocket for the plastic cuffs and covered Melanie as she secured Roscoe's wrists. 'Take his boots off.'

Kerr ducked into the hideout for Roscoe's towel, crossed the workshop and unrolled the hose pipe, trailing it back to the office. 'Stand up,' he ordered. When Roscoe slumped deeper into the chair, Kerr holstered the Glock and dragged him to his feet. He spun him round and crashed him backwards onto the desk, sliding him down until his head hung over the end. Looking for Melanie's nod of assent, he forced the nozzle of the hose into Roscoe's mouth. Face flooded with shock, Roscoe held himself as tight as a man with lockjaw, so Kerr leaned over him, pressing with all his strength until they heard his teeth splinter.

'The clock's ticking, and you know what I'm going to do,' murmured Kerr. Another glance at Melanie. Silence from the prisoner. He twisted the nozzle to release water into Roscoe's mouth. 'If the bomb goes, no way do you get through this.' Roscoe spat and wailed against the flow, arching his back and flailing his legs as water flushed from his mouth and nose. Kerr pulled the hose away. 'Kick again and I'll break your legs. Last chance, then it gets worse.' A look of terror. Groans of disbelief, then silence again.

Kerr grabbed one of the drawers Dodge had upended on the

floor and gestured Melanie to lift Roscoe from the waist. He shoved the drawer beneath Roscoe's backside and pushed his head down again, tilting his whole torso. Splashing water over the towel, he held it high until it dripped on Roscoe's face. Roscoe twisted his head to flash a desperate look at Melanie, as if she, his most violent assailant, might save him from her partner's craziness.

Instead, Melanie shook her head and watched Kerr lay the towel over his face and hose more water. The soaked cloth ballooned outwards in a single, desperate exhalation, then Roscoe's struggle for air sucked it inside his mouth and nostrils, creating a vacuum-packed outline of his face as the body slowly drowned. A slow count to ten before Kerr pulled the towel away, 'Where?' he said quietly, as Roscoe's head thrashed beneath the desk.

Kerr waterboarded him twice more. On the final application, his surrender came on a rapid count of five, the confession diluted with strings of blood and vomit. 'The Dome,' he croaked.

Kerr calmly checked his watch. 'How long?'

Roscoe shook his head, desperately taking in air as Kerr leaned over him again. 'Dunno. I swear.' Kerr stared down into his eyes, looking for the truth, but the only fight left in Bobby Roscoe was for oxygen.

Resolved, Kerr turned off the water and tossed his keys to Melanie. 'Bring the car round.'

Chapter Fifty-Eight

As Melanie dashed from the workshop, Kerr moved away from Roscoe so that he would not hear his call to 1830. Fargo picked up spontaneously, as if the line had been left open. In the background, he could hear Gemma in the comms room. 'She's on the link,' said Fargo. 'What have you got?'

'Target is the O2 Arena and the bomb is in a lorry.'

'And how long do we have?' said Gemma.

'I'm working on it.' There was a crash as Roscoe tipped from the desk onto the hard floor. 'Al, I'm going there myself. Can you get me the external layout?' he said, but Fargo was already calling into the room for everything on the O2, his Cornish voice calm and measured. Kerr could hear Gemma, too, making her report: 'This is Gemma in SO15 comms with additional on the 11.06 Livebait to Greenwich…'

In 1830, Fargo's keyboard clattered as he made his own searches.

'What's on this weekend?'

'Just scrolling the events page…there's an equestrian thing till Sunday afternoon. Show jumping…dressage, exhibitions, fun rides for kids, etcetera. I'm guessing coaches and families from across Europe.'

'Who's organising it?'

'It's a European Union event, everything gold stars on blue. Hold on. Plus three, four logos from sponsors. Here you go. Funded by the EBF. European Banking Federation.'

'So we have bomb and motive.' Outside, Kerr heard Melanie skid the Alfa into the yard and swing round, the car's shadow seeping under the door. He looked at Roscoe again, slumped on the hard floor, moaning in pain and spitting to clear his mouth.

On a shelf behind the desk, he spotted a two litre bottle of white spirit. 'I'm going to get more.'

More shuffling and voices offstage, then Fargo again. 'Thanks, Rosie...John, I'm pinging you the plans now.'

'And I'll touch base as soon as I'm there,' said Kerr, cutting the call. He grabbed the bottle and splashed the turps around Roscoe, seeing his eyes widen with fear. By the time Melanie ducked beneath the door and held out his car keys, he was hosing water over Roscoe's head and slapping his face to revive him. 'I made a quick search of his van,' she said, wrinkling her nose.

'Any phones? Laptops?'

'Nothing. What's the plan?'

Kerr switched the hose to refill the bottle. 'We're going to Greenwich. Help me get him to the car.'

'John, he's a prisoner,' she said, looking doubtful.

'He's a bomber with a lot more to tell.' According to Jack Langton, Melanie was the quickest driver on the Reds, so he closed her hand around the key fob. 'How quickly can you get us there?'

'Euston Road. Angel, Old Street, Aldgate,' she said, knitting her brow. 'Traffic's light. Provided Commercial Road's okay and the tunnel's not blocked...how fast do you need?'

He pulled Roscoe to his feet. 'Like you've never driven before.'

'Okay, but it'll be bumpy in the back,' she said, grabbing Roscoe's arm, 'and very noisy.'

They half-carried, half-dragged Roscoe to the Alfa, grazing his bare feet on the stones. By the rear door he resisted again, so Kerr smashed his face against the edge of the roof and forced him behind the passenger seat. He darted back for the bottle of water, rolled the door shut and clambered behind Melanie. By the time he secured his seat belt Melanie was half a mile away, blue light flashing, siren howling, kicking down as she weaved east through the Saturday traffic and accelerated into clear road.

The radio flicked automatically between two operational

channels. Jack Langton had already redeployed the Reds into a Starburst around Greenwich, and communicated on Tetra Channel Five, while Eighteen updated on the O2 evacuation. With agitation all around, the Alfa's three occupants stayed more or less silent, Melanie at the peak of concentration, Roscoe slumped in his seat, and Kerr figuring how the next hour would play out.

Less than four minutes later it was the dome of Madame Tussauds, not the O2, that sparked the connection in his brain. Screaming along the Marylebone Road past Baker Street, the siren bouncing off walls and windows, a shaft of sunshine against the famous green cupola drew him like a lodestar across the Atlantic to Rich Malone's warning of an attack in London against 'Corona.' The source had been uncorroborated, the information in Spanish, second or third hand, the microphone coverage defective. This had been Washington protecting her interests by passing raw, sketchy intelligence to Kerr. The Americans called it 'covering their ass,' the Brits *Rectum Defende*, but it amounted to the same thing: disclosure followed by deniability, the dark art of intelligence exchange amongst allies. For Kerr, it had been the classic, substandard product people in his business managed every day, but now the target kept him steady as a rock as they hurtled east into Euston Road. Corona had been Rich's genuine gift, one friend sharing with another: not a crown but a dome, a building; an iconic arena, nothing to do with Royalty.

Both channels squawked non-stop. Monotone police voices repeated key words and elongated syllables for clarity, defying the bomb's urgency. Melanie's driving was faultless, the speedometer wavering between seventy and eighty on the straights, plummeting as she negotiated tailbacks and red lights, even murmuring the occasional apology. Buildings, vehicles and traffic jams swept past in a blur, yet Kerr's brain coolly reprocessed the information from the past twelve days as they slid through the giant roundabout at Old Street and careered east towards Aldgate and Limehouse.

He turned to the murderer holding the secret to the threat ahead. Roscoe's face was a bloody mess, his left eye half-closed and nose evidently broken, lips shredded and swollen. Kerr grabbed his chin, forcing his head round. 'Where did they leave it?'

Roscoe fixed Kerr with his good eye, his face twisted with hate, so Kerr punched him again on the side of the head. 'Who told you to hit the O2?'

Then Channel Eighteen came through with a suspect lorry parked on the north side bordering the river, a six-wheeler with its hazard lights flashing. 'Security now evacuating through south doors only. Estimate upwards of twelve, repeat twelve hundred people.'

Kerr absorbed the information as they rocketed through east London, but his attention was on Roscoe's face, suddenly split by a blood-drenched grin. 'Wrong again.'

'What does that mean?' shouted Kerr.

'Doesn't matter, cos you'll still be too fucking late,' he grunted.

They hit another straight stretch of road, Melanie accelerating above eighty as Kerr unclicked his belt and dragged Roscoe down, twisting to make room for him across the back seat. Roscoe's feet kicked violently against the side window as Kerr clambered onto him, then ripped the blood-stained T-shirt over his face and head.

His thighs stabilising him against Roscoe's body, he told Melanie to steady the car. He poured water onto the shirt until the cloth saturated Roscoe's airways, and watched the familiar result: inflation, inhalation, the bloody mask showing every outline of Roscoe's face. They shot into Blackwall Tunnel, the curved walls maximising the siren's wail, the blue light and headlamps strobing the semi-darkness as Roscoe began to drown again, cuffed hands rigid, his back arching so violently that Kerr's head struck the roof.

Kerr pulled away the T-shirt to watch Roscoe choke on his blood and vomit. 'Tell me,' he shouted, but Roscoe shook his head until Kerr hooded him again and poured more water. Roscoe's fingers clawed at Kerr's chest as they shot into the daylight. This time he tried to say something when Kerr desisted, but his voice was too weak to carry above the din.

Kerr slapped him hard. 'Louder. Say it again.' They flashed past a series of giant posters with pictures of racehorses against the EU flag, then the gigantic masts of the Arena came into view and Kerr dragged Roscoe upright as he tried to speak again.

'Not a lorry.'

Kerr leant in close. 'What, then?'

Roscoe's lungs worked frantically, sucking the atmosphere from the Alfa. 'Horsebox,' he croaked.

'A horsebox? Where?'

'Main entrance.' He bent forward slightly to peer over Melanie's shoulder as they careered round a tree-lined curve in the final sprint, and suddenly the Dome towered over them. Roscoe's expression changed again, hatred and fear banished by panic as they drew beneath the target's shadow. 'You're too late,' he gasped. 'Have to turn back.'

Kerr followed Roscoe's eyes to the dashboard clock: 11.48. Sixteen minutes since leaving Willesden. 'Shit, he's set it on the hour.' He twisted Roscoe's chin again. 'It's on for noon, isn't it? What kind of timer? Memopark?'

Roscoe nodded. 'Can't stop it. Nothing you can do,' he panted, as Melanie skidded to a halt by the first car park. Cops were running everywhere with reels of tape and they saw five or six horses being led away to a patch of open ground near the station sign. Melanie pointed through the windscreen. 'Over there. Is that it?' Fifty paces away, parked in sunshine by the main entrance on the south side, was a grey horse box with its side door open. Alongside, bales of hay were piled haphazardly around a picnic table with flowers, a large wicker hamper and bottles of wine in coolers, the backdrop a giant poster of the Dordogne. Welcome to paradise.

'Jesus,' said Kerr, pulling himself forward on the back of the seat. 'Couldn't be worse.' The area was a mass of visitors being directed across the path of the bomb, casual, good-humoured, jokily oblivious to the danger. Blue lights punctured the air, but none appeared to belong to a bomb disposal vehicle: if the explosives officers were already here, they had been sent to the wrong place.

'We should radio it in, John.'

Kerr watched the crowd walking towards them and checked the clock against his watch. 'With a Memopark? Accurate to a couple of minutes?' He turned to Roscoe, murderous. 'You kept the warning vague to catch people getting away, didn't you? Victoria, now Greenwich.'

'You can't go in there.' Beneath Roscoe's injuries, his skin had drained white, as if he had just choked away his last blood. 'Please. All they told me is, this one's a fucking monster.'

'Did he leave the key in the ignition?'

A shake of the head.

Kerr peered ahead again. 'How old is it?'

'Ancient. Fourteen, fifteen years.'

Another time check: 11.53. 'Old enough to hotwire, Mel?'

Melanie nodded and slipped the gears. 'Couple of minutes.'

'What the fuck are you doing?' sobbed Roscoe as Melanie surged forward. She used the siren again, weaving through the evacuees and sliding to a halt by the horsebox as a bunch of local police yelled at them to get clear. Kerr's door clicked open. 'Stay here and watch him,' he said, leaping from the car. He ran to the nearest cop, flashed his ID and demanded his baton. Pushing at a second officer, he whirled around like a crazy man. 'It's a bomb! Run! Bomb! Bomb!' Three pairs of confused officers stared between him and Melanie in the Alfa, instinctively checking their Tasers, so Kerr held his ID high again and kept shouting until reality finally galvanised them into finding their own voices, herding, shoving, ordering everyone to run for their lives.

Kerr beckoned Melanie, smashed the driver's window with a single blow, pulled the door open and ran past her as she attacked the steering column. Struggling to get clear, Roscoe already had the Alfa door open, so Kerr helped him on his way, hauling him into the back of the horsebox and slamming the door as the engine coughed twice and spluttered to life. Kerr shifted a couple of the hay bales as he raced round the vehicle, still yelling with all his strength.

'Am I driving?' said Melanie, but Kerr was already tugging her from the driver's seat. He took off his jacket and handed over the Glock, then his BlackBerry. 'Go.' He leapt behind the wheel, spot-checked the cab for signs of the bomb and revved the engine. 'I want you to help them get people clear, then come for me.'

Melanie protested but Kerr had already rammed the gears into first. He found the hazard lights, sounded the horn and shot forward, knocking over the picnic table as he swung left. Scraping between a couple of posts, he accelerated hard to find himself on a wide gravel footpath, bordered by ornate lamp posts and blocks of modern apartments. To his left, the River Thames, deep and wide. Three minutes. A scattering of dog walkers gesticulating and, from the back, Roscoe hammering in desperation. Kerr stole another look for traces of the bomb, any battery, wire or plastic he could pull, dislodge or smash to make it safe: nothing. Submersion was his only chance and he raced along at twenty-five in third gear, searching for access to the river.

The timber jetty appeared like a mirage as he swerved round a tree-lined curve. Rackety and dilapidated, half the length of a football pitch, it was blocked only by a wire mesh gate. Kerr strapped himself in and swerved across the neatly tended grass. Time remaining: zero.

Wetsuits draped around their waists, a couple of young men were pulling a dinghy on a launching trolley across the access path so Kerr sounded the horn again as he rammed the accelerator to the floor. Just in time, the men leapt clear. Striking the dinghy a glancing blow, Kerr shielded his face as he smashed through the gate and rattled over the loose wooden joists, longing for the water to engulf him, mouth open in a full-throated roar as he breached the safety fence, took to the air and nosedived into the sluggish river.

The seat belt saved Kerr's body but jack-knifed his head against the windscreen as Roscoe crashed through the partition behind him, his head and shoulders trapped in the shattered plywood circle like a guilty man in the stocks. Stretched tightly around his throat was a necklace of three plastic bags filled with Semtex, the terrorist confronted by his bomb. The horsebox drifted downstream, time for Kerr to throw off his shoes and jacket as water gushed into the compartment and engulfed them. He snatched a final look at Roscoe, heaved his shoulder against the door, filled his lungs and slid into the river.

Swimming frantically to get clear, he saw the two dinghy sailors wading towards him, to save or remonstrate. Crabbing for the shore with the current, his feet suddenly touched shingle and he scrabbled to get a foothold, waving at his rescuers to stay back. Strength was deserting him as he staggered through the shallows, then strong arms were pulling him to safety. Voice fading, he tried to fight them off, turning to point at the sinking horsebox as the bomb exploded with a muffled thump and a giant plume of water as high as a house, everything in slow motion until the aftershock flattened them and shattered every window within yelling distance.

Kerr could smell the beach as he turned to look at the river, littered with floating debris. For a few seconds the three of them lay silently in the black mud, Kerr exhausted, his rescuers uncomprehending, the only noise from seagulls and sirens. 'You alright?' said the younger of them, eventually. He glanced at his mate, then frowned at the river, its waters languid again, as if he had imagined everything. 'Anyone else out there?'

Kerr shook his head. The sludge sucked at his knees as he struggled upright. 'Can I borrow a phone?'

Chapter Fifty-Nine

Saturday, 22 October, 14.56, The Queen's Walk

'I've known him for ages, from my days in the Registry. What I don't understand…thing is, you're his daughter, so tell me, Gabi. Why does he have to act like he's bloody James Bond?'

'Oh, Dad's always been on the on the excitable side, ever since I was a kid. When he came to see us in Rome he was always in some sort of scrape with the high-ups. Actually, I think Mum quite liked him being a bit of a rebel, you know, deep down. She would, wouldn't she?'

Sipping from their takeaway Americanos, Gabi and Nancy Sergeyev perched on a bench overlooking the Thames, a short stroll from St Thomas' Hospital. Gabi, returning from Rome to rehearse for a Barbican recital, had caught Melanie's text the moment she landed and come straight from the airport. She slipped off her rucksack, sat back and rotated her shoulders. 'Anyway, doing the right thing doesn't make him a bad bloke, does it?'

'He's a serial risk-taker,' said Nancy. They watched a young family negotiate the stone steps from Westminster Bridge, the mother cradling an infant, dad struggling with the buggy and a toddler. Nancy sighed and lifted her face to the weak afternoon sun. 'And I've got two kids who need looking after.'

'Three,' said Gabi, 'if you take on Dad.'

Nancy swirled her coffee and turned to her. 'Which is why neither of us thinks that's going to happen.'

They sat quietly again, taking in the scene. The autumn sun had stayed with them and strengthened, promising a warm afternoon, and Nancy balanced her cup on the ground to search for her sunglasses. From the other end of the bridge towered Big Ben and, to their right, the London Eye. On the opposite bank, a couple of wide tourist craft manoeuvred expertly around Westminster Pier. 'It's funny,' said Gabi, running a hand through her hair. 'Dad was always threatening to introduce us, but I never thought it would be like this.'

Nancy let out a harsh laugh, her anxiety leaking anger. 'With him lying in a hospital bloody bed, you mean? Battered, bruised… drips everywhere and…Christ knows what?' An amphibious duck boat was labouring upstream against the tide, its bright yellow hull low in the water. 'Just about says it all, doesn't it?'

Nancy had bumped into Gabi at the hospital, both rushing to find Kerr, reassured by Melanie's texts but scared to take her at her word. He had already been whisked from A and E when they arrived, another great sign, according to Melanie, though Nancy guessed she had arranged this to guard his privacy. Melanie had led them to a private area off the waiting room to tell the story of his heroism while, high on a wall outside, a TV looped footage of the O2 Arena, bomb debris on the river bank and row upon row of shattered windows.

Summoned on a borrowed mobile, avoiding the masses of police descending on Greenwich, Melanie had reached Kerr through an ecology park at the other end of the footpath. Shoeless, his clothing drenched and heavy with mud, Kerr had scarcely managed to walk up the shingle to the Alfa. Melanie had acted quickly, ramping up the heater and racing him to St Thomas'. By the time Finch's team reached the O2, Kerr was already in triage, naked beneath a white gown, face battered beneath the smile, only half-joking about discharging himself.

'The point is, Nancy, from what he's told me, I really think you're just what he's been looking for all these years,' said Gabi.

'After his latest stunt? I don't think so.' Nancy stared at her. 'Gabi, I'm talking about Rome, not this thing today.'

Gabi paused as the realisation sunk in, then gave a shriek of laughter. 'Dad and Mum, you mean? You really believe she's still into him? Nancy, that is *so* not true.' Gabi slipped her shades over her forehead. 'And you think I'm covering for him?'

Nancy turned away to gaze across the river.

'Well, let me put your mind at rest. Mum just is not interested in the slightest. That's the honest truth. She has a boyfriend and they go back for ever.'

'How long is that?'

'Nearly three years. In fact…yes. Tell you what,' she said, rummaging in her rucksack, 'I'll prove it.' She took out a pair of trainers, a hairbrush and and a paperback, *Witch Light* by Susan Fletcher, then her ten inch tablet in its scuffed maroon case. She switched it on, cussed the low battery and clicked onto a folder. 'Here you go. Robyn's birthday, this time last year. She had a do at the flat. Don't ask me why, it wasn't a special one, but that's Mum for you. Everyone totally hammered.'

'You took these?'

'Photographer, bar person and chucker-outer. Keeping Mum in order. I did a sort-through when I got back to London.' Shifting closer to Nancy, she angled the screen away from the sun. There were the usual shots of partygoers jostling in the *soggiorno* or crammed into the kitchen around the drink. Robyn, made up in a black, tailored skirt and low cut white blouse, was everywhere, with the images growing lopsided and blurry as the evening went on. 'As you can see, I was as squiffy as anyone…here we are. Miguel turned up a bit late and from here it's just the two of them goofing around. You'll see Mum is totally loved-up.' In the back pocket of her jeans, Gabi's mobile rang. 'They've been having sex for ever… and this is my man checking in…straight up, Nancy, you've got nothing to worry about. I mean…Hi, babe, hang on…he's not exactly Dad, is he?' she whispered, darting away for privacy.

The photographs were of Robyn with a handsome man in his fifties in a black linen shirt and cotton trousers with flip-flops. A few showed them smoking on the balcony in the twilight, the camera picking out the man's face more clearly than inside the flat. The effect on Nancy was electric. By the second shot, she had made a tentative connection; by the fifth, a smiling head and shoulders close-up, she was utterly convinced. She scrolled to and fro, startled, her certainty growing with each image, then searched for her own mobile.

A few paces away she could hear Gabi speaking Italian, using her hand for emphasis as she looked over the river, probably talking about her dad's bravery. Nancy swung away, shaded the tablet from the sun and grabbed the clearest three images on her mobile. She quickly checked them for quality, her mind buzzing with recovered memories and tangled emotions. Relief, trepidation for Kerr and irrational rage against Robyn fought each other as she drained her coffee, knowing she had to get away. She went up to Gabi and gently touched her arm, holding up her phone. 'Babysitter. Gotta go,' she mouthed, then blew a kiss before Gabi could react and hurried for the bridge, dialling even before she mounted the steps.

•••

Saturday, 22 October, 15.21, St Thomas' Hospital

The duty sister who made sure Kerr behaved himself was from the Seychelles. Her name was Nur, and Melanie knew she had recently kicked out her abusive and unfaithful husband, a homicide detective from Fulham. Having patched up a number of injured surveillance officers over the years, she was on first name terms with Melanie and Jack Langton and, because their work was secret, provided special treatment in zero waiting time. She knew about discretion, too: when Melanie walked in with her arm around Kerr's shoulders, she lifted her head to the breaking news on TV, waited for Melanie's nod of confirmation, then quietly took over in a flurry of triage, x-rays, blood tests and just-to-be-on-the-safe-side antibiotics. She found a private space for him, too, a plaster room in the fracture clinic crowded with walking frames, moon boots and folded wheelchairs.

Kerr had banged his shoulder escaping from the horsebox, his head ached from crashing against the windscreen, and every muscle was protesting from the struggle in the river. In the corridor outside he heard Melanie arguing with a pair of aggressive cops pulling rank, then Nur's voice, calm and authoritative, sending them away until the morning.

As soon as Melanie left, taking his wet clothes in a plastic sack, Nur threatened to confiscate his BlackBerry unless he agreed to stay overnight for observation. 'You're the boss,' said Kerr, sliding down the bed.

He began dialling Rich Malone in Washington as soon as Nur was out of earshot, then cancelled it for an incoming from 1830.

'You're still there?' said Fargo.

'I survived. Thanks for asking.'

'Mel already told us,' said Fargo, chuckling. 'Just to warn you, the Bull is sending two of his finest to ask about a headless torso floating downriver with its wrists cuffed.'

'Hospital already told them to bugger off,' said Kerr, stretching.

'And the commander's going to stall everyone until he's seen you for the welfare bit. John, can you talk?'

'I can listen.'

'You'll have a missed call there from Polly Graham. You were trying to walk on water at the time, so she rang me instead. Will Tommy's release you tonight?'

'I'm escaping as soon as Mel brings clothes.'

'So best you hear this now. Polly says she's found the bombmaker.'

'Jesus.' Kerr winced as he pushed himself up on the pillows. 'European? Is he ACI?'

'Not European extremist.'

Kerr frowned. 'Irish?'

'Think again.'

Kerr gingerly stretched forward to peer into the corridor. 'Al, I've got Sister Nur threatening to snatch my phone. Let's not play twenty questions.'

'The terrorist is one of the good guys.'

'What are you talking about?'

'One of ours. When you bumped into Polly this morning

she told you the recovered device was too perfect, right? Like something out of the engineering manual? Well, now we know why.'

'Who is it?'

'Not confirmed yet, so we're being careful.'

'But she had a fingerprint. A partial.'

'Middle finger of the right hand. Moment she got back to Porton she ran the mark through the computer. It pinged up five points of similarity with the suspect for a bank robbery three years ago. West Mids have a warrant out for him.'

'What's his name?'

'Jonathan Tranter, forty-eight years old and ex-military. English, born in Harrogate. Army records have him as Jonny Tranter, a bomb disposal officer in Belfast during the eighties.'

'Right or left-handed?'

'Left. He did three tours, a warrant officer seconded to explosive ordnance, EOD. No regiment shown, which suggests a freelancer.'

The secrecy immediately swept Kerr a mile downriver to St Katherine's Docks and Thursday's meeting with Vanessa Gavron. He found himself in The Headsail again, absorbing Gavron's account of her editor's shadowy army career and hatred of the IRA.

'Gavron told me Charles Brandon worked for Fourteen Intell. You think there's a tie-in here?'

'Quite possible, though Brandon was a few years earlier.'

'So we need to search for linkages. Places they served, lines of command, any possible crossovers.'

'Already on it. The MOD weekend duty officer blanked us till Monday morning but the commander's sorting it. Once we get access we'll put everything through the wringer. Anyway, Jonny Tranter is a hero, obviously. The army lost count of the number of bombs he made safe. But also a genius engineer, according to Polly, expert at reconstructing IRA improvised devices for instruction purposes. He was so brilliant the Real IRA tried to make out he planted a couple of devices attributed to them. John, the man becomes a legend to both sides. Then in September 2002 he gets dishonourably discharged. No reason given, but West Mids Counter Terrorism Unit have him as a contact of UFL. That's "Union First and Last".'

'Have we heard of them?'

'We're looking at the blog now.'

'What does Polly say about this?'

'A military bomb disposal officer making devices for terrorists? A rogue in her own profession? Well, she's gutted, isn't she? People she works alongside at Porton will know of this bandit. If it's true, there's going to be hell to pay.'

'So who's broken the news to the Bull?'

Fargo left a moment's silence at the other end of the line. 'Actually, Polly's asking us to keep the trace in-house until we're certain.'

'We're talking evidence in a live terrorist operation, Al.'

'But Tranter is still a tentative ID. She needs more time.'

'To do what?'

'She called the lab in Belfast and they still have Tranter's reconstructed devices in store. Apparently, bomb disposal officers use the same tools and keep them for ever. Luck, superstition, who knows? If Jonny Tranter used the same kit for the Gloucester Road bomb, she'll find identical markings under the microscope. Striation traces on the screw heads, cuts in the wood, all that stuff. Even the way the Semtex is pressed out.'

'The bombmaker's signature.'

'Just as she promised.' Fargo let the silence hang again, waiting for Kerr to respond. 'It's just a few hours, John, and the Bull is going to be up to his eyes at the O2.'

'That's not the point.'

'Okay. But we owe her.'

Another pause. 'Let me call Ritchie.'

Chapter Sixty

Before Kerr could try Rich Malone again, a Chinese student nurse dropped by to check his blood pressure and tell him Sister Nur was occupied with a hit and run. 'Hey, buddy. You beat me to it,' said Malone without preamble, to a background of engine noise and honking. Kerr wondered why his friend was driving through Washington on a Saturday morning.

'Is this a bad time?' He could hear young voices, too, and U2's 'Beautiful Day' playing at high volume.

'It's my weekend with the kids,' said Malone, 'but I was gonna call you, anyway.'

'You've seen the news?'

'About that guy driving the bomb into the River fucking Thames? You bet,' said Malone, intemperate as ever. Kerr had never inquired about Malone's domestic circumstances, but guessed his children would grow up fast. 'And the nutcase was you, right? No bullshit, John. We'll just check with your ops room. Are you hurt?'

'Stuck in the ER but everything's good. Look, I'm calling to thank you, Rich.'

Malone's voice veered from the hands-free as he turned to keep the kids in check. 'For what?'

'The Corona tip.'

'What about it?'

'The Crown. It was the O2, right? Your source was good and we joined the dots. Eventually.' Kerr paused as the music dropped, waiting for Malone's assent. 'Rich? You know, the Dome? Hey, pal, I'm grateful. And I want any more you can give me.'

'No, that's not it,' said Malone.

Kerr frowned. The kids sounded boisterous but Malone's voice had dropped a notch. Caught off guard or distracted, he drifted away again, and Kerr strained to hear. 'You talking to me?'

'I'm *en route* to the office. My pal in the DEA says his source had another crash meet this morning.'

'Goldhawk?'

'Just after you took your dive in the river.'

'Same targets?'

'And place. Sean Brogan with the John Doe in the brothel. No time to wire Goldhawk.'

'Is that because their job here failed?'

'John, you're not getting this.'

'You want me to come over again?'

'No. That's not it. Goldhawk says they're talking about a *future* attack. I'm telling you Corona hasn't happened yet.'

'Hold on.' Melanie slipped into the room with a grab bag of clothes as Kerr absorbed the blow. He ripped out his saline drip, rotated his hand for Melanie to turn away and slid from the bed. 'Future, as in "soon"?' he said, wriggling into his pants and chinos.

'As in "imminent," buddy. So you can forget the O2 Arena. Greenwich was a taster for the main event. Which is why I'm dropping the kids at their ma's and going in for the full spiel.'

'Okay.' Melanie held the phone as Kerr pulled a blue polo shirt over his head and nudged into his moccasins. 'Do they know anything about the target?'

'Whatever, my pal's not sharing on the phone. They'll be notifying MI5 tonight.'

'But you'll give me a heads-up, yeah?'

'Soon as I have the readout.'

'Rich, I owe you again.'

'He's sending the cleaned up recording from the earlier meeting, too. It's not brilliant. A lot of gaps and cut-outs.'

'But you'll ping it across?'

'How good's your Spanish?' Malone managed a short laugh. 'It's secret. You think I'm gonna send it to the frigging ER?'

Kerr glanced at Melanie, already checking the corridor to make their escape. 'I'll be secure in twenty minutes,' he said, as she shot him a thumbs up.

Melanie had found a shortcut to the hospital car park through the boiler room. 'Did they recover anything at Roscoe's?' said Kerr, above the noise of the machinery.

'The van was clean. Still searching the workshop.' She shouldered the fire door into the car park. 'What did Rich want?'

'We need to check with the Palace again. I'll tell you on the way.'

'Whatever it is, let us handle it.' Melanie zapped the key fob, searching the gloom for the Alfa's hazard lights. 'Right now you need to concentrate on Nancy.'

'She's called you?'

'She's already at yours,' said Melanie over her shoulder. 'And mega peed off with you.'

At his bedside Nancy had been as calm and contained as Gabi, so the change brought him a pulse of alarm. He caught up with Melanie and took her arm. 'What's going on?'

'Something private between you two,' said Melanie, easing aside to open the passenger door for him. 'Why would she share with me?'

They clicked into their seat belts, inhaling the dregs of Bobby Roscoe's stale sweat and fear. 'Melanie, what's wrong?'

She gave a shrug and started the engine. 'Only you can say, apparently.'

•••

Saturday, 22 October, 16.08, Kerr's Apartment

A driver from the Reds was waiting for Melanie outside Kerr's Islington apartment. Melanie parked the Alfa, tossed Kerr the keys, ordered him to rest ('Lock yourself away at Nancy's for a couple of days. No ifs or buts') and scooted across the street.

Kerr's refurbished top floor apartment was light and airy, with its original high ceilings and cornices. There were two ensuite bedrooms off the living area, which stretched from front to back, filled with natural light. French windows led onto a spacious balcony and he found Nancy there with a chilled glass of wine, her back to him, distracted by the Saturday afternoon hubbub below. Sometimes, when Karl had the children to stay overnight, they would make dinner here, or visit a local restaurant by Chapel Market, then linger on the balcony until bed called. Nancy was wearing the same clothes she had worn at the hospital, light slacks with flat shoes and a lime sweater, and he wondered where she had been for the past three hours. He hoped with all his heart that she had come to wait for him, not to return his key.

Padding across the wooden floor in his bare feet, Kerr recognised her giant tote bag beneath the glass dining table, zipped and bulked out of shape. He stepped onto the balcony and bent to kiss her neck. She must have heard him above the din of the street for she turned at the last instant, grazing her hair against his injured face.

'Oh God, sorry,' she said, reaching to touch him as he found her lips. She waved her glass as he pulled a chair close. 'I helped myself.'

'Nance, I'm just so glad to see you.'

'Don't be. I've come to save you from yourself.' She paused while Kerr stared at her, then nodded at the bedroom, where Kerr kept his encrypted laptop in a wall safe. 'I'm sending you an email, and it's not good.' Perplexed, he collected his laptop, then disappeared into the kitchen for another glass and the opened bottle of Sancerre. When he returned, Nancy had come inside, scrolling through her iPhone at the dining table. She sipped her wine in silence while Kerr checked his Inbox. There was a brief email from Fargo with the subject 'Purple,' a police epithet for the Royal Family. 'Spoke with Melanie. Core principals by helicopter to Norfolk yesterday, returning to London Monday evening. I gave Prot a heads-up. Can you speak?'

Nancy's email popped up a second later. 'Recognise anyone?'

she said, as Kerr clicked onto the photographs grabbed from Gabi's tablet.

Kerr made a face. 'How did you get them?'

'Robyn threw herself a birthday party last year, apparently,' said Nancy.

'Yeah, Gabi mentioned it. She was referee and bouncer. So what's the story?' He leaned into her. 'You're worried I was there and didn't tell you?'

Nancy laughed. 'Oh, I think we're a long way past that.' She pointed at the screen. 'And Robyn's already got a boyfriend, hasn't she?'

Kerr shrugged. 'She doesn't tell me about her personal life.'

'I bet.' She regarded Kerr for a moment, then poured him some wine. 'Does lover boy ring any bells?'

Kerr's eyes dropped to the floor, suddenly glimmering with suspicion. He reached down and heaved Nancy's bag onto the table. 'What have you got in here?'

'When we left the hospital, Gabi and I had a chat, getting to know each other. Then I walked to the Yard to find Gemma. She got me into the Registry. First time in yonks.'

'Why would she do that?'

'Because I asked her.'

'But you're not security cleared any more.'

'Carol was on. We still have lunch and I haven't gone over to the Russians. Did you know she had to destroy the digital images of European terrorists? The heirs to Action Directe, Red Brigades, all gone. Baader-Meinhof Gang *kaput*, as if it never existed. Some EU phooey, according to Carol. It's like I wasted twelve years of my life. Unless it's a psycho narcissist tosser with a beard, no-one's interested, apparently. All the bosses in blinkers, like every other threat has evaporated. Is that true, John?'

Kerr gave a short laugh. 'Not any more.'

'So Carol, being Carol, secretly retains the paper files, squirrels them away in a security cabinet everyone's forgotten about.'

Nancy unzipped the bag and reached inside for a bulging pink folder headed Secret in black capitals, its contents tagged with string. Yellowing photographs were glued or stapled to the pages, releasing coils of dust into the sunshine as she leafed through them. 'The original subject files were culled years ago but she kept photographs with a copy of the front folio,' she said, as Kerr slowly shook his head. 'My whole working life in the Branch is in here, John, my initials on every page.' She opened the file to folio thirty-six. 'Donate Lucrecia Poncheti, member of *Brigate Rosse*. Bank robber, political extremist and weapons expert. A zealot who advocates political assassination to incite revolution. Ring any bells?'

Kerr studied a police mugshot, a smiling close-up from a family album and two surveillance photographs, all faded with age. 'Long time ago, Nance,' he said, shaking his head.

Nancy traced the bio with her finger. 'Here we are. Milan 1983. Took a bullet in the chest but pulled through, unfortunately. His comrades smuggled him into France, which is how he stayed free. But he couldn't resist the lure of Rome, right?'

'What are you getting at?'

'Did you know Robyn was having it off with a terrorist?'

Kerr stared at her, lost for words. The glue holding the photographs to the paper was cracked and flaky, and one of the surveillance shots dropped to the table. Nancy held it against the image on Kerr's laptop. 'Same thug, different generation. Tell me you can see the likeness.'

Stapled to the page was a brown envelope filled with more stills which Kerr spilled onto the table, as if they might give him a way out. 'He looks taller in the surveillance pics. Leaner.' Kerr sifted through every shot, doubtful, then relieved. 'Different colouring, hairline.'

'Same bullet wound, though,' said Nancy, quick as a flash. She sorted the close-ups for an image with Poncheti's upper chest exposed, pointing at a mark beneath the left clavicle. 'See? Now look again.' On the laptop, Robyn's boyfriend had his left arm around her shoulders, stretching his shirt to reveal the same dark, circular smudge.

Kerr breathed something inaudible, a murmur of defeat. He turned to her. 'Look, you know how I met Robyn.'

'In your undercover op, yes.'

'As an activist with International Prisoners' Aid. The Branch never had her down as a member of *Brigate Rosse*. A contact, at most.' Kerr touched his injured face, playing for time, looking for for an escape. 'Christ, for all we know, Donate Poncheti may turn out to be one of the *penitenti*.'

'And that makes everything alright?'

'Nance, she's a trained nurse. Worked for years with radical street lawyers in Rome. Civil rights and social justice right across Europe. Robyn is a libertarian. Her life is Spirito e l'Anima, not terrorism, and in Belfast it nearly got her killed.'

Suddenly, Kerr's BlackBerry was ringing with Justin's name on the screen. 'So they're both angels,' said Nancy.

'I'm saying, don't jump to conclusions…let me take this.'

Justin was in a busy street somewhere, with raised voices competing around him. 'I've only got a couple of minutes, boss.'

'You okay?'

'In Broadway Market, getting us some fruit and veg before it closes. Look, I was out of order yesterday and I'm sorry.'

'No need. We're good. Anything on the O2?'

'Nothing, but I think we may have a situation here.'

'Is that from Costello?'

'She wants me to fly someone out of the country tomorrow evening. I know you're not happy about…you know…but I told her I'm up for it. Can you do the necessary from Clacton?'

'Who's asking her?'

'Didn't say. We haven't been out of her flat since we got back.'

'Do you have any idea where Luca is hiding?'

'Isn't that one for the Reds?'

There was a space, filled with raised voices selling off bananas and strawberries. 'Boss, I've done my bit, haven't I?'

'I'm asking you. Justin, who's protecting this guy?'

'I don't think Gina knows. Sorry.'

'Hold on.' Kerr glanced at the photographs scattered on the table, shot Nancy a glance and put the phone on speaker. 'So what does he look like?'

'Boss, they took loads of stills at the beach before we left.' Justin sounded mystified. 'Hasn't Mel shown you?'

'I'm sending you some images right now. Tell me if you recognise the man.' Kerr slanted the screen for Nancy to tap Justin's number into her iPhone and forward the photographs of Robyn with Donate Poncheti. 'So did you get into Costello's laptop?'

'In the morning, depending how pissed she gets tonight...hold on.' Kerr and Nancy sat quietly for almost a minute, listening to the sounds of the market. 'Yeah, that's Luca, one hundred percent. Who's the girlfriend?'

'No-one.'

'So can I tell Gina I'll do it?'

'I'll speak with the commander. Get away again tonight and call me.'

Kerr sensed Nancy's look of reproach as he cut the call. 'Robyn may know nothing about this,' he said, dropping the BlackBerry onto the table.

'Christ, that's some hold she's got over you,' said Nancy as Kerr headed for the balcony. 'And you've got incoming from the US of A.'

Rich Malone's email was headed 'US State Department Personal and Confidential Malone/Kerr,' with an attachment but no explanatory text.

'You want privacy?' said Nancy.

Kerr shook his head. 'This is State doing me a favour. Remember Sean Brogan?'

'The IRA man on the run? Trained the gangsters in Columbia? Of course. You hungry?'

'Don't you want to hear his voice again?'

Nancy shrugged, already heading for the kitchen. 'I want moussaka.'

Kerr opened the audio file and listened to the monotone preamble from Goldhawk's handler. Ten seconds of silence in the ether as Nancy opened and closed the microwave door, then male voices in Spanish, muffled through the brothel's partition wall. The voice of the John Doe, excitable, argumentative, a verbal helter skelter, then Brogan's slow bass cutting across his rhythm, faltering Spanish overlaid with hard Belfast. The IRA man was just as Kerr remembered him from other secret recordings years ago, the ideologue bomber and shooter, untouched by doubt, his authority threatened by no man on earth.

Kerr stayed with the voices for another five minutes, listening in vain for Corona, hoping Malone had got it wrong. In the kitchen behind him, the clatter of cutlery and pinging of the microwave; from Santa Fe, flamenco guitars and distant, shrill laughter from girls entertaining clients in the bar downstairs, a kaleidoscope of distractions. He understood why the DEA had been so embarrassed about the recording, with its snatches of conversation fractured by long silences where the wire had failed. Even cleaned up, the quality was confusing and substandard, an intelligence officer's nightmare, the defence attorney's dream. In the kitchen, the microwave pinged but the audio died again, a silence stretching so long that Kerr reached for the keyboard as Nancy called to him. Then, suddenly, a loud crack: an explosion, gunfire; no, the sound of a door being smashed open, an interloper, a gatecrasher, and Goldhawk too late or weak to prevent it, then a hard voice speaking English as Kerr froze and dipped his head to the laptop.

'For fuck's sake, Sean. I haven't got all fucking night. If I miss my flight cos of this, he's dead.'

A woman's voice, powerful, equal to Brogan's but clear as a bell. Unmistakably Robyn, mother of his child, his past and present racing down the wire. 'Don't take any more shit. Tell him I need to know *when*.'

Kerr stayed silent for a long moment, head teeming, the words refusing to come. Then Nancy was at his shoulder. 'I heard,' she said, softly, reading his face. 'That's your radical, isn't it, your *libertarian*, chasing human bloody rights in Columbia?'

'I think I just found Javelin,' muttered Kerr.

'Yes. I think so, too.' Nancy perched on her chair and made him face her. 'So who are we going to tell?'

Chapter Sixty-One

Nancy allowed Kerr to come home with her, as Melanie had hoped. Her invitation suggested it was out of pity, not reconciliation, yet Kerr welcomed the chance to recover lost ground and assimilate Robyn's betrayal beyond the reach of Finch's cold callers. He had not been inside Nancy's house since Tuesday, the night before his visit to Rome, and felt a surge of pleasure as he crossed the threshold. Amy and Tomas had evidently missed him, racing down the hall from the kitchen as Nancy paid the teenage babysitter from next door. The children revitalised his sense of belonging, especially when, upstairs, he saw Nancy had saved his page in Horrid Henry.

Later, while Nancy got them ready for bed, Kerr settled in the kitchen and called Dodge to talk through the day's events. He sounded slurry with drink and anxiety, and it took Kerr a long time to convince him all was not lost, that he and Melanie would shield him from the scrutiny of others while he came to terms with himself.

Kerr's hope for an evening's respite from his own physical and mental shocks quickly evaporated. Within moments, Bill Ritchie rang from the office to chide him for leaving hospital and to press for everything on Bobby Roscoe. Evidently, Ritchie had endured a call from the Bull about his intelligence failures and inability to keep Kerr in check. 'He's seeing the Commissioner tonight. Says you killed his prime suspect and washed away his forensics. She's going to love that.'

'He's got a point,' said Kerr.

'Finch wants a prisoner in handcuffs, TV lights outside the Old Bailey, and what do we give him? A torso in the morgue with everyone in the dark.' Ritchie sounded weary, and Kerr guessed he would have driven from home in his weekend clothes. He pictured the commander behind his desk in the gloomy, half-deserted Yard, surrounded by crates to be packed for the move, the windows turning cold and black in the twilight.

'I'm sorry, Bill, but there was no other way.'

'Yesterday he accuses me of obstructing MI5, now we're running a parallel European operation without telling him.'

'But what choice do we have, with him and Toby Devereux still fixated on the IRA?'

'I know,' said Ritchie. He gave a deep sigh. 'So what do I tell the Commissioner?'

'The truth.' In less than three minutes, Kerr reduced the tracing, confession and death of Bobby Roscoe to the rapid disruption of a major bomb attack: a clear and present danger, lethal and inescapable. In a blend of fact, omission and dissembling, Kerr indicted himself, absolved Melanie and credited Dodge with a brilliant agent operation over several frenetic days.

Ritchie sounded both irritated and impressed. 'Where is Dodge now?'

'In purdah, which is why he's not telling you this himself.'

'Where, in purdah?'

'Harrow. He's exhausted, so I sent him home. Doctor's orders. Flu.'

'Stress.'

'Without Dodge we would never have got to Roscoe, which is a big deal, right? We had less than one hour to find the bomb.'

'Very adroit,' said Ritchie, unmoved. 'And when do I get the true version?'

Kerr paused. 'Bill, I need you to give me some slack. Just a few more hours.' He suddenly realised Nancy was in the kitchen, listening to everything, her look of disbelief matching Ritchie's voice.

Ritchie muttered something inaudible. 'Did Polly Graham get back?'

'Searching the Belfast lab right now. The minute she verifies this maverick ex-squaddie as the bombmaker, Finch gets his manhunt and top of the bill on *News at Ten.*'

'So let me know.'

'And Polly's not the only story here. Gina Costello has asked Justin to exfiltrate someone from the UK tomorrow, same set-up as before.'

'Who's the lucky passenger?'

'Luca, almost certainly. That's Donate Lucrecia Poncheti. *Brigate Rosse* veteran, old style, serious player. Bad news. We're running him past European liaison.'

'Where is he right now?' said Ritchie.

'The intel has him at Bayswater, Benita's address. No sightings yet.'

'Jesus.'

'It's alright. Whatever he's been sent to do, we'll contain this through surveillance.'

'How? You just told me you don't know where he is.'

'I'm relying on Justin to guide us in.'

Ritchie stayed silent for a moment. 'So what the hell am I looking at here?'

'A campaign by Anti-Capitalist Insurrection, playing out exactly as we warned at the Silver Scrum this time last week. We've identified Roscoe, Gina Costello, Maria Benita Consuela and this Luca dude, who may be preparing to do something tomorrow. We don't know. It may just be a recce for an attack down the line. Or a money transfer.'

'But it means I have to share this tonight,' said Ritchie.

'Too risky. Listen, Benita has led us to the door of Wymark Corporate Solutions. The CEO is a millionaire big shot called Philip Deering, and he's been holding cosy meetings with the Bull. In secret.'

'Can you prove this?'

'Would I tell you otherwise?' Kerr listened to the children upstairs, still wide-awake, and hoped they were excited because he had come home. He reached for Nancy's hand as she brushed past him to fill the kettle.

'What's the worst case?' said Ritchie, eventually.

'Drugs funding terrorism. Cocaine for bombs, with Wymark doing the laundering. Alan Fargo's team are following the money, and it's a long trail. I've got the Reds in Fulham covering Deering's house right now, and his finance chief.'

'I'm talking about Derek Finch.'

'Deering has bought him. He's got the Bull deep in his pocket, and it's full of dirty money.'

'Does he know that?'

'Is the Bull a dupe or conspirator, you mean?' Kerr gave a short laugh. 'Want to hear what Vanessa Gavron said to me two days ago? "Take another look at your boss". Exact words.'

'A grudge is not evidence of corruption, John.'

'It's another brick in the wall, and I'm asking you to keep Finch on the other side until we sort this.'

'High stakes.' The commander's voice dropped to a murmur again, arguing with himself. 'Will Justin give us Luca in time?'

'Trust me.'

Another pause on the line. 'Okay.'

•••

Sunday, 23 October, 08.51, The Fishbowl

Kerr woke early, with Nancy beside him but Robyn in his head. A cloud of foreboding had followed him upstairs to bed and there was an awkwardness with Nancy, still wary as she steered him from the spare room, compromising with kind words over intimacy. Hovering over Kerr all night had been the trials he would face today: revelations about Robyn, his operative still in harm's way and, if Rich Malone and Justin were right, the spectre of more bloodshed from another attack, imminent yet unsighted.

On waking, Kerr found smudges of dried blood on the pillow from his injured face. He twisted onto his back, troubled by the gaps in his team's knowledge, the debilitating famine of hard facts. When secrets about the enemy's intentions were in short supply, MI5 analysts and media experts would talk about 'intelligence deficits', or 'missing tiles in the mosaic'. Many euphemisms for failure had emerged over the years, all wasted on cops in the front line, for whom the information vacuum meant carnage at Victoria and Cheapside, bodies blasted out of recognition and families torn apart. The business of SO15's intelligence unit was to predict, warn and disrupt; today, if Kerr failed, he knew the Bull would twist misfortune into neglect and missing clues into dereliction, with blame levelled at Commander Bill Ritchie.

Kerr lay quietly, jeopardy floating over him like a shroud. He tried to weigh his defeat by the terrorists against success in uncovering the Bull's corruption, but the scales refused to settle. The only certainty was that Sunday would be a day of endurance.

Shortly after eight, still reeling from the proof of Robyn's betrayal, he crept downstairs to the kitchen. Pummelled and wrung out, his body had seized up overnight, so he spent a few minutes curling and stretching to unlock his back and shoulders. He filled the kettle, then forced himself into a flurry of press-ups until he heard it click off, punishing his toes against the cold, unforgiving tiles. Pouring boiling water into the teapot, he struggled to contain his feelings. Anger? Certainly. Humiliation? Yes, a deep sense of shame for himself, pity for Gabi and doubt about his own judgment. Nancy's evidence had tainted Robyn, yet Kerr had been wrong about them both. His scepticism and credulity left him feeling physically sick as he poured milk over shredded wheat, sliced a banana and forced himself to eat while he planned the day's moves. He would have to break the news to Gabi very soon, and the prospect chilled him. He padded upstairs with a cup of tea for Nancy, then took a shower.

'You're staying home with us today, right?' said Nancy, still bleary when he returned, towel around his waist. She sat up as

Kerr dressed in yesterday's clothes. 'Resting. Isn't that what Bill Ritchie told you?'

'Have to pop to the office first,' he said, plumping her pillow against the headboard. Next door, the children were stirring, evidently disturbed by the shower. 'We'll take them to the park.'

'For God's sake, John.' Nancy swept a hand through her hair in irritation. 'You look a bloody wreck.'

'It's alright.' Kerr's first task was a call to Vanessa Gavron, and it could not be from here. He bent to kiss her. 'Be straight back, promise,' he lied.

It took him ten minutes to drive to the Yard through the quiet Sunday streets, a couple more to reach the Fishbowl and search his Inbox for 1830's satnav readout on Gavron's Saab. The journalist was on voicemail but called back five minutes later, to the ding of a solitary church bell.

'Work or worship?' said Kerr, spooning coffee into his stained mug. 'Still harassing the priest?'

'What do you want?'

'Just calling to say thanks.'

'For what?' said Gavron, then laughed. 'Are you talking about the Bull?'

'I'm taking a close look at him and the signs are promising. There you go. Thank you.'

'So when do I get the exclusive?'

'Listen, I'm seeing Robyn soon. Where did you say you two met?'

'I didn't.'

'Tell me now,' said Kerr, smoothly.

'Like I said before, ask her yourself.'

Kerr took a breath as he scrolled down. 'Vanessa, at this moment I'm guessing you're parked outside St Jude's church in Haringey, right? Family Mass? Waiting for the man?' Kerr sensed Gavron shifting in her seat, fiddling with her camera. 'Is it Ducketts Road or Green Lanes today?'

'This is my story, for Christ's sake.'

'An abusing priest linked to terrorism? It's my investigation.'

'From my source.'

'And I promise to look after you both.' Silence again, the bell insistent. 'It's a simple question, Vanessa.'

'I bumped into Robyn in a bar in Colombia, okay?' said Gavron, anger stifled by resignation. 'Bogota, not far from the airport.'

'What were you there for?'

'I'd been following an Olympics story in Rio.'

'You cover sport, too?'

'A government long firm fraud. Alleged. Then a couple of days in Bogota on the way home.'

'Working?'

'Sightseeing. Robyn and I got chatting. Shouting, rather. It was crowded. Everything very sociable, no big deal.'

Images of Robyn flooded Kerr's brain. He was with her by the river and on the houseboat, her suntanned face laughing at him, her body tricking his, a picture of fulfilment on the eve of the bombing campaign. 'Was she with anyone?'

'Couple of locals and a big Irish bloke, which is probably how I got sucked in. Guinness and shots all round. Why? You're jealous?'

'Curious.'

'Jesus, she warned me you were a tricky bastard.'

'No, she didn't. Date?'

'Ages ago. I'll get back to you.'

'Do it now.'

Gavron exhaled down the line. 'I was overnighting to Heathrow. It would be a Tuesday, four, five weeks back. We ended up on the same flight.'

'What seats?'

'Premium economy for me. Robyn was standby, back of the plane. What's that got to do with anything?'

'And when you landed?'

'I drove to the office. Robyn connected to Belfast.'

Kerr scrolled through his calendar. Robyn had caught up with him in Hammersmith on the penultimate Friday in September. 'How about Tuesday the twentieth of last month?'

'Sounds about right.'

'No, Vanessa. Look it up.'

Sounds of irritation, a thud as Gavron dropped her phone, then more muttering as she swiped through the diary. Waiting, Kerr tried to make sense of his thoughts as Robyn's deception unravelled. When they met in Rome, she had implied a lengthy stay in Belfast researching sectarianism and child abuse by paramilitaries, a story strengthened by Dodge's confession; and her claim that the report for Spirito e l'Anima was in its third draft suggested a project lasting weeks or months.

Gavron joined him again. 'September twentieth? Yeah, that's the one.'

Three days: unless she was lying, too, Vanessa Gavron's travel schedule gave Robyn less than seventy-two hours in Belfast. She had blended fact and fabrication to dupe him. And if her subterfuge was bold, its implication was shattering: Robyn, the mother of his daughter, had diverted him from Javelin, the extremist, using truth to frame republican dissidents. Even as he absorbed this body blow, another question hammered inside his brain: what had Robyn done to provoke the IRA, to ignite such rage that they would stalk her to Hammersmith and place a bomb beneath her car?

Suddenly, Alan Fargo was filling the doorway, waving a sheet of paper and mouthing something.

'Still there?' said Gavron.

'Sorry,' he murmured into the phone, beckoning Fargo inside. 'Vanessa, thanks. I owe you.'

Gavron was still signing off as Kerr cut the call.

'Polly just got back,' said Fargo.

'It's him?'

'Jonny Tranter, plus some interesting history. His father was also a soldier. In eighty-seven, Christopher Tranter was ambushed by the IRA and murdered in cold blood. He was thirty-nine and young Jonny was already learning how to disarm bombs.'

'Was dad special forces?'

'Paras. A veteran, obviously. The rest is vague and unusual. Christopher and a partner were in plain clothes in an unmarked car in Belfast. No armed escort or back-up. Personal weapons only. They took a wrong turn, got jammed in by a black taxi and set upon by a mob. The pal fired a couple of shots and got away, but they dragged dad to waste ground, stripped him naked, beat him half to death then shot him in the head.'

'Did we know about this?'

'It was a fuck-up. Why would we? The army didn't even release the true names. Christopher's body has never been recovered. He's one of the Disappeared you never hear about.'

'So when did Jonny Tranter spin off the rails?'

'The day they started giving terrorists get-out-of-jail cards.'

'Okay. Can Polly help us find him?'

Fargo smiled and shook his head. 'We can do it ourselves. Christopher's widow is Amelia. She went through a couple more bad marriages. In two thousand and five, she accepted an offer from Christopher's best buddy at Sandhurst.'

Kerr stared hard, then snatched the paper from Fargo's hand. A bolt of lightning shot through him as he deciphered the scrawl. 'Are you sure about this?'

Fargo nodded. 'Our bombmaker's step father-in-law is Philip Deering.'

In an instant Kerr was revitalised, the long night's paralysing regrets banished as he snatched back control. 'I'll brief the commander,' he said, grabbing his office phone as the BlackBerry vibrated in his hand and priorities fizzed through his head, letting him know exactly what he had to do. 'We need to get photographs of Tranter to the Reds.'

'Done. And Justin's cleared for Clacton tonight.'

'So we need him to insert the Echo Chip as soon as.'

'He must have done it first thing. Mercury is streaming Costello's emails right now.'

It was Jack Langton on the mobile, speaking in riddles to avoid confusion with target code names. 'John, we're getting movement here. Boss Man and Sunny Jim both left home five minutes ago. That's Fulham and Dulwich, and they're busy on the hands-free. Best guess is they're headed for the Mayfair office to talk about the thing in the river.'

Kerr was estimating the number of watchers required for an uncertain number of targets at four plots suddenly becoming mobile. 'Can you manage this, Jack?'

'It's tight, because we're also watching for Airplane Man outside the Artist's house.'

'Portobello. Who's covering there?'

'Melanie took over at six, nothing doing yet. Look, provided everyone assembles at the office and stays put, I'm okay. Any more players, it gets tricky.'

'Jack, I'll come right back to you.'

Chapter Sixty-Two

Sunday, 23 October, 09.21, safe house, Finsbury Park

The M1 traffic from Luton was busy enough for Jonny Tranter's Fiat Punto van to pass unnoticed among the airport taxis and shuttle buses, trucks and day trippers making their way south towards the capital. He had pulled grey overalls over his jeans and sweatshirt, staying cool with the driver's window lowered and the visor down. Alert for bored traffic cops, he was careful to keep below seventy, except when a bunch of girls flashing him from the back of a coach forced a shift to the outside lane.

On the radio, LBC buzzed around Saturday's foiled attack on the O2 Arena, with prattling foreign schoolkids and anyone in range overstating their brush with death. Somehow the attack had been spun towards Brexit, with talk of xenophobia and the youngsters agreeing that hatred would never divide London from Europe. '*Nous sommes Londres*', promised an overwrought, horsey crowd from Normandy, as Tranter scornfully shook his head.

Talk of the unnamed hero cop who had driven the horsebox into the river made his temples throb, for the brilliant plan had been scuppered by Bobby Roscoe's cowardice, not some insane dive to the bottom of the Thames. Tranter carried a new Glock pistol in his battered army shoulder holster and felt for it now, snug beneath the overalls, waiting for his anger to subside. He leant out of the window for a couple of seconds, offering his head to the wind, then stabbed the Classic FM button.

By the time the motorway petered out at Hendon, Bobby Roscoe had embedded himself in Tranter's brain, the weakling resurrected as his nemesis. Against orders, he found himself heading for Willesden, a short detour to the south, careful not to excite the speed cameras along the North Circular Road. In less than fifteen minutes he had crossed the canal, slowing for the approach to Roscoe's workshop.

Evidently, the area around Betta Tyre and Exhaust remained a major crime scene, with three police vehicles parked haphazardly beyond a length of police tape, including a white van marked Police Evidence Recovery. Twisting in his seat as he crawled past, he glimpsed five scientific officers working inside the workshop, their coveralls stark white in the gloom. Heading east through sleepy traffic, he felt for the clear, sealed plastic bag hidden inside the glove compartment. The pouch held metal shavings, wire fragments and microscopic traces of Semtex, genuine clues creating a false evidence trail to save him from Roscoe's dereliction. He breathed easily again. In a few hours the cops would be sniffing around a different scene, drawing the wrong conclusion from real evidence, with every shred luring them away from Jonny Tranter.

By ten o'clock he was dipping beneath the railway bridge in Seven Sisters Road, giving way to a clutch of hoodies, ashen-faced, glassy-eyed, up early or home late. Outside a block of council flats workmen were loading a flatbed truck with dumped mattresses, worn tyres and a sofa as he turned for the safe house. He passed Muslims walking to the mosque, Christians heading for church and dog walkers skimming Sunday tabloids while their pets defecated. An elderly man washed a Nissan Micra, its handwritten For Sale sign peeling from the windscreen; in a tiny front garden, kids skipped around a mother tending window boxes. They had murdered his father in Victorian terraces just like these. Here was London's melting pot slopped into a single street, everyone poor and rubbing along, taking turns at the back of life's queue. He drove slowly between the lines of parked cars as the street came to life, searching for number 17A and its amateur bombers. With Bobby Roscoe gone, the brothers would be holed up in the basement, waiting for rescue and cocaine. He crunched over a rolling drinks can, looking for a place to park.

Reaching the end of the street, he turned around in the shadow of St Peter's church and found a gap three car lengths away from the safe house. Unobserved, he slipped the evidence pouch into his overalls pocket, unfolded himself from the van and descended the crumbling steps to the dank basement. He paused to take in the brown, slanted door and barred window, then pressed his ear to the glass. The only muffled sound came from the TV and he imagined the fear triggered by the O2 fiasco and Roscoe's death. He stretched on tiptoe to glance along the street, then stooped to pull on blue plastic shoe covers. A cat appeared from behind a cracked terracotta pot and rubbed itself against his leg as he transferred the Glock to his left pocket. He paused to stroke the mottled fur, then gently pushed it away before slipping on latex gloves.

The brothers would be expecting him, awaiting exfiltration in the event of Roscoe's elimination or arrest. He took a deep breath to compose himself, then tapped the coded knock with his car key, three-two-three. Almost immediately he heard a key turn, then the door opened and a wide-eyed face stared at him, whiter than the sheet covering the window. Unshaven in shorts and filthy vest, he was barefoot and slow to make way. They had never met, so Tranter glanced at the withered right knee to satisfy himself: Kenny the cripple, frightened, not to be relied upon. No threat, either.

'We've been fucking desperate,' said Kenny. 'Waiting for you all night.'

Tranter ignored him and stepped into a fug of sweat, feet and bad breath, reassuring himself they had not moved from the hideout. It took only a couple of seconds to assess their sleazy building site of piled rubble, cracked plaster, lifeless cabling and workmen's trestles. The TV was blaring from the far side but neither of the folding chairs was occupied. Tranter hesitated by the pine table Roscoe had used to demonstrate his bombs, scanning for firearms. 'Where's your brother?' he said, just as Fin appeared from the bathroom. He was naked, rubbing his hair with a towel, unaware of another presence. In different circumstances Tranter would have reprimanded Kenny for opening the front door without armed cover; now, it was for the best. Then Fin looked across, instinctively covering himself.

'What fucking kept you?' Disadvantaged, he tried to play catch-up as Tranter moved to narrow the gap, his Belfast accent harsh, entitled. 'How long are we supposed to survive in this dump?'

The boy's miscalculation made Tranter laugh. 'Is that why you're getting yourself all spruced up? To walk away?' Aware of Kenny at his shoulder, he glared from one brother to the other, no-hopers redolent of the gangsters who had tortured his father. He closed his hand around the Glock. 'Who'd want to save a pair of losers like you?'

Then he caught Fin's eyes flicker over his protective clothing, his covered hands and shoes, the shrewd one sensing danger where Kenny saw only cocaine. Fin must have left his weapon in the makeshift kitchen, for he was on the move as Tranter weaved around the bed to reach him in four easy strides, his own gun already rising. The race lost, Fin swung to fight with his hands, making his chest an easy target. Tranter fired a pair of rounds into his heart, then shot him twice in the face, just as boys like these had done to his dad.

Fin catapulted backwards, crashing the TV to the floor. The Sky reporter continued to deliver her terrorism update to the ceiling, her mouth still working beside the naked corpse. Fin's features were scarcely recognisable, his nose and right eye lost, right cheek hidden beneath a mat of glossy hair. More blood meandered around his chest hair to drip, drip, drip onto the TV screen, as if his heart was still pumping.

Tranter ripped the TV plug from the wall and turned his sights on Kenny. 'They tell me you're the little shit who bottled it at Gloucester Road,' he said, filling the silence left by the television. Kenny remained transfixed, a picture of shock and disbelief, when he should urgently have been considering his own position. His muteness irritated Tranter, so he lowered the Glock and shot him in his right leg, obliterating the scars from his fist kneecapping.

Kenny screamed and collapsed to the floor. 'My work of art, and you handed it to them,' said Tranter, stooping to wrench his knee. 'Do you have any idea of the trouble you caused? The shit flying my way because of you?'

Tranter had hoped for a lash of retaliation, anything to fan the flames. Instead, the boy writhed in agony, sobbing like a baby, his eyes filled with dread. Before Tranter could speak again, he let out a full-throated scream that must have reached the street, so Tranter silenced him with a single headshot. He watched him flop away, curling like a foetus within touching distance of his brother.

Tranter pocketed the Glock, took out the evidence pouch, sprinkled its contents onto the pine table and stepped into the yard. The cat was peering at him again by the wheelie bin as he peeled off the gloves and overshoes, stuffing them into his pocket. He snatched a final glance along the pavement as the creature slipped between his legs, darted up the steps and led the way to his van.

Chapter Sixty-Three

Sunday, 23 October, 11.23, Kerr's Alfa Romeo

Beyond the Fishbowl's dusty blinds the autumn sky looked promising, though Kerr saw only a storm about to break. On edge, he retrieved his Glock from the safe and headed out in the Alfa.

He was feeding into the traffic around Marble Arch when Jack Langton came through on Tetra Five, the encrypted surveillance channel. 'We have Boss Man and Sunny Jim arriving at the Mayfair location…stand by…plus a grey Fiat van parking in the mews now…UI male out of the vehicle and entering the office.'

'Polly's guy?'

'Very likely.'

'Any others?' said Kerr.

'No. Boss Man used the main door key and deactivated the alarm.'

'If they disperse, can the Reds cover all three targets?'

'It'll be rough and ready, but yes, not a problem,' said Langton, without drawing breath.

'Okay. Sightings of the Artist? Airplane Man?'

Melanie broke in before Langton could speak. 'Dead as a dodo at Portobello.'

Kerr rammed his foot down. 'With you in four minutes, Mel.' He pretended it was an impulsive decision, though images of Donate Lucrecia Poncheti with Robyn had eclipsed everything since last night's revelations.

Langton again, his voice low. 'John, how do you want to play this?'

It was a loaded question that reduced Kerr to silence as he shot into Hyde Park Place, stringing out the make or break time. For the twelve armed surveillance officers listening in, John Kerr was the ranking officer on the ground, without oversight from the Bull or Bill Ritchie. In the eye of London's most vicious bombing campaign since 7/7, it fell to him to arrest the targets or keep them in play, risking more bloodshed. Langton was drawing him into the classic intelligence officer's dilemma, the long game against executive action.

Melanie was on Tetra again, quietly urgent, severing his thoughts as he accelerated to seventy along the Bayswater Road. 'Make it quicker. I've got the Artist in a rush to a blue Audi A4, checking something, glove compartment or dash…now returning inside.'

'I'm sending back-up,' said Langton.

'Negative, Jack. Cover the Wymark end.' Kerr had flipped the siren now, and had to raise his voice. 'We'll take this in mine.'

In less than a minute he spotted the Red Team's ancient Volvo parked on the street adjoining Maria Benita Consuela's. As he smoked to a halt, Melanie was already sprinting along the tarmac.

'Move,' she said, clambering aboard. 'Benita's coming out again.'

Kerr edged into the corner, just in time to see Consuela dip inside the Audi. Then a man followed her, cradling a brown holdall and moving fast.

'Airplane Man,' said Melanie. 'With the bag he collected in Scheveningen.'

Luca, instantly recognisable from twenty car lengths, flooding Kerr with adrenaline as he craned forward, knuckles white on the steering wheel but his body reinvigorated, Saturday's pain banished. He fixed on the man folding himself into the passenger seat, agile and strong, face tanned, hair glossed back. He imagined him with Robyn, the smooth dude with a jagged past, another of her secrets. Then Melanie was offering water. 'You okay?'

Kerr shook his head, drifting forward. He sensed danger, not from Luca but deep inside himself.

'Not yet or we'll show out,' she said, unscrewing the bottle for him. 'Drink.'

Kerr braked and swallowed some water, his eyes never leaving the target as he wiped his mouth with the back of his hand. Melanie's eyes were on him again, uncertain. 'Want me to drive?'

Kerr dropped the bottle into the cup holder, watching Luca tug his seat belt as the Audi pulled away. 'I'm fine.' He kept a safe distance as they passed Consuela's flat, stealing a glance into the community garden where they had executed Avril Knight. Was it jealousy, vengeance or hatred stabbing at him? Melanie was murmuring into Tetra as Kerr silently examined his motives, all of them unbecoming.

Sunday morning traffic was building as they drove west to join the M4 at Chiswick. Consuela set a gruelling pace from the start, with Kerr playing every trick to achieve 'visibility unseen,' the goal of all surveillance officers. She trespassed into bus lanes to undertake, chanced her luck at amber lights, accelerated aggressively above the limit and braked hard for speed cameras. For the pursuers, every turn, junction and tailback became a challenge.

'Rubbish driver or surveillance conscious?' said Kerr, exasperated after his third near loss.

'She's erratic but it's Sunday,' said Melanie. 'And you're out of practice.'

They had been on the move less than fifteen minutes when Alan Fargo came on the hands-free. 'Guys, has Justin given any hint or worry about his personal security?'

'Why?'

'I'm reading Echo Chip live. Luca just tasked Gina Costello to find a different pilot for tonight.'

'Any reason?'

'Must be suspicious, and he'll be feeding that into Gina.'

Kerr ran a fourth set of lights as he grappled with a new quandary. Then Melanie was looking at him, expectant, making his decision easy. 'Okay, I'm pulling Justin out,' he said, quietly, 'soon as I get this sorted.'

'And we're tracking you M4 westbound,' said Fargo. 'You think Luca's going to risk Heathrow, instead?'

In the near distance to their left, Kerr watched an Airbus 380 rise in slow motion, its Emirates logo picked out by the sun. 'No,' he said. 'This guy's come here to do something.'

They followed the Audi onto the M25 before pressing further west along the M40 towards Oxford, with Kerr, Melanie and everyone in 1830 racking their brains for possible targets.

Melanie spotted them a second before Kerr, a string of flashing blue lights inflating in her rear-view mirror, a mile back but closing fast. Seconds later a shiny black BMW 7 Series flashed past with a silver Jaguar in its slipstream and a Land Rover Discovery tailgating at ninety plus.

Without a word, Melanie speed-dialled on Kerr's mobile. Karl Sergeyev answered on the first ring, as if he had been expecting the call. 'Good morning, John. What's up?'

'I want you to call Number Ten and check the PM's diary for me,' said Kerr.

'No need. I'm with him.'

Kerr frowned in concentration at the fading convoy as the threat suddenly deepened. 'Well, you just steamed past us. Is the Foreign Sec there?'

'My man's away, so the office put me on reserve.'

Kerr imagined Sergeyev in the BMW, rear nearside, diagonal to the driver. 'What's the programme?'

'The PM making reassuring noises to the president of the European Banking Federation about Brexit and our love of all things European.'

'Martin Bergmann? They sponsored yesterday's equestrian thing at the O2.'

'So even more to talk about. They're travelling together, best buddies since their Harvard days. Private visit, low-key, no statements. Bergmann's got something extracurricular lined up tonight in London, then last flight out. Excuse me, John. Are you telling me we have a problem?'

'You're headed for Chequers, yes?'

'Eventually. PM wants to buy him a pint before lunch.'

'In the schedule?'

'It's a photo opportunity, so of course. England and Germany all smiles. Sweetness and light at the local.'

'Which one?'

'Hold on.' From the front seat, a woman's voice gave the answer before Karl could ask. And in that split second the kaleidoscope in Kerr's head stopped spinning, its teeming pieces slipping into place, settling his next move.

'The Crown,' said Sergeyev.

Chapter Sixty-Four

Sunday, 23 October, 11.57, Kerr's Alfa Romeo

Corona. In a flash, Kerr was strolling with Rich Malone by the Reflecting Pool in Washington, listening to his friend dissemble about technical failure and fractured intelligence. Unwittingly, Karl Sergeyev had just drawn him a new route map: the Royal Family and O2 both false trails, his true destination a modest pub in deepest Buckinghamshire.

'Karl, where is this place?'

'The wilds north of Pulpit Hill, seven minutes from Chequers.'

'Who did the recce?'

'The PM's regular team…hold on.' Kerr could hear other voices, anxious and quieter now, full of questions. 'Good. Thank you…John? Yes, he drops in there, sometimes with his wife and kids. Plus a TV crew. He took Obama last year. The staff are trustworthy and discreet, everyone vetted. It's low risk, no big deal.'

'Karl, the pub is cancelled. Change the plan, make an excuse. It's not going to happen.'

Up ahead, the Audi suddenly veered from the middle lane to leave the motorway, tearing down the slip road. 'She's definitely headed their way,' said Melanie quietly, checking her phone map.

Without braking, Kerr managed to slide between a truck and a caravan to make the exit. 'Karl, you take the PM and Bergmann to Chequers. Stay there until I call you. Understood?'

'Can you tell me what's going on?'

'The moment I know myself.'

'I believe the PM will not like that,' he said, carefully. Beneath the understatement, Kerr sensed Sergeyev watching the other protection officers in the car. 'Guy is with both principals in the Jaguar. Would you like to speak with him?'

'No. I want you to handle this for me,' said Kerr, sniffing the cordite from a hundred turf wars. 'If the top man plays up, I'll come to Chequers and explain.'

Sergeyev responded in a beat. 'I understand, John.' Kerr imagined the Russian's body language in the BMW, the back-up officer about to call the shots. There would be no questions, excuses or conditions, no backsliding. 'Operational reasons. You can rely on me,' was all he said, before cutting the call. It was classic Sergeyev, courteous and dutiful, the protector unafraid to take on the most powerful man in the land.

'We're getting close,' said Melanie. 'Six miles.' They were speeding north on a single carriageway, with Kerr four vehicles back and Consuela overtaking at the slightest opportunity. Clearing the traffic around Princes Risborough, Kerr began to close the gap.

'Are you carrying?'

'Yes,' said Melanie. 'And I think we have to do a hard stop.'

Dead on cue, Consuela reacted as if she had been listening to every word. The Audi surged forward, passing three cars in a row, then braked violently to swing across the traffic into a lane signposted 'The Old Mill.' By the time Kerr could follow, the Audi was almost out of sight, racing into a distant bend between tall hedgerows, the winding, pockmarked lane just wide enough for two cars to squeeze past.

For Kerr, this was a release. Stealth abandoned on the main road, he roared in pursuit, a petrolhead finally breaking cover. Consuela constantly misread the lane or drove blind, taking a double bend so recklessly that she almost crashed into an oncoming Nissan, black smoke whipping from her tyres as their door mirrors collided. Because the lane was too narrow to pass safely, Kerr sat on her tail and flipped the siren, watching Luca's angry, jerking head as he glared behind and yelled at Consuela.

The chase ended after three miles on the approach to the mill, where the lane snaked across the river. Kerr had to use brakes and gears to kill his speed but Consuela ignored the warning signs, rounding a blind left-hander onto a hump back bridge so fast that she took off, overshooting the bend on the other side. The Audi slithered on a skin of wet mud, glanced off a wall lining the river and catapulted into a stone gate post.

From the top of the ancient bridge, Kerr and Melanie were caught in the eerie, post-crash stillness, the only sounds the cawing of crows, steam hissing from the smashed engine and the faint rush of the mill stream. 'Both air bags deployed,' said Melanie.

Movement inside the Audi, then the thud, thud, thud of Luca's shoulder heaving open the passenger door, his hands clawing at the airbag to escape. He was suddenly out of the car with the holdall, looking back at them, evidently uninjured. He reached into the bag, then the sun glinted on something in his hand.

'Gun!' Both Alfa doors clunked open in a single movement as Kerr and Melanie rolled beneath the rise of the bridge, Glocks drawn. Then rapid fire from an automatic weapon punctured the air, with more flapping and rustling as birds took off from a thousand branches and Luca ran into the field, clutching the bag to his chest. They immediately sprinted for the Audi, Melanie pulling open the driver's door to check for signs of life while Kerr covered her.

'She's alive,' said Melanie, her fingers at the pulse in Consuela's neck.

'Stay with her,' shouted Kerr, already on the run.

The field rose gently from the lane to a huge dilapidated barn, built of ancient red bricks, blackened timbers and clay roof tiles. From inside came the rise and fall of a powerful tractor engine, its driver evidently unaware of the drama unfolding by the stream. Twenty metres away, tracing the hedgerow along the left perimeter, Kerr waited for Luca to disappear inside the giant double doors before running to an isolated oak a bus length from the barn. He heard the rapid putter of the machine gun, then the tractor fell silent as he sprinted the last stretch and risked a look inside. The barn was filled with rectangular hay bales stacked into neat pillars, a warehouse of fodder intersected by an earthen track stretching forty paces to the far wall. The muddy tractor was to his left, its elderly driver lying dead on the ground where Luca had thrown him, blood radiating from his neck, his face frozen in shock. Then more gunfire came from deep inside the barn and a stun grenade detonated with a snap and a blinding flash, igniting the carpet of straw.

It was the turning point, fight or flight, the moment Kerr could have retreated to await armed back-up; instead, as flames flooded the ground, he dived through the dense smoke for the nearest bales, determined to draw Luca from cover.

The next hail of shots came from a different place along the far wall, somewhere to the right, Luca searching for his own way out. Smoke billowed through the barn, carried in the draught from the open doors. It fanned the flames, cutting off Kerr's escape as a second grenade rolled down the track, too close this time, mesmerising. The explosion blasted away the Glock and threw him violently against the unyielding bales. He lay prone, his sight impaired, hearing blunted, only his sense of smell warning him he would soon choke to death. Somewhere close by Luca was calling to him in Italian, hunting his prey.

The grenade had ignited a second seat of fire that curled across the ground to join the first and lick at the towers of hay. The machine gun spat again into the swirling smoke above Kerr's head as he shuffled to recover the Glock and recoiled into the hay. Bare arms peppered with hot ash, he scarcely noticed the pain, trapped in a pincer movement between his assassin and the blaze. Then Luca appeared through the smoke to his right side, a ghost with a machine gun ready to fire, Kerr an unmissable target the second he turned his head.

In the next instant another sound rose above the crackling fire, the rattle of the tractor starting up and crunching into gear. It drew Luca's eyes straight ahead as he looked for Kerr high in the cab, not crouched nearby in the smouldering hay. The engine throbbed louder, closer, as powerful headlights pierced the smoke and Kerr saw Melanie sweep past, the lethal spikes of the bale stacker pointing at waist height.

Luca was firing to kill the driver when he should have been saving himself, for the central spike pierced his waist as cleanly as a harpoon, whipping him from his feet as the tractor swayed down the track, his legs dangling uselessly from the bailer. On elbows and belly, Kerr dragged himself from cover to watch the tractor charge the end wall, smashing through the ancient brick and timbers to safety in the field beyond.

With black smoke funnelling through the barn and most of the bales alight, Kerr was only dimly aware of Melanie's silhouette as she flitted back through the rubble, calling his name. Nothing came when he tried to shout back but she was suddenly crouched beside him, yelling into his ear, then hauling him through the chasm into the fresh air, just as the whole wall collapsed in a storm of dust and sparks and the fire took hold of the roof, its embers pricking the sky like the remnants of Chinese lanterns.

Ten metres from the blazing building, Kerr slumped against the giant tractor tyre, camouflaged by smoke but finding lungfuls of fresh air. 'Didn't know you could drive one of these?' he wheezed.

Melanie looked shattered, with dust rising from her clothes and her face smudged grey from ash or shock. 'I can't. Obviously,' she said, already dialling.

Kerr broke into a spasm of coughing, then gripped her arm. 'Thank you, anyway.'

While Melanie worked the phone, Kerr hauled himself up against the wheel to study the tractor's mangled front end. Luca's body had erupted on impact with the wall, leaving his innards trailing to the grass and his handsome face unrecognisable. Only one of his eyes remained, fixed in disbelief. Reviving fast, Kerr stretched, examined himself for injuries and tucked the Glock into the small of his back.

'Ready?' he said, as Melanie cut the call.

Shielding her face from the heat, Melanie stared at him, incredulous. 'John, whatever you're thinking, forget it. We almost died in there.'

Kerr was already making his way slowly down the field. 'But we're not finished.'

He was already level with the barn and she had to lift her voice above the inferno. 'Are you crazy?'

Kerr wiped his face on the filthy polo shirt and turned to beckon her, his voice strengthening again. 'I want you to look for something in the Audi.'

•••

They separated at the gate, Kerr returning to the Alfa, high on the bridge. He opened the driver's window and drank deeply from Melanie's water, taking in the scene. Seven cars were stranded in the lane and a clutch of pensioners encircled the Audi, peering at Consuela beneath the deflated airbag. A single local patrol car had arrived, its blue light flashing as the young PC darted between lane and field, searching for the connection between a car crash and a blazing barn.

Kerr watched Melanie identify herself, a desperado claiming to be with the good guys, adding to the cop's puzzlement. Then a roar from the field distracted him and the rubberneckers as the barn collapsed in a whirlwind of fire and falling masonry. Kerr was edging down the bridge as Melanie quickly reached across Consuela's body, grabbed something from the dashboard and joined him. Sirens were approaching from the main road as Kerr weaved around the police car and sped away. 'Any good?'

Melanie nodded, clicking into her seat belt as she worked the Audi's TomTom satnav and pointed to the red marker on the screen. 'You were right.'

'They're strangers here,' shrugged Kerr. 'How else would they know where to go?'

In her free hand Melanie held her phone map, with the Crown

already located. 'Okay. The pub is about half a mile further down but she's directing us right, three hundred metres past the mill.'

They drove between water meadows to the turn, then climbed steadily to the hamlet of Linton, a three way junction around a triangle of green with a war memorial and a pub serving five squat cottages. Kerr swung into a winding, one-track lane that suddenly climbed so steeply he needed first gear, cursing as the encroaching hedgerows whipped the bodywork.

'We've arrived, according to this,' said Melanie.

Suddenly the road levelled and cleared as the hedges petered out to a dry stone wall. A field bordered one side with sweeping views across the county and, to the right, a thatched cottage with a sign, 'Let by Stapes and Coggles.'

They abandoned the Alfa, knocked on the front door and peered through the tiny windows, front and back. Against the garden wall lay a bunch of fence posts, so Kerr picked the largest, smashed the kitchen window and stood back for Melanie to climb inside and open the back door. Unfurnished and smelling of damp soot, there was a small living room with low beams and the original fireplace and, up the narrow stairs, a bathroom and two bedrooms with sloping ceilings.

Melanie coughed in the stale air. 'How many years since anyone lived here?' she said, then followed Kerr's eyes from the hatch in the ceiling above them to recently disturbed dust on the rough wooden floor. Standing on his clasped hands, she reached up to open the hatch and release the loft ladder. She climbed into the roof space, gave a low whistle and made room for Kerr to join her.

Beneath the square casement window were a telescope on a tripod and, lying ready on a metal table, a black sniper rifle. Kerr ducked beneath the oak rafters and hooked the curtain aside. The assassins had chosen the perfect vantage point, high and uncluttered. Beyond fields to the left a veil of smoke drifted over the mill; but the telescope was already calibrated on the low, whitewashed stone walls of the Crown pub, less than a quarter of a mile across open farmland, its terrace, garden and car park visible to the naked eye.

Hands clear, like detectives viewing a murder weapon, they peered at the rifle, then Melanie took her turn at the telescope. 'Which one do you think they were going for?'

Kerr was already dialling Jack Langton. 'Does it matter?'

'Two for the price of one?'

'Jack. Anything happening?'

'Still at Wymark.'

'We've got a situation here. My guess is your targets will be on the move very soon.'

'What's the plan?'

This time, Kerr answered in a flash. 'Hard arrest.'

Chapter Sixty-Five

Robyn had evidently told the manager of the Anchor to expect John Kerr, for he unhooked the houseboat keys and handed them across the bar without question. The row of moored boats was floating on the tide and Kerr was careful as he made his way along the ramshackle pier, gripping the butcher's bike on the stern to pull himself aboard. Inside, inhaling the familiar odour of grease and diesel, he remembered his first visit here and settled on the threadbare divan to wait.

Kerr had spent Sunday evening in Bill Ritchie's kitchen in Finchley, north London, recounting the drama near Chequers while the commander and his wife made supper. Today he felt drained by what Ritchie called his 'lively' weekend, with no prospect of a respite any time soon.

His risk-benefit gamble had been settled in Mayfair just before two o'clock the previous afternoon with the ambush of Philip Deering, finance chief 'Sunny Jim' Walker and bombmaker Jonny Tranter as they dispersed outside Wymark Corporate Solutions. Before they could reach their vehicles, Jack Langton's Reds had thrown them to the cobbled street with guns at their heads, then rushed them in separate cars to Paddington Green, the high security unit designed to contain terrorists.

Early this morning the Bull had placed himself sick from an undisclosed illness, with SO15's clique of senior detectives immediately falling as silent as their boss. Later, Kerr and Melanie would meet a team of independent examiners to justify the murders of Bobby Roscoe and Donate Lucrecia Poncheti. In the meantime, investigation-wise, John Kerr was unavailable, with Ritchie fielding calls from his eyrie on the eighteenth floor.

Soon, the pier creaked and the boat dipped as Robyn climbed aboard, the star player Kerr had held back from everyone. He hauled himself up as she appeared in the narrow doorway and stood facing him, neither of them willing to break the silence. She was wearing a fleece over tracksuit bottoms and carrying a soft overnight bag, like a woman returning to court for sentencing.

Kerr blinked first. 'Flight okay?' Robyn had agreed to take the first easyJet out of Rome, a one-way ticket.

She tried a laugh. 'Better than the *carabinieri* at the door.'

Surrender in London or extradition from Rome: those had been the only options when Kerr had rung her from Nancy's house. 'I spoke with Gabi.'

Robyn dropped the bag onto the divan and flipped Kerr her passport. 'I know.'

She had wanted Kerr to be the one to break the news to their daughter. By the end of their late night call, Gabi had moved through shock and disbelief to agonising remorse. 'All this because of some stupid photograph at a party?' she had sobbed. 'I try to convince Nancy you're a good guy and look what happens. This is all my fault.'

Robyn produced a bottle of Barolo from her bag and stood it on the narrow drop leaf table. 'Oh, for God's sake,' she groaned, as Kerr shook his head, then squeezed past to fetch plastic wine glasses from the cabinet, just as she had done before. She poured them each a drink and sat opposite, resting against the back cushion. For a bereaved woman facing life imprisonment, Robyn looked remarkably relaxed. 'Where do you want me to start?'

'It's your story.'

'The clue's in the title, right? Anti-Capitalist Insurrection?… One for the road, John. Please,' she said, sliding his glass across in exasperation. 'Blitz the banksters across Europe, first stop London because they're fatter. Greedier.'

Kerr took a sip. 'Let's have some players.'

'Well, the IRA won't be getting the Nobel Peace Prize any time soon. Have you followed their anti-imperialist spiel over the years? The dissidents were in bed with us from the start, Marxists with anti-caps.'

'Who was the matchmaker?'

'An IRA fugitive called Sean Brogan. He runs the cocaine operation out of Colombia and set up the contact. Funding through Spain, bombs from Belfast. That was the plan.'

'How long ago?'

'Spring. Beginning of April, I think. I was in Belfast for six weeks on the Spirito project I told you all about. Perfect cover. That's when we agreed the targets and timings.'

'So what went wrong?'

'Brexit.' Robyn drained her glass, poured more wine and made a face. 'The result no-one expected. Suddenly, everyone's talking about Scottish independence and a united Ireland. For the IRA it's ballots, not bombs all over again, winner takes all without firing a shot. Suddenly our operation is a distraction, a mega threat to their political campaign and whatever shady deal they're cooking up with Westminster. They pulled the plug overnight.'

'Who?'

'A back-stabbing bastard called Tommy Molloy.'

Kerr gave a low whistle. 'He's still Army Council,' he said. 'Leader of the pack.'

'Yes. We had to find another way PDQ or call it off. And where's the insurrection in that?'

'So in walks Philip Deering?'

'Not exactly.' Dropping her eyes, she frowned and gently chopped the table top with her hands, a classic Robyn mannerism. 'Wymark were already laundering the money from Bobby Roscoe's end-user coke markets. London and Manchester, with Amsterdam the export hub for Europe. And creaming a nice percentage off the top through Benita's ex, who runs the accounts in Galicia.'

'What made Deering take the next step?'

'Don't pretend you don't know.' She drank some wine, looking at him. 'He's in the nick, isn't he? Ask him yourself.'

'I want to hear it from you.'

'Because that's the deal, right?' Robyn gave a harsh laugh and nudged his glass. 'Anyway, we're dicking around in Rome, wondering what to do, when Benita tells us Philip Deering hates the IRA more than the banks and wants revenge.'

'For what?'

'This guy is your typical Sandhurst shite, tours of duty in Belfast and an obsession about Westminster capitulating to the IRA, like the British Empire just lost India all over again. He's Tommy Molloy with a silver spoon, and you don't want to get too close.'

Beneath them something was gently knocking against the hull, driftwood, or a bottle trapped between the boats.

'So why risk Belfast again?'

'To warn Tommy not to renege on our deal. Give him a last chance before we hit Victoria.'

'Or else?'

'Or else.'

Kerr wiped his mouth and studied her, sceptical but impressed. 'You're telling me you threatened Tommy Molloy?'

'Told him to his face he was a cynical, calculating, treacherous bastard. Why not? It's all true.'

'Did you say what you were planning with Wymark?'

'Not in as many words. But they tried to assassinate me anyway, in the middle of our private jig-jig, remember?' she said, nodding through the window to Hammersmith Bridge. 'With you jumping around up there, chucking things?'

'And you making secret deals with soldiers from opposing armies. Christ, talk about sleeping with the enemy.'

'Being pragmatic.'

'Hypocritical.'

Eyes widening, her face reddened by wine or self-restraint, Robyn shot him a glare of reproach. 'It is what it is,' she said, eventually. 'Anyway, Plan B worked a treat. ACI provided the explosives from France. Deering came up with the old IRA code words and a bombmaker better than anyone Molloy could find.'

'Who put the bombs down?'

'They didn't say and I didn't ask.' Robyn shrugged. 'That was Bobby Roscoe's department. But it was an awesome stitch-up. Bash the banks and frame the IRA. What's not to like?'

'But what's the point? If you can't claim the attacks for ACI?'

'You really don't fucking get it, do you?' said Robyn, her voice rising a notch as the drink kicked in. 'This is about stirring up Europe, not taking credit. Inciting the thousands of people the banksters have robbed and cheated. Our mission is to rock the boat and swim away. No labels. No egos.'

'Luca?'

'Including Luca.' She flinched and her face flushed a deeper red.

Kerr took a breath. 'How did you get him into the UK?'

'That was Gina.' She paused for a moment. 'Costello? She's the ACI front line, so don't act like I'm telling you something new. Gina does the ACI propaganda, social media, open activism and cross-border courier work. She recruited a Brit for us, a pilot. He smuggled Luca in on Friday.'

Kerr looked out to the river, waiting and hoping. 'Where are they now?'

'No idea. His name is Jay and she wants to use him for the next phase. End of.'

'She trusts someone that new?'

Robyn shrugged. 'She's up the duff.'

Kerr had been worrying about Justin all night. Robyn's answer, flat and offhand, banished his initial relief at a stroke. Absorbing the blow, he concentrated on a cabin cruiser chugging towards the bridge. 'Avril Knight trusted Benita, too, didn't she?'

'And deserved everything she got. Did you know she was chief investment something or other in Trade and Industry? Just when governments across Europe were letting banks off the hook?

Bungs and bonuses as usual while they conned everyone this shit could never happen again? Plus, she hated the political surrender to the IRA as much as Deering. Probably more, however much she tried to hide it.'

'Why did you mark her as a traitor?'

'The sign on her body? It's what they did to that old spook who went over to threaten them. Avril Knight was a legitimate ACI target but we made it look like a second IRA execution. Another win-win.'

'Which Benita planned right from the start?'

'Used sex to get to her, you mean?' Robyn laughed. 'Well, you'd know all about that, wouldn't you?'

They spent the *touché* moment in silence, listening to a pair of seagulls patter across the roof. Again, Kerr broke first. 'We had a name for you…well, not you, obviously, because I only knew for sure on Saturday night.'

'You going to tell me?'

'Javelin. Code for the ACI activist who co-ordinated the campaign. The go-between for the bombs and the trafficking. That's why I had to see you first.'

'Before you turn me in.'

'To hear it from your own lips.'

Robyn fired straight back. 'Because you think I'm incapable of this?'

'It's unbelievable.'

'Don't insult me, John. It's how we met, remember?'

'I mean, that you would put our daughter through this.'

Robyn laughed. 'Gabi is as radical as me and anyone in *Brigate Rosse*. You think she's embarrassed to bear Gabriella Forini's name? What is it with you? Do you believe I lost my passion the day I gave birth? Why should motherhood blunt idealism?'

'Robyn, it's an incredibly high price.'

'Life in prison? You think I care what happens to me?'

'For the people you murdered, I mean. Their families.'

'What about the real victims? The workers who killed themselves because the banksters stole or destroyed everything they had? Homes and jobs lost, lives and families torn apart. People in despair taking the only way out.' She regarded him carefully, then exhaled and dropped her voice. 'Look, ours is a story of bonuses and bankruptcies. Wealth and misery rolling across Europe. Suicides unreported. Disabilities ignored, benefits slashed. People are suffering. Should they let the banks get away with it? Accept a lifetime of austerity because of those bastards? No. So our campaign is to punish the guilty, agitate the angry and ignite Europe. Watch the EU implode, John. There's nothing you can do to stop it.'

Kerr searched her eyes, as if seeing her for the first time, striving for the right words. Then she looked past him, her voice quiet and calm. 'You think I'm callous? That I should feel guilty about a few poncey Londoners with pensions and big houses and six-figure savings accounts? Don't condemn me, John. When was it ever possible to have peace *and* justice?' She finished her wine and fell silent, watching the river. 'I can see those swans again.'

Kerr took the bottle and eased round the table as Robyn looked up at him, her face and voice suddenly brightening. 'So what's it to be?' she smiled, crossing her wrists. 'Cuff or fuck?'

Kerr turned away to put the glasses in the tiny sink, weighed by a deep sadness. 'You betrayed me, Robyn.'

She swivelled round to touch his arm. 'John, I don't belong to you.'

Epilogue

Monday, 24 October, 21.47, Parsons Green

Parked in the crowded street outside Justin's address, Kerr sat in the Alfa, listened to Classic FM and waited. Home for Justin and his partner was a flat on the first floor of a grand Edwardian house, not far from Putney Bridge. Arriving after nine, Kerr had peered up to the living room window, hoping to see light, then rung the bell for Flat 2, knowing it was pointless, for Melanie had already told him that Louise was working her physio clinic at the Royal Free in Hampstead.

Kerr recognised her by the street light the moment she turned the corner from the tube, still wearing her scrubs beneath a light jacket, a bulky canvas bag over her shoulder, door key ready. Her head was lowered, deep in thought, so he tried a smile as he got out of the car and called her name, anxious not to alarm her.

Louise looked surprised, then pleased, immediately holding out her hand.

'Wasn't sure if you would recognise me,' said Kerr.

'How are you, John?' she said, then her face clouded. 'This is about Justin?'

Inside, she went around flicking on lights and clearing a mug and cereal bowl from the coffee table. For the second time that day he declined a drink. 'But don't let me stop you,' he said, as she cleared space for him on the sofa. He heard the running tap in the kitchen, then his eyes flickered to her belly as she returned with water in a pint glass.

'Melanie told me you dropped by to see her and I feel bad this has taken so long.'

Bare feet tucked beneath her in the armchair, Louise shook her blonde hair free of its bun and nodded at the TV. 'I've seen the news, John. A lot happening.'

'I expect Justin's told you.'

'He's not been here,' she said, abruptly. 'Well, only once since I called on Mel. We don't talk much these days. She probably told you. He manufactured another row, then buggered off as soon as poss. What's new?'

'I think you called him a "closed book"?'

'Really?' She flashed a smile and shifted in the chair. 'I was being polite, obviously.'

'He's done a fantastic job for us,' said Kerr, toying with his BlackBerry.

Justin had sent his text message three hours earlier, while Kerr was at Paddington Green with Robyn. 'Need space so going away with GC to think things through…not having her persecuted for this…dumping phone now don't come for me…will let you know when sorted…sorry boss take care.'

'So when do I get him back?'

'There's ongoing stuff on the European side we're not making public. A follow-up mission. Justin's cover as a pilot is our only chance to wrap this up.'

'Where is he right now?'

'Europe.' The previous evening, according to Alan Fargo, Justin's Cessna had unexpectedly taken off from Clacton, as planned. Henk Jansen, the Dutch liaison officer, had sent CCTV footage of Justin leaving Rotterdam airport with Gina Costello. The two had climbed into the back of a waiting Citroen and been driven off at speed.

'That's a big ball park.'

Kerr smiled. 'Sorry, Louise. That's all I can share right now. It's a tough assignment that no-on else could manage. I have to know you're alright with it.'

'Do I have any choice?'

'Of course.'

'Is he in danger?'

'Justin may not be in touch for a while but I promise to get him safely back to you. That's what I came to say.'

'Okay. Thanks.' She saw the car key in his hand and stood to let him go. 'You should get some sleep.'

Kerr faced her. 'Louise, I know what you're going through.'

She absently touched her stomach. 'So how long? Days? Weeks?'

Kerr held out his hand. 'Soon. But it's complex, bound to take some time.' Her grip was strong. 'This is personal for me, too, Louise. You can be very proud of him. Just as we are.'

THE END

http://www.roger-pearce.com/

The former Commander of Special Branch at New Scotland Yard, Roger Pearce was responsible for surveillance and undercover operations against terrorists and extremists, the close protection of government ministers and visiting VIPs, and other highly sensitive assignments.

He was also Director of Intelligence, charged with heading covert operations against serious and organised criminals.

After leaving the Yard he was appointed Counter-Terrorism Adviser to the Foreign Office, where he worked with government and intelligence experts worldwide in the campaign against Islamist terrorism.

Roger Pearce has degrees in Theology from Durham University and Law from London University. He is also a barrister-at-law. Married with three adult children, he has homes in London and Miami and was European Security Director of a leading, high profile global company.

In Agent of the State, The Extremist, Javelin and future titles, the author draws upon his knowledge and first hand experience of a career in national security at every level.

Urbane Publications is dedicated to
developing new author voices, and publishing
fiction and non-fiction that challenges, thrills and
fascinates. From page-turning novels to innovative
reference books, our goal is to publish what
YOU want to read.

Find out more at
urbanepublications.com